The **BABY-SITTERS CLUB**

Kristy's Great Idea

Ann M. Martin

The BABY-SITTERS CLUB

Kristy's Great Idea

A GRAPHIC NOVEL BY
RAINA TELGEMEIER

AN IMPRINT OF

NEW YORK   TORONTO   LONDON   AUCKLAND   SYDNEY   MEXICO CITY   NEW DELHI   HONG KONG   BUENOS AIRES

Library of Congress Cataloging-in-Publication Data is available.

ISBN 0-439-80241-5 (hardcover)   ISBN 0-439-73933-0 (paperback)

10 9 8 7 6 5 4 3 2 1   06 07 08 09

First edition, April 2006
Lettering by Comicraft
Edited by David Levithan & Janna Morishima
Book design by Kristina Albertson
Creative Director: David Saylor
Printed in the U.S.A.

This book is for Beth McKeever Perkins,
my old baby-sitting buddy.
With Love
(and years of memories)
A. M. M.

Thanks to Dave, Mom, Dad, Amara, Will, Grandma, Diane, Bruce,
the Roman family, the Rigores family, the Cuevas family, K.C., Marisa,
Jason, my editors, my friends, my co-workers,
and my fellow comic artists.
R. T.

Chapter 1

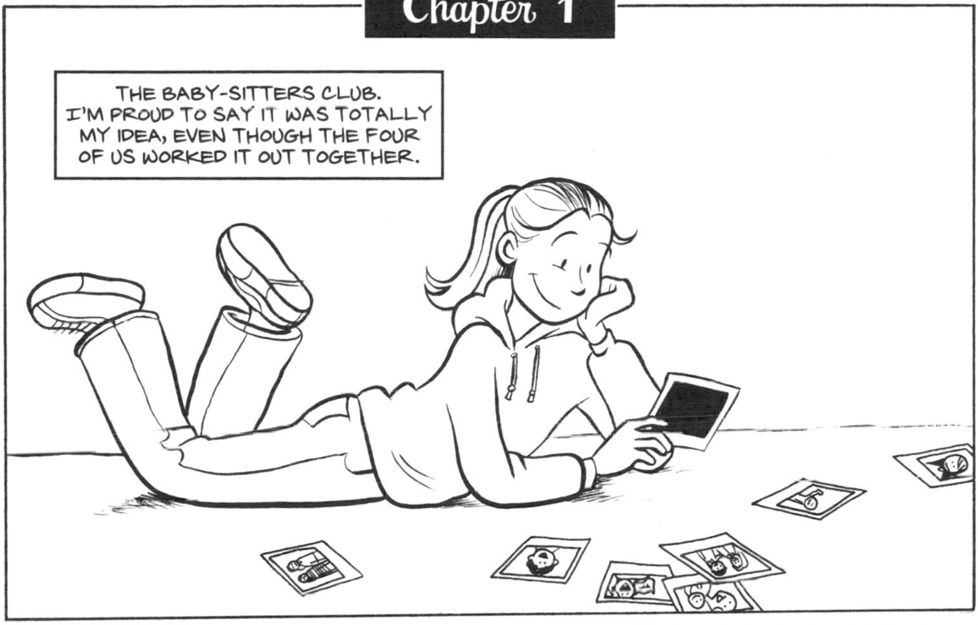
THE BABY-SITTERS CLUB. I'M PROUD TO SAY IT WAS TOTALLY MY IDEA, EVEN THOUGH THE FOUR OF US WORKED IT OUT TOGETHER.

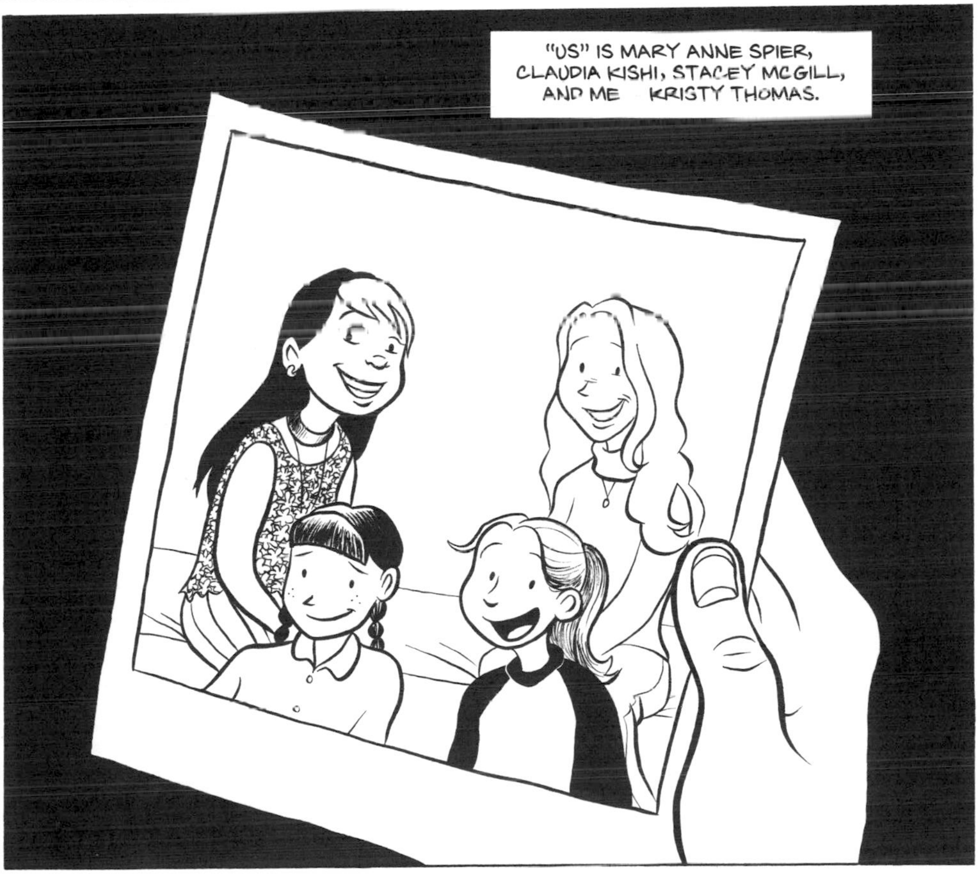
"US" IS MARY ANNE SPIER, CLAUDIA KISHI, STACEY MCGILL, AND ME — KRISTY THOMAS.

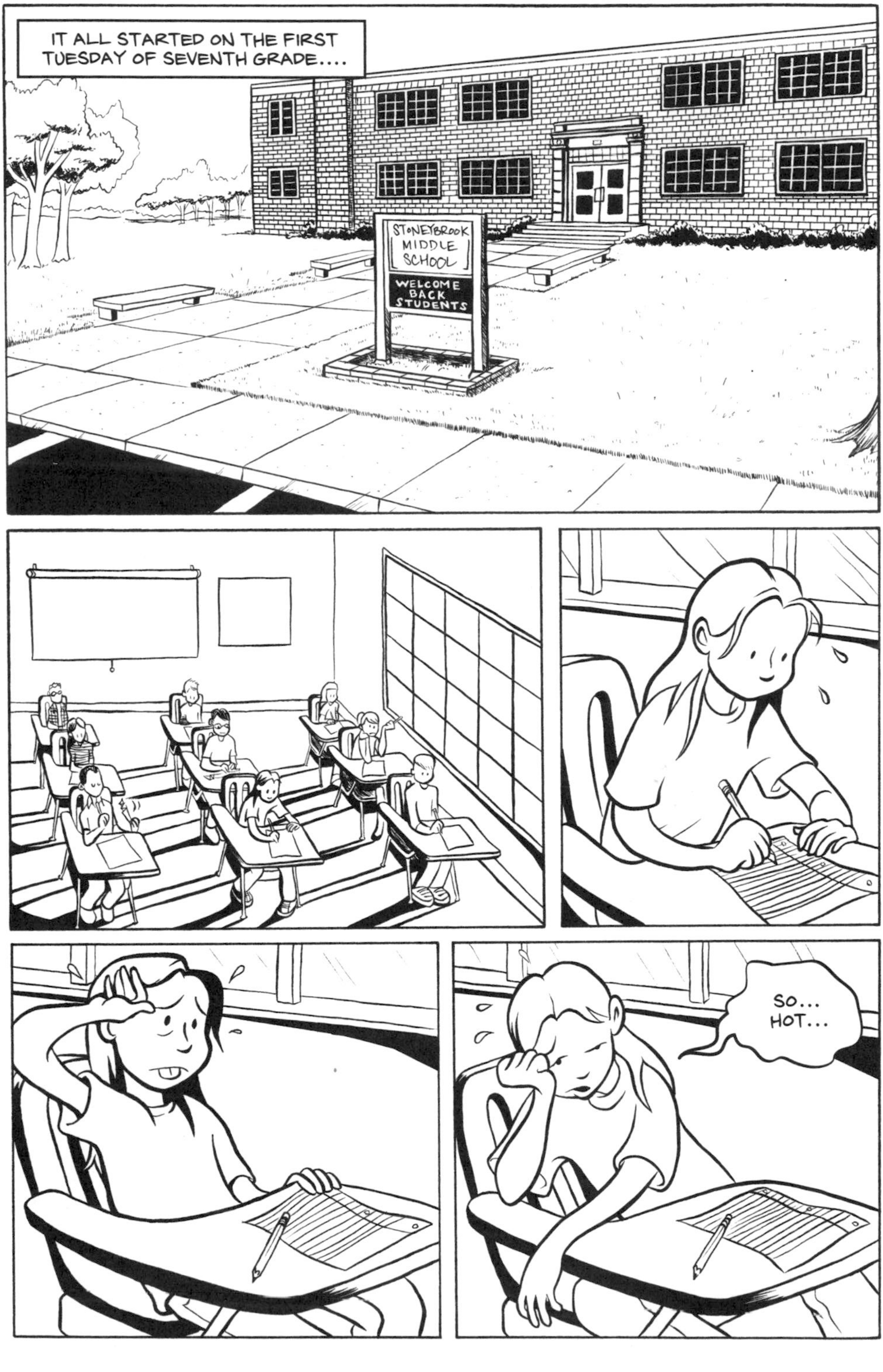
IT ALL STARTED ON THE FIRST TUESDAY OF SEVENTH GRADE....
STONEYBROOK MIDDLE SCHOOL
WELCOME BACK STUDENTS
SO... HOT...

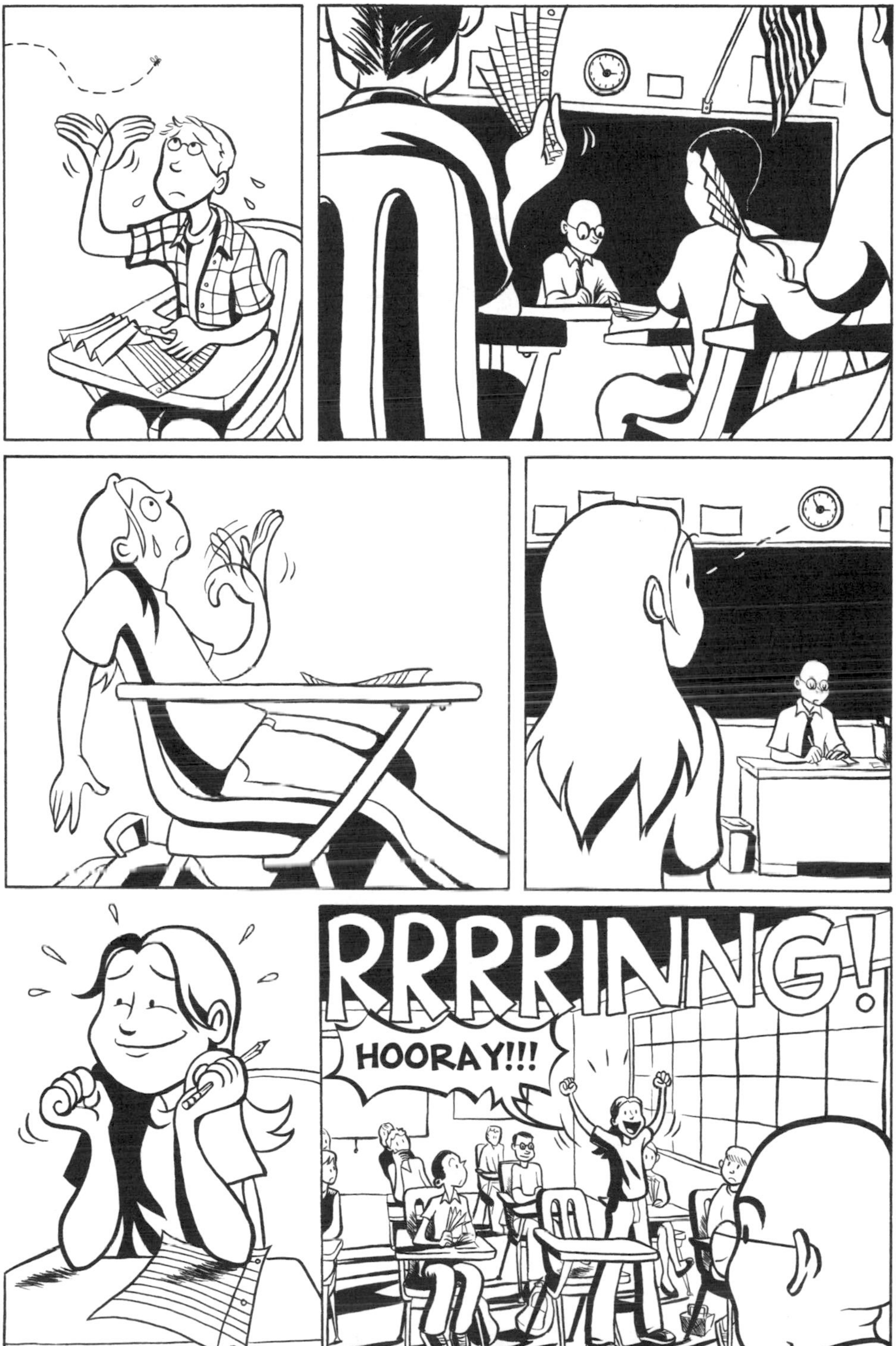
RRRRINNG!
HOORAY!!!

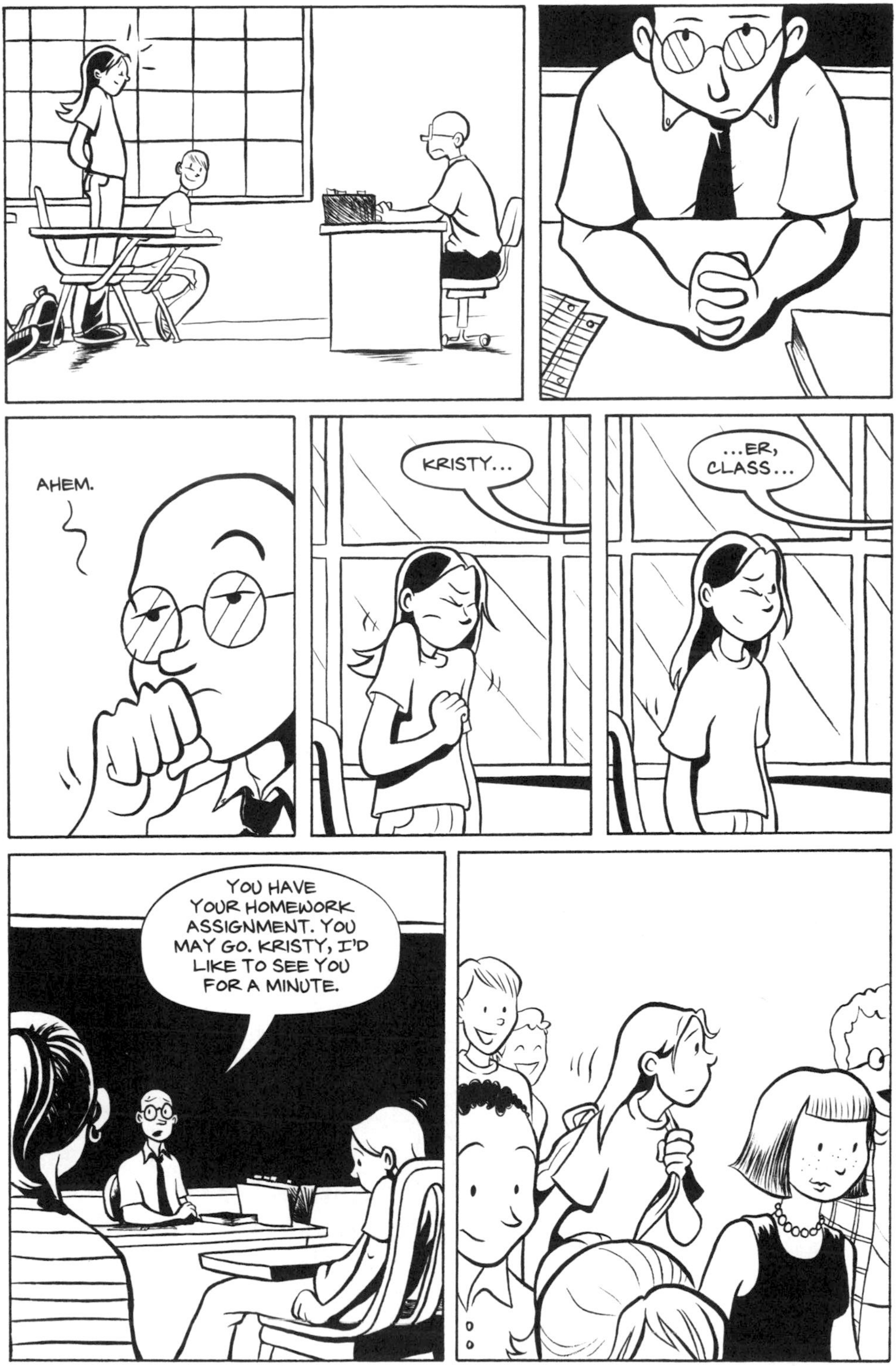
AHEM.
KRISTY...
...ER, CLASS...
YOU HAVE YOUR HOMEWORK ASSIGNMENT. YOU MAY GO. KRISTY, I'D LIKE TO SEE YOU FOR A MINUTE.

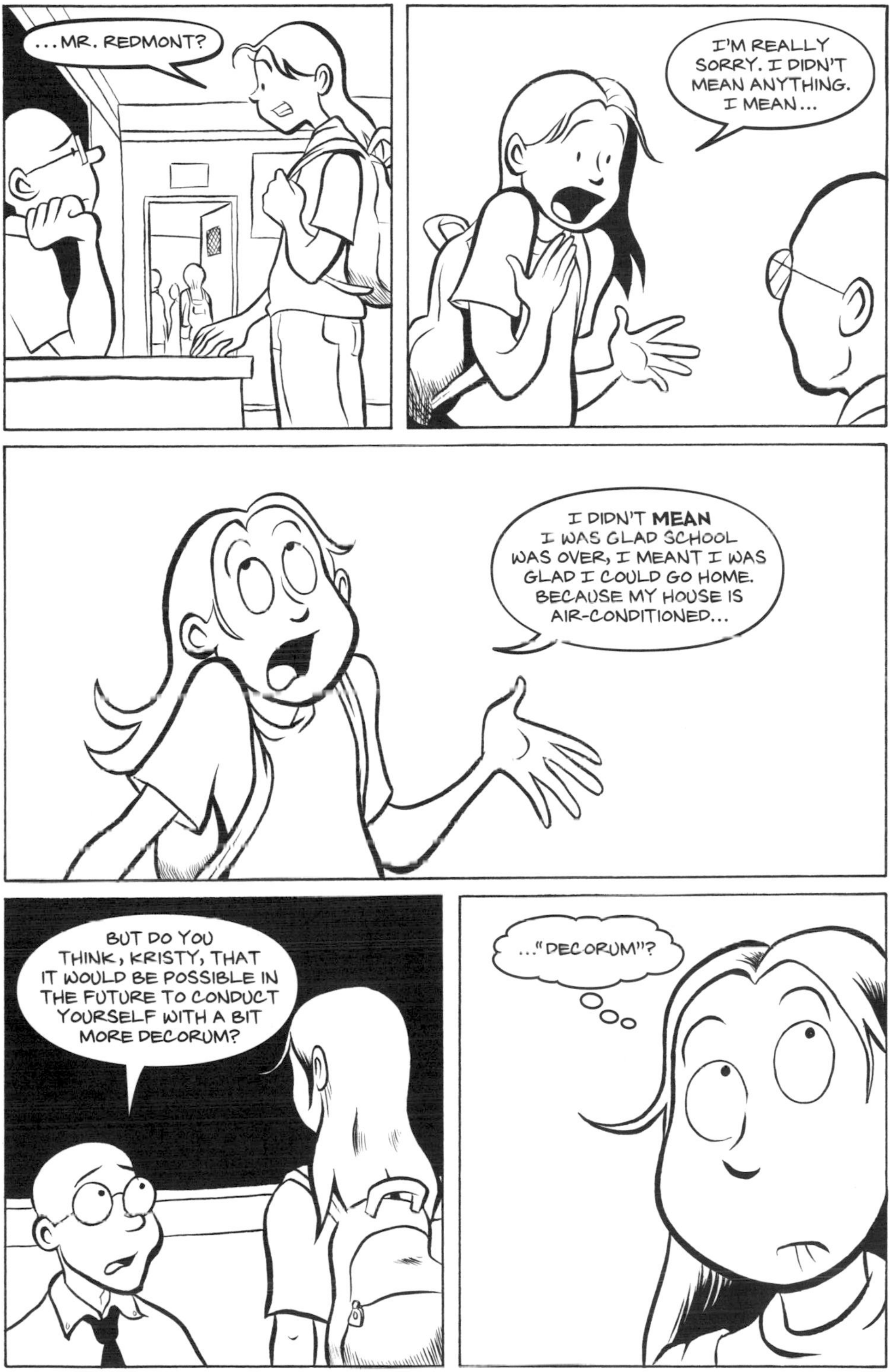
...MR. REDMONT?
I'M REALLY SORRY. I DIDN'T MEAN ANYTHING. I MEAN...
I DIDN'T **MEAN** I WAS GLAD SCHOOL WAS OVER, I MEANT I WAS GLAD I COULD GO HOME. BECAUSE MY HOUSE IS AIR-CONDITIONED...
BUT DO YOU THINK, KRISTY, THAT IT WOULD BE POSSIBLE IN THE FUTURE TO CONDUCT YOURSELF WITH A BIT MORE DECORUM?
..."DECORUM"?

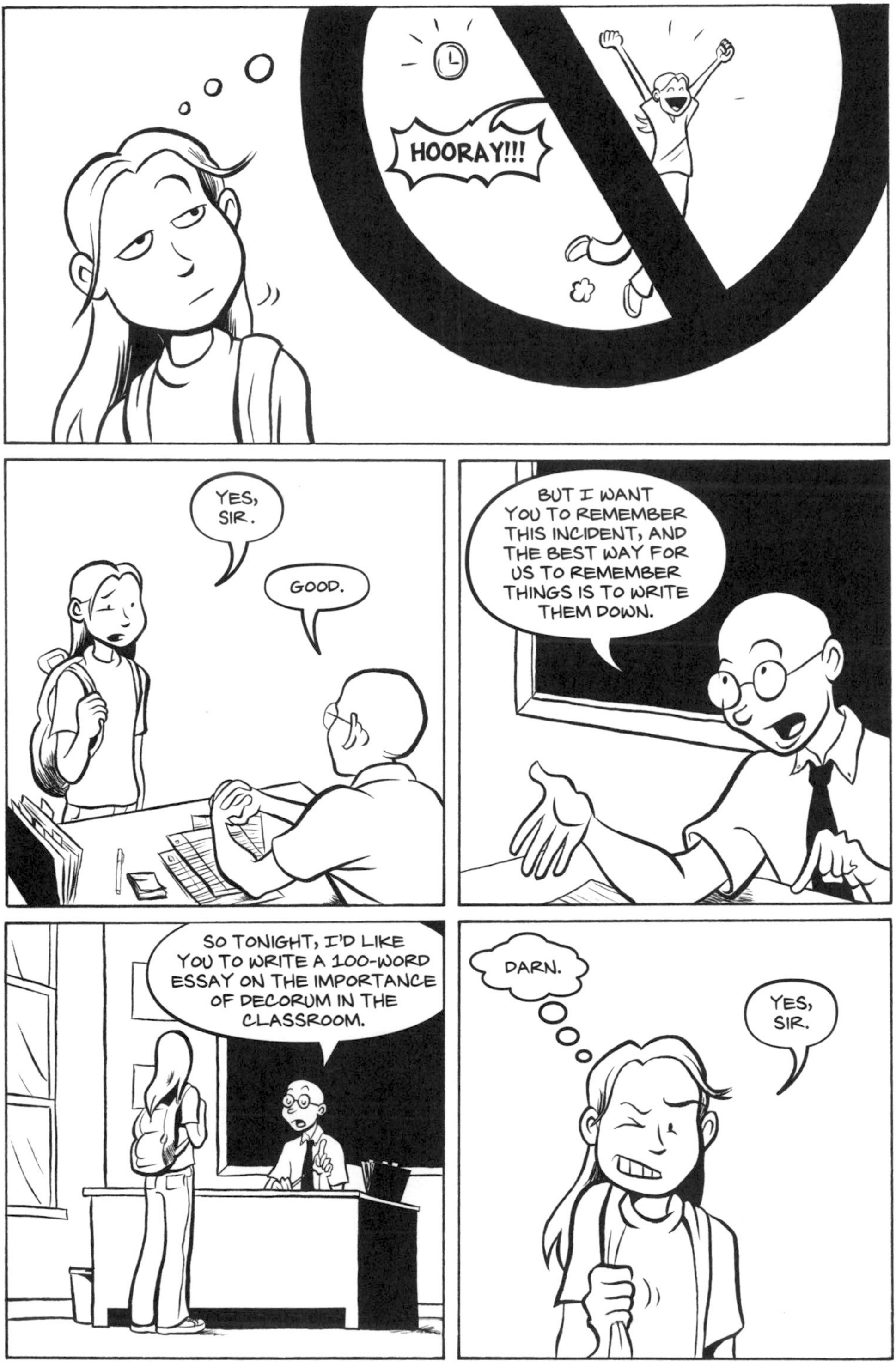
HOORAY!!!
YES, SIR.
GOOD.
BUT I WANT YOU TO REMEMBER THIS INCIDENT, AND THE BEST WAY FOR US TO REMEMBER THINGS IS TO WRITE THEM DOWN.
SO TONIGHT, I'D LIKE YOU TO WRITE A 100-WORD ESSAY ON THE IMPORTANCE OF DECORUM IN THE CLASSROOM.
DARN.
YES, SIR.

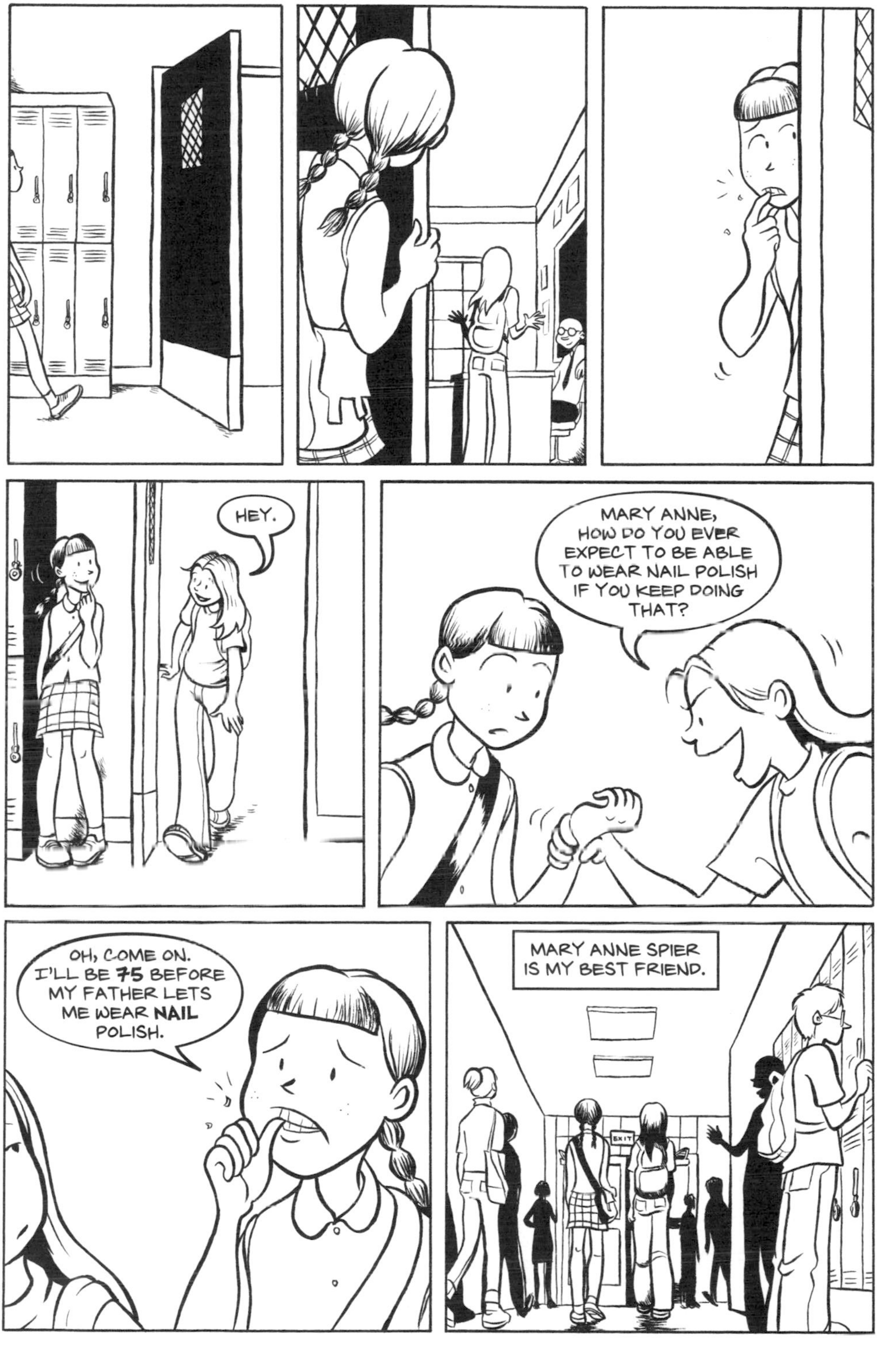
HEY.
MARY ANNE, HOW DO YOU EVER EXPECT TO BE ABLE TO WEAR NAIL POLISH IF YOU KEEP DOING THAT?
OH, COME ON. I'LL BE 75 BEFORE MY FATHER LETS ME WEAR NAIL POLISH.
MARY ANNE SPIER IS MY BEST FRIEND.
EXIT

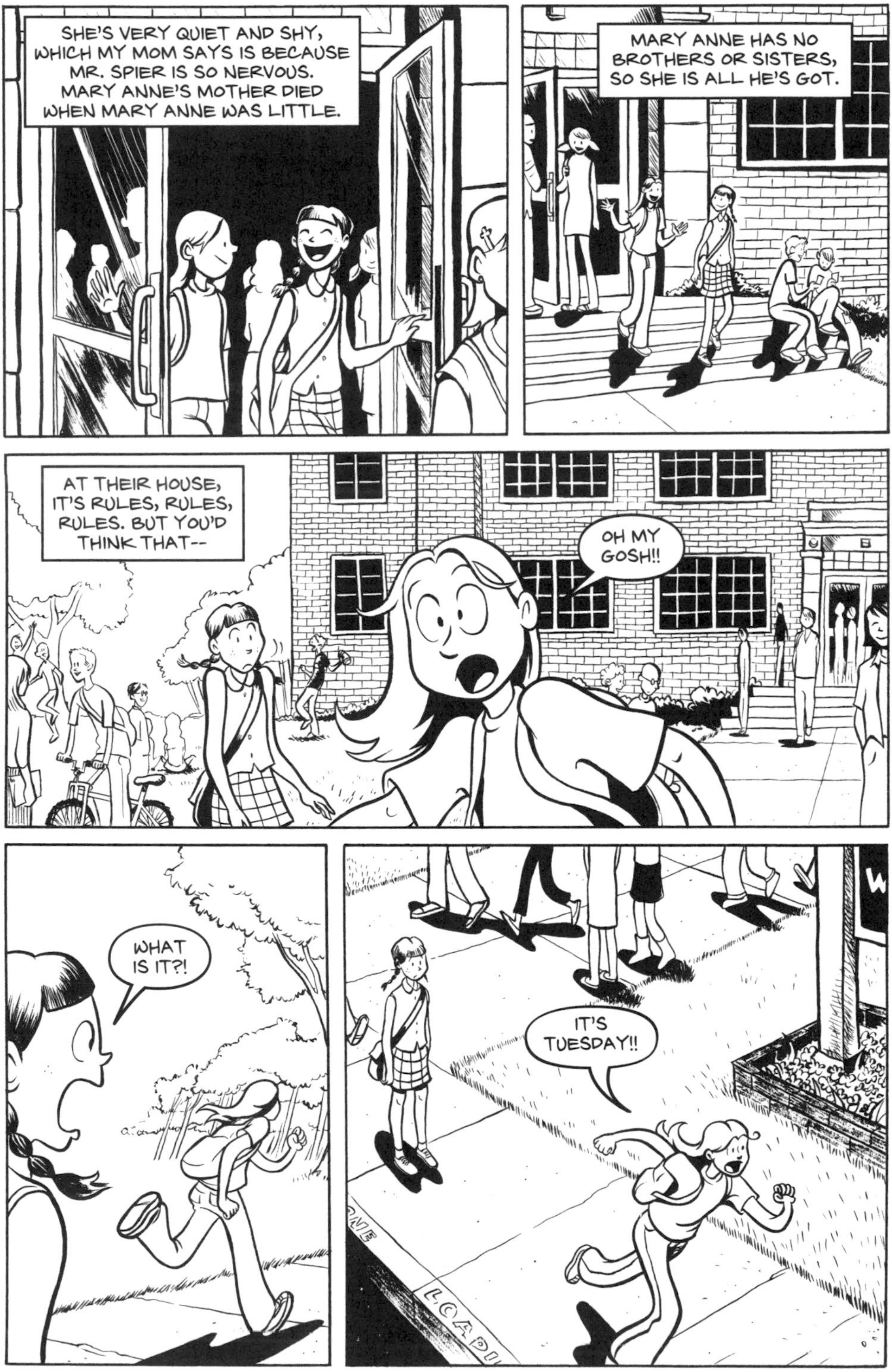
SHE'S VERY QUIET AND SHY, WHICH MY MOM SAYS IS BECAUSE MR. SPIER IS SO NERVOUS. MARY ANNE'S MOTHER DIED WHEN MARY ANNE WAS LITTLE.
MARY ANNE HAS NO BROTHERS OR SISTERS, SO SHE IS ALL HE'S GOT.
AT THEIR HOUSE, IT'S RULES, RULES, RULES. BUT YOU'D THINK THAT--
OH MY GOSH!!
WHAT IS IT?!
IT'S TUESDAY!!

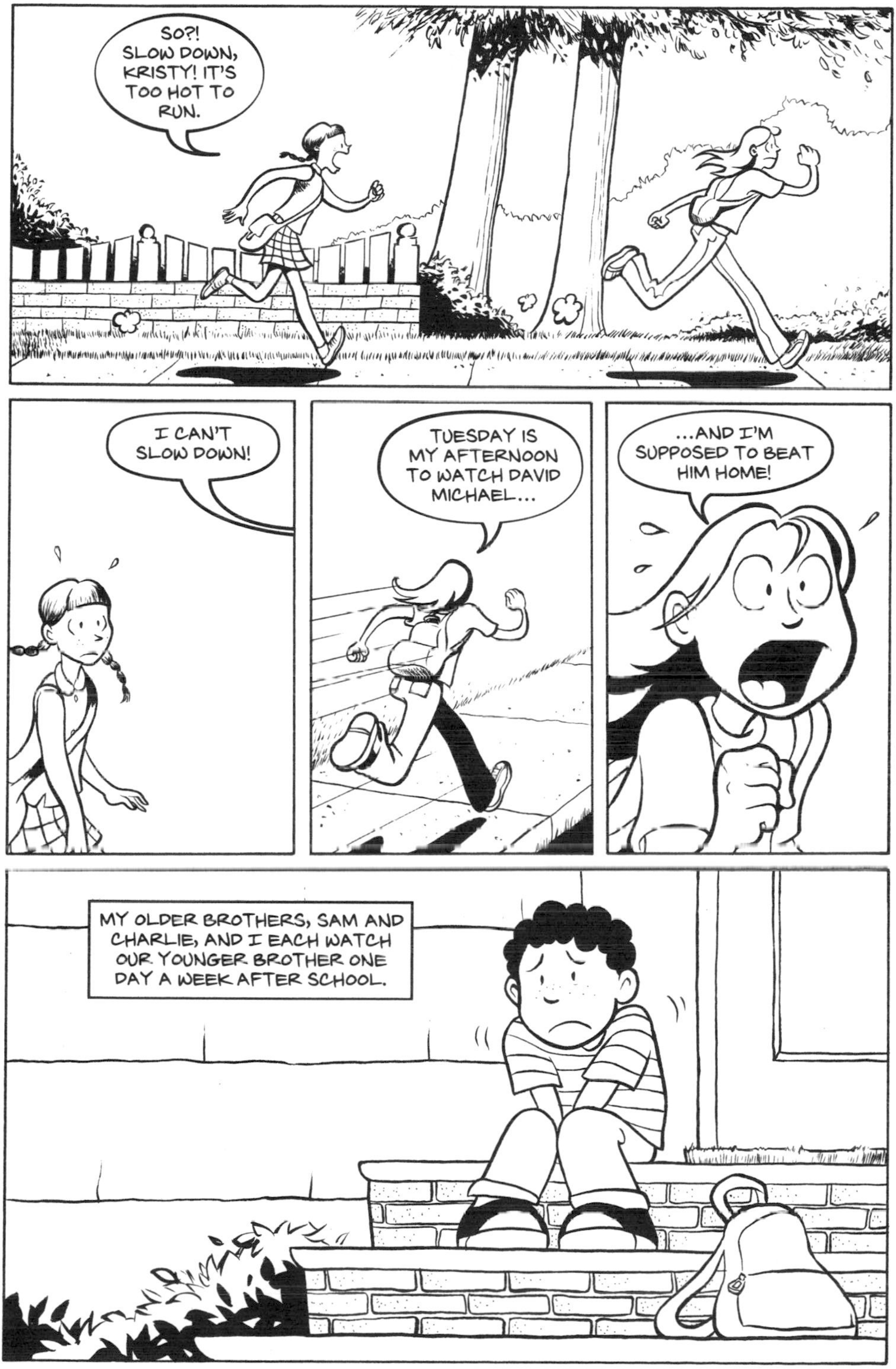
SO?! SLOW DOWN, KRISTY! IT'S TOO HOT TO RUN.
I CAN'T SLOW DOWN!
TUESDAY IS MY AFTERNOON TO WATCH DAVID MICHAEL...
...AND I'M SUPPOSED TO BEAT HIM HOME!
MY OLDER BROTHERS, SAM AND CHARLIE, AND I EACH WATCH OUR YOUNGER BROTHER ONE DAY A WEEK AFTER SCHOOL.

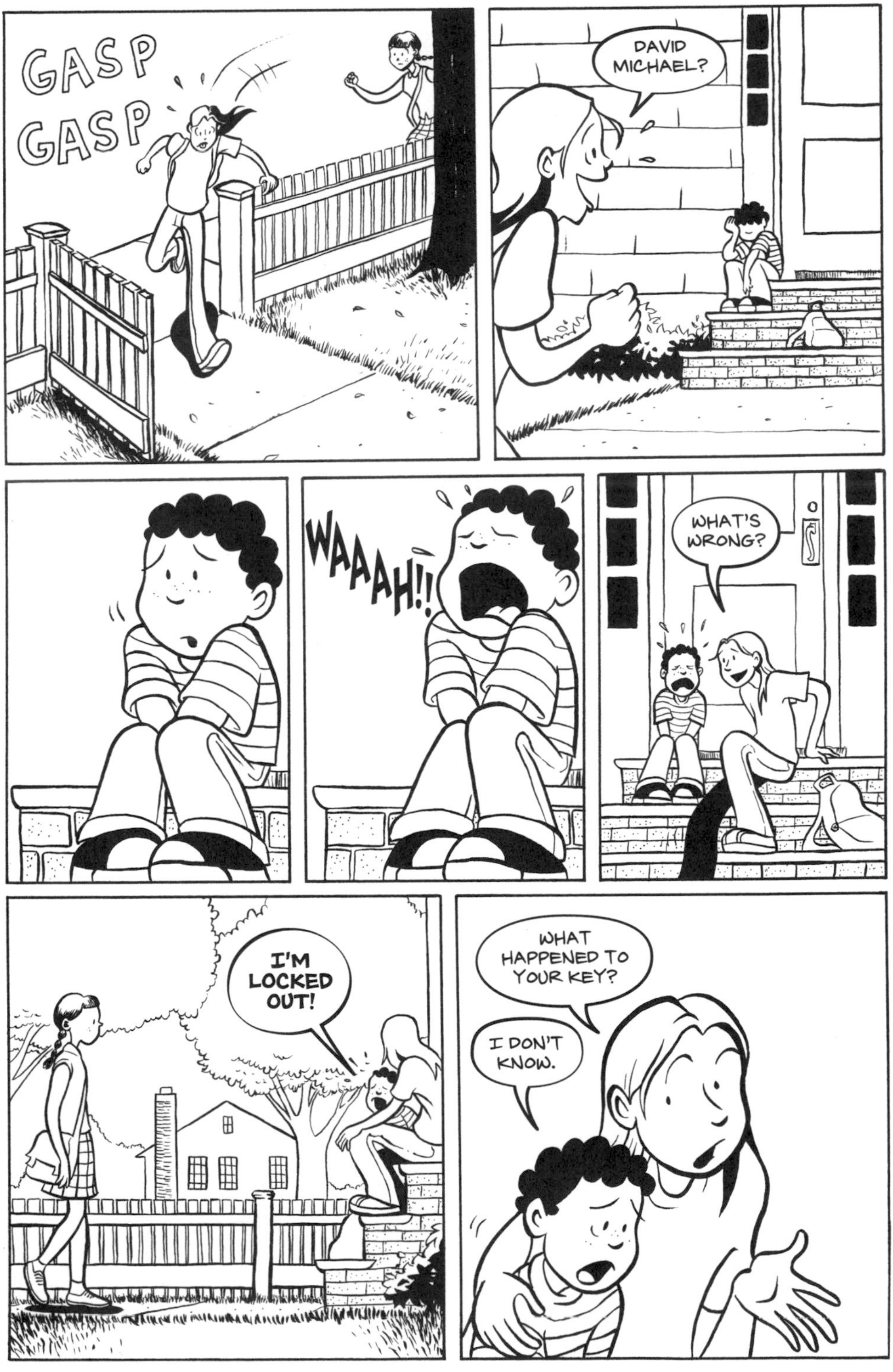

GASP
GASP
DAVID MICHAEL?
WAAAH!!
WHAT'S WRONG?
I'M LOCKED OUT!
WHAT HAPPENED TO YOUR KEY?
I DON'T KNOW.

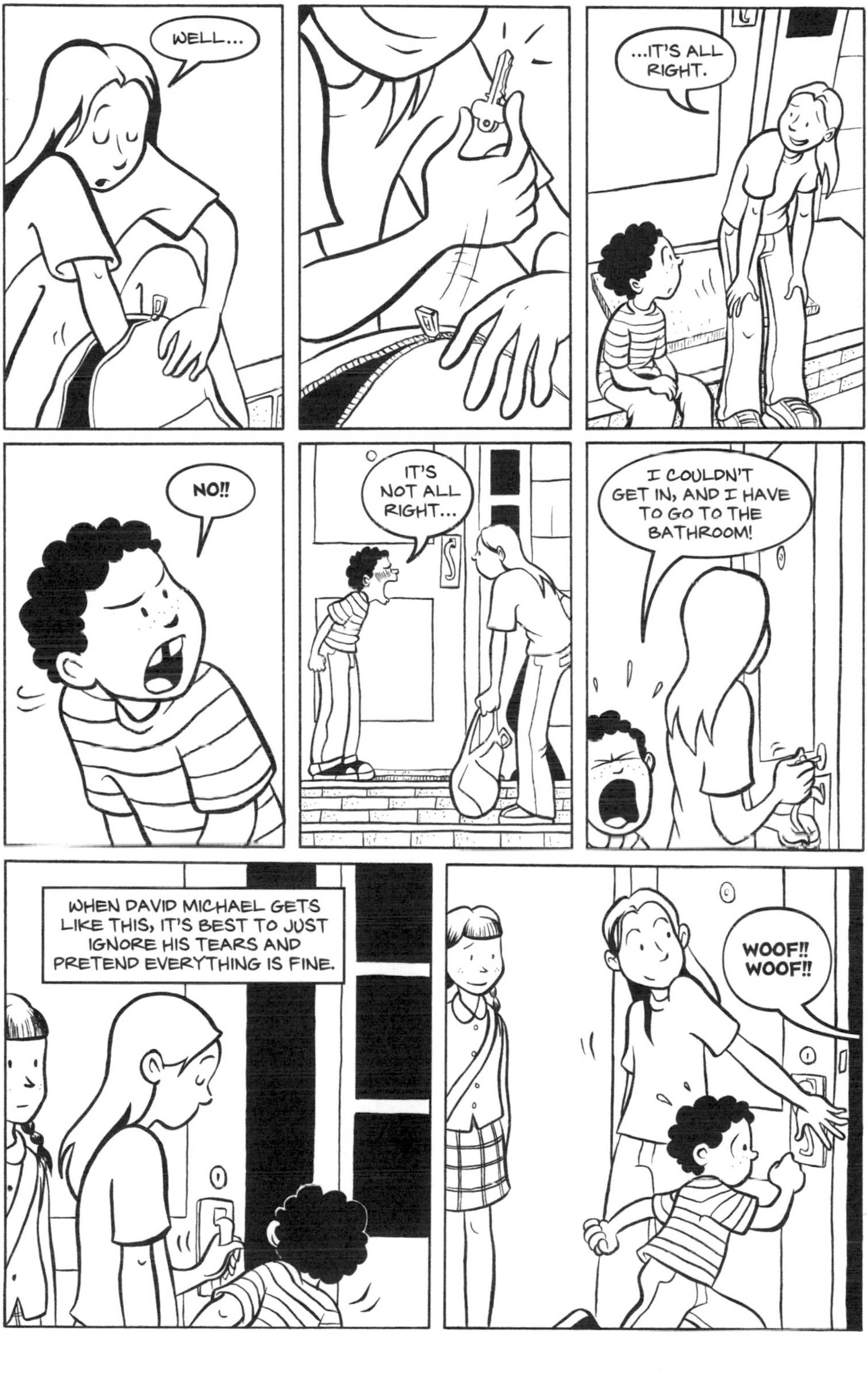
WELL...
...IT'S ALL RIGHT.
NO!!
IT'S NOT ALL RIGHT...
I COULDN'T GET IN, AND I HAVE TO GO TO THE BATHROOM!
WHEN DAVID MICHAEL GETS LIKE THIS, IT'S BEST TO JUST IGNORE HIS TEARS AND PRETEND EVERYTHING IS FINE.
WOOF!! WOOF!!

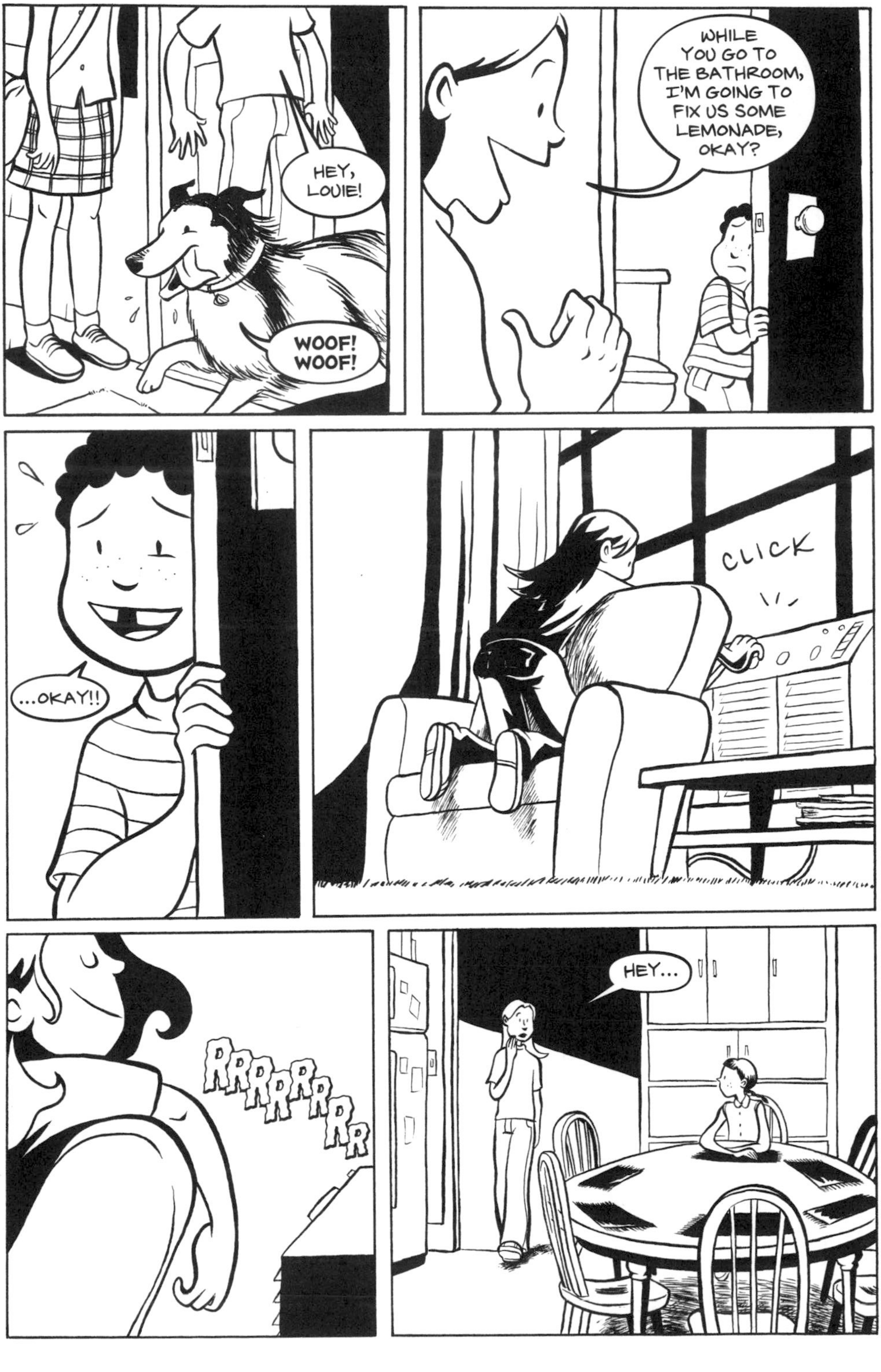
HEY, LOUIE!
WOOF! WOOF!
WHILE YOU GO TO THE BATHROOM, I'M GOING TO FIX US SOME LEMONADE, OKAY?
...OKAY!!
CLICK
RRRRRRRRR
HEY...

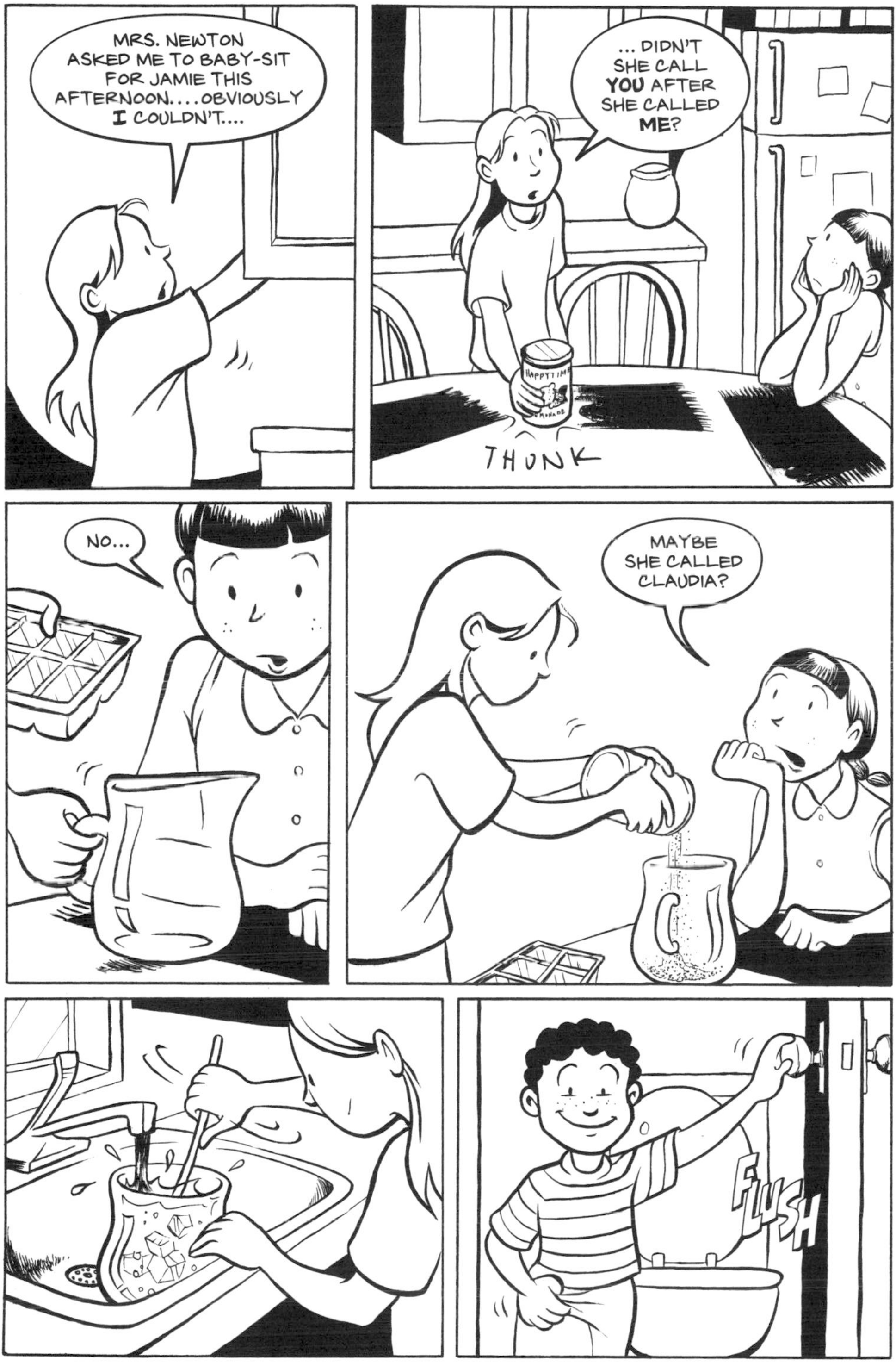
MRS. NEWTON ASKED ME TO BABY-SIT FOR JAMIE THIS AFTERNOON....OBVIOUSLY I COULDN'T....
...DIDN'T SHE CALL YOU AFTER SHE CALLED ME?
HAPPYTIME LEMONADE
THUNK
NO...
MAYBE SHE CALLED CLAUDIA?
FLUSH

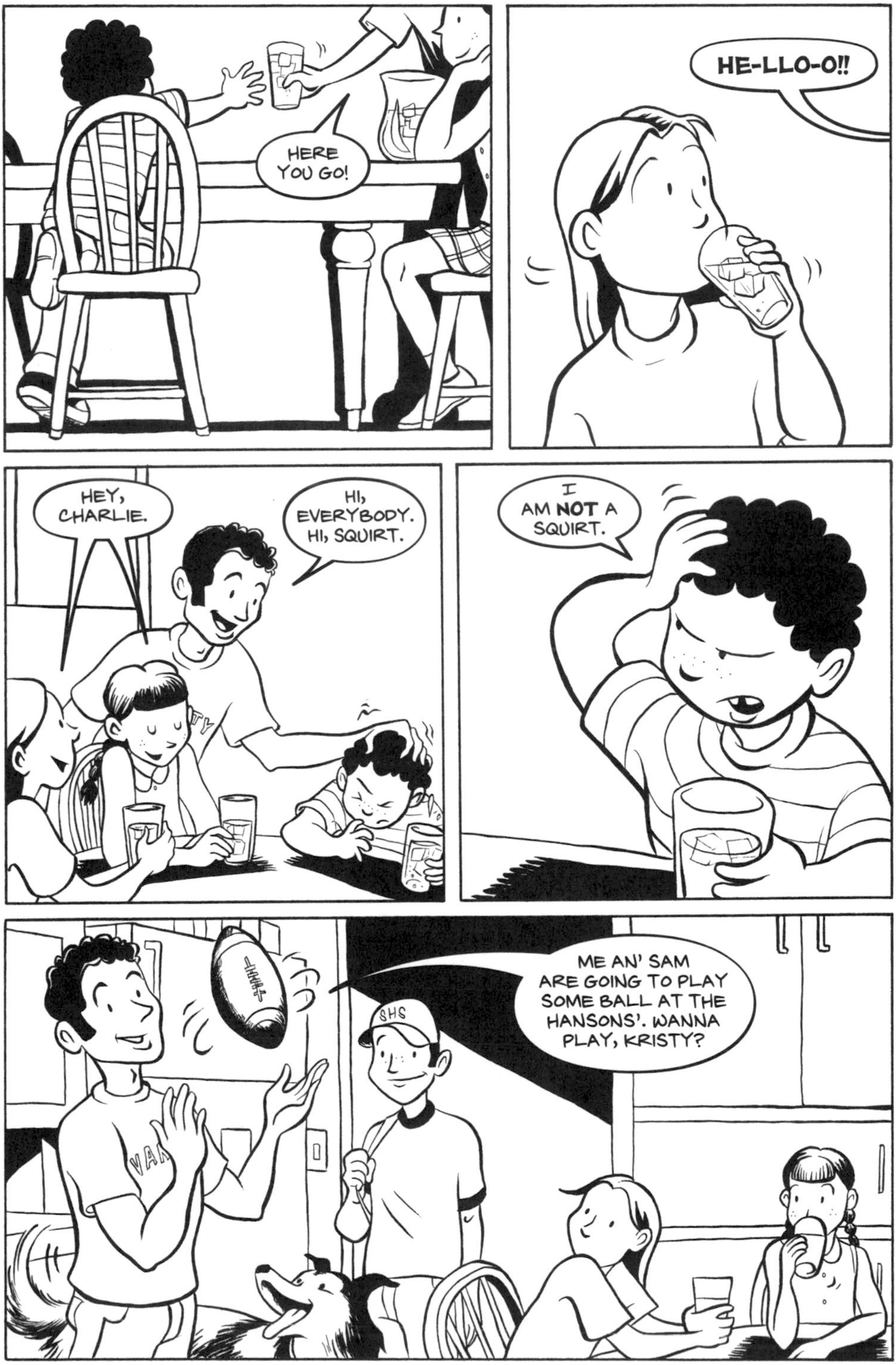
HERE YOU GO!
HE-LLO-O!!
HEY, CHARLIE.
HI, EVERYBODY. HI, SQUIRT.
I AM **NOT** A SQUIRT.
ME AN' SAM ARE GOING TO PLAY SOME BALL AT THE HANSONS'. WANNA PLAY, KRISTY?

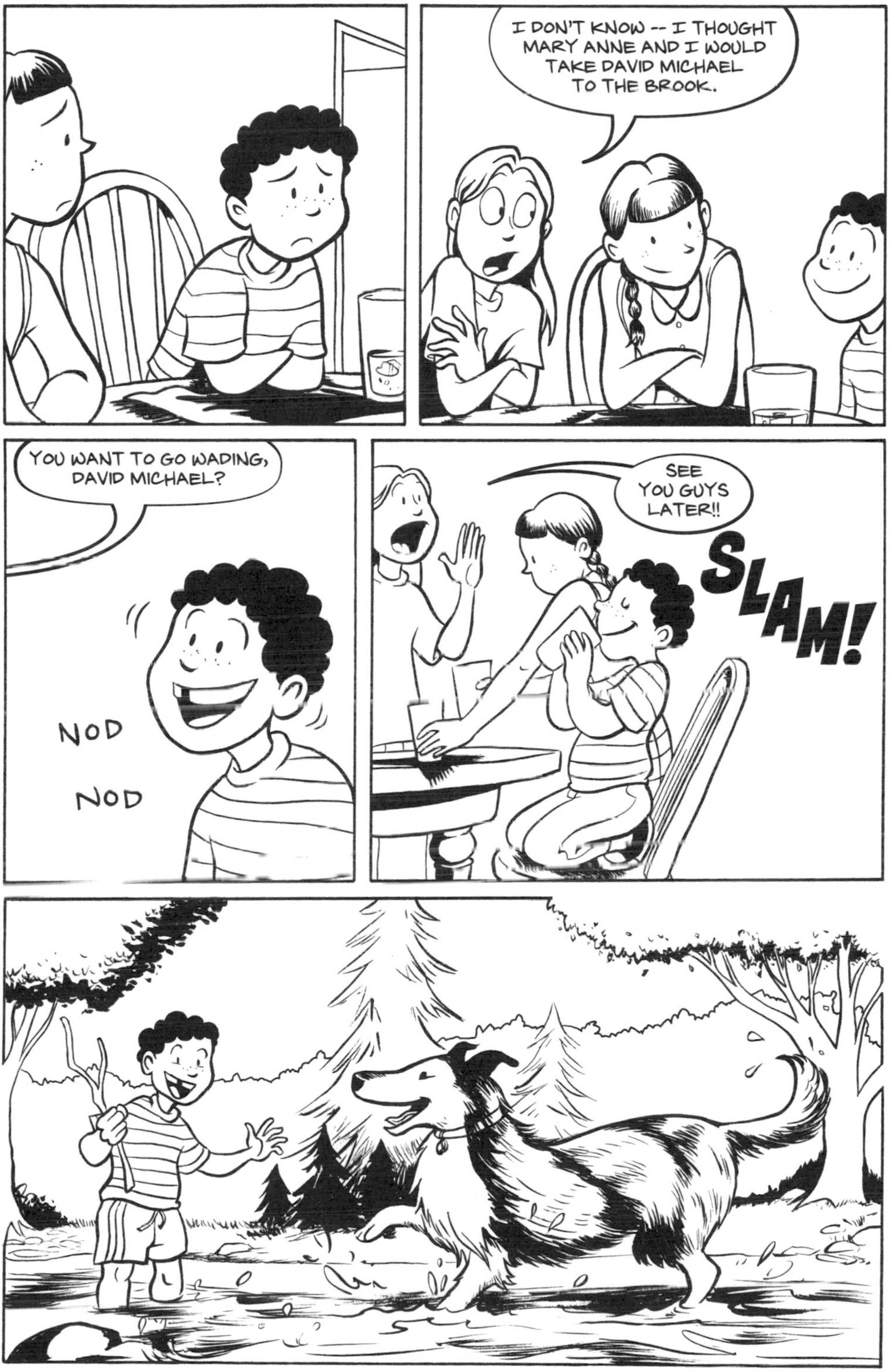
I DON'T KNOW -- I THOUGHT MARY ANNE AND I WOULD TAKE DAVID MICHAEL TO THE BROOK.
YOU WANT TO GO WADING, DAVID MICHAEL?
NOD
NOD
SEE YOU GUYS LATER!!
SLAM!

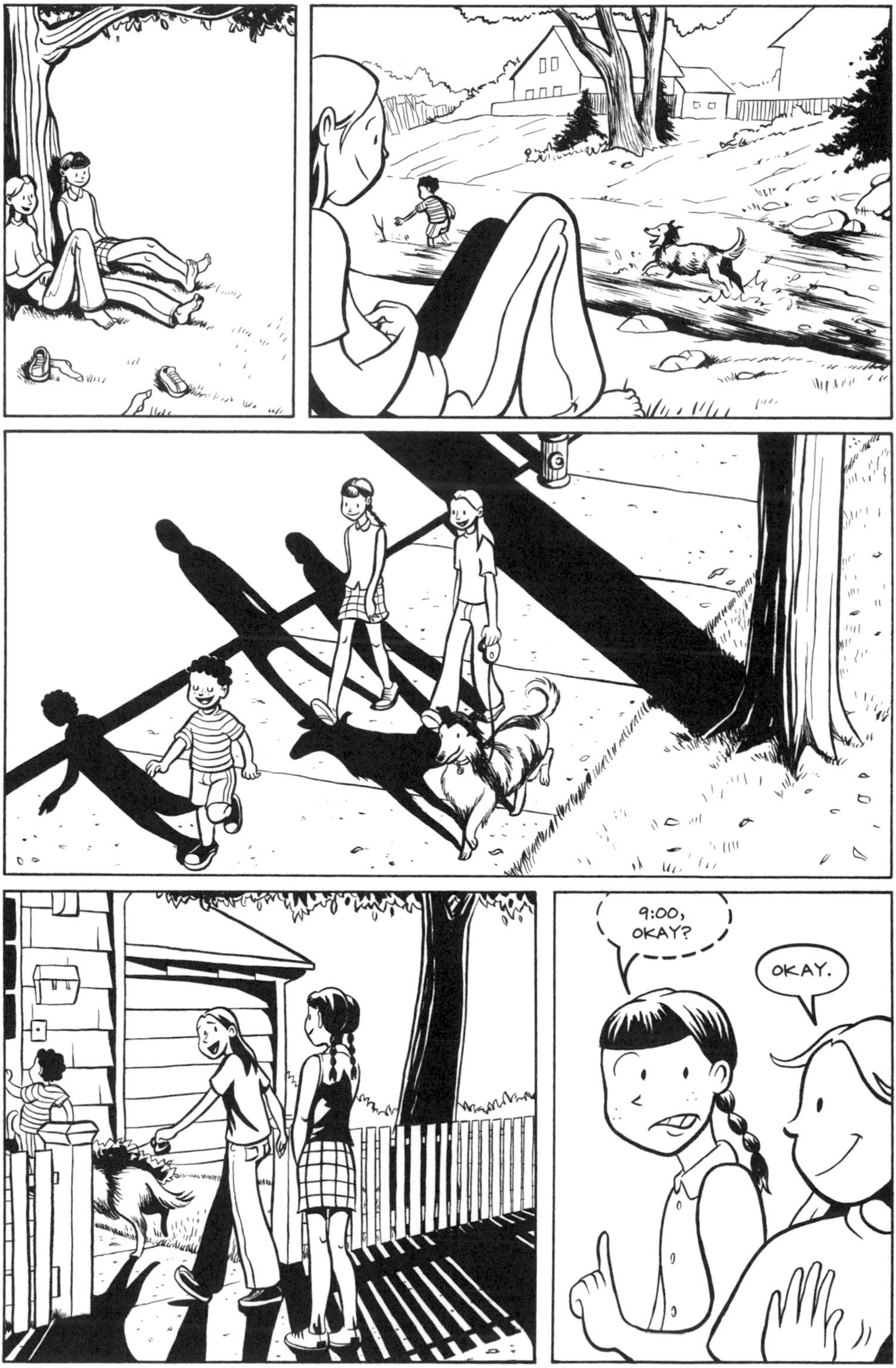
9:00, OKAY?
OKAY.

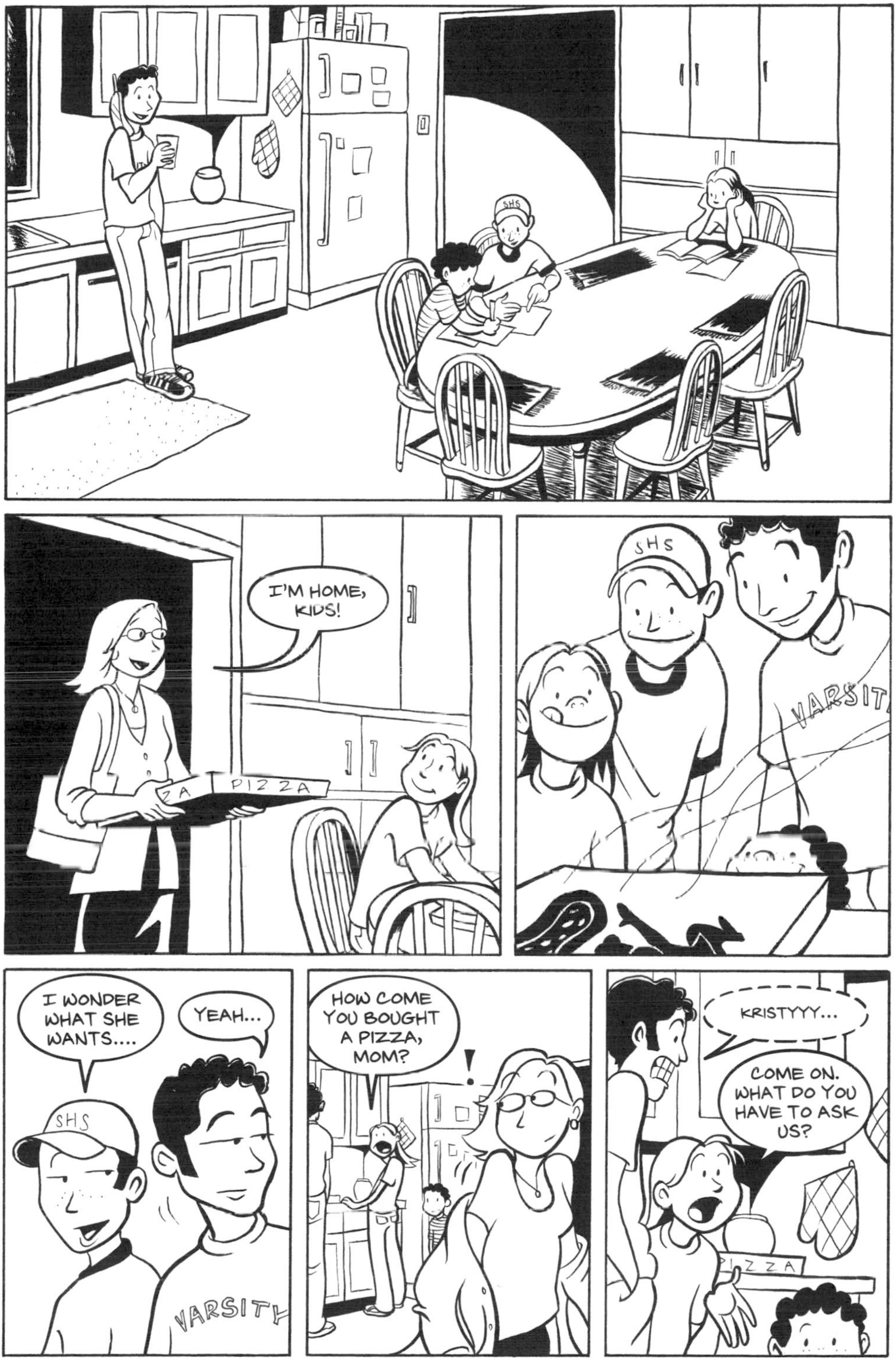

I'M HOME, KIDS!
PIZZA
I WONDER WHAT SHE WANTS....
YEAH...
HOW COME YOU BOUGHT A PIZZA, MOM?
!
KRISTYYY...
COME ON. WHAT DO YOU HAVE TO ASK US?

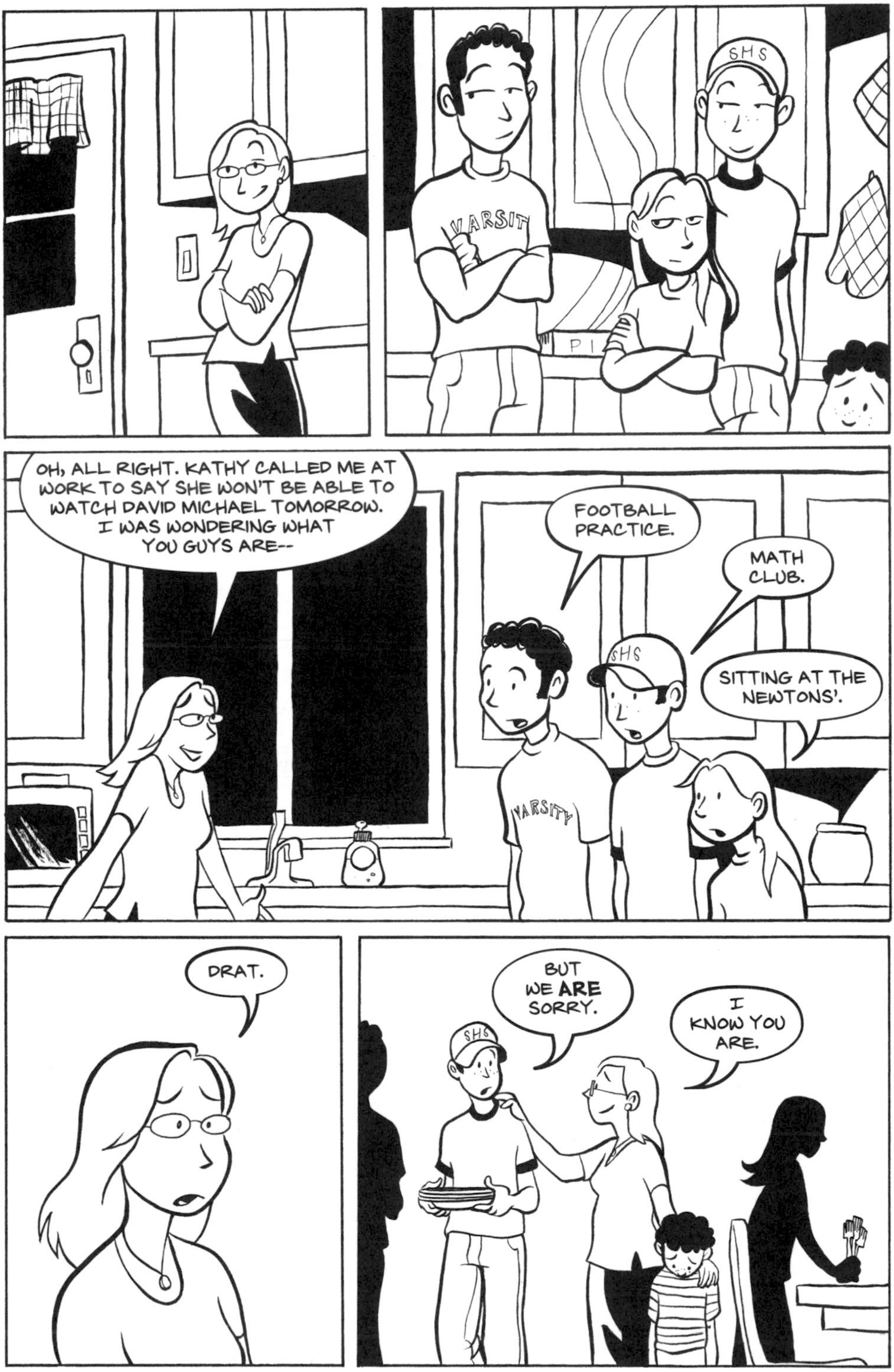
OH, ALL RIGHT. KATHY CALLED ME AT WORK TO SAY SHE WON'T BE ABLE TO WATCH DAVID MICHAEL TOMORROW. I WAS WONDERING WHAT YOU GUYS ARE--
FOOTBALL PRACTICE.
MATH CLUB.
SITTING AT THE NEWTONS'.
DRAT.
BUT WE **ARE** SORRY.
I KNOW YOU ARE.

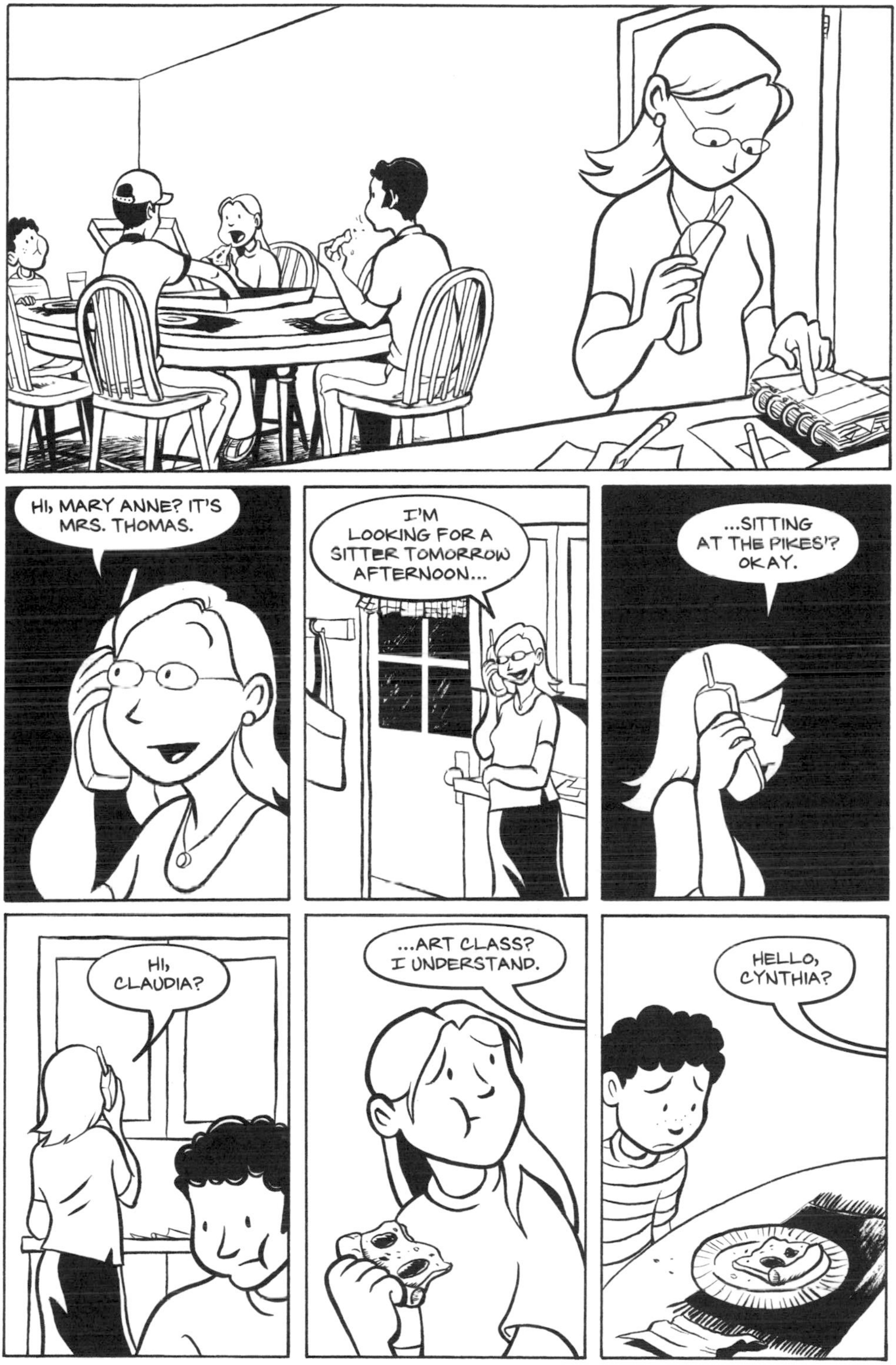
HI, MARY ANNE? IT'S MRS. THOMAS.
I'M LOOKING FOR A SITTER TOMORROW AFTERNOON...
...SITTING AT THE PIKES'? OKAY.
HI, CLAUDIA?
...ART CLASS? I UNDERSTAND.
HELLO, CYNTHIA?

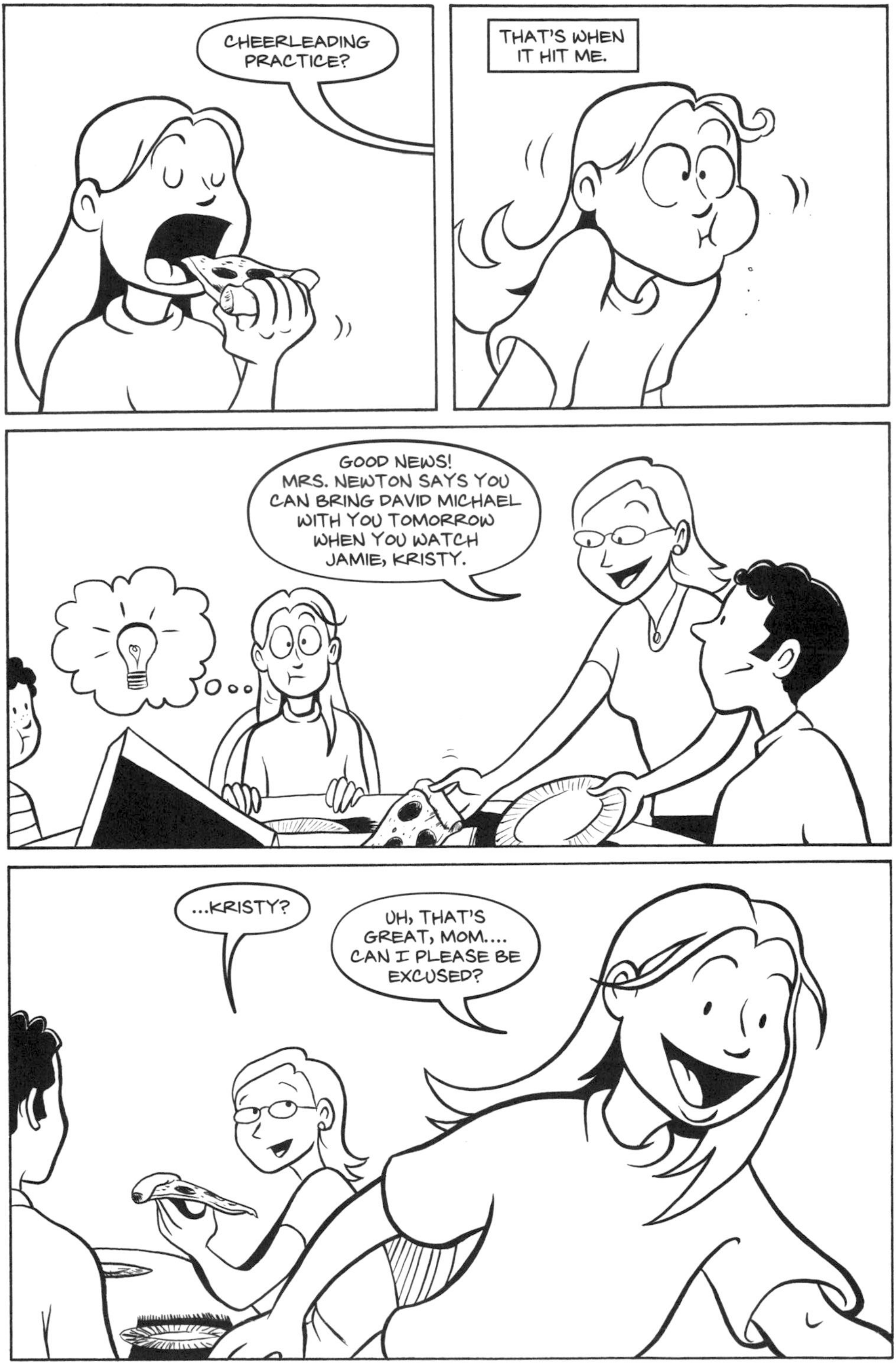
CHEERLEADING PRACTICE?
THAT'S WHEN IT HIT ME.
GOOD NEWS! MRS. NEWTON SAYS YOU CAN BRING DAVID MICHAEL WITH YOU TOMORROW WHEN YOU WATCH JAMIE, KRISTY.
...KRISTY?
UH, THAT'S GREAT, MOM.... CAN I PLEASE BE EXCUSED?

Chapter 2

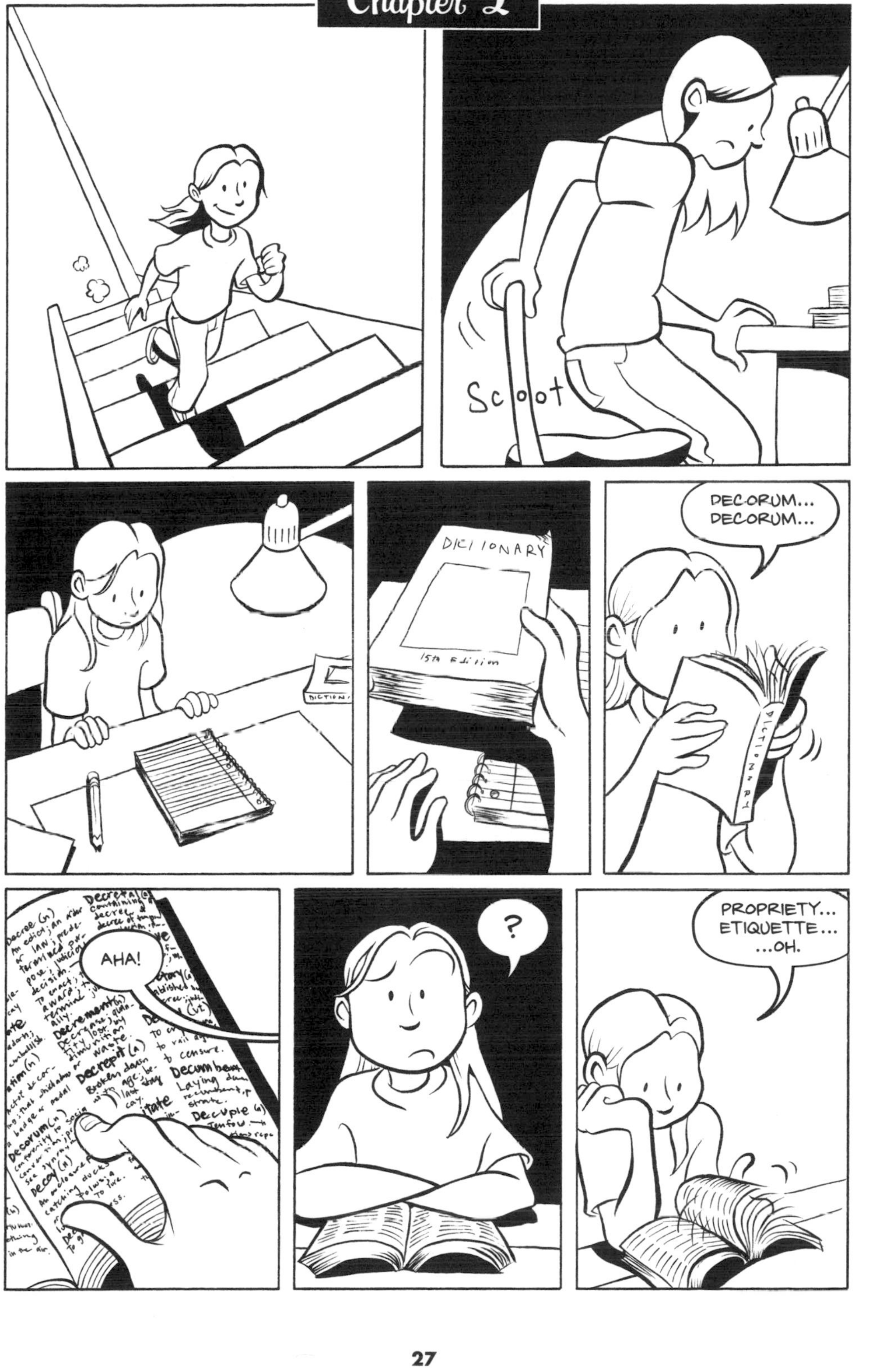

Scoot
DICTIONARY
15th Edition
DECORUM... DECORUM...
DICTIONARY
AHA!
?
PROPRIETY... ETIQUETTE... ...OH.

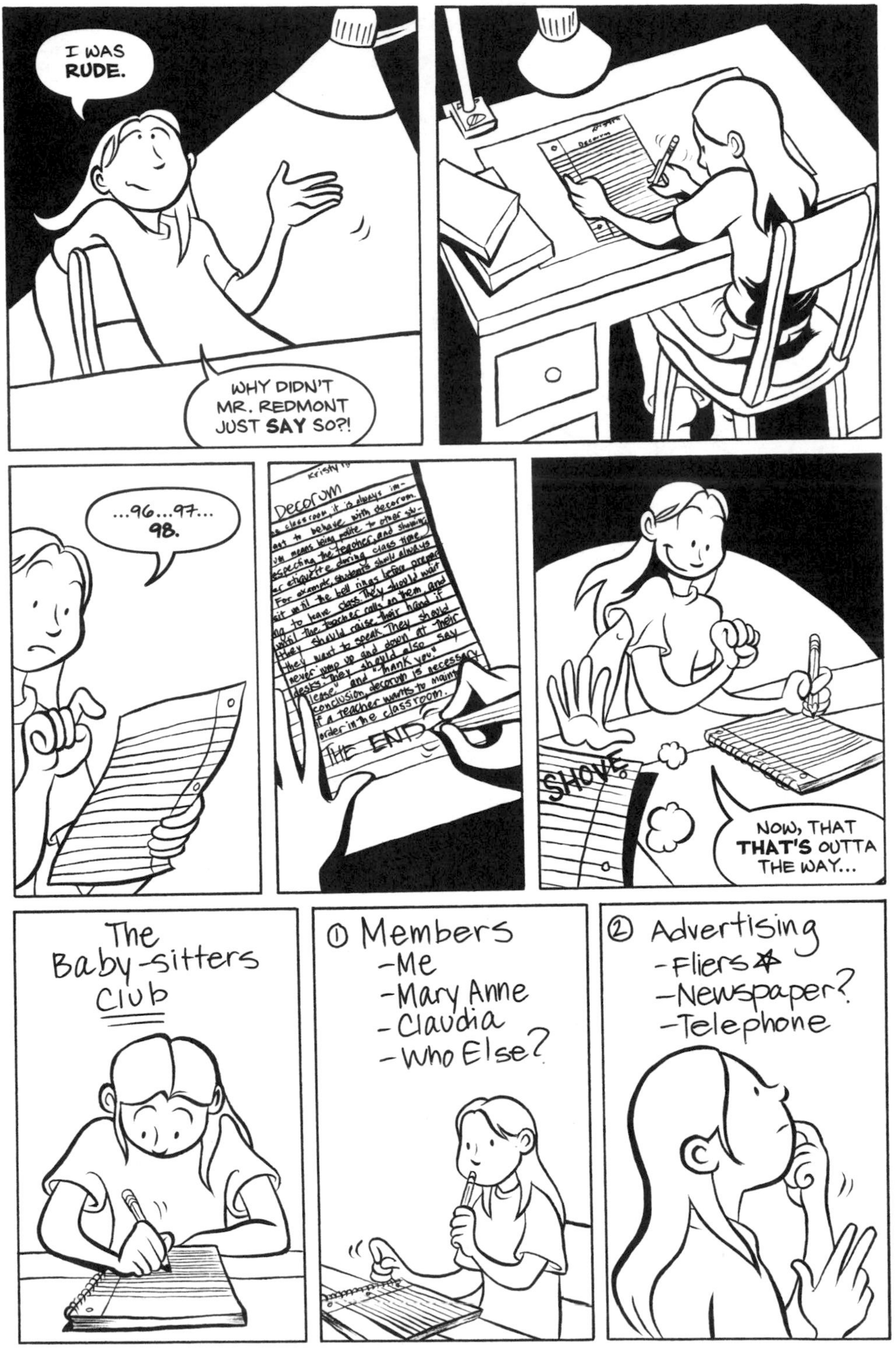
I WAS RUDE.
WHY DIDN'T MR. REDMONT JUST SAY SO?!
...96...97... 98.
Decorum
THE END
SHOVE
NOW, THAT THAT'S OUTTA THE WAY...
The Baby-sitters Club
① Members
-Me
-Mary Anne
-Claudia
-Who Else?
② Advertising
-Fliers
-Newspaper?
-Telephone

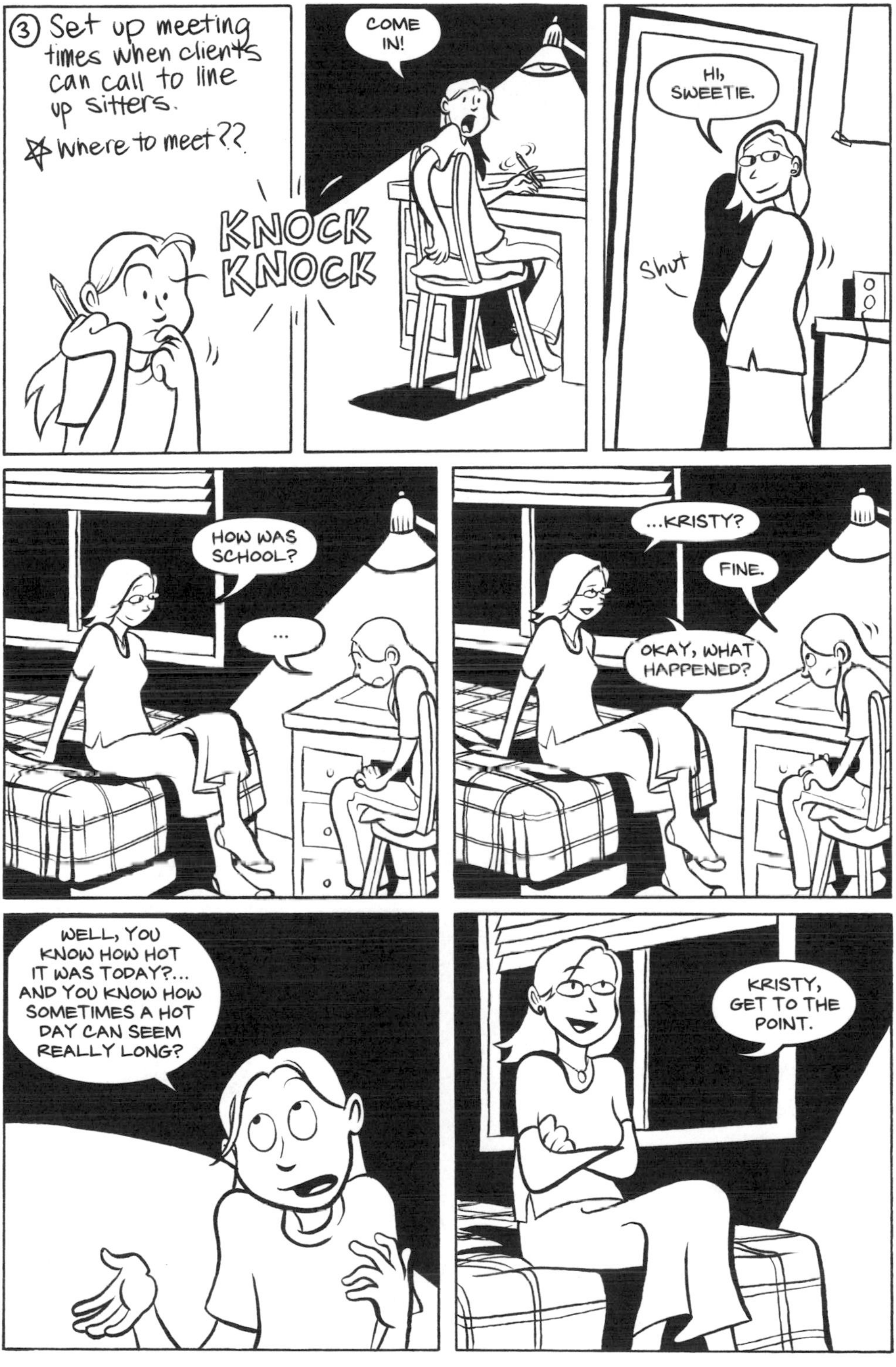
③ Set up meeting times when clients can call to line up sitters.
✡ Where to meet??
KNOCK KNOCK
COME IN!
HI, SWEETIE.
Shut
HOW WAS SCHOOL?
...
...KRISTY?
FINE.
OKAY, WHAT HAPPENED?
WELL, YOU KNOW HOW HOT IT WAS TODAY?... AND YOU KNOW HOW SOMETIMES A HOT DAY CAN SEEM REALLY LONG?
KRISTY, GET TO THE POINT.

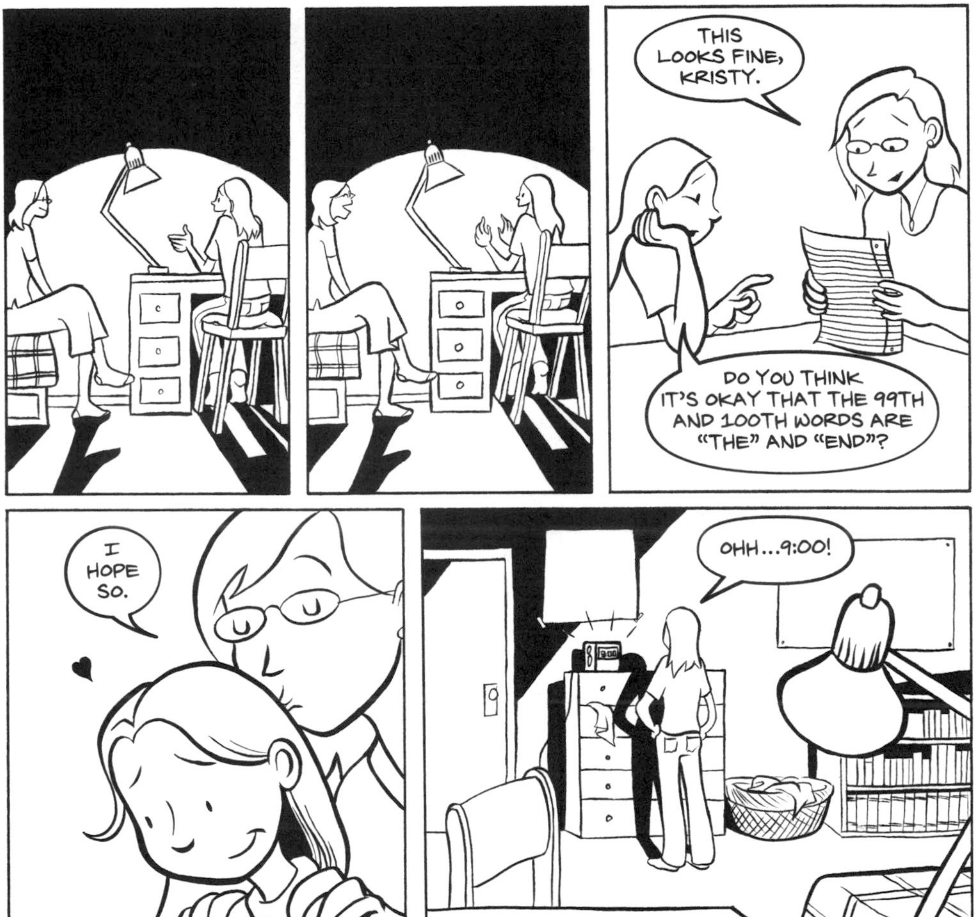
THIS LOOKS FINE, KRISTY.
DO YOU THINK IT'S OKAY THAT THE 99TH AND 100TH WORDS ARE "THE" AND "END"?
I HOPE SO.
OHH...9:00!
CLICK

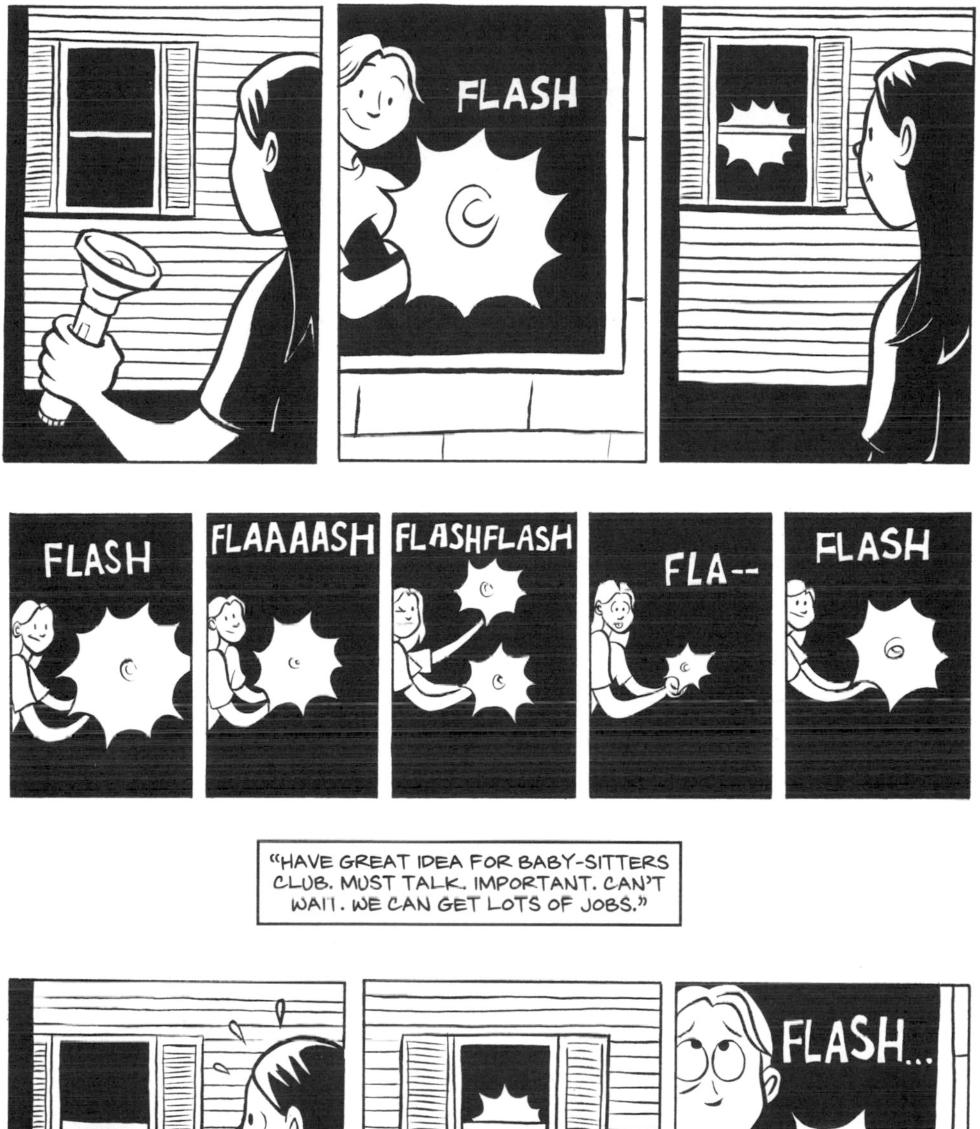
FLASH
FLASH
FLAAAASH
FLASHFLASH
FLA--
FLASH
"HAVE GREAT IDEA FOR BABY-SITTERS CLUB. MUST TALK. IMPORTANT. CAN'T WAIT. WE CAN GET LOTS OF JOBS."
"WHAT?"
FLASH...
"HAVE IDEA. BABY-SITTERS CLUB. MUST--"

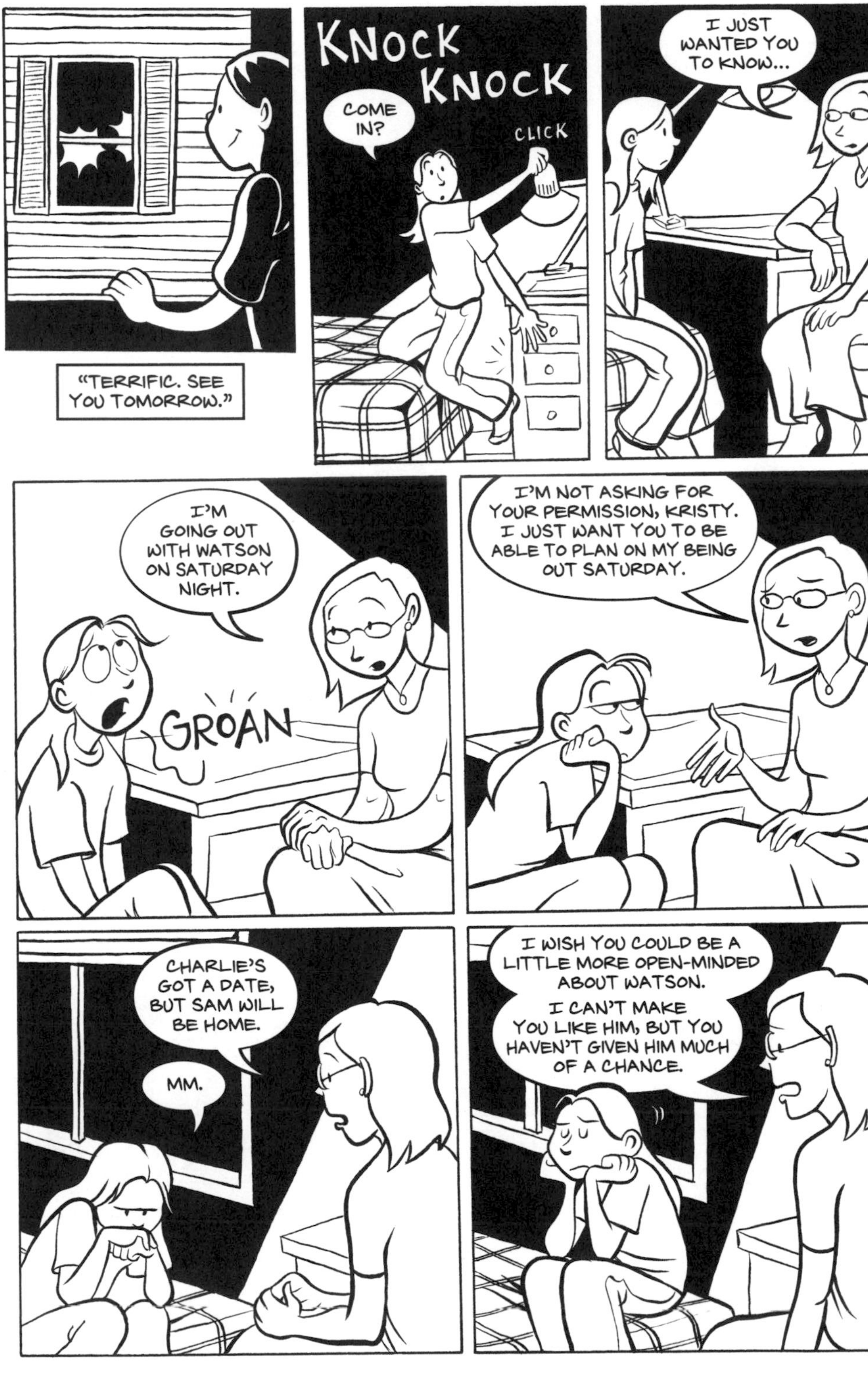
"TERRIFIC. SEE YOU TOMORROW."
KNOCK KNOCK
COME IN?
CLICK
I JUST WANTED YOU TO KNOW...
I'M GOING OUT WITH WATSON ON SATURDAY NIGHT.
GROAN
I'M NOT ASKING FOR YOUR PERMISSION, KRISTY. I JUST WANT YOU TO BE ABLE TO PLAN ON MY BEING OUT SATURDAY.
CHARLIE'S GOT A DATE, BUT SAM WILL BE HOME.
MM.
I WISH YOU COULD BE A LITTLE MORE OPEN-MINDED ABOUT WATSON.
I CAN'T MAKE YOU LIKE HIM, BUT YOU HAVEN'T GIVEN HIM MUCH OF A CHANCE.

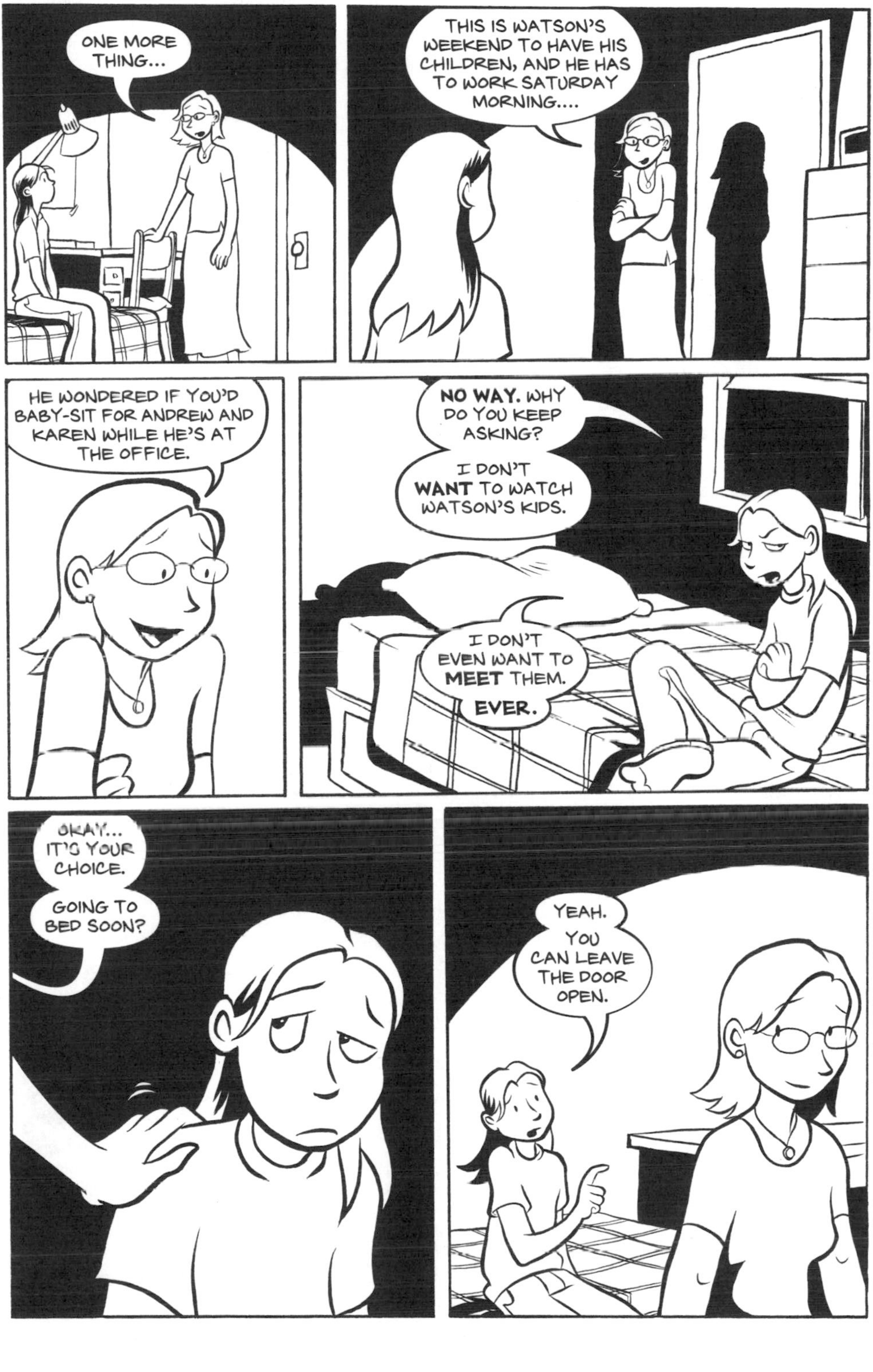
ONE MORE THING...
THIS IS WATSON'S WEEKEND TO HAVE HIS CHILDREN, AND HE HAS TO WORK SATURDAY MORNING....
HE WONDERED IF YOU'D BABY-SIT FOR ANDREW AND KAREN WHILE HE'S AT THE OFFICE.
NO WAY. WHY DO YOU KEEP ASKING?
I DON'T WANT TO WATCH WATSON'S KIDS.
I DON'T EVEN WANT TO MEET THEM.
EVER.
OKAY... IT'S YOUR CHOICE.
GOING TO BED SOON?
YEAH.
YOU CAN LEAVE THE DOOR OPEN.

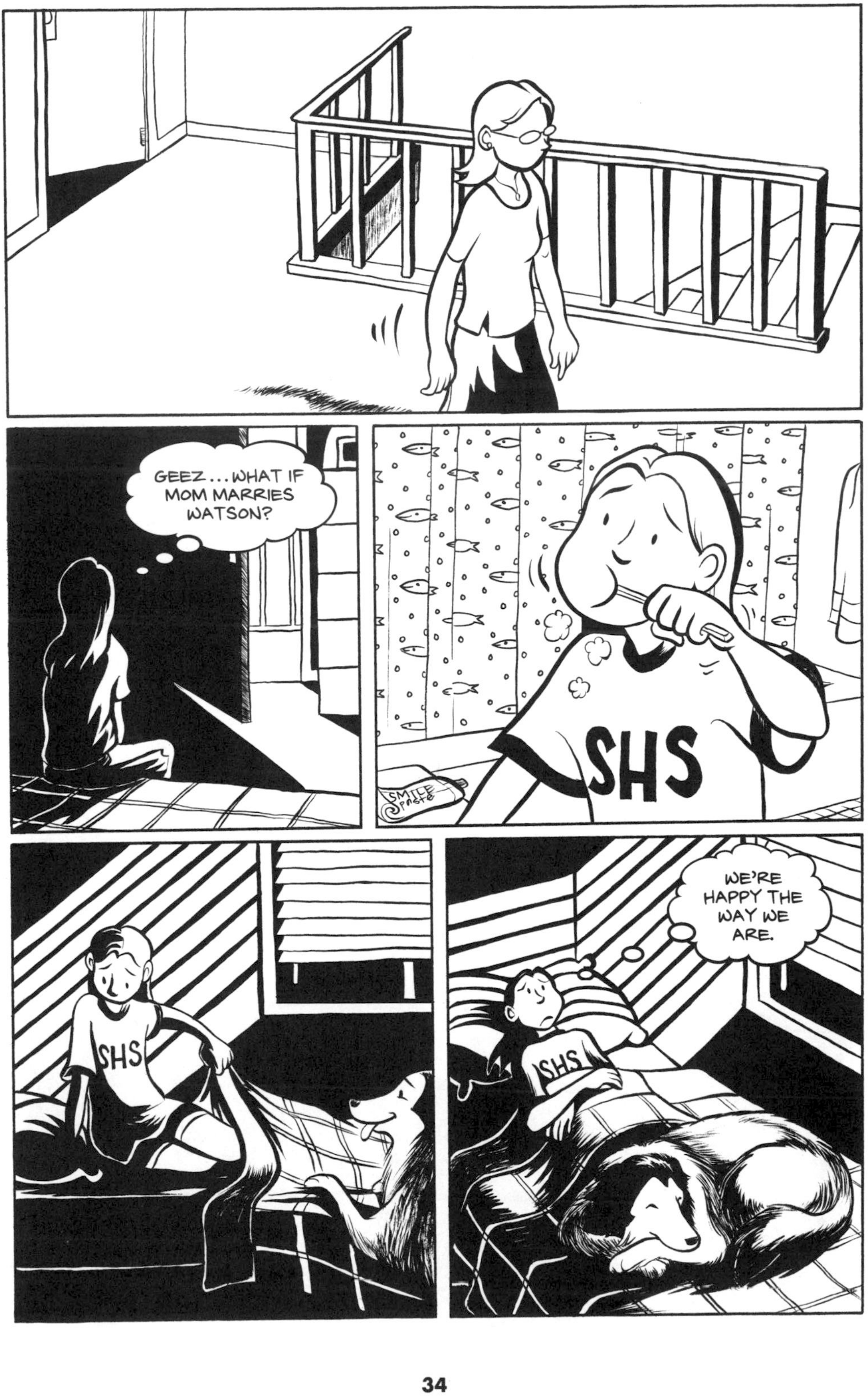
GEEZ... WHAT IF MOM MARRIES WATSON?
SHS
SMILE paste
SHS
WE'RE HAPPY THE WAY WE ARE.
SHS

Chapter 3

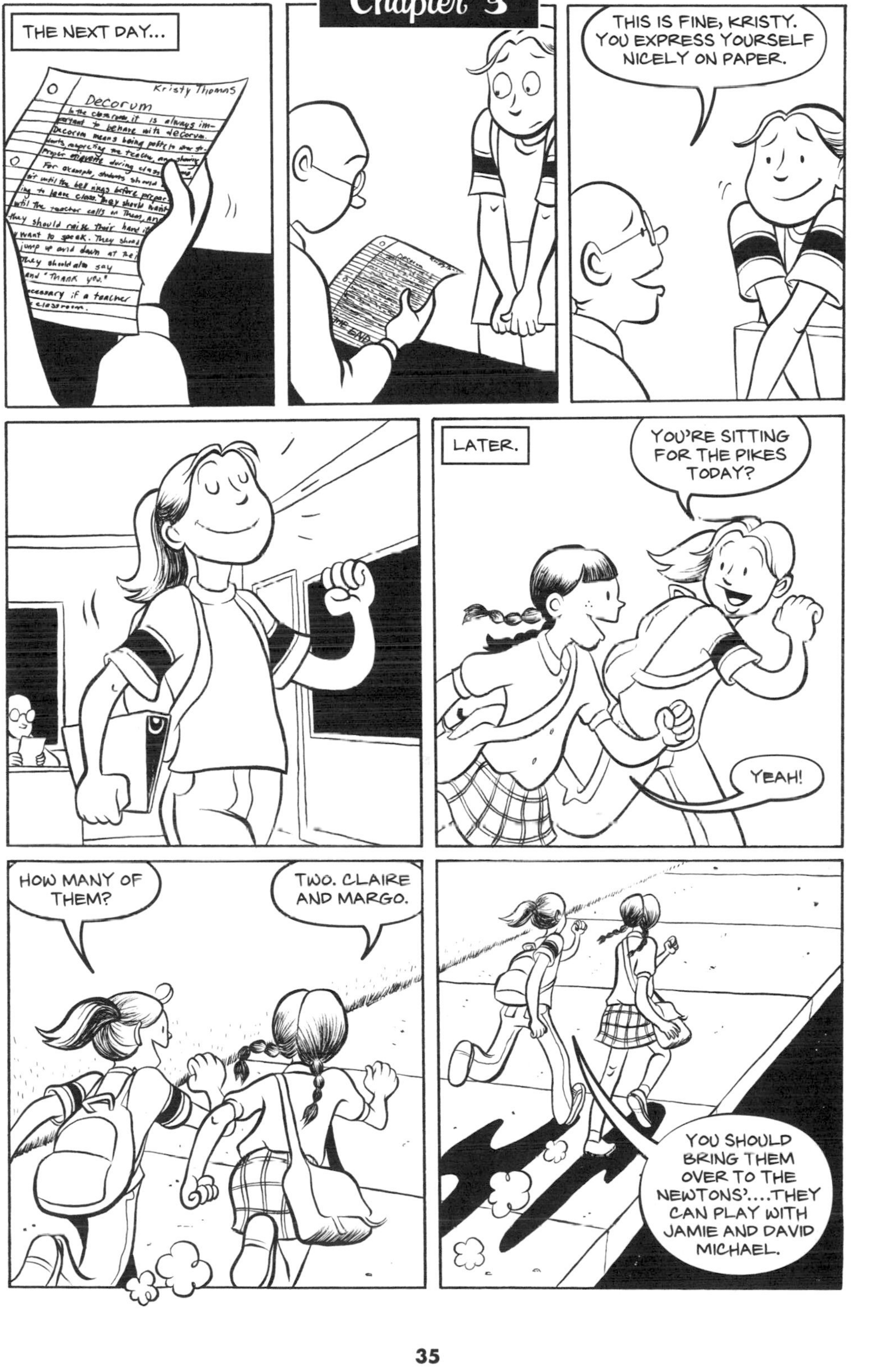

THE NEXT DAY...
Kristy Thomas
Decorum
THIS IS FINE, KRISTY. YOU EXPRESS YOURSELF NICELY ON PAPER.
LATER.
YOU'RE SITTING FOR THE PIKES TODAY?
YEAH!
HOW MANY OF THEM?
TWO. CLAIRE AND MARGO.
YOU SHOULD BRING THEM OVER TO THE NEWTONS'....THEY CAN PLAY WITH JAMIE AND DAVID MICHAEL.

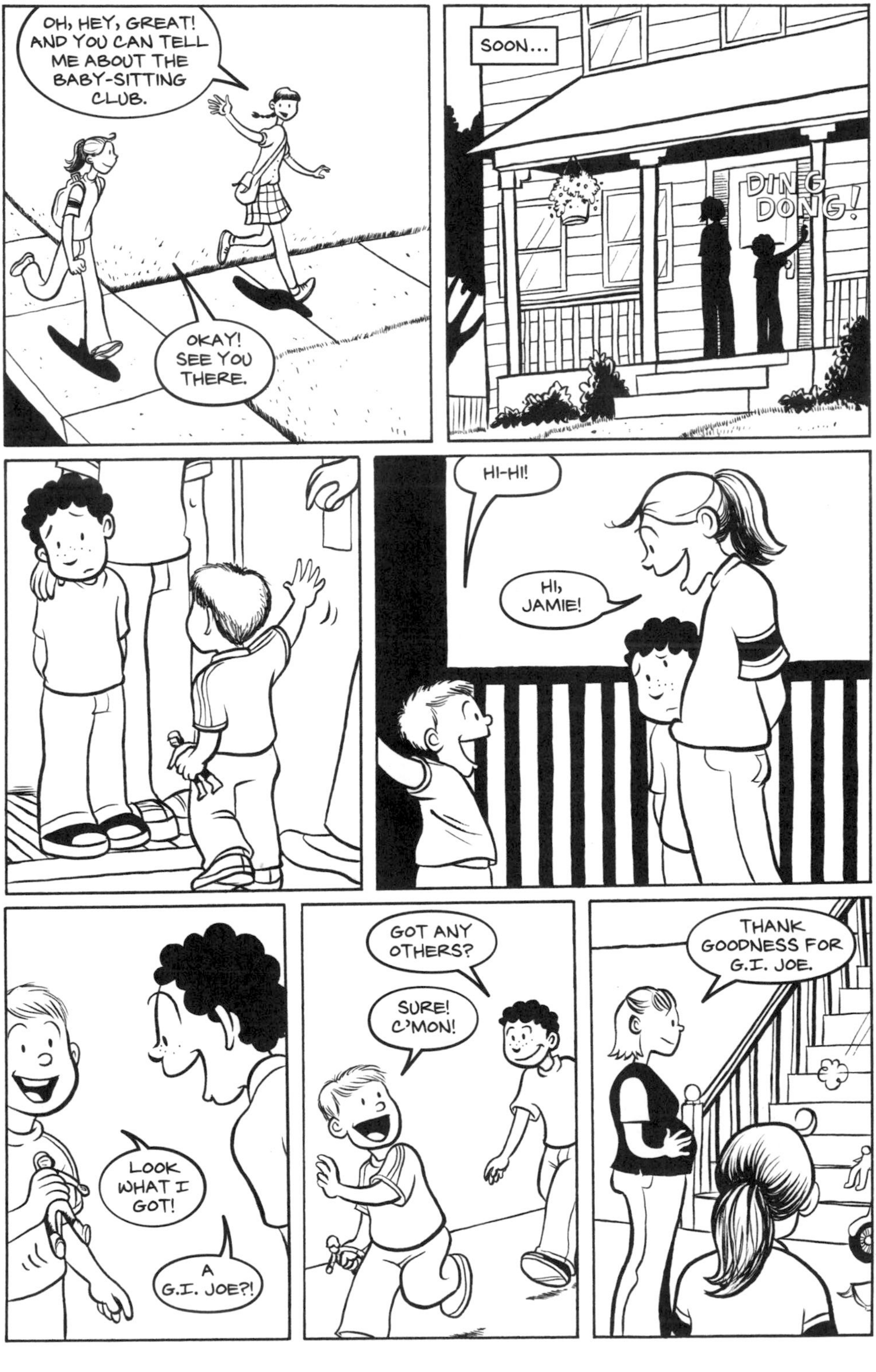
OH, HEY, GREAT! AND YOU CAN TELL ME ABOUT THE BABY-SITTING CLUB.
OKAY! SEE YOU THERE.
SOON...
DING DONG!
HI-HI!
HI, JAMIE!
LOOK WHAT I GOT!
A G.I. JOE?!
GOT ANY OTHERS?
SURE! C'MON!
THANK GOODNESS FOR G.I. JOE.

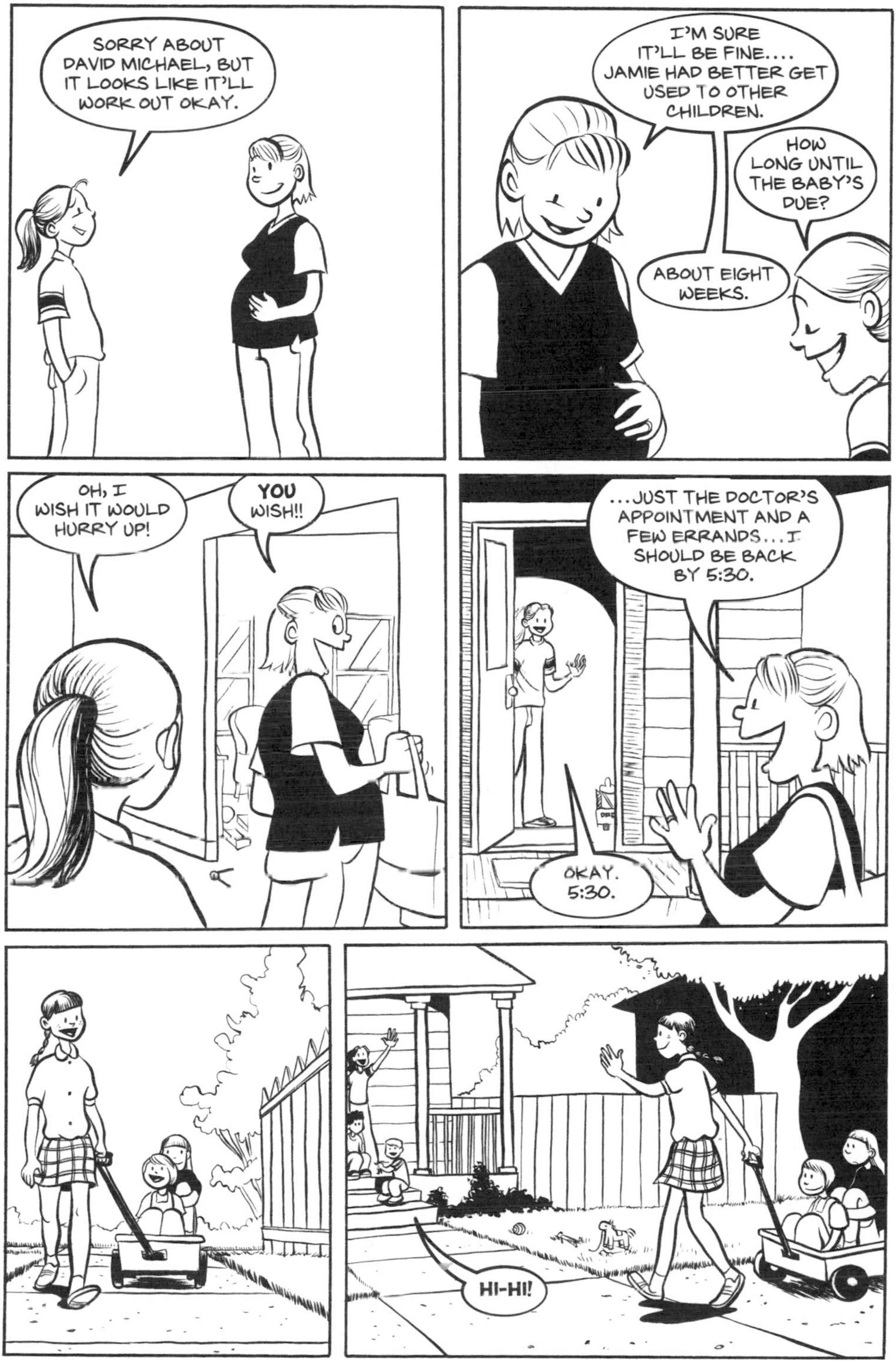
SORRY ABOUT DAVID MICHAEL, BUT IT LOOKS LIKE IT'LL WORK OUT OKAY.
I'M SURE IT'LL BE FINE.... JAMIE HAD BETTER GET USED TO OTHER CHILDREN.
HOW LONG UNTIL THE BABY'S DUE?
ABOUT EIGHT WEEKS.
OH, I WISH IT WOULD HURRY UP!
YOU WISH!!
...JUST THE DOCTOR'S APPOINTMENT AND A FEW ERRANDS... I SHOULD BE BACK BY 5:30.
OKAY. 5:30.
HI-HI!

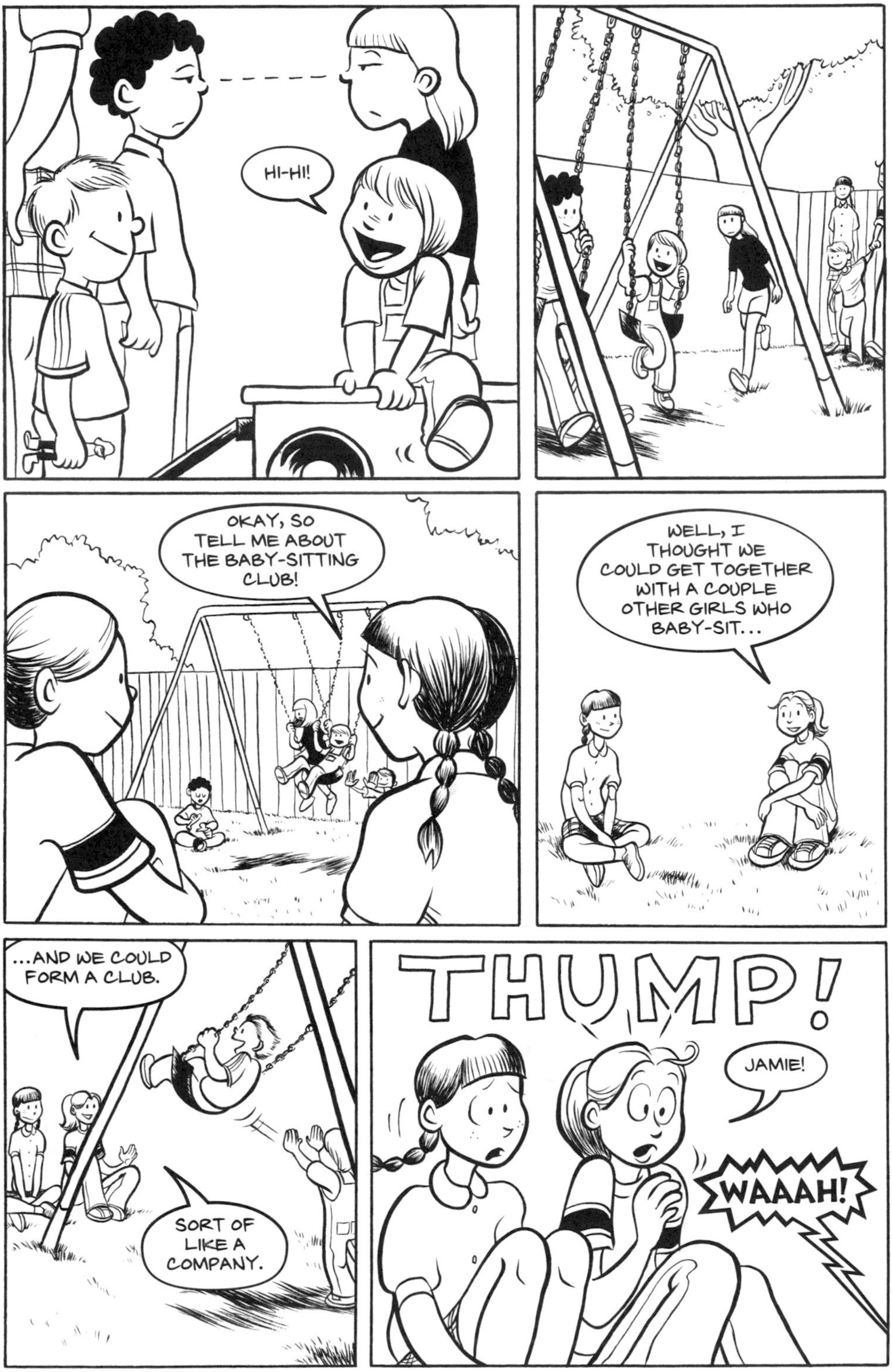
HI-HI!
OKAY, SO TELL ME ABOUT THE BABY-SITTING CLUB!
WELL, I THOUGHT WE COULD GET TOGETHER WITH A COUPLE OTHER GIRLS WHO BABY-SIT...
...AND WE COULD FORM A CLUB.
SORT OF LIKE A COMPANY.
THUMP!
JAMIE!
WAAAH!

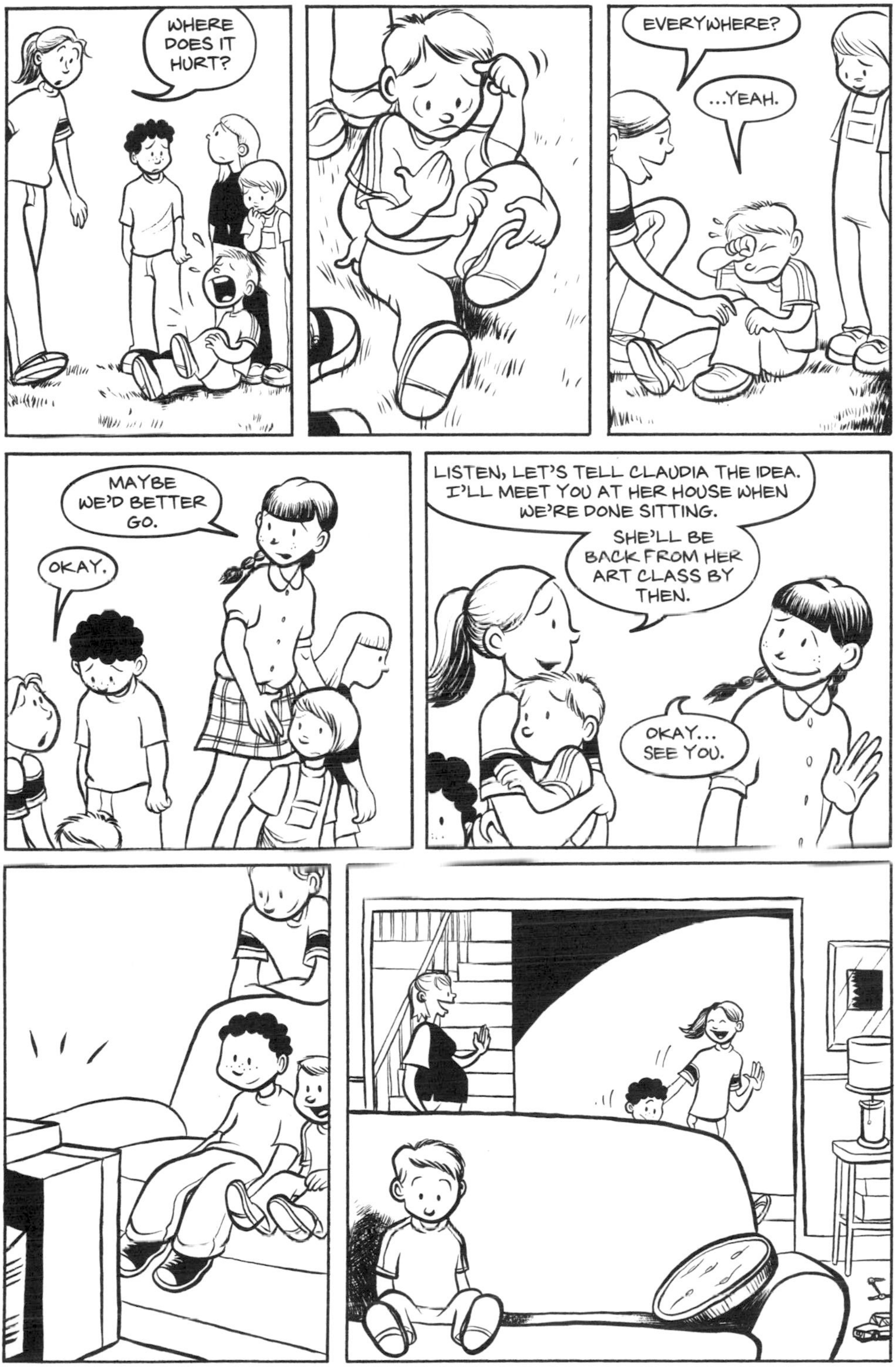
WHERE DOES IT HURT?
EVERYWHERE?
...YEAH.
MAYBE WE'D BETTER GO.
OKAY.
LISTEN, LET'S TELL CLAUDIA THE IDEA. I'LL MEET YOU AT HER HOUSE WHEN WE'RE DONE SITTING.
SHE'LL BE BACK FROM HER ART CLASS BY THEN.
OKAY... SEE YOU.

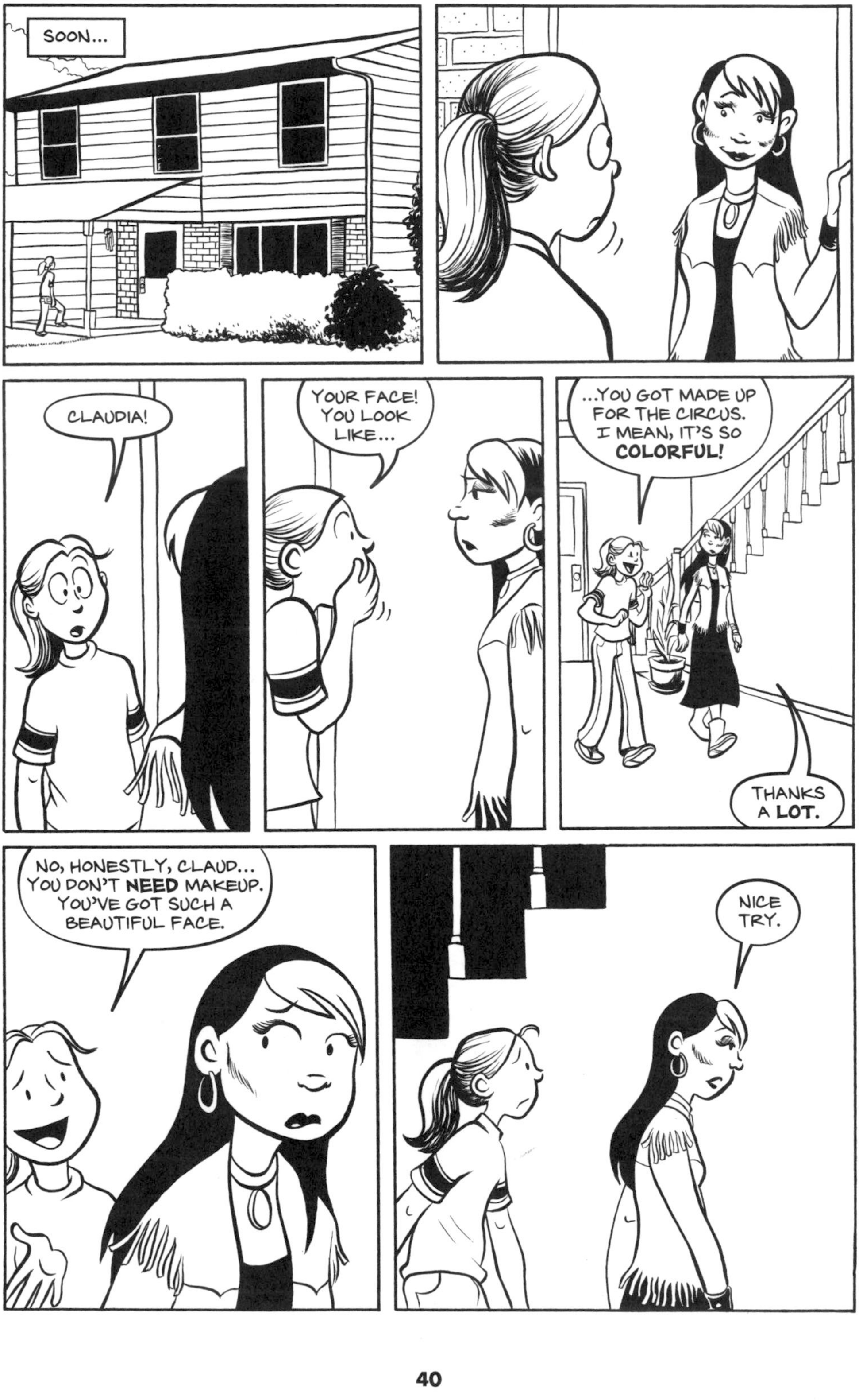
SOON...
CLAUDIA!
YOUR FACE! YOU LOOK LIKE...
...YOU GOT MADE UP FOR THE CIRCUS. I MEAN, IT'S SO **COLORFUL!**
THANKS A **LOT.**
NO, HONESTLY, CLAUD... YOU DON'T **NEED** MAKEUP. YOU'VE GOT SUCH A BEAUTIFUL FACE.
NICE TRY.

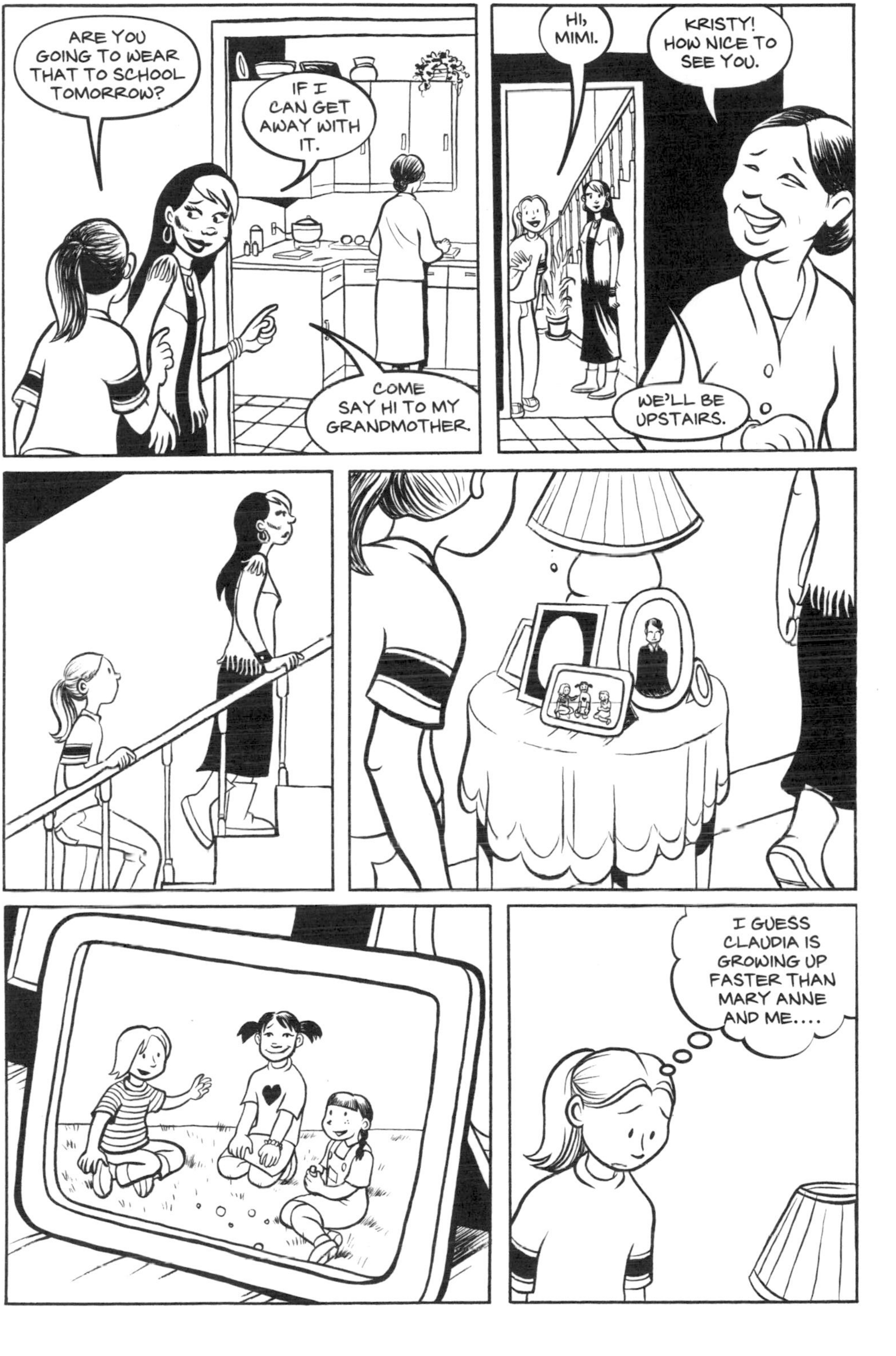

ARE YOU GOING TO WEAR THAT TO SCHOOL TOMORROW?
IF I CAN GET AWAY WITH IT.
COME SAY HI TO MY GRANDMOTHER.
HI, MIMI.
KRISTY! HOW NICE TO SEE YOU.
WE'LL BE UPSTAIRS.
I GUESS CLAUDIA IS GROWING UP FASTER THAN MARY ANNE AND ME....

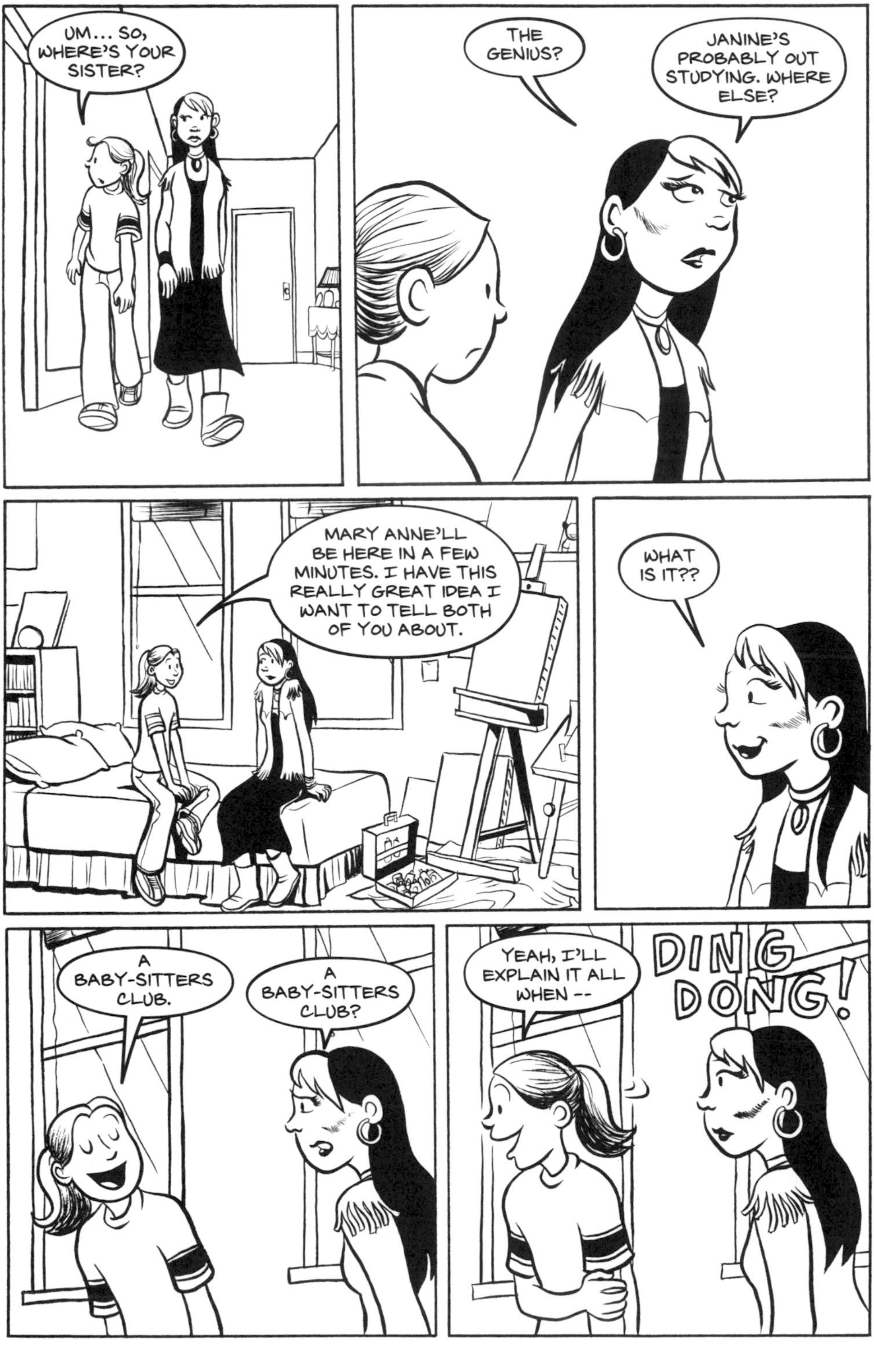
UM... SO, WHERE'S YOUR SISTER?
THE GENIUS?
JANINE'S PROBABLY OUT STUDYING. WHERE ELSE?
MARY ANNE'LL BE HERE IN A FEW MINUTES. I HAVE THIS REALLY GREAT IDEA I WANT TO TELL BOTH OF YOU ABOUT.
WHAT IS IT??
A BABY-SITTERS CLUB.
A BABY-SITTERS CLUB?
YEAH, I'LL EXPLAIN IT ALL WHEN --
DING DONG!

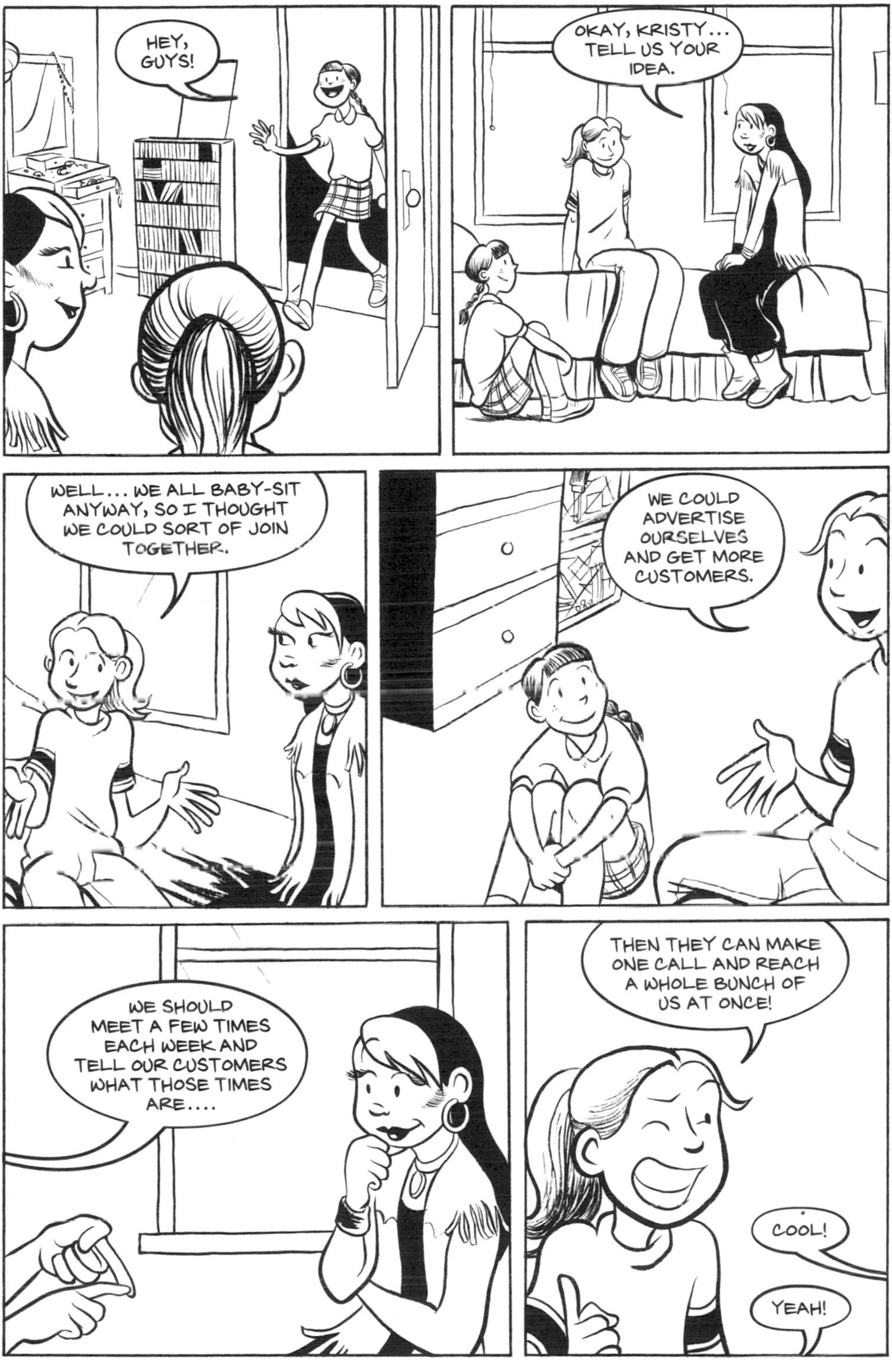
HEY, GUYS!
OKAY, KRISTY... TELL US YOUR IDEA.
WELL... WE ALL BABY-SIT ANYWAY, SO I THOUGHT WE COULD SORT OF JOIN TOGETHER.
WE COULD ADVERTISE OURSELVES AND GET MORE CUSTOMERS.
WE SHOULD MEET A FEW TIMES EACH WEEK AND TELL OUR CUSTOMERS WHAT THOSE TIMES ARE....
THEN THEY CAN MAKE ONE CALL AND REACH A WHOLE BUNCH OF US AT ONCE!
COOL!
YEAH!

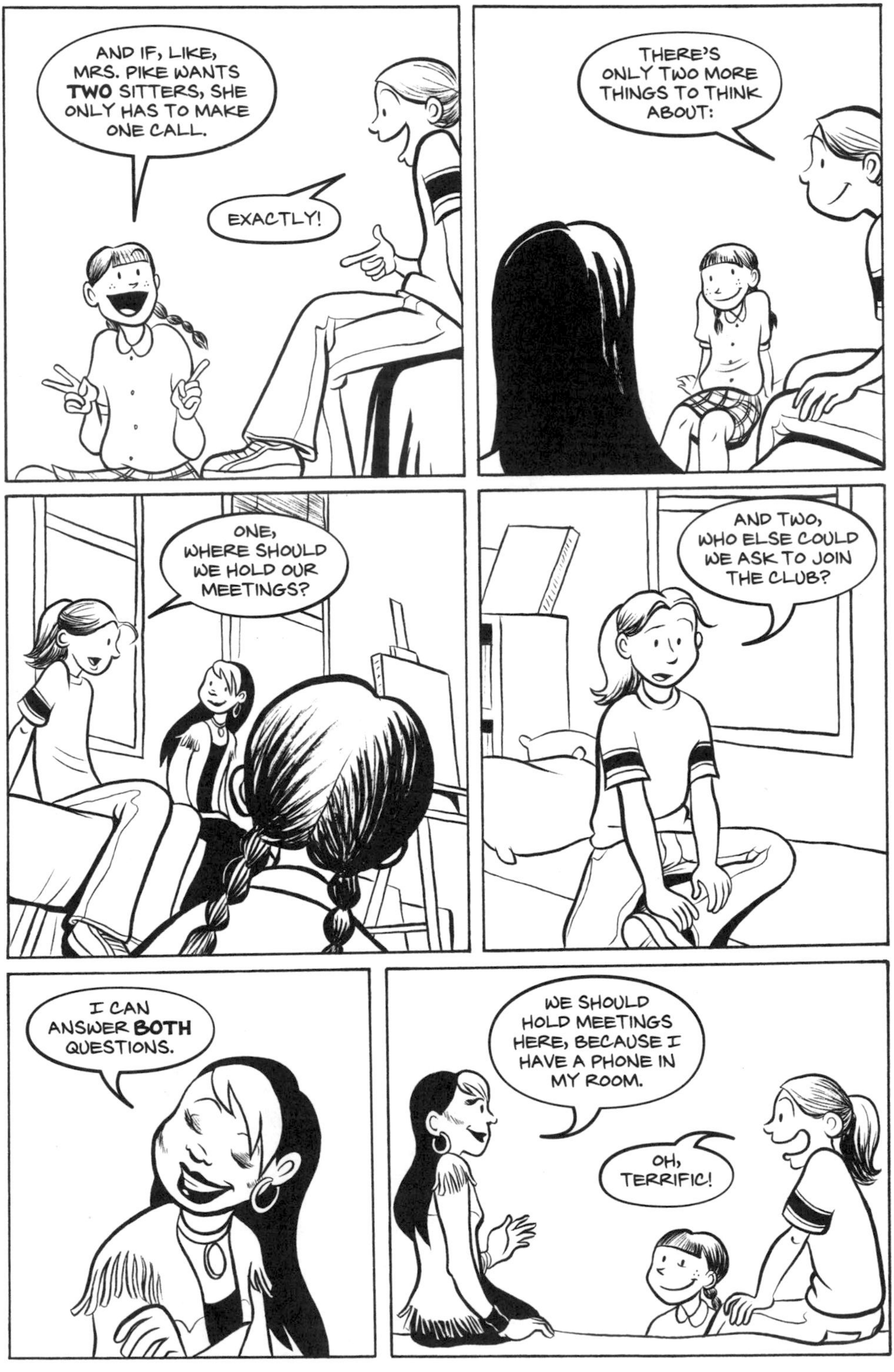
AND IF, LIKE, MRS. PIKE WANTS **TWO** SITTERS, SHE ONLY HAS TO MAKE ONE CALL.
EXACTLY!
THERE'S ONLY TWO MORE THINGS TO THINK ABOUT:
ONE, WHERE SHOULD WE HOLD OUR MEETINGS?
AND TWO, WHO ELSE COULD WE ASK TO JOIN THE CLUB?
I CAN ANSWER **BOTH** QUESTIONS.
WE SHOULD HOLD MEETINGS HERE, BECAUSE I HAVE A PHONE IN MY ROOM.
OH, TERRIFIC!

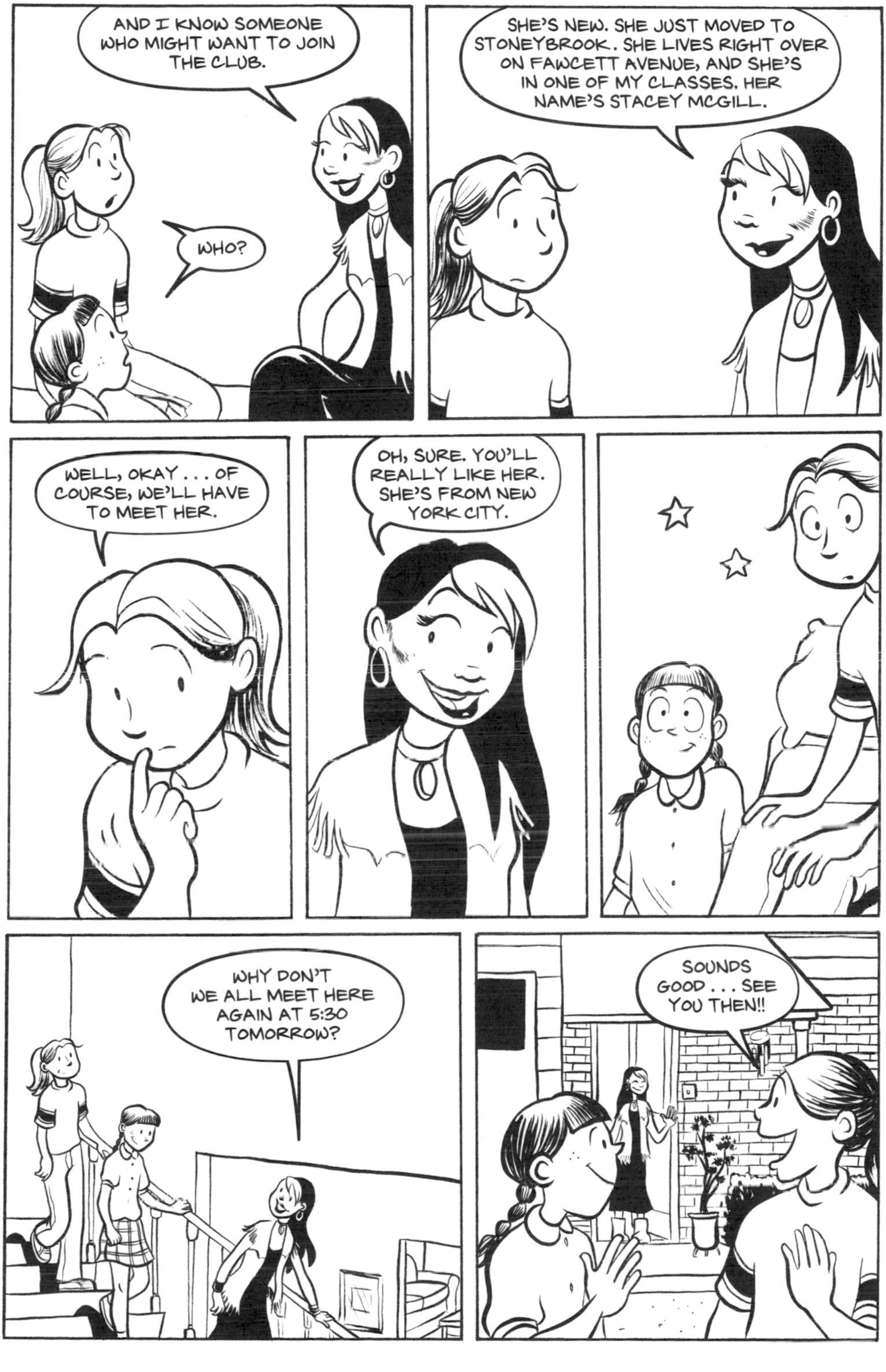
AND I KNOW SOMEONE WHO MIGHT WANT TO JOIN THE CLUB.
WHO?
SHE'S NEW. SHE JUST MOVED TO STONEYBROOK. SHE LIVES RIGHT OVER ON FAWCETT AVENUE, AND SHE'S IN ONE OF MY CLASSES. HER NAME'S STACEY MCGILL.
WELL, OKAY . . . OF COURSE, WE'LL HAVE TO MEET HER.
OH, SURE. YOU'LL REALLY LIKE HER. SHE'S FROM NEW YORK CITY.
WHY DON'T WE ALL MEET HERE AGAIN AT 5:30 TOMORROW?
SOUNDS GOOD . . . SEE YOU THEN!!

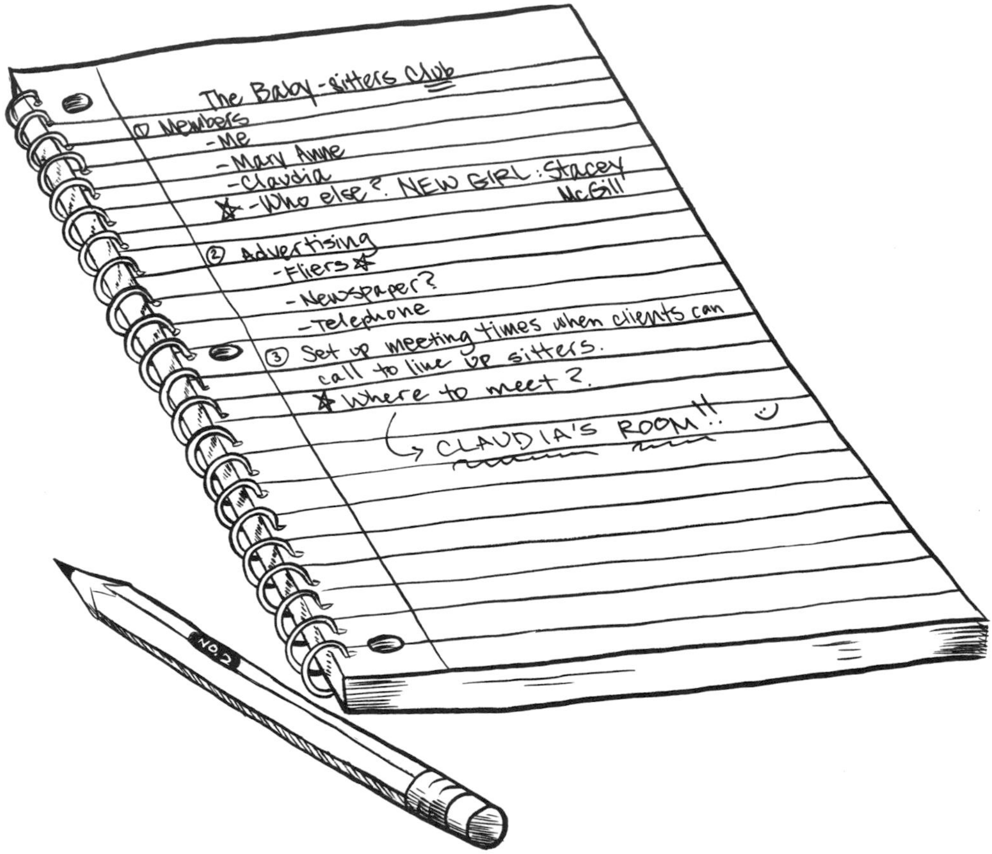
The Baby-sitters Club
① Members
-Me
-Mary Anne
-Claudia
-Who else? NEW GIRL: Stacey McGill
② Advertising
-Fliers
-Newspaper?
-Telephone
③ Set up meeting times when clients can call to line up sitters.
Where to meet?
CLAUDIA'S ROOM!!
NO. 2

Chapter 4

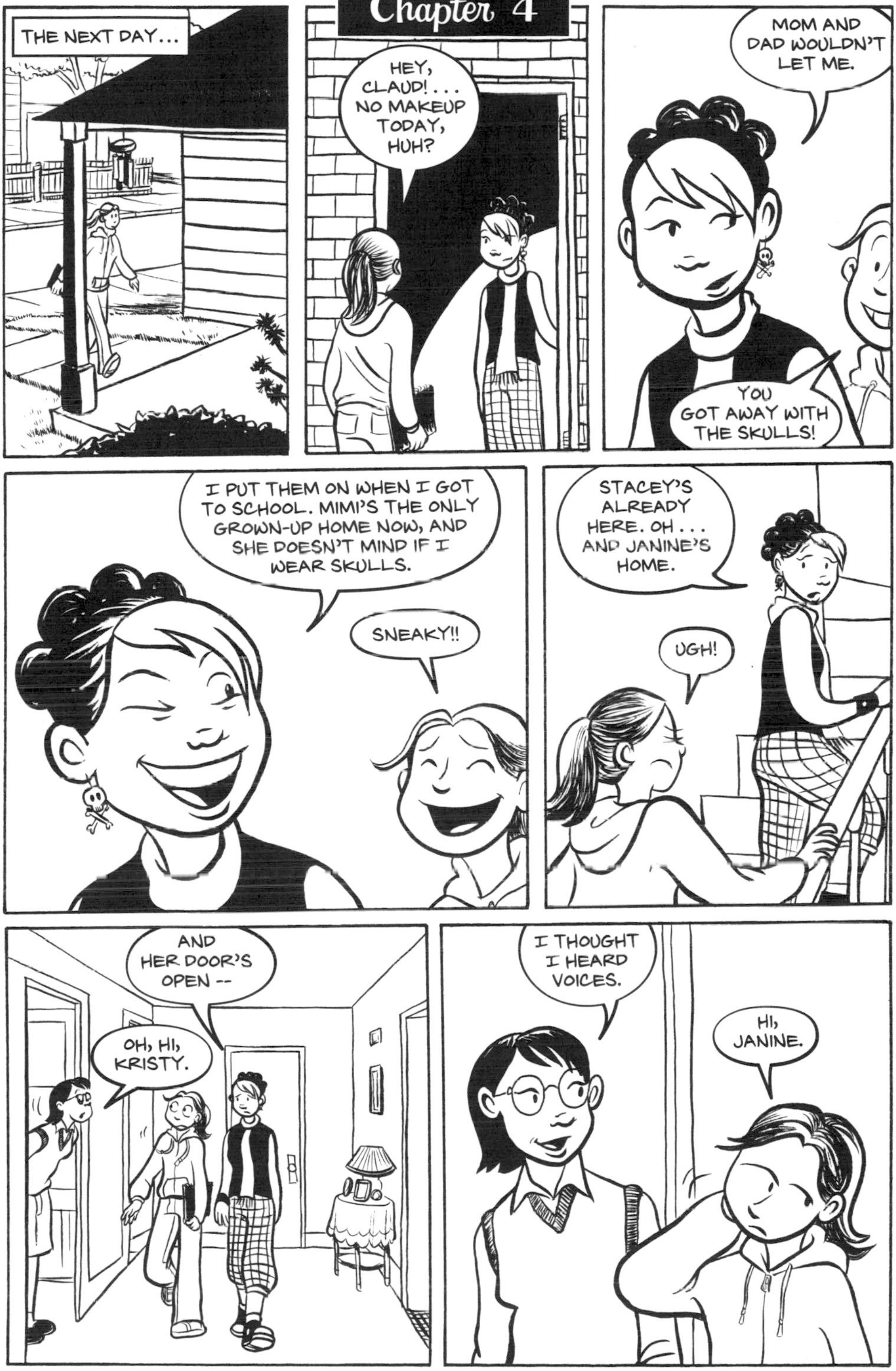
THE NEXT DAY...
HEY, CLAUD! . . . NO MAKEUP TODAY, HUH?
MOM AND DAD WOULDN'T LET ME.
YOU GOT AWAY WITH THE SKULLS!
I PUT THEM ON WHEN I GOT TO SCHOOL. MIMI'S THE ONLY GROWN-UP HOME NOW, AND SHE DOESN'T MIND IF I WEAR SKULLS.
SNEAKY!!
STACEY'S ALREADY HERE. OH . . . AND JANINE'S HOME.
UGH!
AND HER DOOR'S OPEN --
OH, HI, KRISTY.
I THOUGHT I HEARD VOICES.
HI, JANINE.

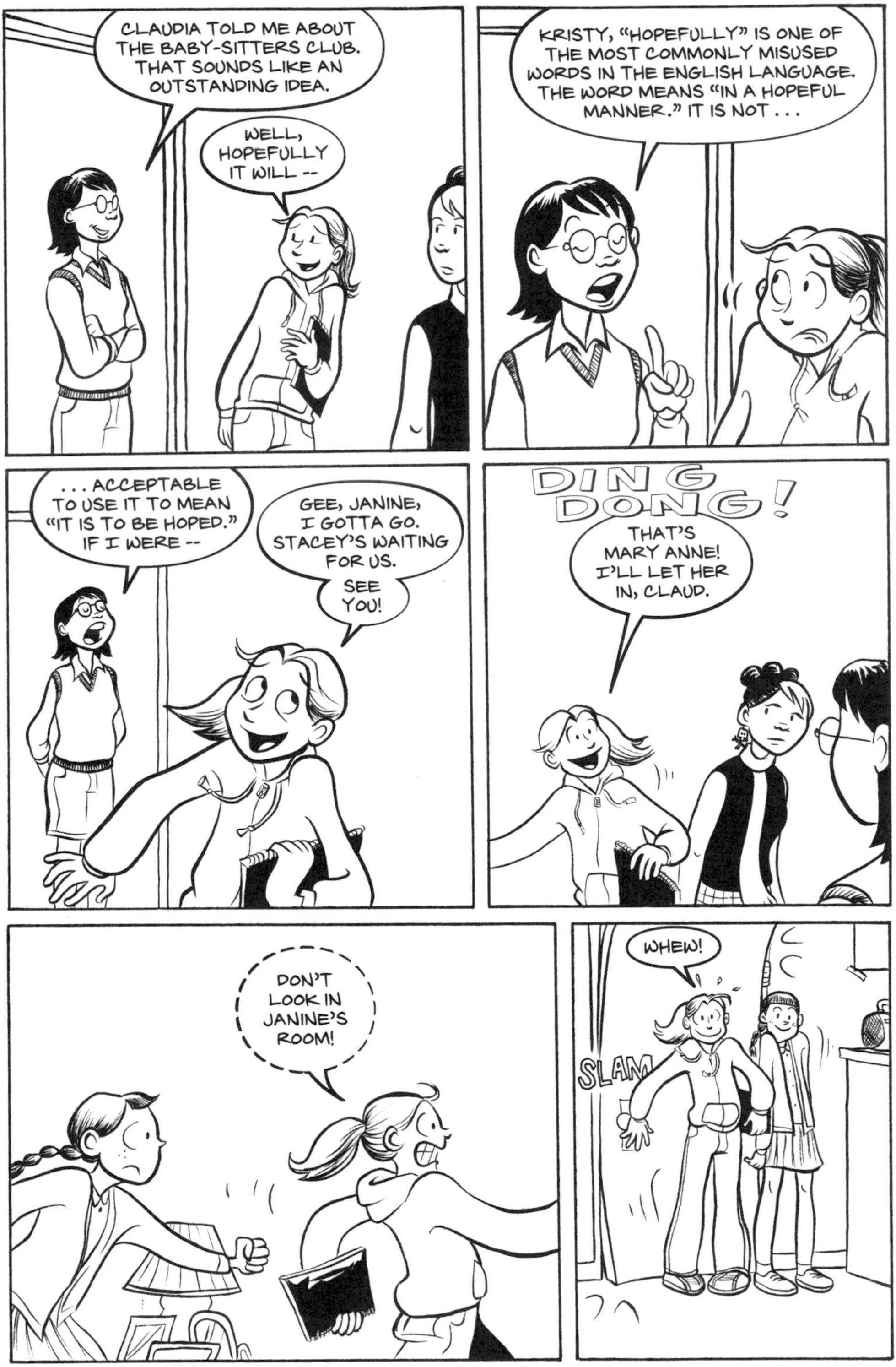
CLAUDIA TOLD ME ABOUT THE BABY-SITTERS CLUB. THAT SOUNDS LIKE AN OUTSTANDING IDEA.
WELL, HOPEFULLY IT WILL --
KRISTY, "HOPEFULLY" IS ONE OF THE MOST COMMONLY MISUSED WORDS IN THE ENGLISH LANGUAGE. THE WORD MEANS "IN A HOPEFUL MANNER." IT IS NOT . . .
. . . ACCEPTABLE TO USE IT TO MEAN "IT IS TO BE HOPED." IF I WERE --
GEE, JANINE, I GOTTA GO. STACEY'S WAITING FOR US.
SEE YOU!
DING DONG!
THAT'S MARY ANNE! I'LL LET HER IN, CLAUD.
DON'T LOOK IN JANINE'S ROOM!
WHEW!
SLAM

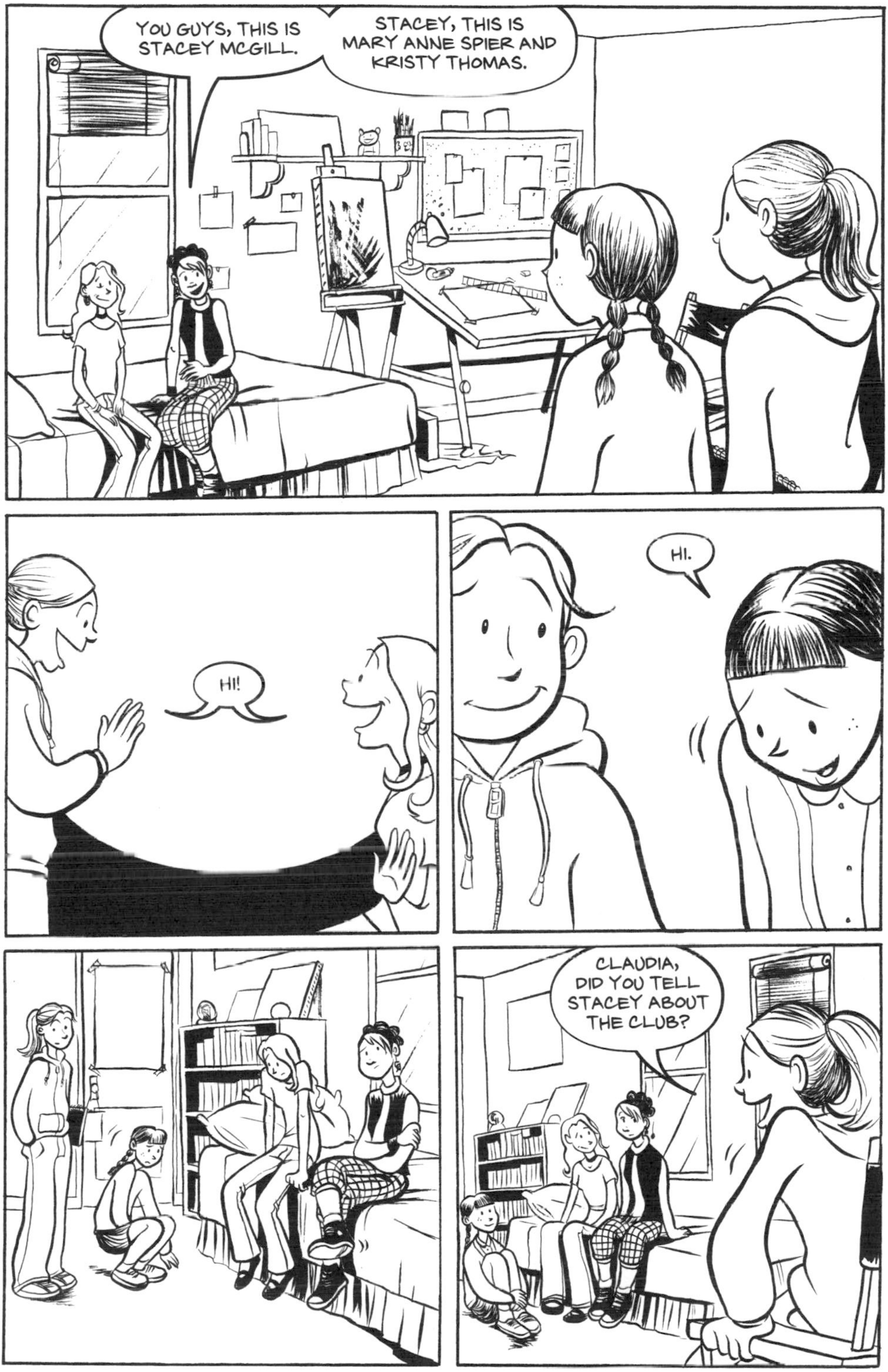
YOU GUYS, THIS IS STACEY MCGILL.
STACEY, THIS IS MARY ANNE SPIER AND KRISTY THOMAS.
HI!
HI.
CLAUDIA, DID YOU TELL STACEY ABOUT THE CLUB?

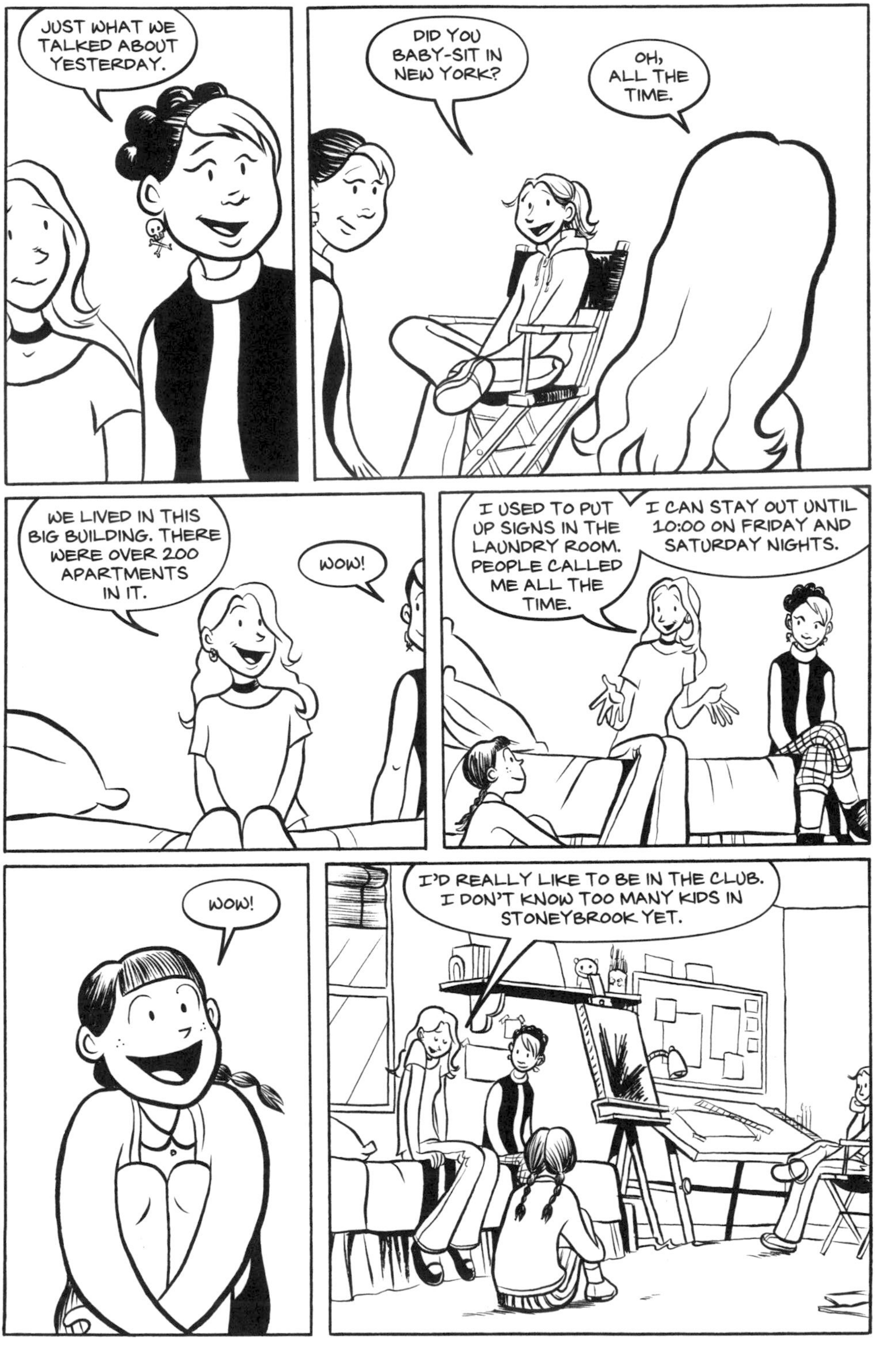
JUST WHAT WE TALKED ABOUT YESTERDAY.
DID YOU BABY-SIT IN NEW YORK?
OH, ALL THE TIME.
WE LIVED IN THIS BIG BUILDING. THERE WERE OVER 200 APARTMENTS IN IT.
WOW!
I USED TO PUT UP SIGNS IN THE LAUNDRY ROOM. PEOPLE CALLED ME ALL THE TIME.
I CAN STAY OUT UNTIL 10:00 ON FRIDAY AND SATURDAY NIGHTS.
WOW!
I'D REALLY LIKE TO BE IN THE CLUB. I DON'T KNOW TOO MANY KIDS IN STONEYBROOK YET.

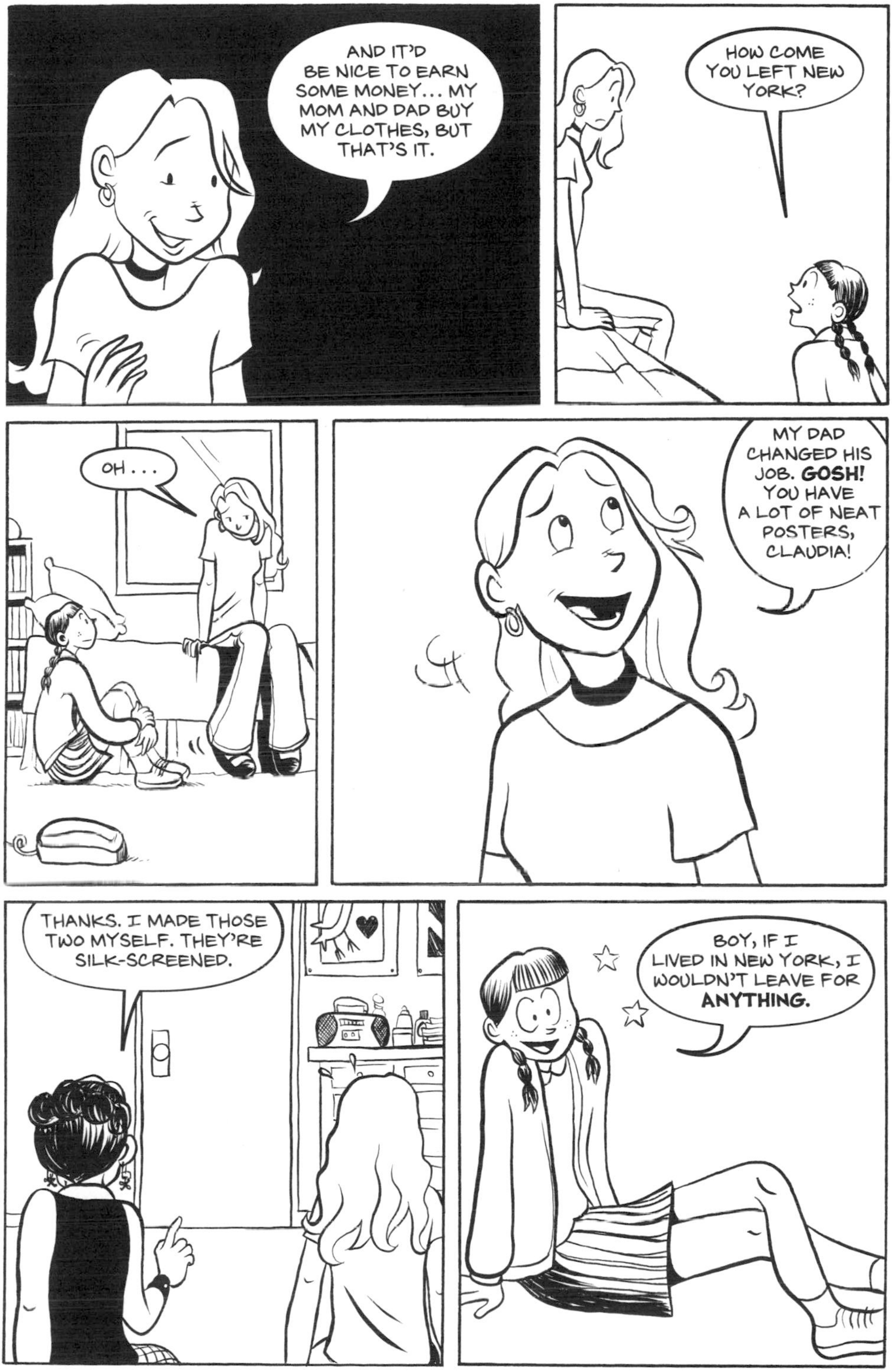
AND IT'D BE NICE TO EARN SOME MONEY... MY MOM AND DAD BUY MY CLOTHES, BUT THAT'S IT.
HOW COME YOU LEFT NEW YORK?
OH...
MY DAD CHANGED HIS JOB. **GOSH!** YOU HAVE A LOT OF NEAT POSTERS, CLAUDIA!
THANKS. I MADE THOSE TWO MYSELF. THEY'RE SILK-SCREENED.
BOY, IF I LIVED IN NEW YORK, I WOULDN'T LEAVE FOR **ANYTHING.**

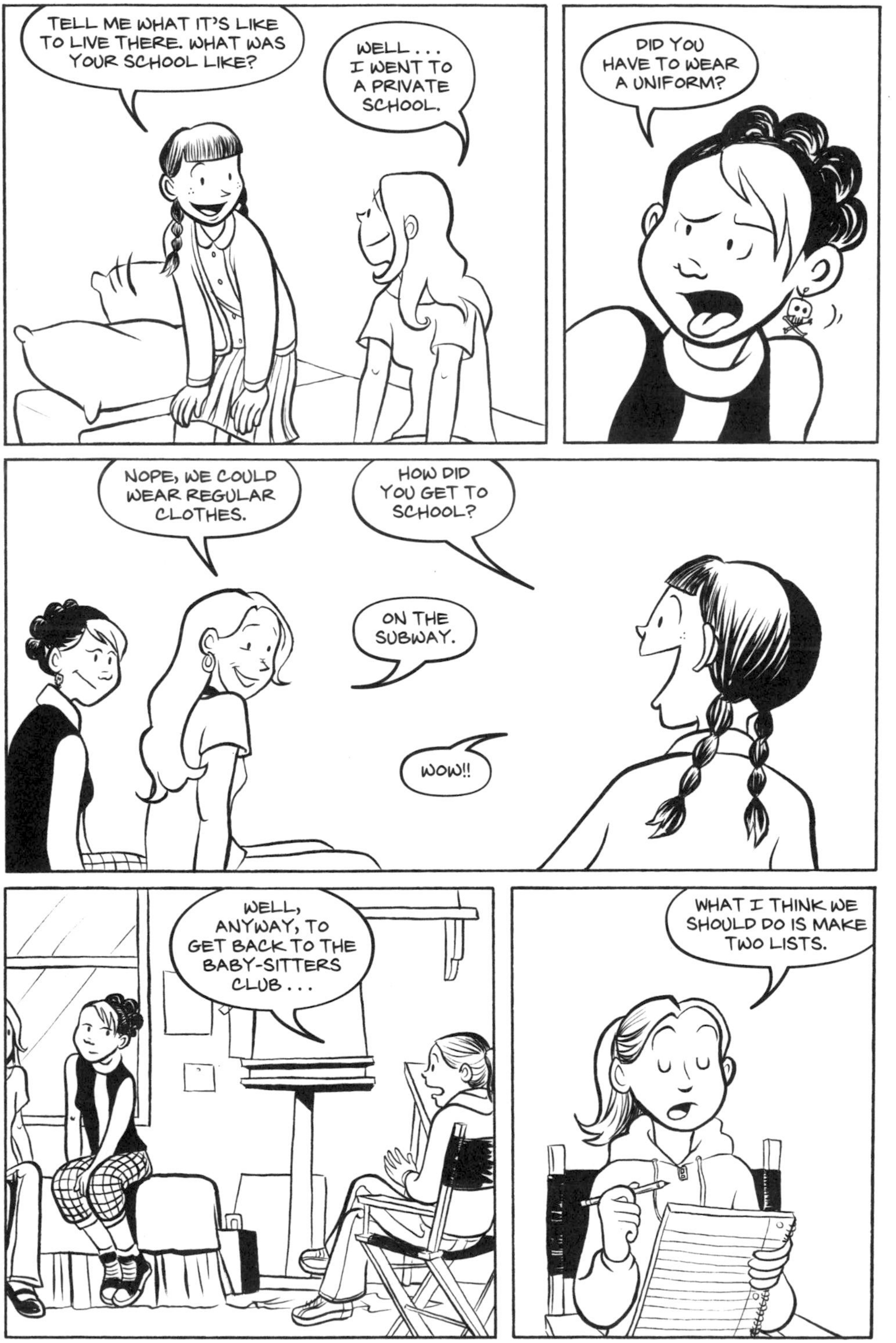
TELL ME WHAT IT'S LIKE TO LIVE THERE. WHAT WAS YOUR SCHOOL LIKE?
WELL . . . I WENT TO A PRIVATE SCHOOL.
DID YOU HAVE TO WEAR A UNIFORM?
NOPE, WE COULD WEAR REGULAR CLOTHES.
HOW DID YOU GET TO SCHOOL?
ON THE SUBWAY.
WOW!!
WELL, ANYWAY, TO GET BACK TO THE BABY-SITTERS CLUB . . .
WHAT I THINK WE SHOULD DO IS MAKE TWO LISTS.

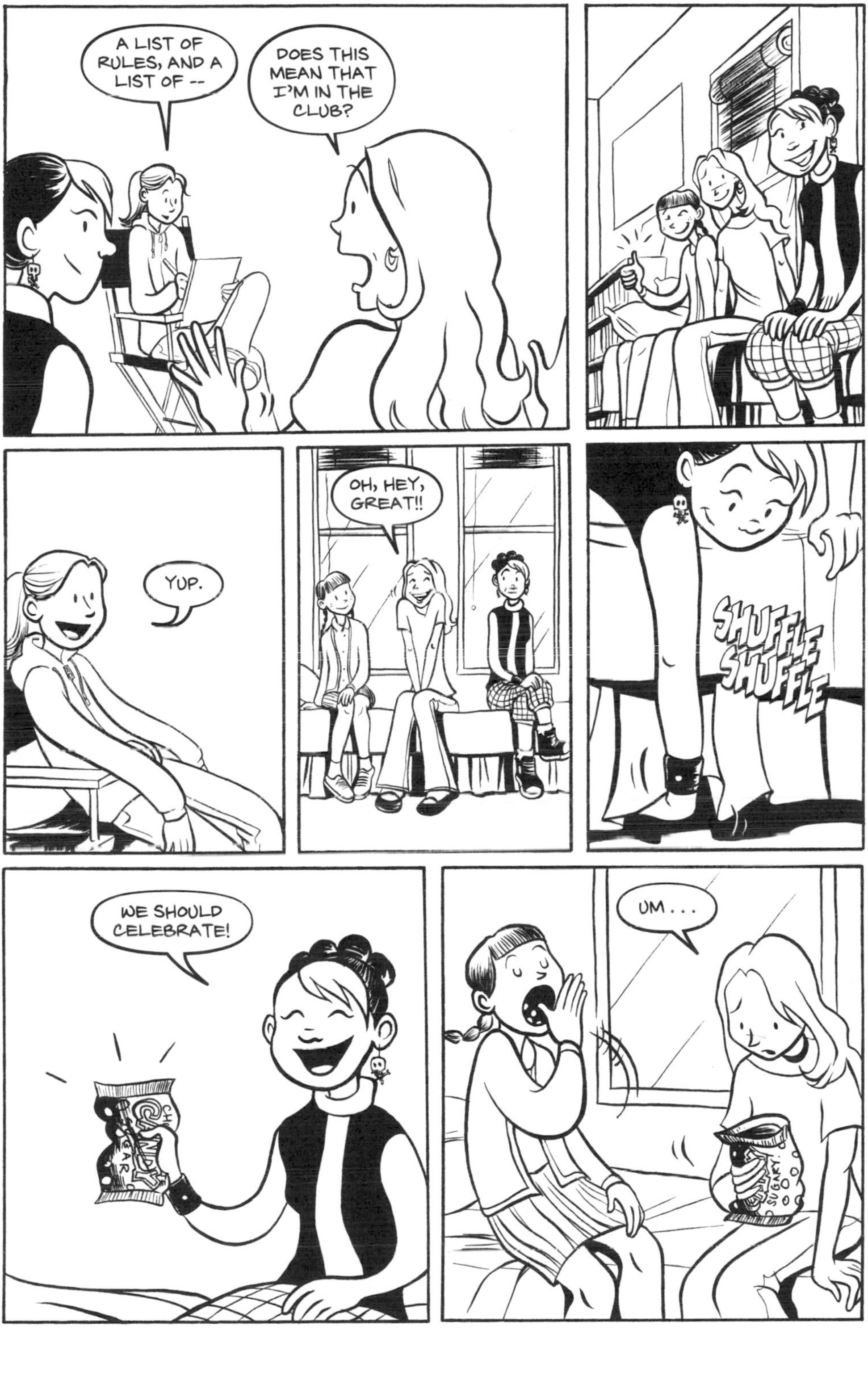

A LIST OF RULES, AND A LIST OF --
DOES THIS MEAN THAT I'M IN THE CLUB?
YUP.
OH, HEY, GREAT!!
SHUFFLE SHUFFLE
WE SHOULD CELEBRATE!
UM . . .

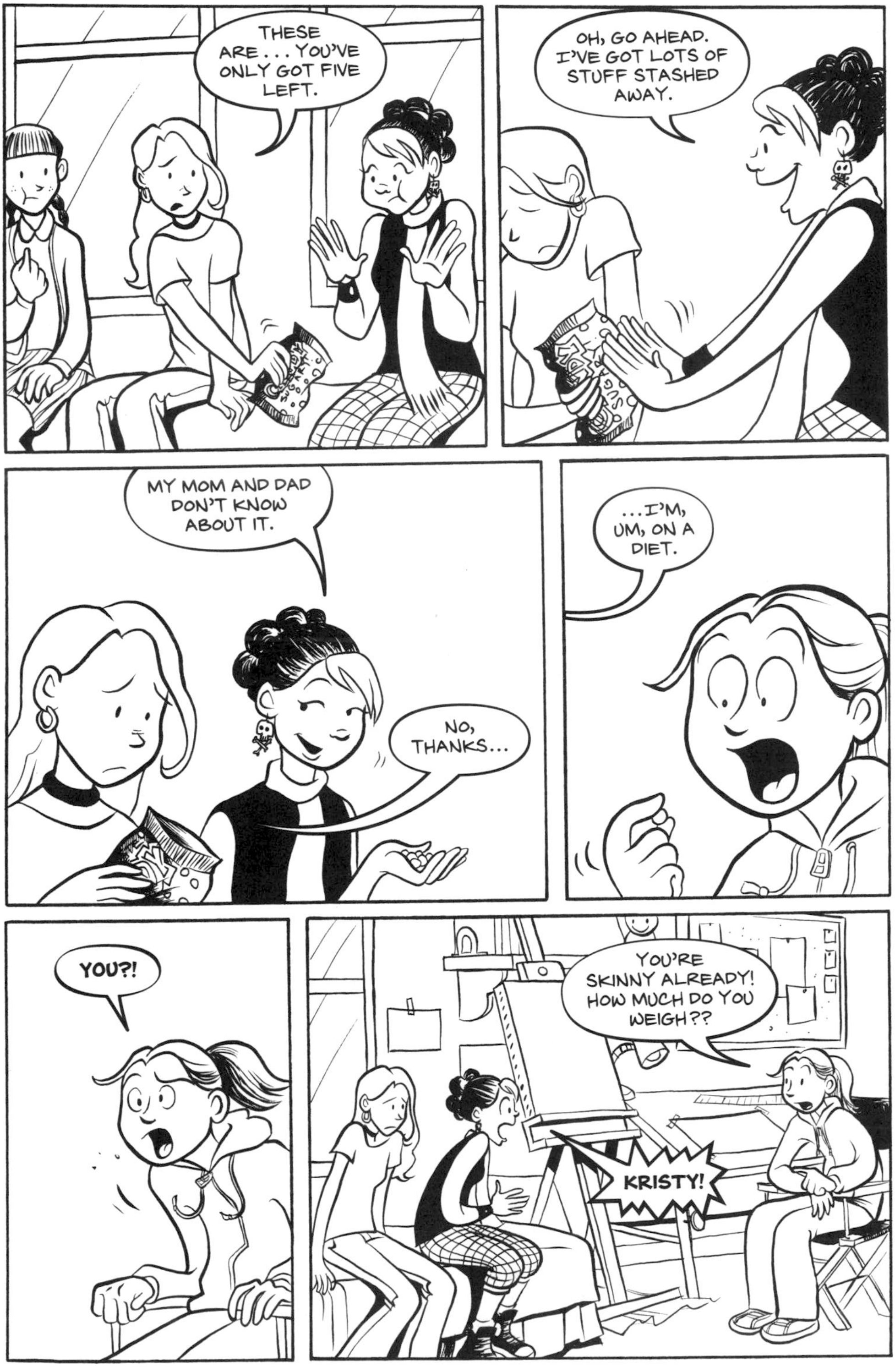
THESE ARE... YOU'VE ONLY GOT FIVE LEFT.
OH, GO AHEAD. I'VE GOT LOTS OF STUFF STASHED AWAY.
MY MOM AND DAD DON'T KNOW ABOUT IT.
NO, THANKS...
...I'M, UM, ON A DIET.
YOU?!
YOU'RE SKINNY ALREADY! HOW MUCH DO YOU WEIGH??
KRISTY!

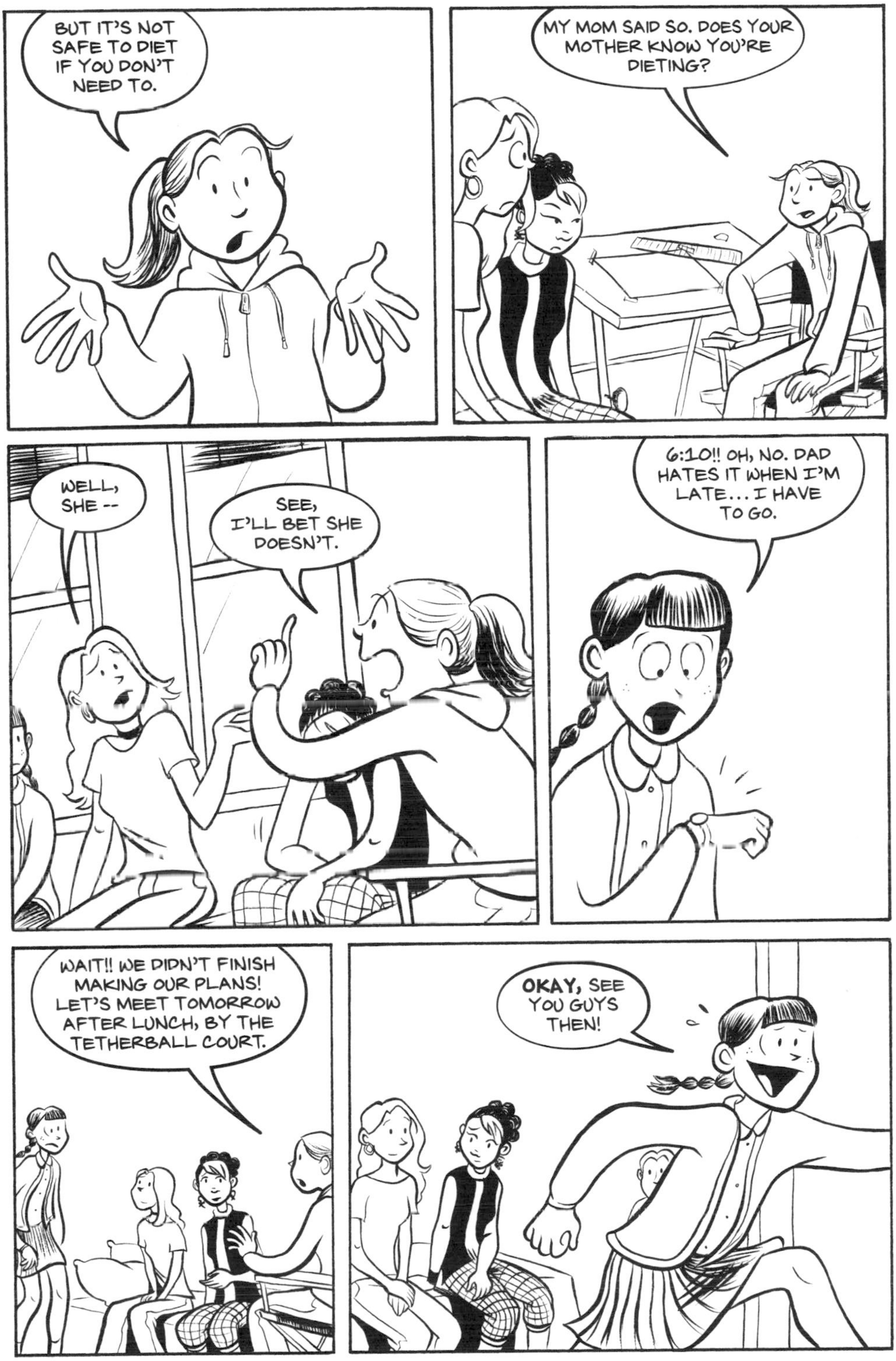
BUT IT'S NOT SAFE TO DIET IF YOU DON'T NEED TO.
MY MOM SAID SO. DOES YOUR MOTHER KNOW YOU'RE DIETING?
WELL, SHE --
SEE, I'LL BET SHE DOESN'T.
6:10!! OH, NO. DAD HATES IT WHEN I'M LATE... I HAVE TO GO.
WAIT!! WE DIDN'T FINISH MAKING OUR PLANS! LET'S MEET TOMORROW AFTER LUNCH, BY THE TETHERBALL COURT.
OKAY, SEE YOU GUYS THEN!

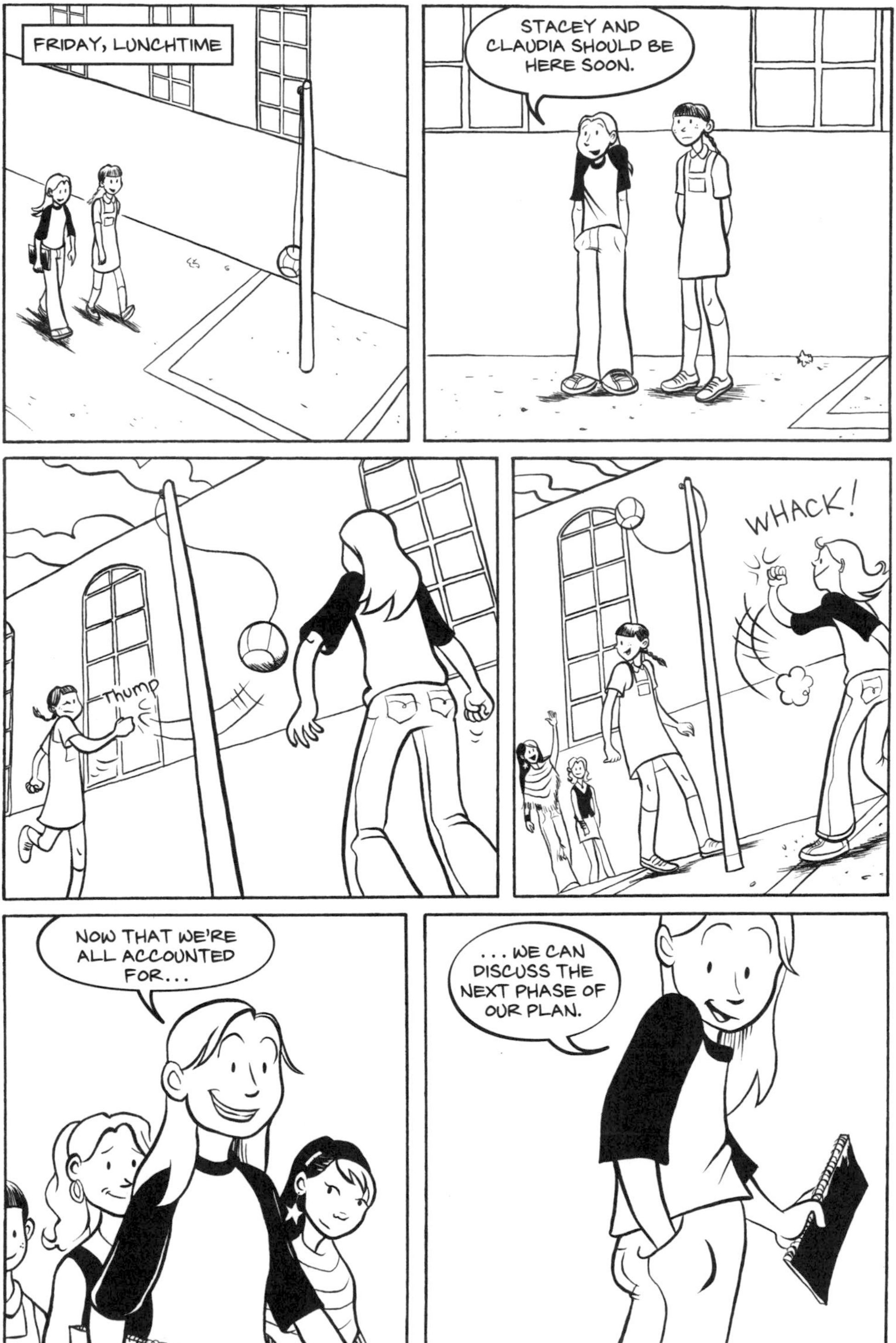
FRIDAY, LUNCHTIME
STACEY AND CLAUDIA SHOULD BE HERE SOON.
Thump
WHACK!
NOW THAT WE'RE ALL ACCOUNTED FOR...
...WE CAN DISCUSS THE NEXT PHASE OF OUR PLAN.

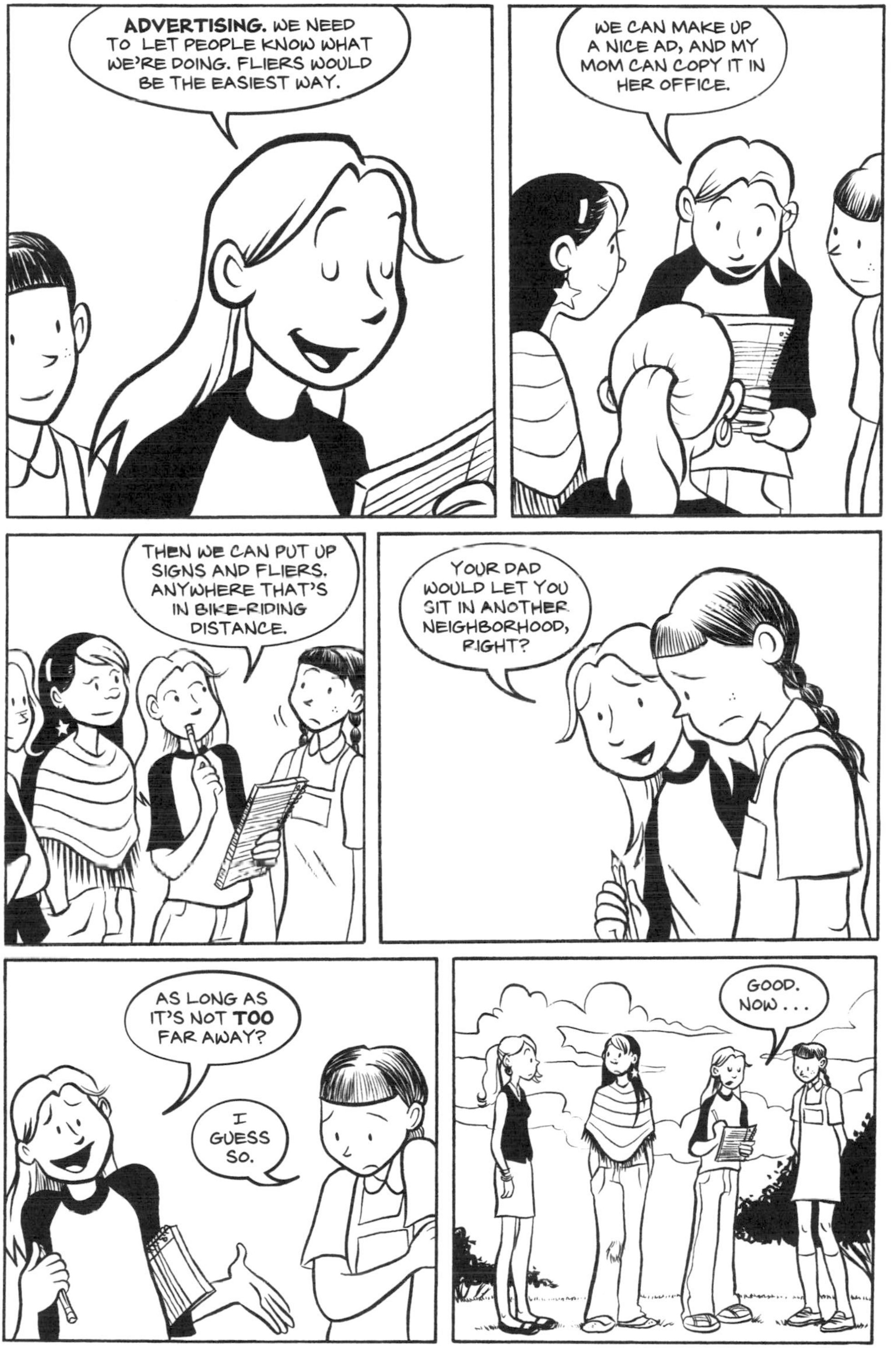
ADVERTISING. WE NEED TO LET PEOPLE KNOW WHAT WE'RE DOING. FLIERS WOULD BE THE EASIEST WAY.
WE CAN MAKE UP A NICE AD, AND MY MOM CAN COPY IT IN HER OFFICE.
THEN WE CAN PUT UP SIGNS AND FLIERS. ANYWHERE THAT'S IN BIKE-RIDING DISTANCE.
YOUR DAD WOULD LET YOU SIT IN ANOTHER NEIGHBORHOOD, RIGHT?
AS LONG AS IT'S NOT TOO FAR AWAY?
I GUESS SO.
GOOD. NOW . . .

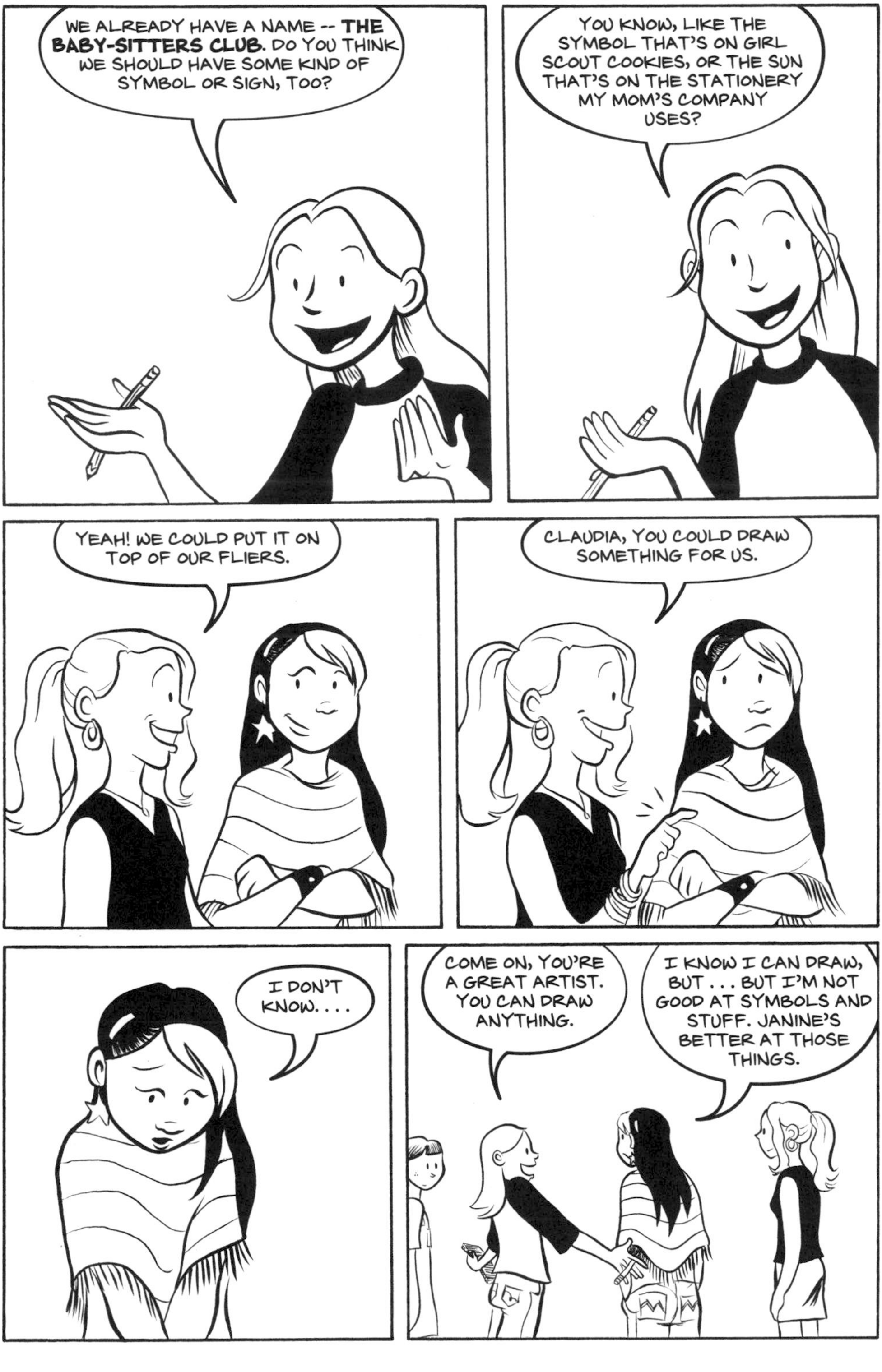
WE ALREADY HAVE A NAME -- **THE BABY-SITTERS CLUB**. DO YOU THINK WE SHOULD HAVE SOME KIND OF SYMBOL OR SIGN, TOO?
YOU KNOW, LIKE THE SYMBOL THAT'S ON GIRL SCOUT COOKIES, OR THE SUN THAT'S ON THE STATIONERY MY MOM'S COMPANY USES?
YEAH! WE COULD PUT IT ON TOP OF OUR FLIERS.
CLAUDIA, YOU COULD DRAW SOMETHING FOR US.
I DON'T KNOW. . . .
COME ON, YOU'RE A GREAT ARTIST. YOU CAN DRAW ANYTHING.
I KNOW I CAN DRAW, BUT . . . BUT I'M NOT GOOD AT SYMBOLS AND STUFF. JANINE'S BETTER AT THOSE THINGS.

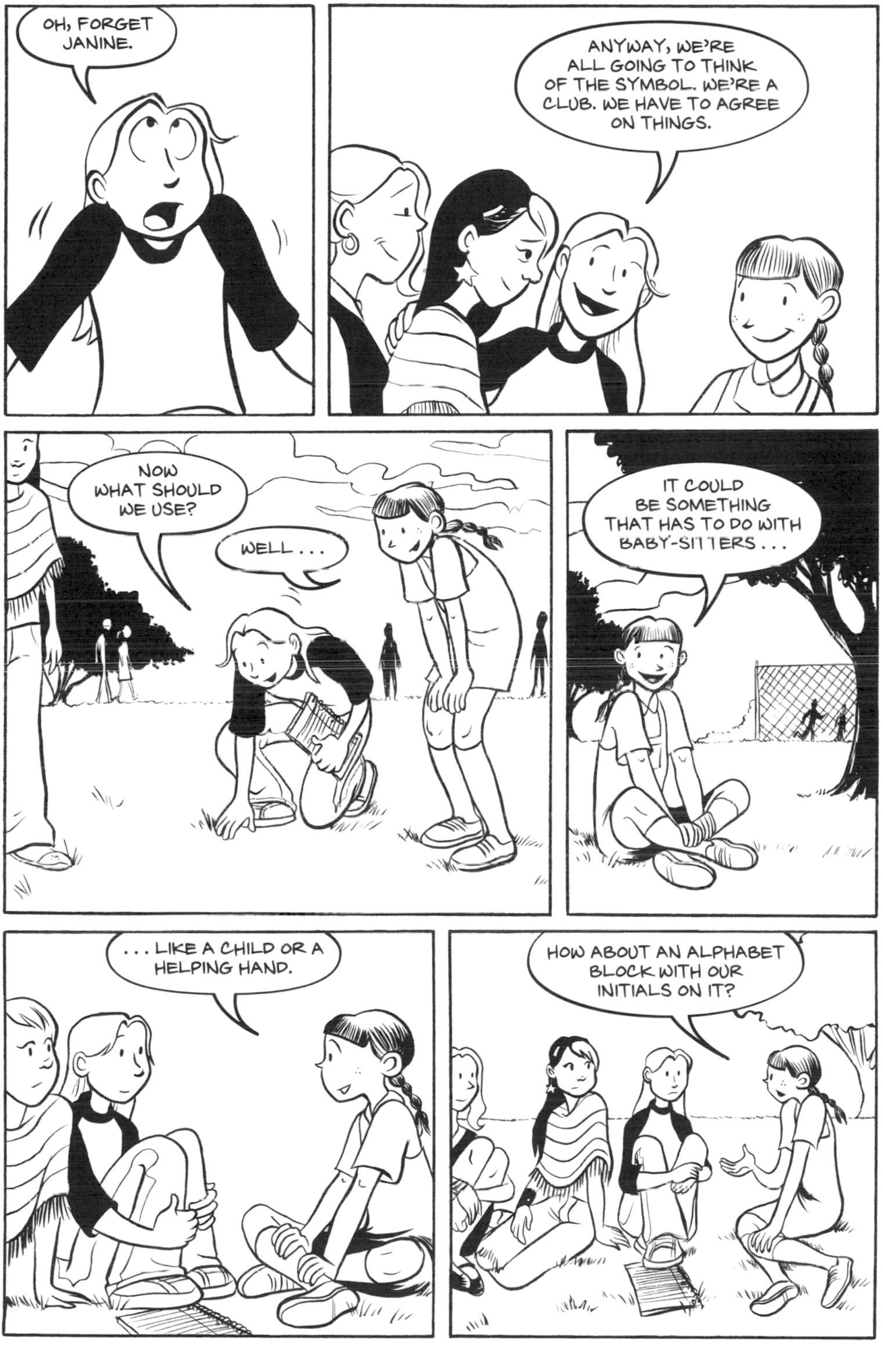
OH, FORGET JANINE.
ANYWAY, WE'RE ALL GOING TO THINK OF THE SYMBOL. WE'RE A CLUB. WE HAVE TO AGREE ON THINGS.
NOW WHAT SHOULD WE USE?
WELL . . .
IT COULD BE SOMETHING THAT HAS TO DO WITH BABY-SITTERS . . .
. . . LIKE A CHILD OR A HELPING HAND.
HOW ABOUT AN ALPHABET BLOCK WITH OUR INITIALS ON IT?

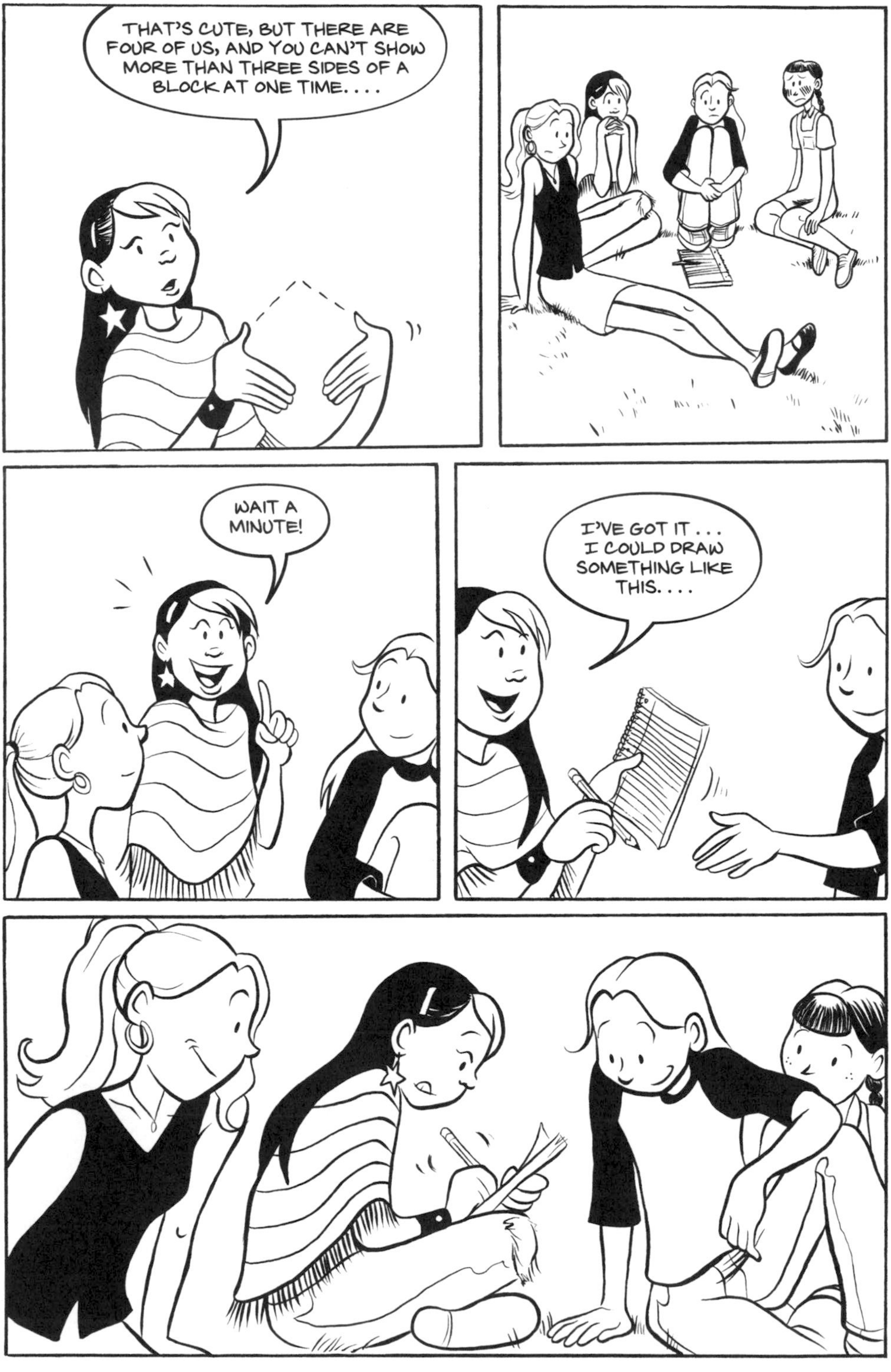

THAT'S CUTE, BUT THERE ARE FOUR OF US, AND YOU CAN'T SHOW MORE THAN THREE SIDES OF A BLOCK AT ONE TIME. . . .
WAIT A MINUTE!
I'VE GOT IT . . . I COULD DRAW SOMETHING LIKE THIS. . . .

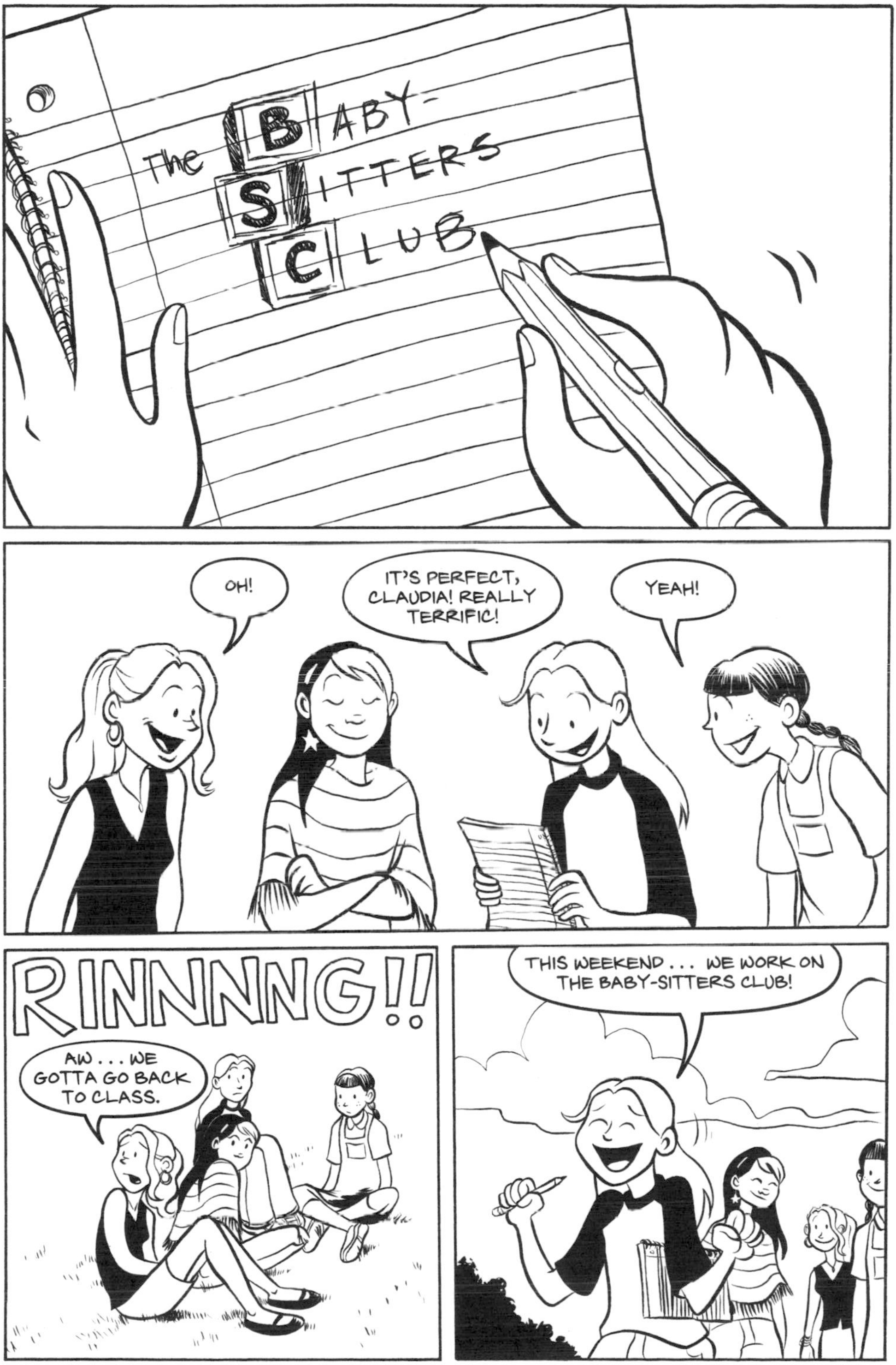
The BABY-SITTERS CLUB
OH!
IT'S PERFECT, CLAUDIA! REALLY TERRIFIC!
YEAH!
RINNNNG!!
AW . . . WE GOTTA GO BACK TO CLASS.
THIS WEEKEND . . . WE WORK ON THE BABY-SITTERS CLUB!

Chapter 5

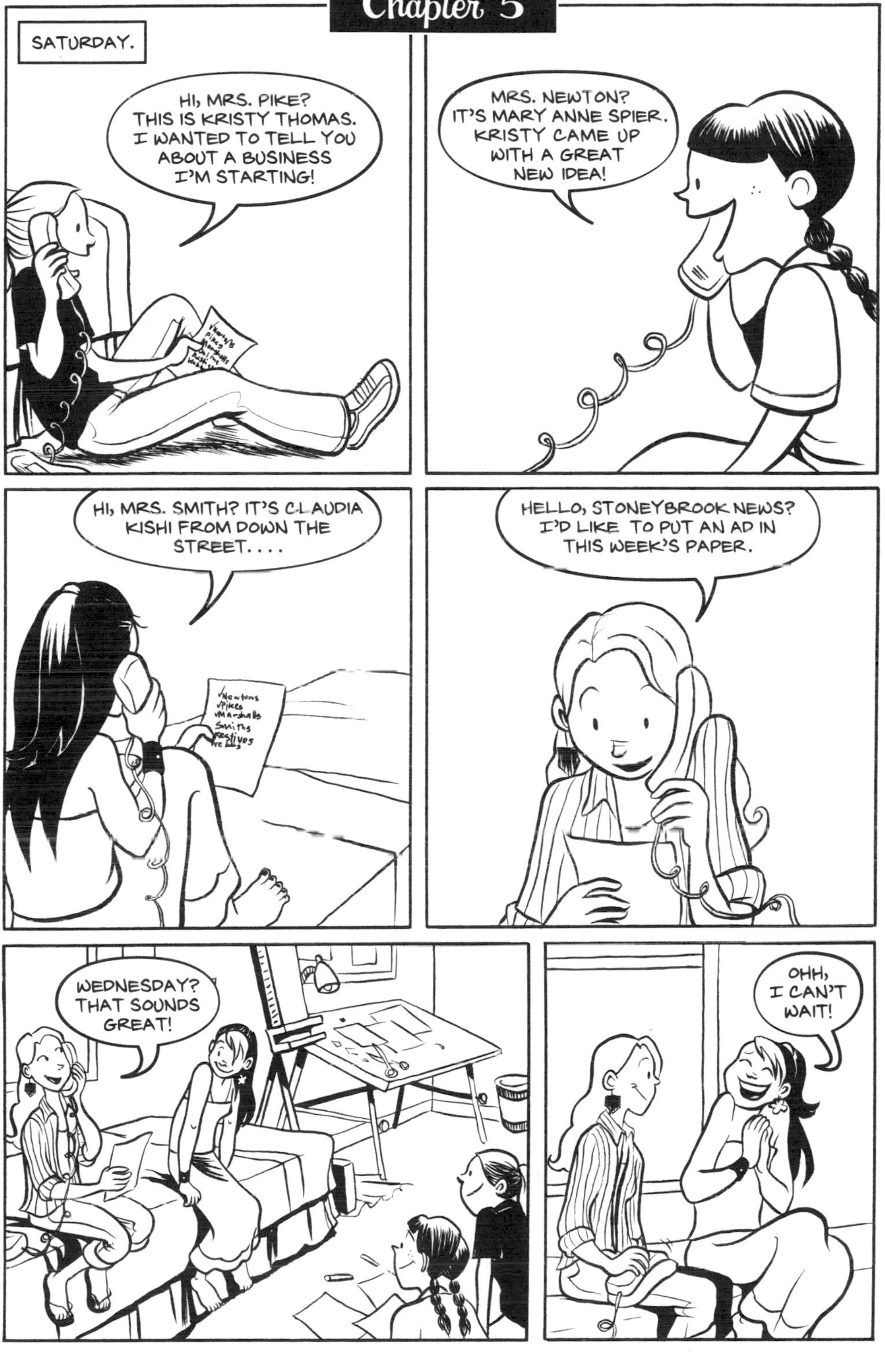

SATURDAY.
HI, MRS. PIKE? THIS IS KRISTY THOMAS. I WANTED TO TELL YOU ABOUT A BUSINESS I'M STARTING!
MRS. NEWTON? IT'S MARY ANNE SPIER. KRISTY CAME UP WITH A GREAT NEW IDEA!
HI, MRS. SMITH? IT'S CLAUDIA KISHI FROM DOWN THE STREET. . . .
HELLO, STONEYBROOK NEWS? I'D LIKE TO PUT AN AD IN THIS WEEK'S PAPER.
WEDNESDAY? THAT SOUNDS GREAT!
OHH, I CAN'T WAIT!

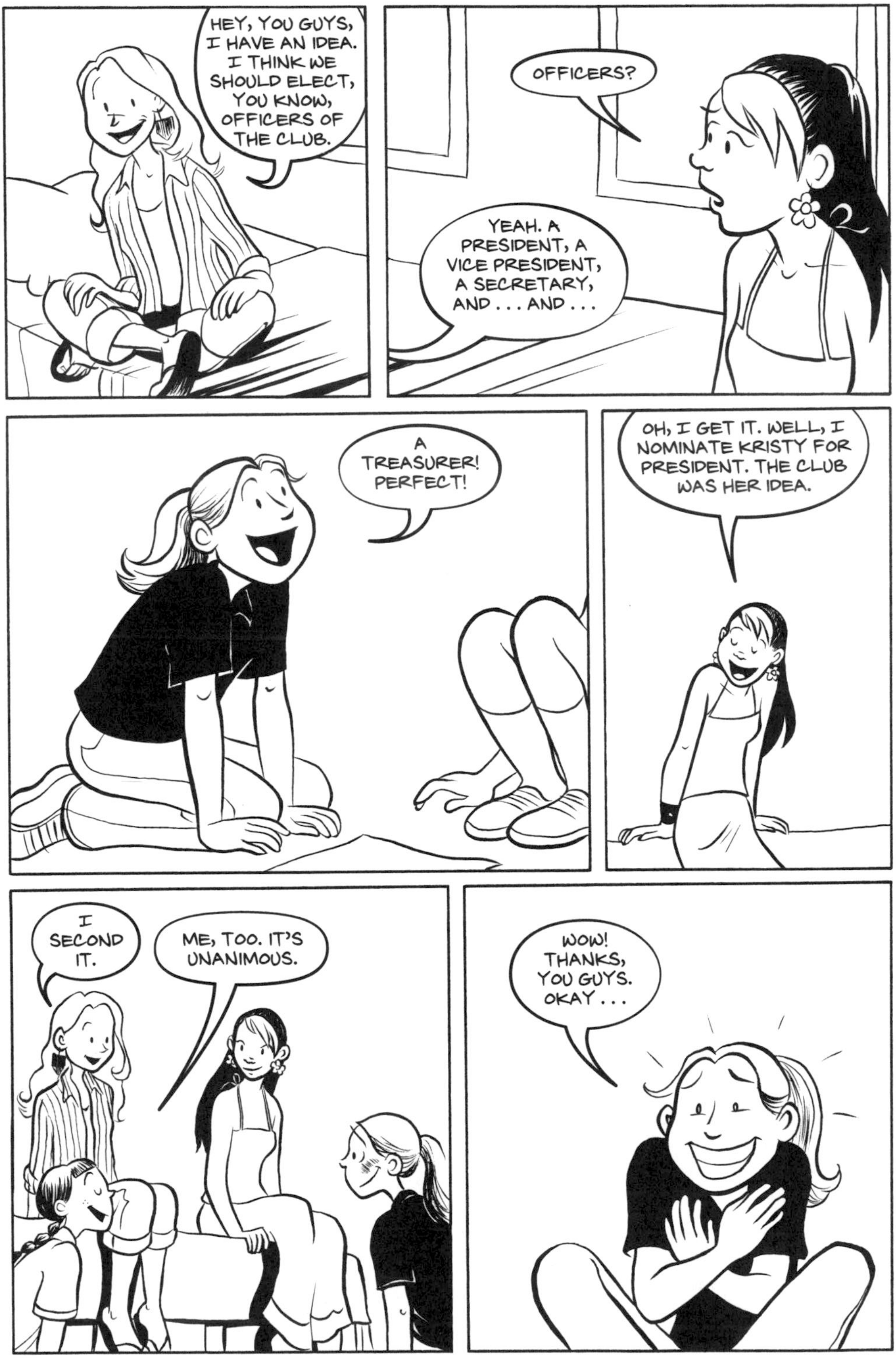
HEY, YOU GUYS, I HAVE AN IDEA. I THINK WE SHOULD ELECT, YOU KNOW, OFFICERS OF THE CLUB.
OFFICERS?
YEAH. A PRESIDENT, A VICE PRESIDENT, A SECRETARY, AND . . . AND . . .
A TREASURER! PERFECT!
OH, I GET IT. WELL, I NOMINATE KRISTY FOR PRESIDENT. THE CLUB WAS HER IDEA.
I SECOND IT.
ME, TOO. IT'S UNANIMOUS.
WOW! THANKS, YOU GUYS. OKAY . . .

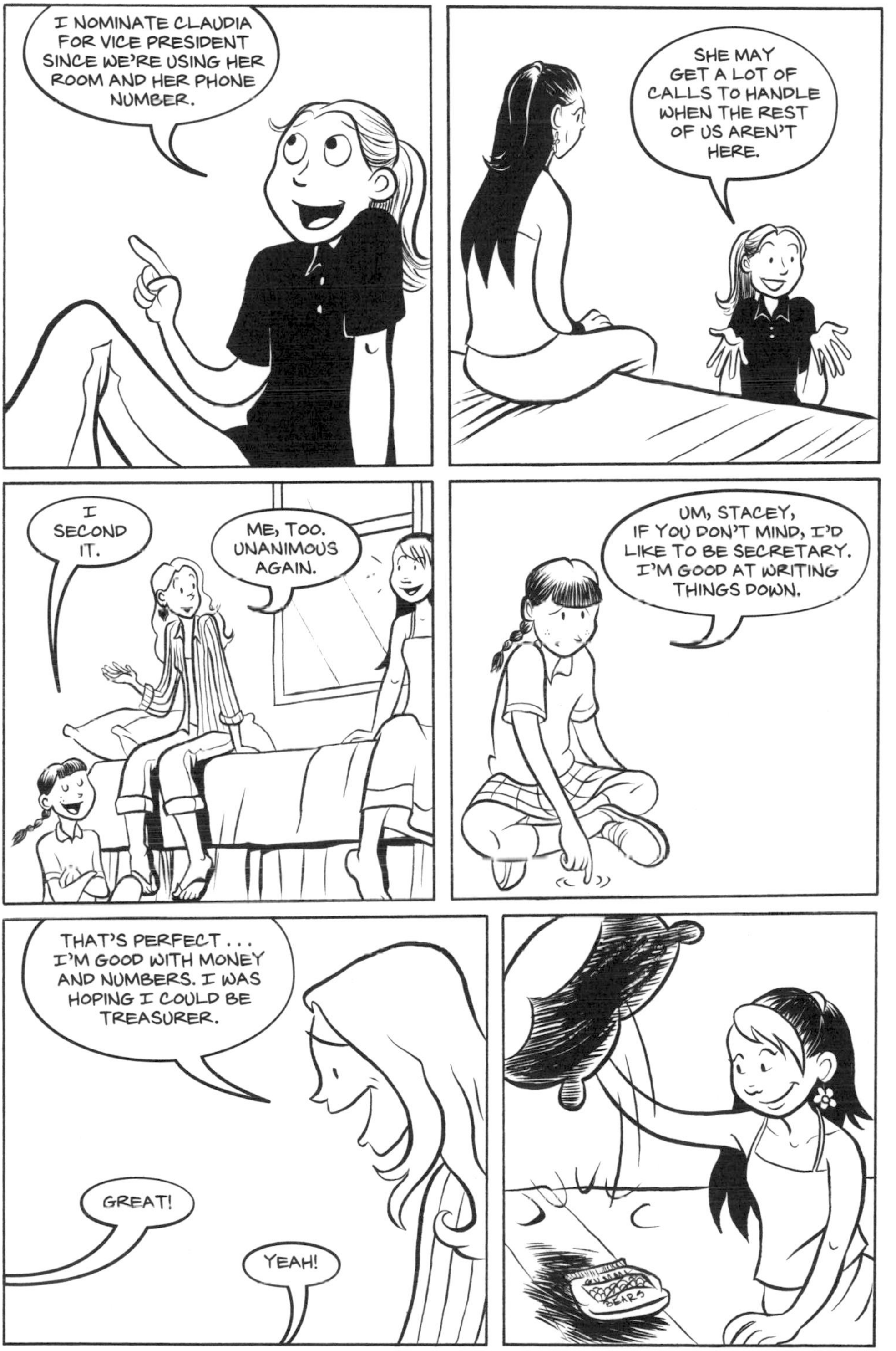

I NOMINATE CLAUDIA FOR VICE PRESIDENT SINCE WE'RE USING HER ROOM AND HER PHONE NUMBER.
SHE MAY GET A LOT OF CALLS TO HANDLE WHEN THE REST OF US AREN'T HERE.
I SECOND IT.
ME, TOO. UNANIMOUS AGAIN.
UM, STACEY, IF YOU DON'T MIND, I'D LIKE TO BE SECRETARY. I'M GOOD AT WRITING THINGS DOWN.
THAT'S PERFECT . . . I'M GOOD WITH MONEY AND NUMBERS. I WAS HOPING I COULD BE TREASURER.
GREAT!
YEAH!

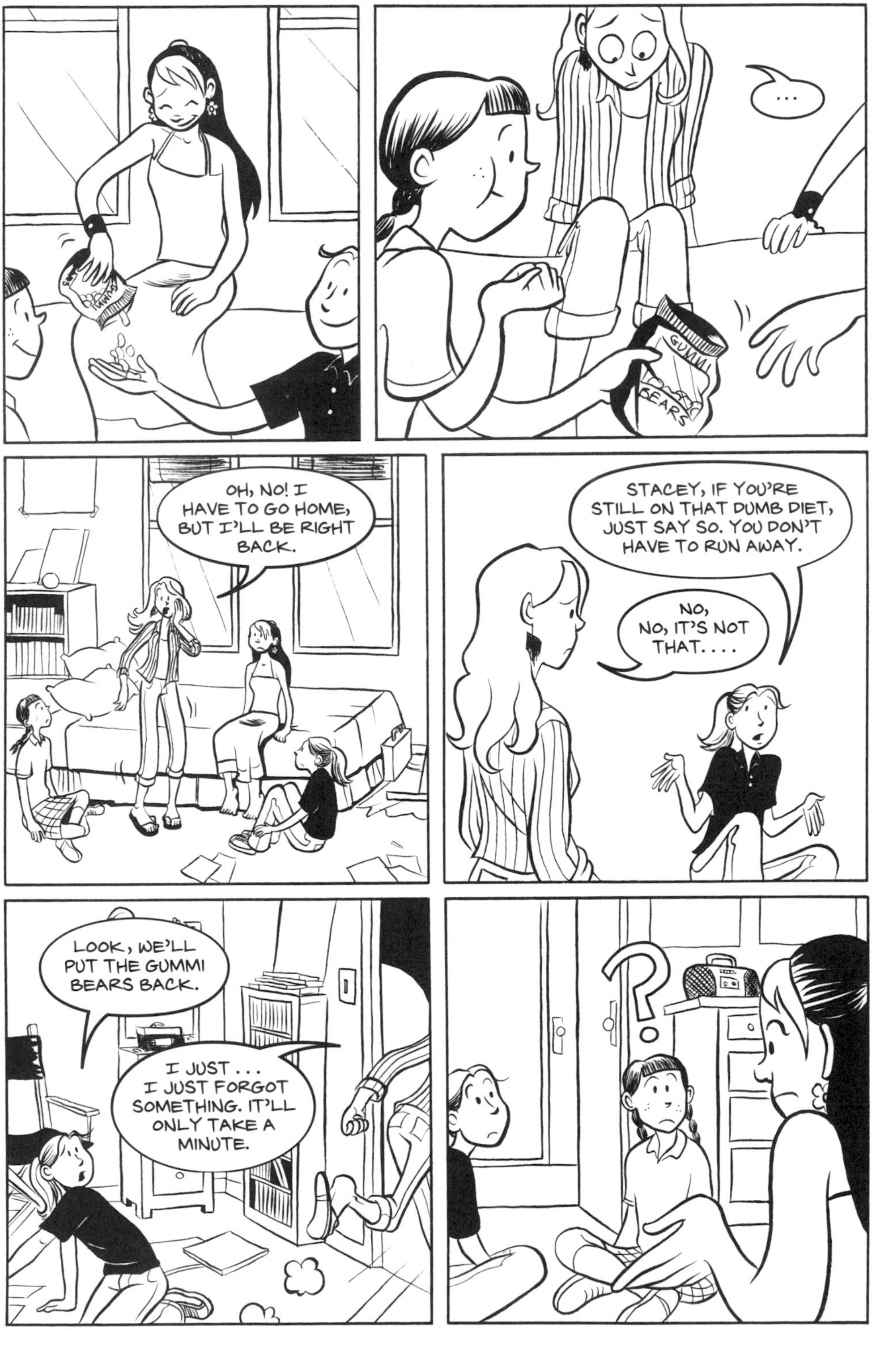
GUMMI BEARS
GUMMI BEARS
...
OH, NO! I HAVE TO GO HOME, BUT I'LL BE RIGHT BACK.
STACEY, IF YOU'RE STILL ON THAT DUMB DIET, JUST SAY SO. YOU DON'T HAVE TO RUN AWAY.
NO, NO, IT'S NOT THAT. . . .
LOOK, WE'LL PUT THE GUMMI BEARS BACK.
I JUST . . . I JUST FORGOT SOMETHING. IT'LL ONLY TAKE A MINUTE.
?

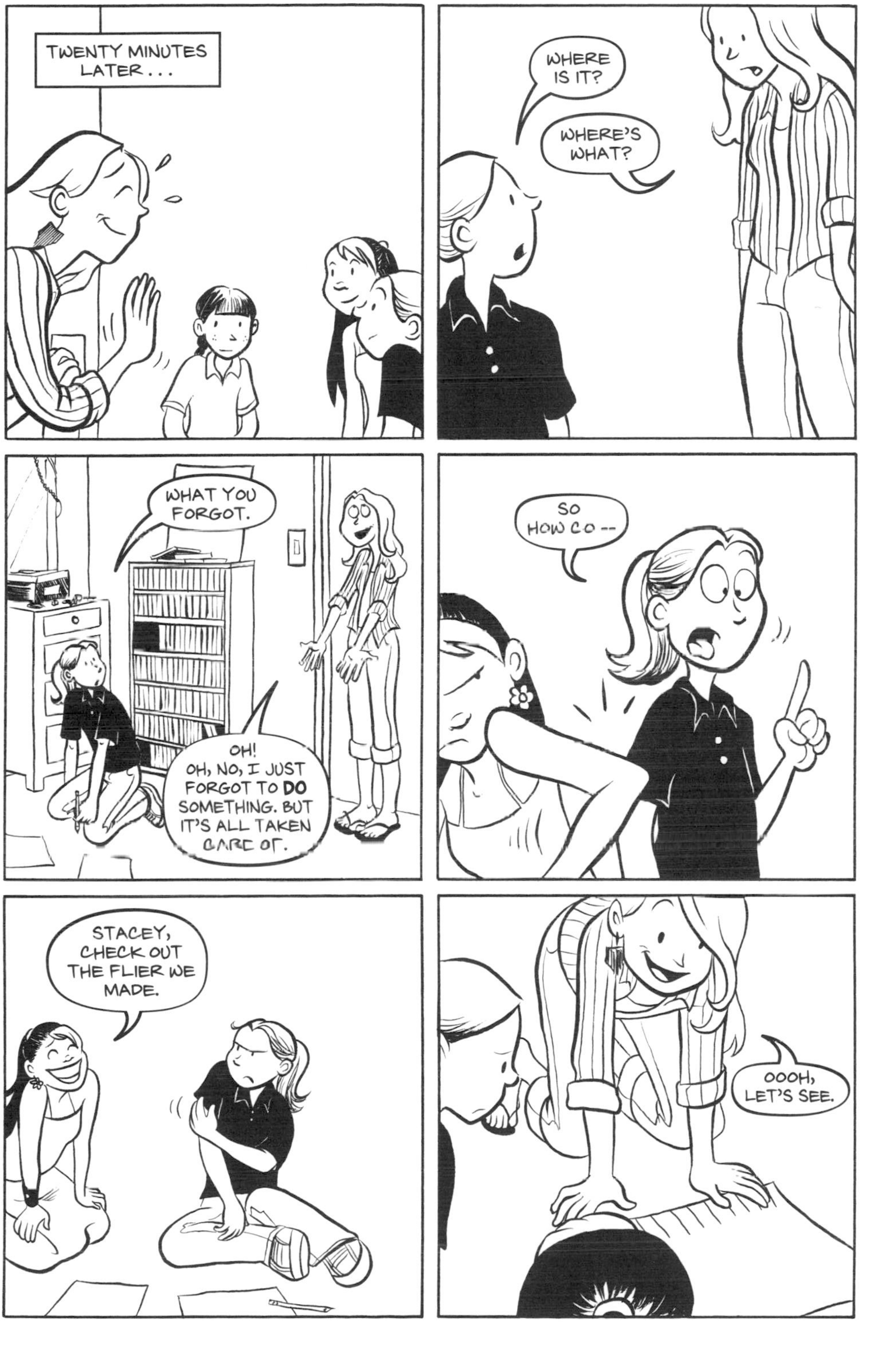
TWENTY MINUTES LATER . . .
WHERE IS IT?
WHERE'S WHAT?
WHAT YOU FORGOT.
OH! OH, NO, I JUST FORGOT TO **DO** SOMETHING. BUT IT'S ALL TAKEN CARE OF.
SO HOW CO --
STACEY, CHECK OUT THE FLIER WE MADE.
OOOH, LET'S SEE.

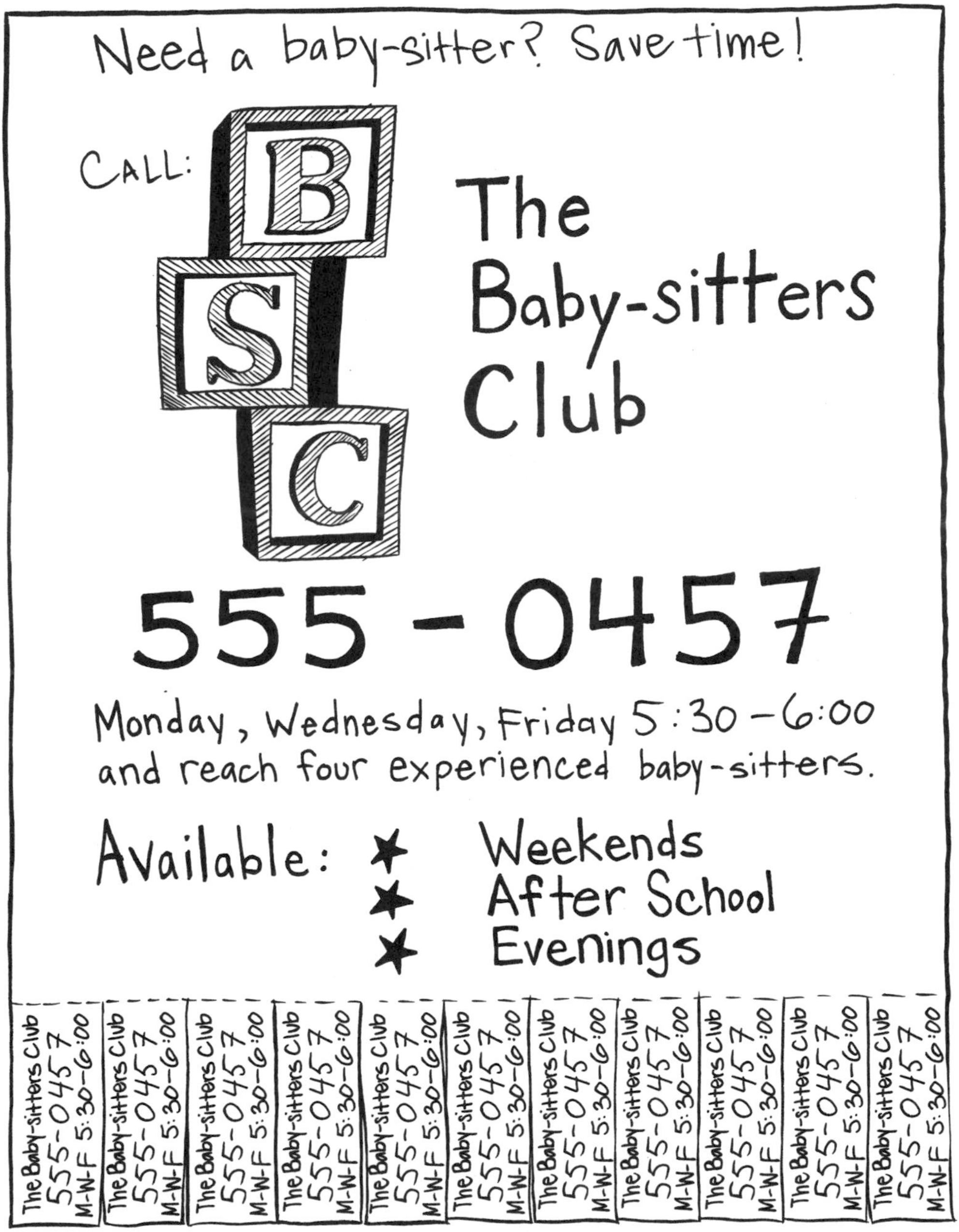
Need a baby-sitter? Save time!
CALL:
BSC
The Baby-sitters Club
555-0457
Monday, Wednesday, Friday 5:30-6:00
and reach four experienced baby-sitters.
Available: ★ Weekends ★ After School ★ Evenings
The Baby-sitters Club 555-0457 M-W-F 5:30-6:00
The Baby-sitters Club 555-0457 M-W-F 5:30-6:00
The Baby-sitters Club 555-0457 M-W-F 5:30-6:00
The Baby-sitters Club 555-0457 M-W-F 5:30-6:00
The Baby-sitters Club 555-0457 M-W-F 5:30-6:00
The Baby-sitters Club 555-0457 M-W-F 5:30-6:00
The Baby-sitters Club 555-0457 M-W-F 5:30-6:00
The Baby-sitters Club 555-0457 M-W-F 5:30-6:00
The Baby-sitters Club 555-0457 M-W-F 5:30-6:00
The Baby-sitters Club 555-0457 M-W-F 5:30-6:00
The Baby-sitters Club 555-0457 M-W-F 5:30-6:00

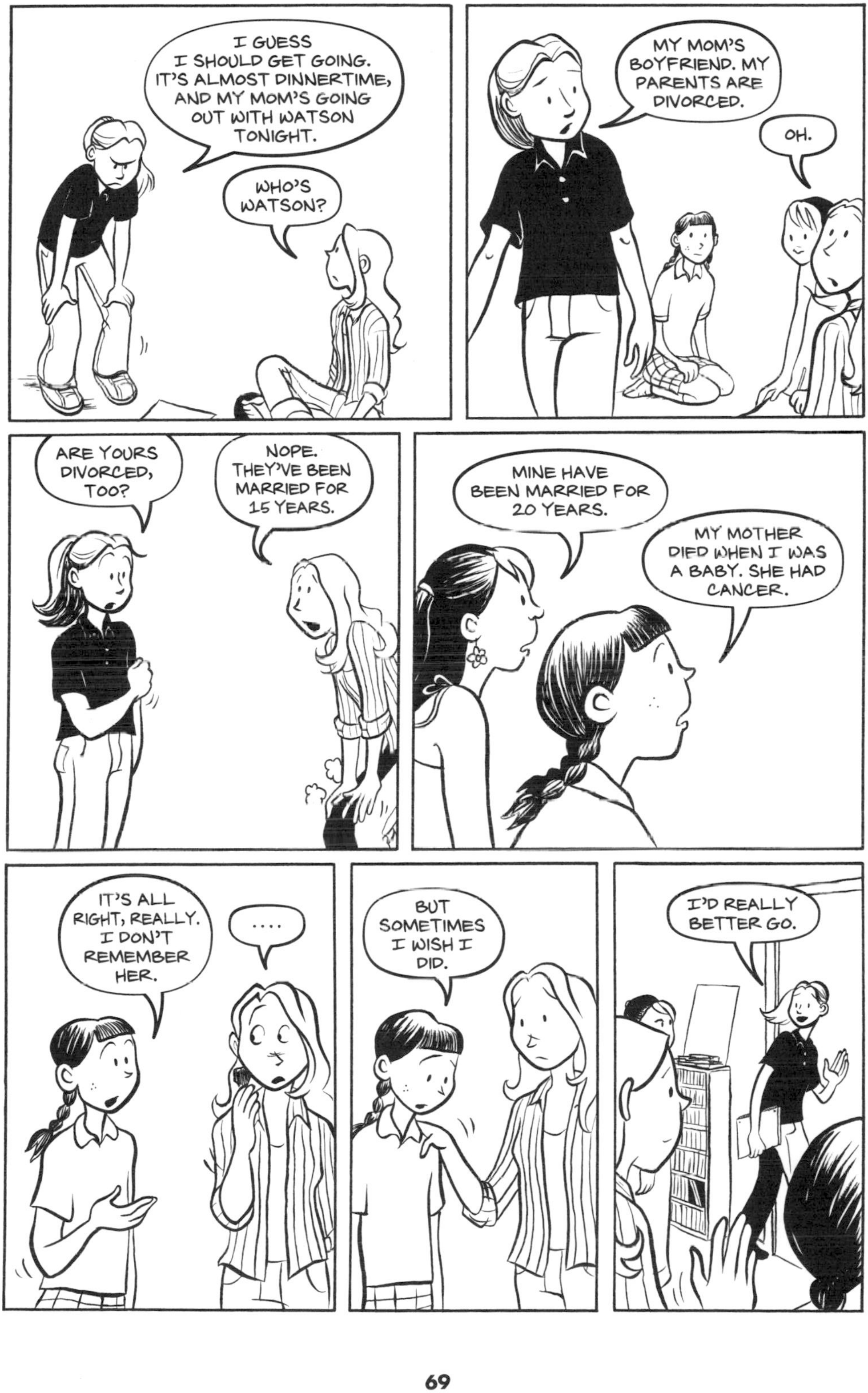
I GUESS I SHOULD GET GOING. IT'S ALMOST DINNERTIME, AND MY MOM'S GOING OUT WITH WATSON TONIGHT.
WHO'S WATSON?
MY MOM'S BOYFRIEND. MY PARENTS ARE DIVORCED.
OH.
ARE YOURS DIVORCED, TOO?
NOPE. THEY'VE BEEN MARRIED FOR 15 YEARS.
MINE HAVE BEEN MARRIED FOR 20 YEARS.
MY MOTHER DIED WHEN I WAS A BABY. SHE HAD CANCER.
IT'S ALL RIGHT, REALLY. I DON'T REMEMBER HER.
....
BUT SOMETIMES I WISH I DID.
I'D REALLY BETTER GO.

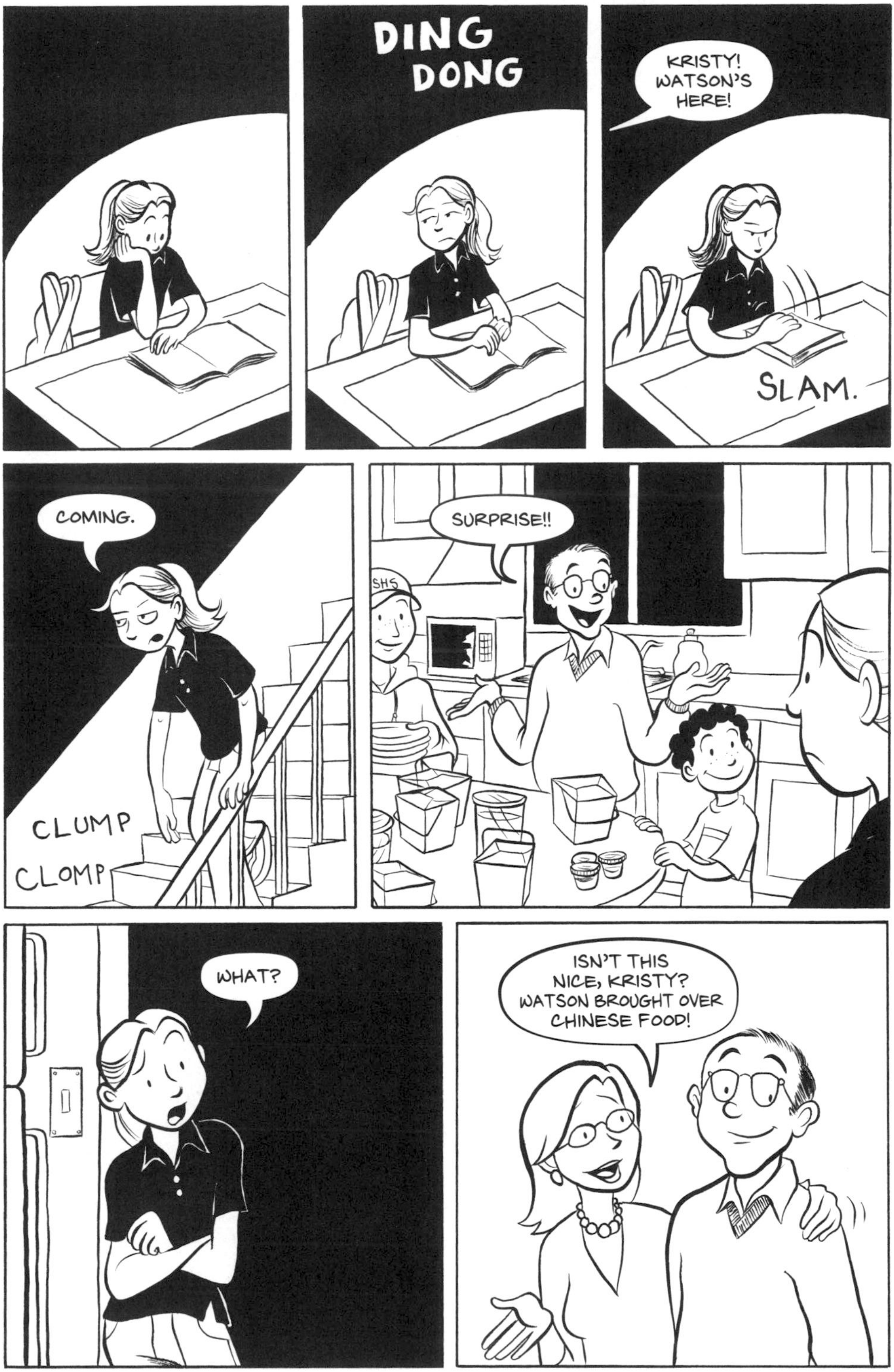
DING
DONG
KRISTY! WATSON'S HERE!
SLAM.
COMING.
CLUMP
CLOMP
SURPRISE!!
SHS
WHAT?
ISN'T THIS NICE, KRISTY? WATSON BROUGHT OVER CHINESE FOOD!

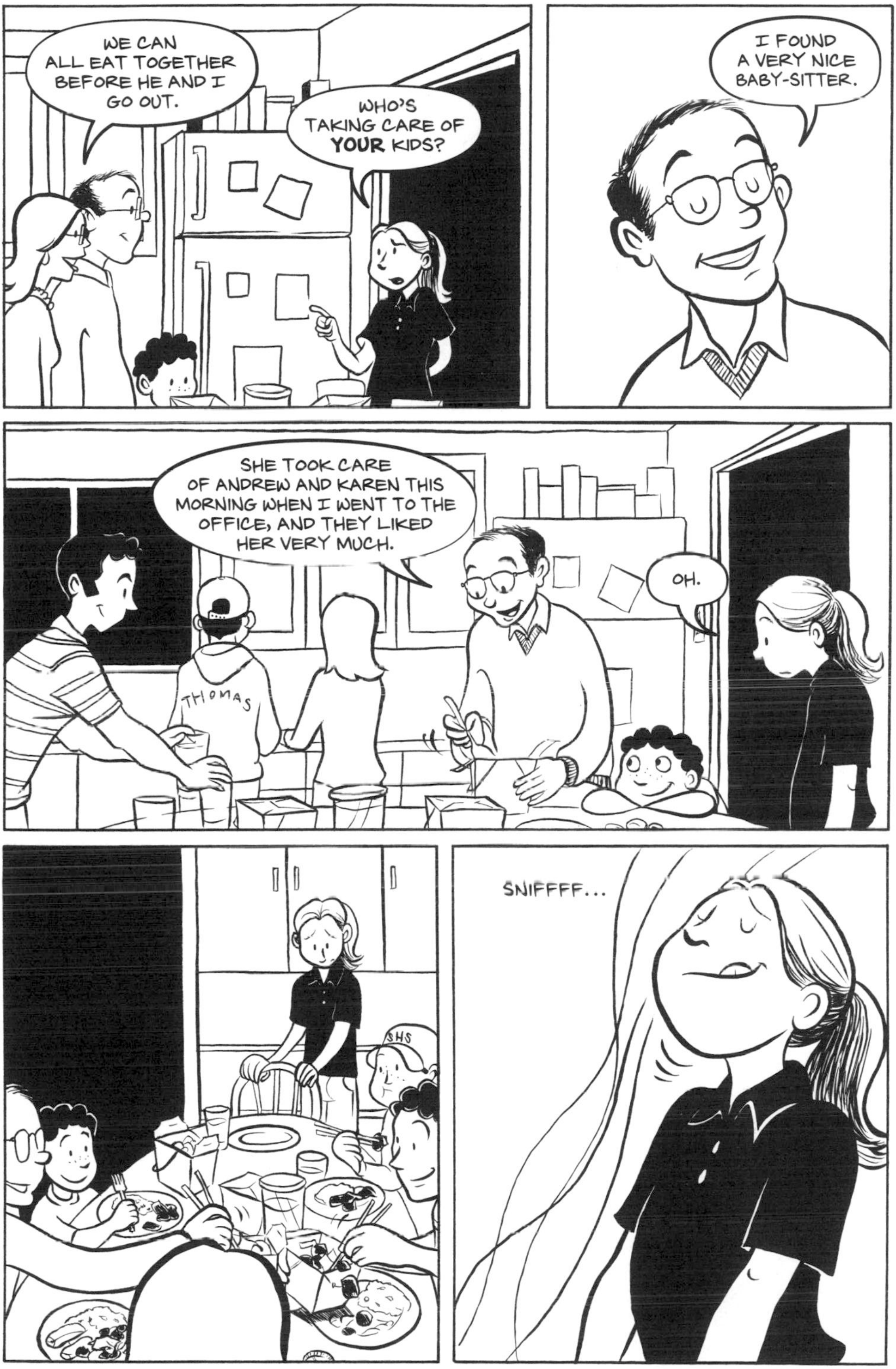
WE CAN ALL EAT TOGETHER BEFORE HE AND I GO OUT.
WHO'S TAKING CARE OF **YOUR** KIDS?
I FOUND A VERY NICE BABY-SITTER.
SHE TOOK CARE OF ANDREW AND KAREN THIS MORNING WHEN I WENT TO THE OFFICE, AND THEY LIKED HER VERY MUCH.
OH.
THOMAS
SHS
SNIFFFF...

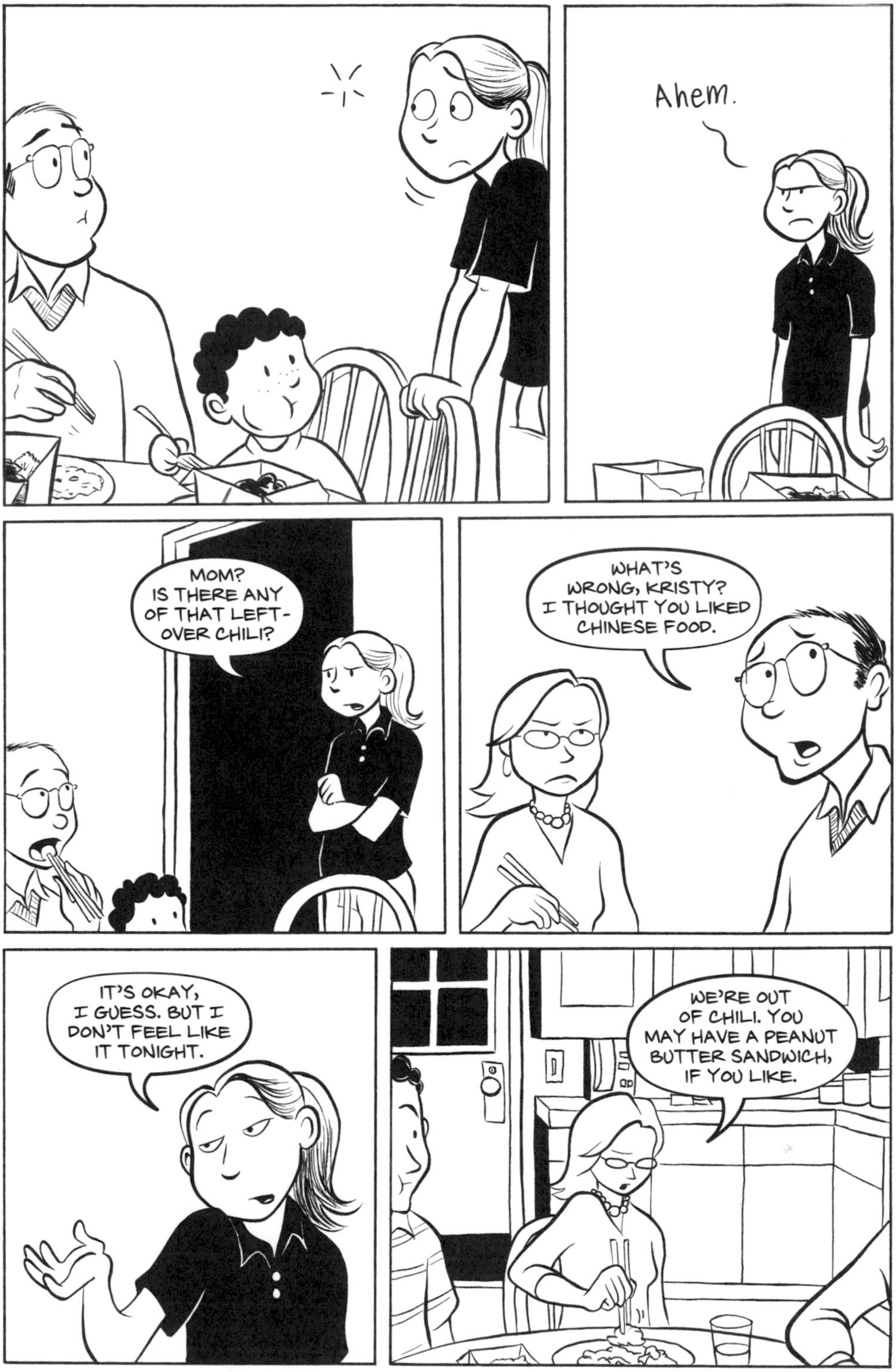
Ahem.
MOM? IS THERE ANY OF THAT LEFT-OVER CHILI?
WHAT'S WRONG, KRISTY? I THOUGHT YOU LIKED CHINESE FOOD.
IT'S OKAY, I GUESS. BUT I DON'T FEEL LIKE IT TONIGHT.
WE'RE OUT OF CHILI. YOU MAY HAVE A PEANUT BUTTER SANDWICH, IF YOU LIKE.

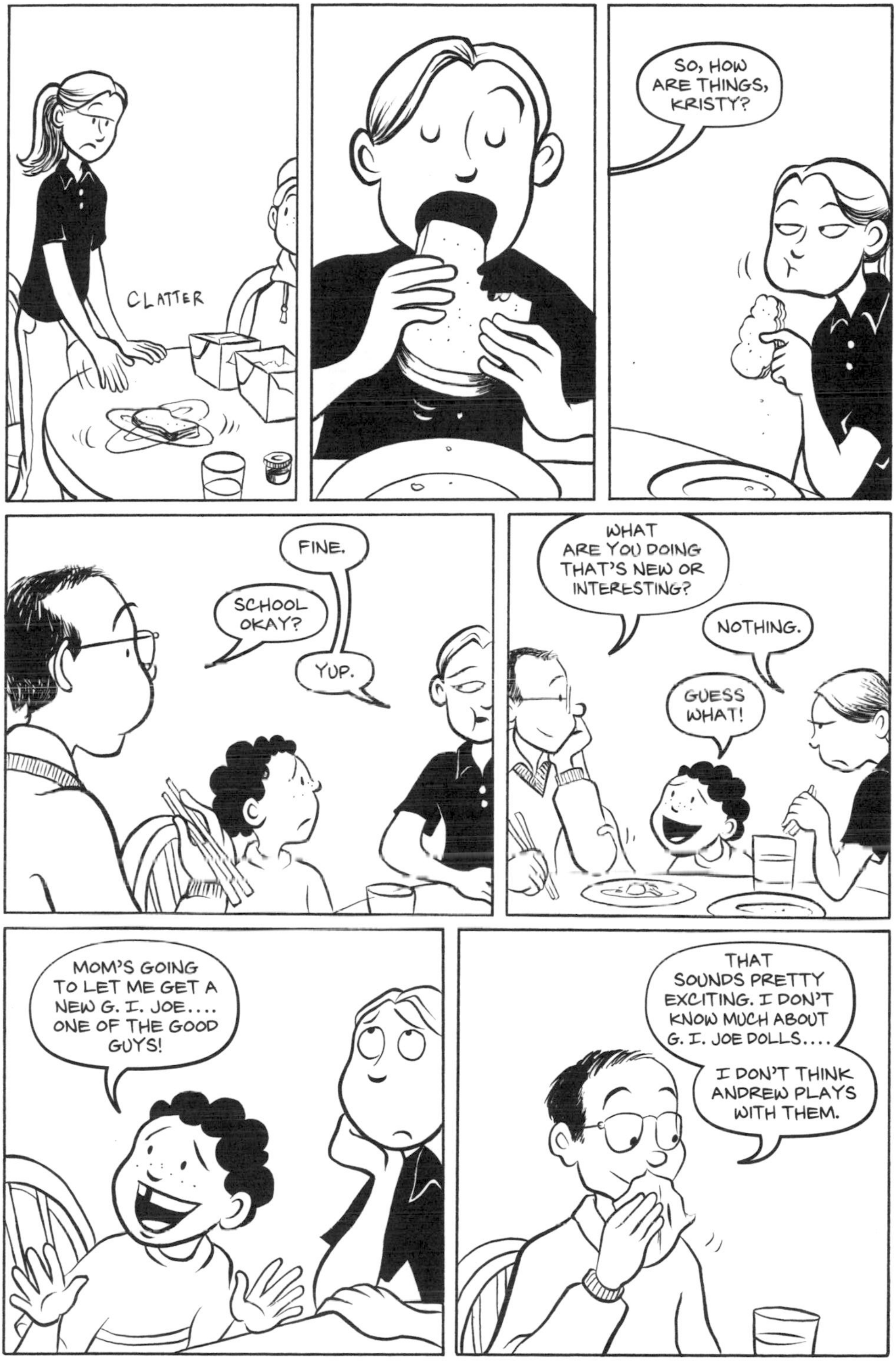
CLATTER
SO, HOW ARE THINGS, KRISTY?
FINE.
SCHOOL OKAY?
YUP.
WHAT ARE YOU DOING THAT'S NEW OR INTERESTING?
NOTHING.
GUESS WHAT!
MOM'S GOING TO LET ME GET A NEW G. I. JOE.... ONE OF THE GOOD GUYS!
THAT SOUNDS PRETTY EXCITING. I DON'T KNOW MUCH ABOUT G. I. JOE DOLLS....
I DON'T THINK ANDREW PLAYS WITH THEM.

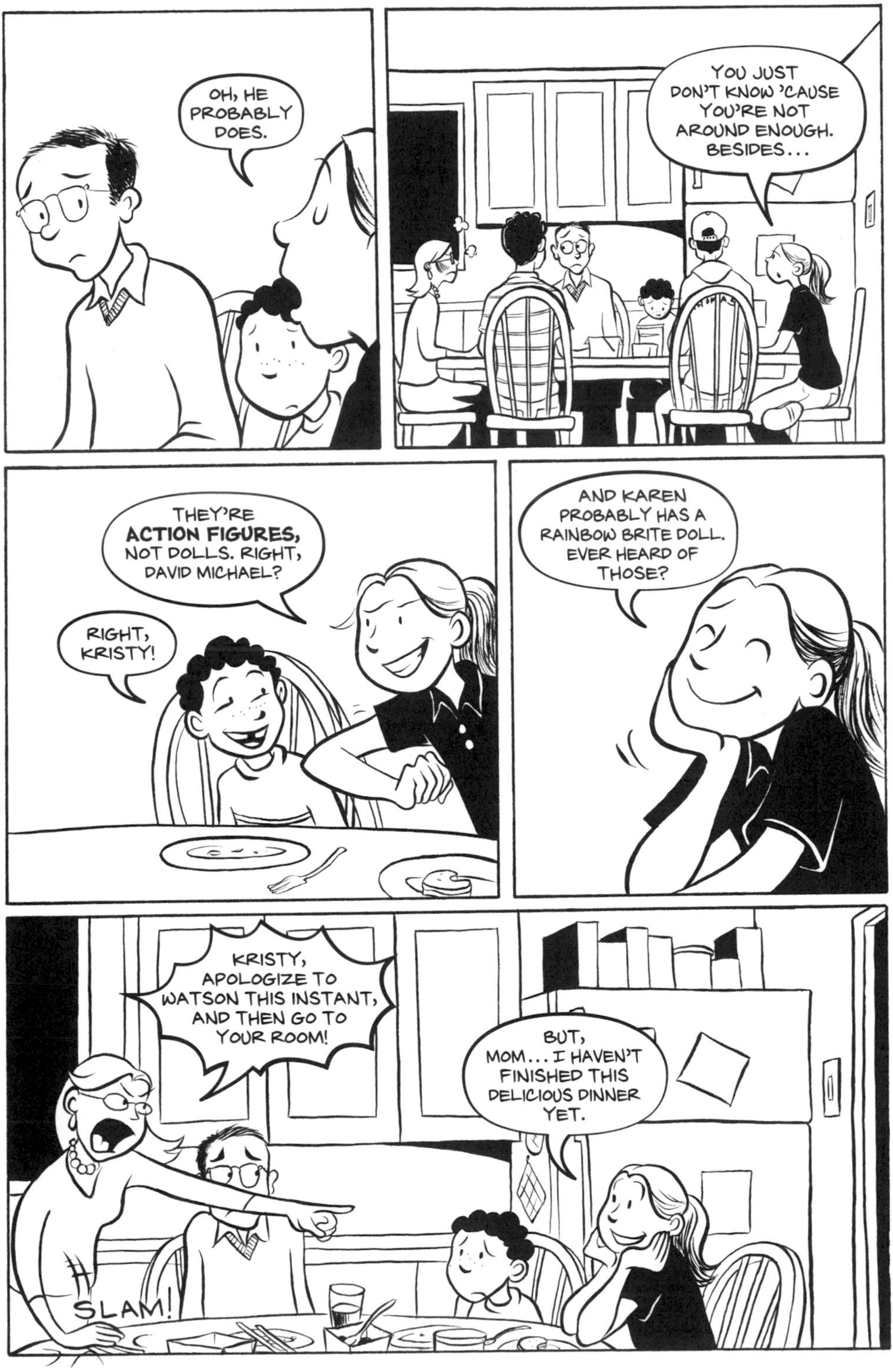
OH, HE PROBABLY DOES.
YOU JUST DON'T KNOW 'CAUSE YOU'RE NOT AROUND ENOUGH. BESIDES...
THEY'RE **ACTION FIGURES,** NOT DOLLS. RIGHT, DAVID MICHAEL?
RIGHT, KRISTY!
AND KAREN PROBABLY HAS A RAINBOW BRITE DOLL. EVER HEARD OF THOSE?
KRISTY, APOLOGIZE TO WATSON THIS INSTANT, AND THEN GO TO YOUR ROOM!
BUT, MOM... I HAVEN'T FINISHED THIS DELICIOUS DINNER YET.
SLAM!

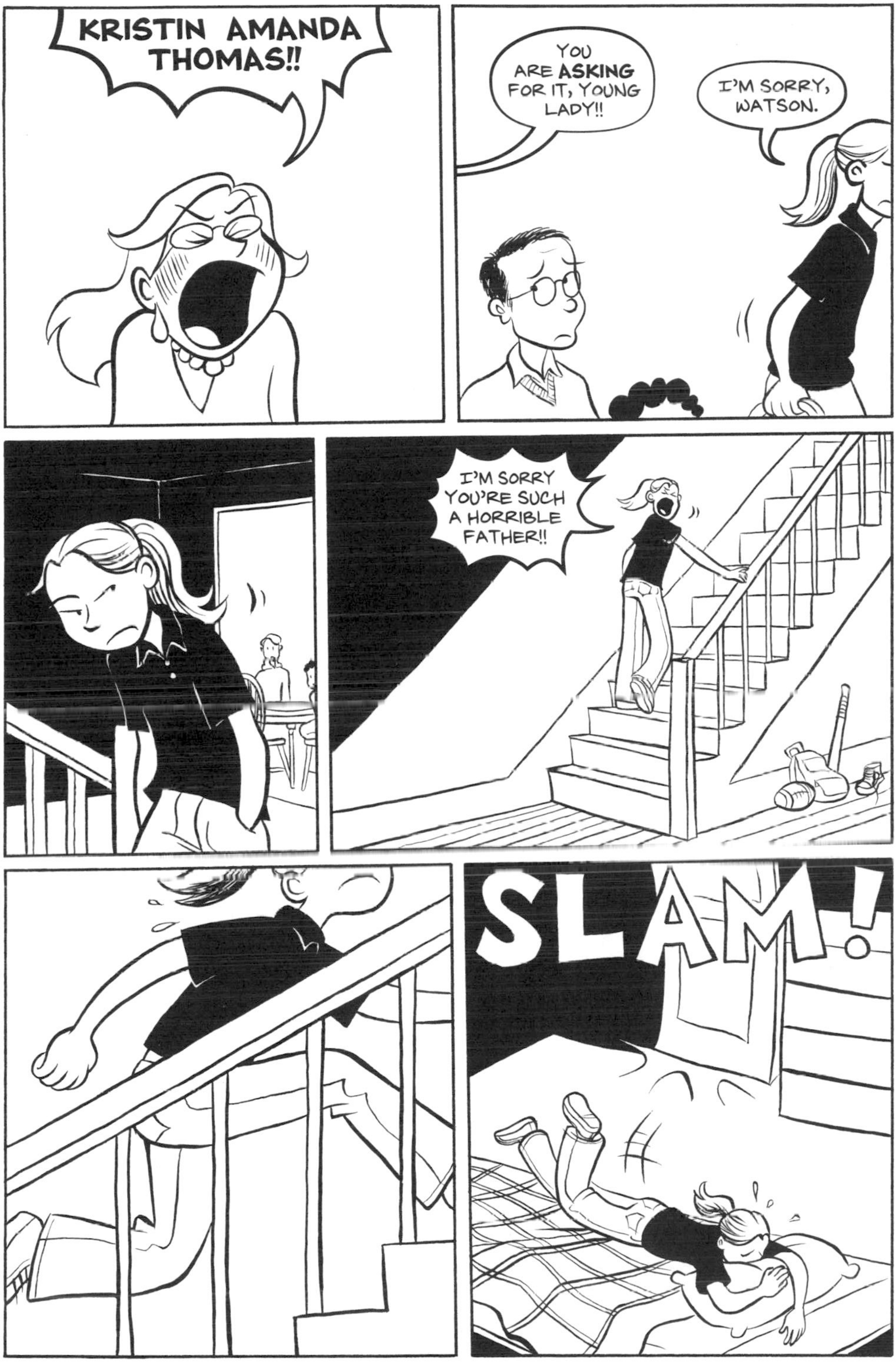
KRISTIN AMANDA THOMAS!!
YOU ARE ASKING FOR IT, YOUNG LADY!!
I'M SORRY, WATSON.
I'M SORRY YOU'RE SUCH A HORRIBLE FATHER!!
SLAM!

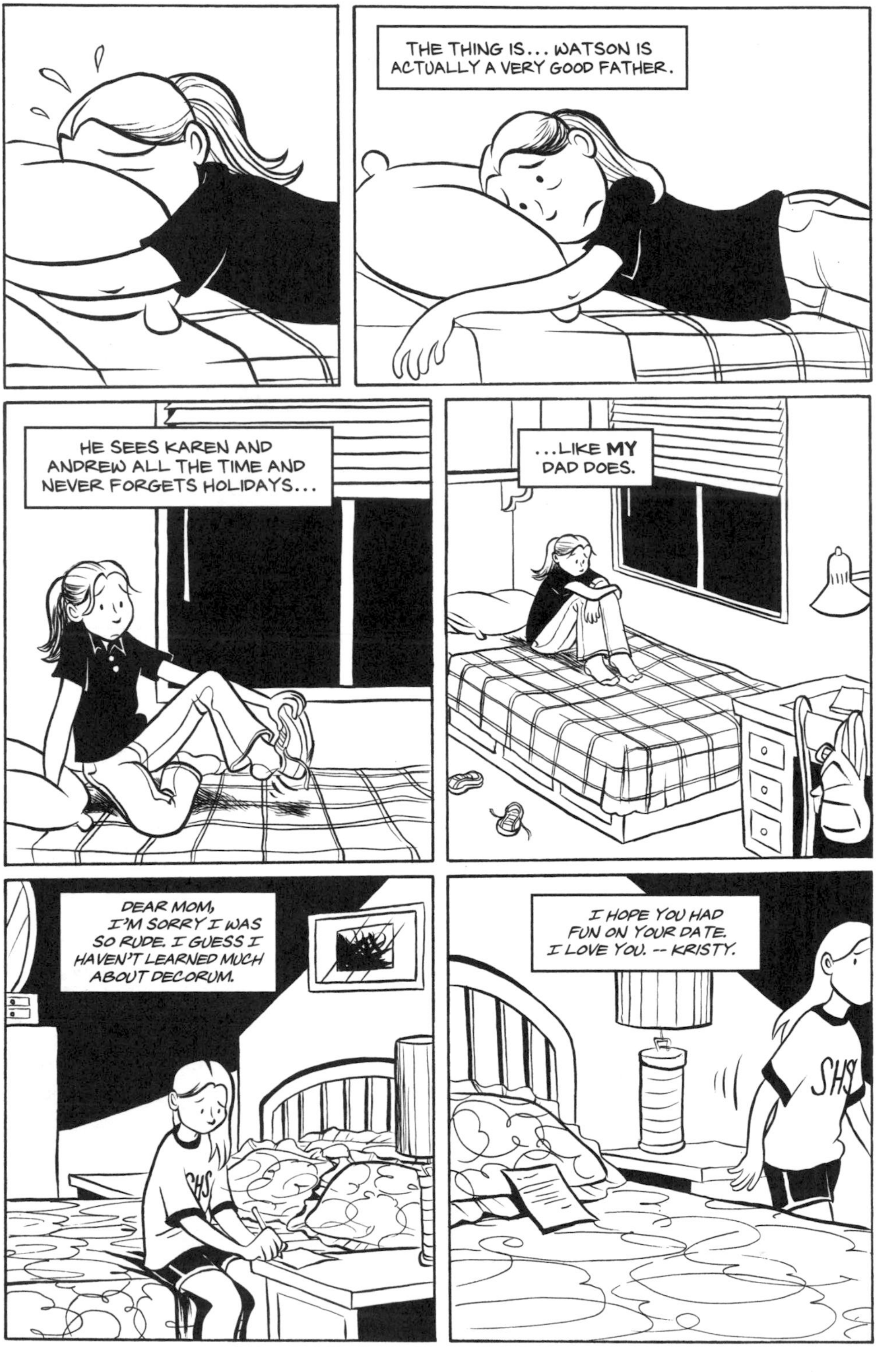
THE THING IS... WATSON IS ACTUALLY A VERY GOOD FATHER.
HE SEES KAREN AND ANDREW ALL THE TIME AND NEVER FORGETS HOLIDAYS...
...LIKE **MY** DAD DOES.
DEAR MOM, I'M SORRY I WAS SO RUDE. I GUESS I HAVEN'T LEARNED MUCH ABOUT DECORUM.
I HOPE YOU HAD FUN ON YOUR DATE. I LOVE YOU. -- KRISTY.
SHS
SHS

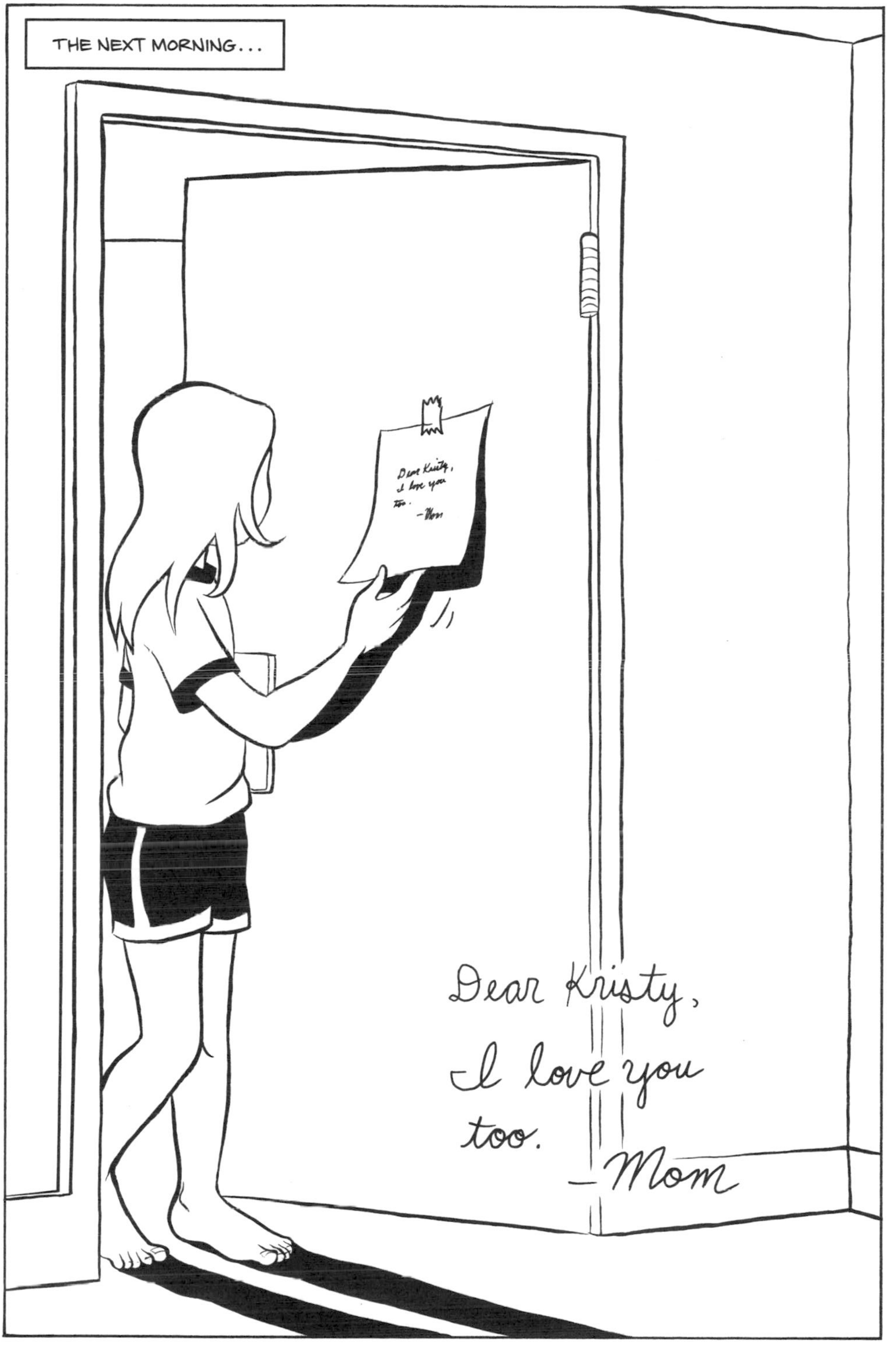
THE NEXT MORNING...
Dear Kristy,
I love you
too.
—Mom
Dear Kristy,
I love you
too.
—Mom

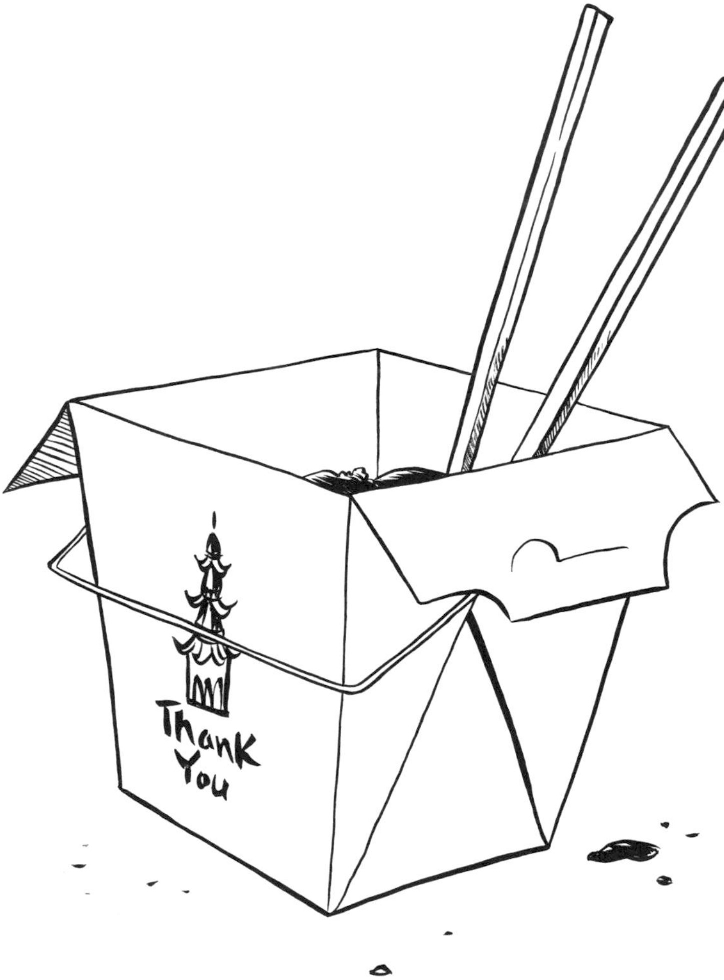
Thank You

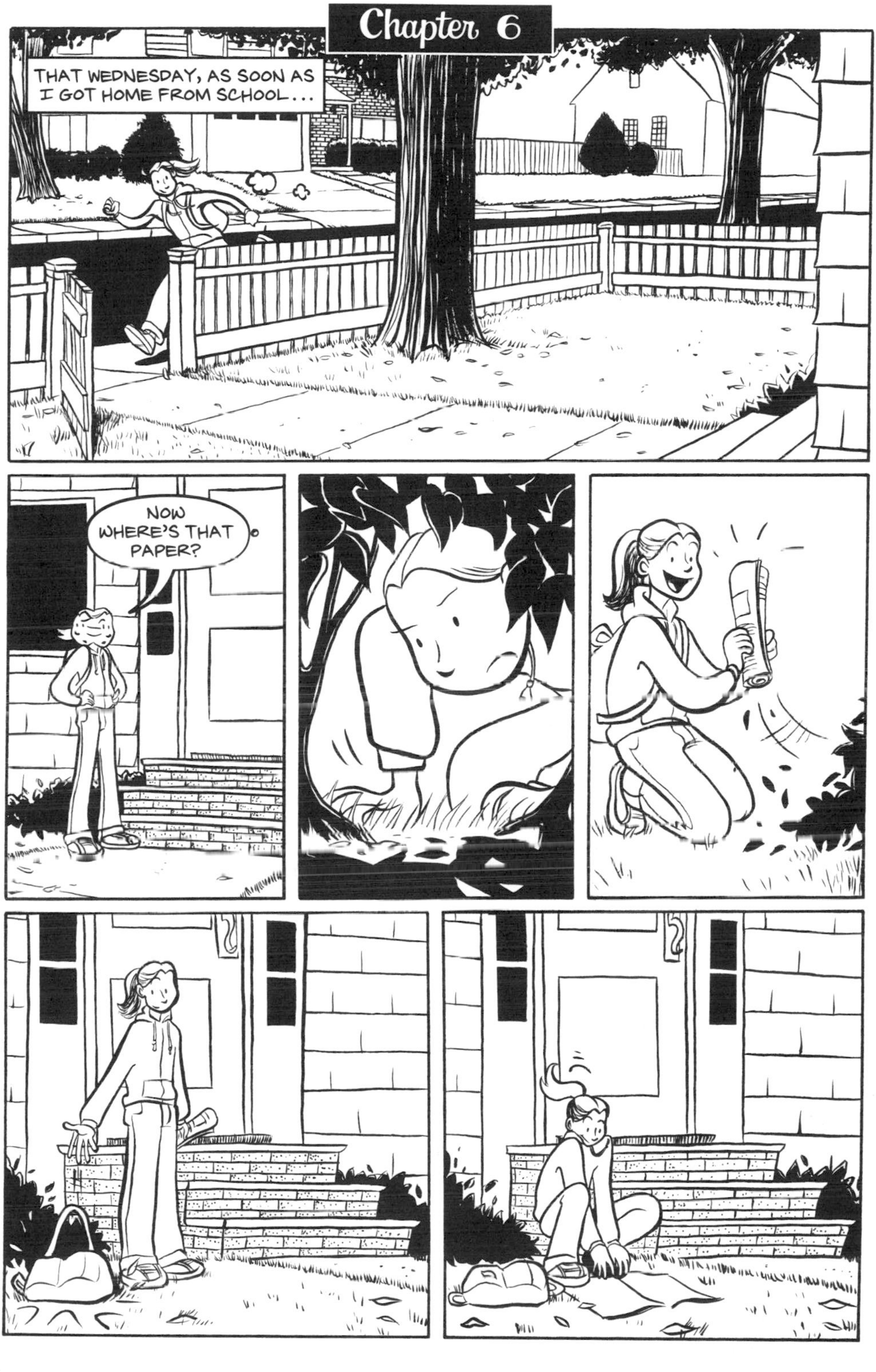
Chapter 6
THAT WEDNESDAY, AS SOON AS I GOT HOME FROM SCHOOL...
NOW WHERE'S THAT PAPER?

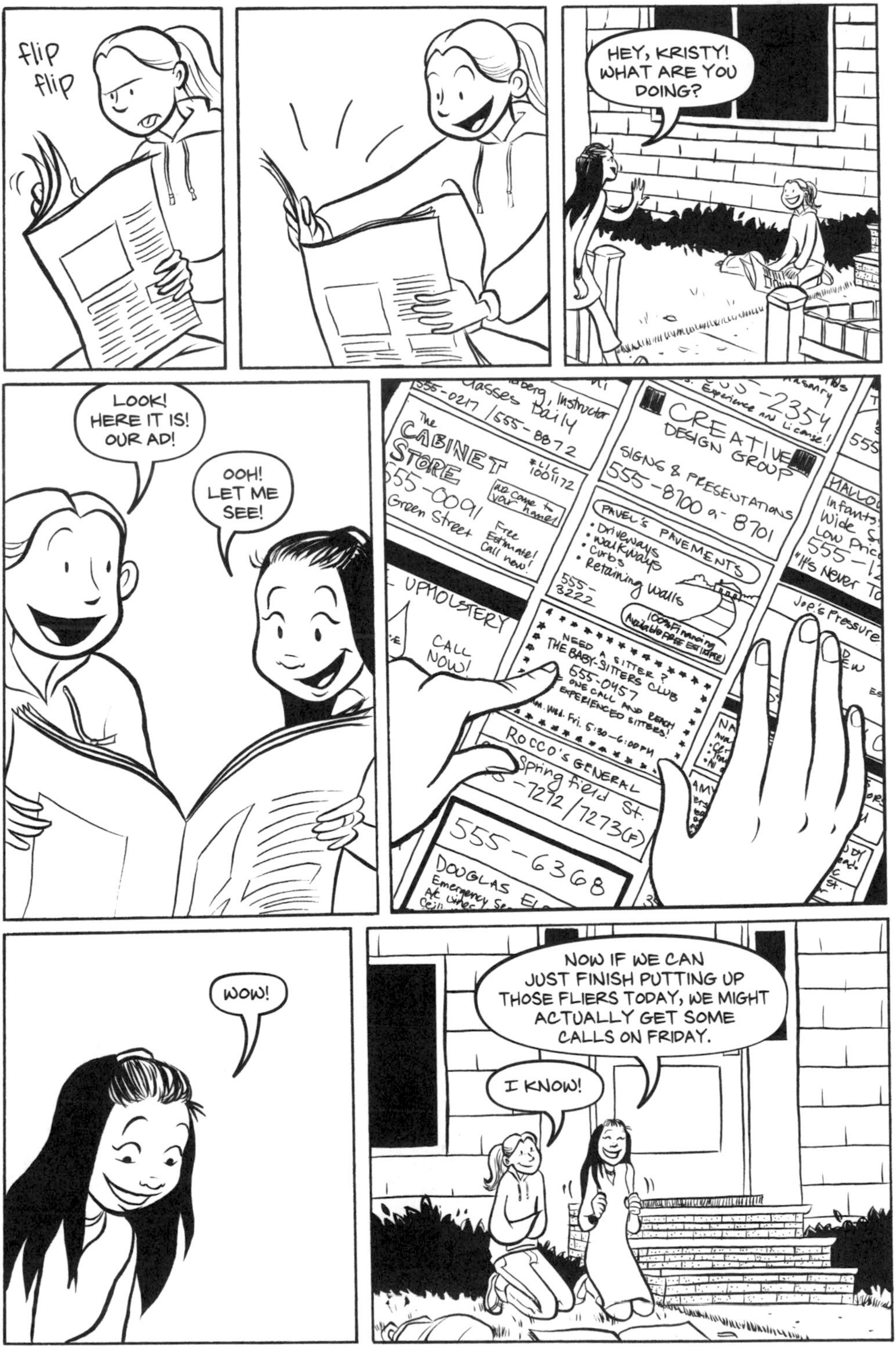
flip flip
HEY, KRISTY! WHAT ARE YOU DOING?
LOOK! HERE IT IS! OUR AD!
OOH! LET ME SEE!
CREATIVE DESIGN GROUP
SIGNS & PRESENTATIONS
555-8700 a-8701
The CABINET STORE
555-0091
Green Street
Free Estimate! Call now!
PAVEL'S PAVEMENTS
• Driveways
• Walkways
• Curbs
• Retaining Walls
555-3222
UPHOLSTERY
CALL NOW!
NEED A SITTER?
THE BABY-SITTERS CLUB
555-0457
ONE CALL AND REACH EXPERIENCED SITTERS!
ROCCO'S GENERAL
Spring field St.
7272/7273(F)
555-6368
DOUGLAS
Emergency
WOW!
NOW IF WE CAN JUST FINISH PUTTING UP THOSE FLIERS TODAY, WE MIGHT ACTUALLY GET SOME CALLS ON FRIDAY.
I KNOW!

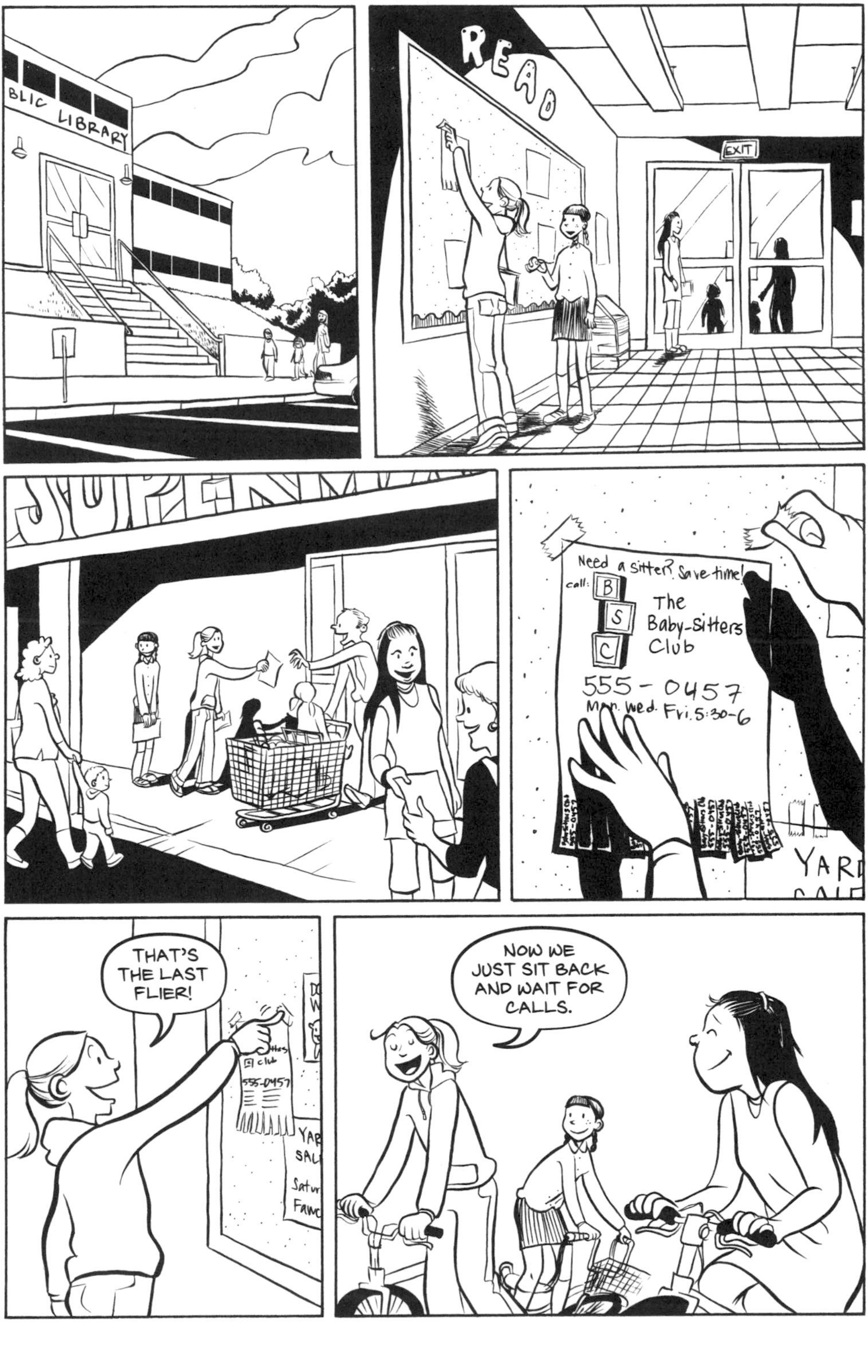
BLIC LIBRARY
READ
EXIT
Need a sitter? Save time!
call:
BSC
The Baby-Sitters Club
555-0457
Mon. Wed. Fri. 5:30-6
YARD
THAT'S THE LAST FLIER!
NOW WE JUST SIT BACK AND WAIT FOR CALLS.

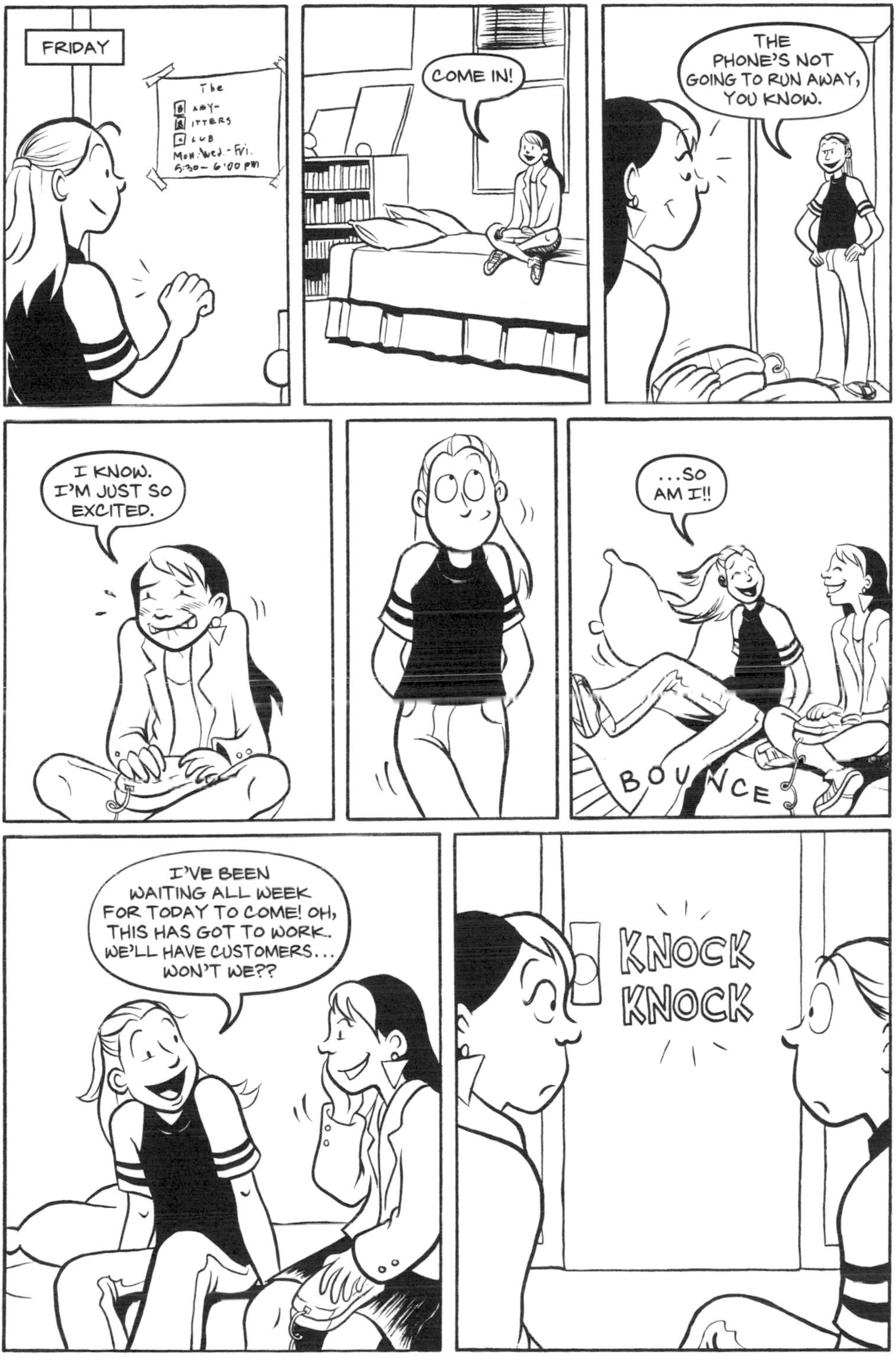
FRIDAY
The
B ABY-
S ITTERS
C LUB
Mon. Wed. - Fri.
5:30 – 6:00 pm
COME IN!
THE PHONE'S NOT GOING TO RUN AWAY, YOU KNOW.
I KNOW. I'M JUST SO EXCITED.
...SO AM I!!
BOUNCE
I'VE BEEN WAITING ALL WEEK FOR TODAY TO COME! OH, THIS HAS GOT TO WORK. WE'LL HAVE CUSTOMERS... WON'T WE??
KNOCK KNOCK

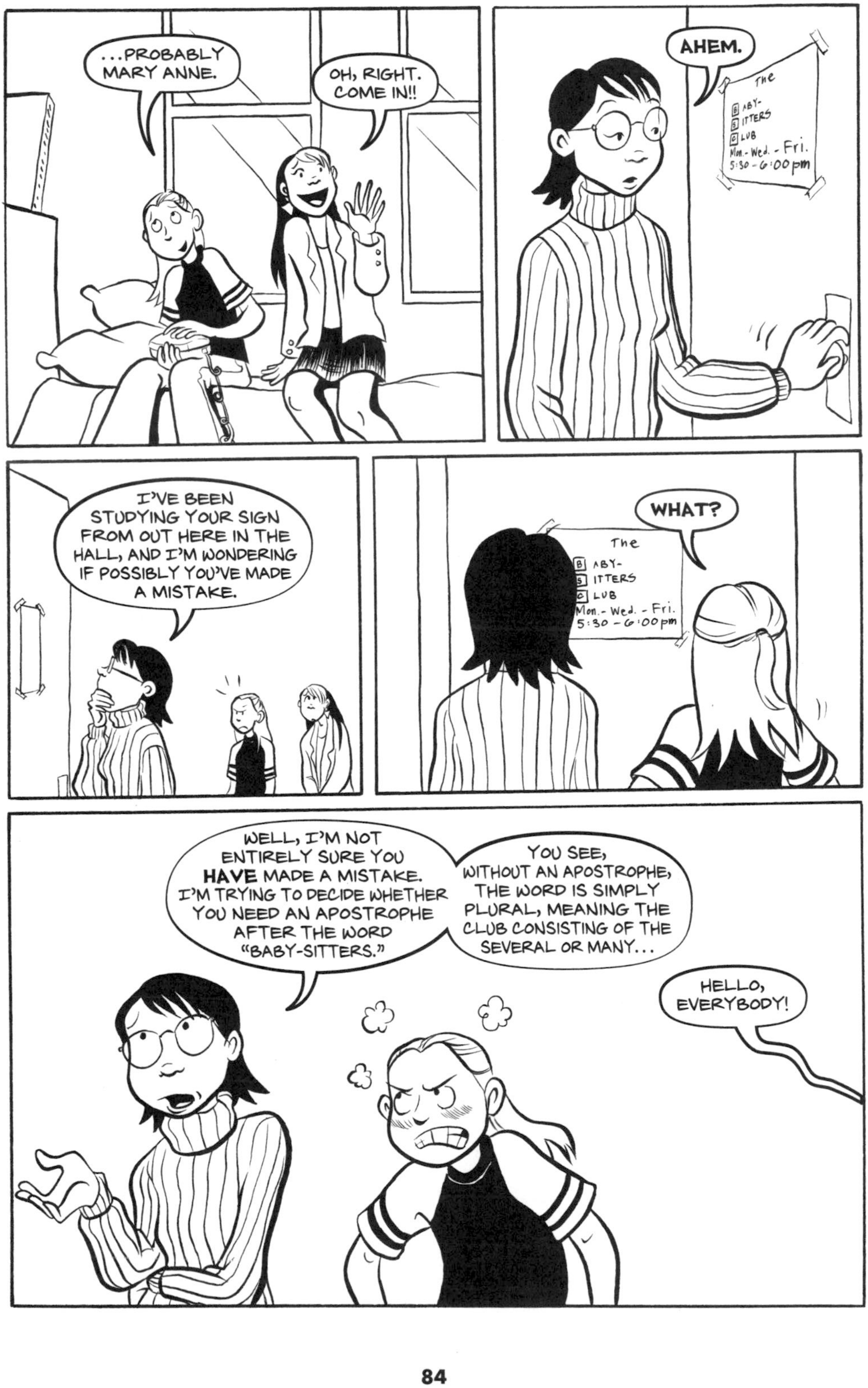
...PROBABLY MARY ANNE.
OH, RIGHT. COME IN!!
AHEM.
The B ABY- S ITTERS C LUB Mon. - Wed. - Fri. 5:30 - 6:00 pm
I'VE BEEN STUDYING YOUR SIGN FROM OUT HERE IN THE HALL, AND I'M WONDERING IF POSSIBLY YOU'VE MADE A MISTAKE.
WHAT?
The B ABY- S ITTERS C LUB Mon. - Wed. - Fri. 5:30 - 6:00 pm
WELL, I'M NOT ENTIRELY SURE YOU **HAVE** MADE A MISTAKE. I'M TRYING TO DECIDE WHETHER YOU NEED AN APOSTROPHE AFTER THE WORD "BABY-SITTERS."
YOU SEE, WITHOUT AN APOSTROPHE, THE WORD IS SIMPLY PLURAL, MEANING THE CLUB CONSISTING OF THE SEVERAL OR MANY...
HELLO, EVERYBODY!

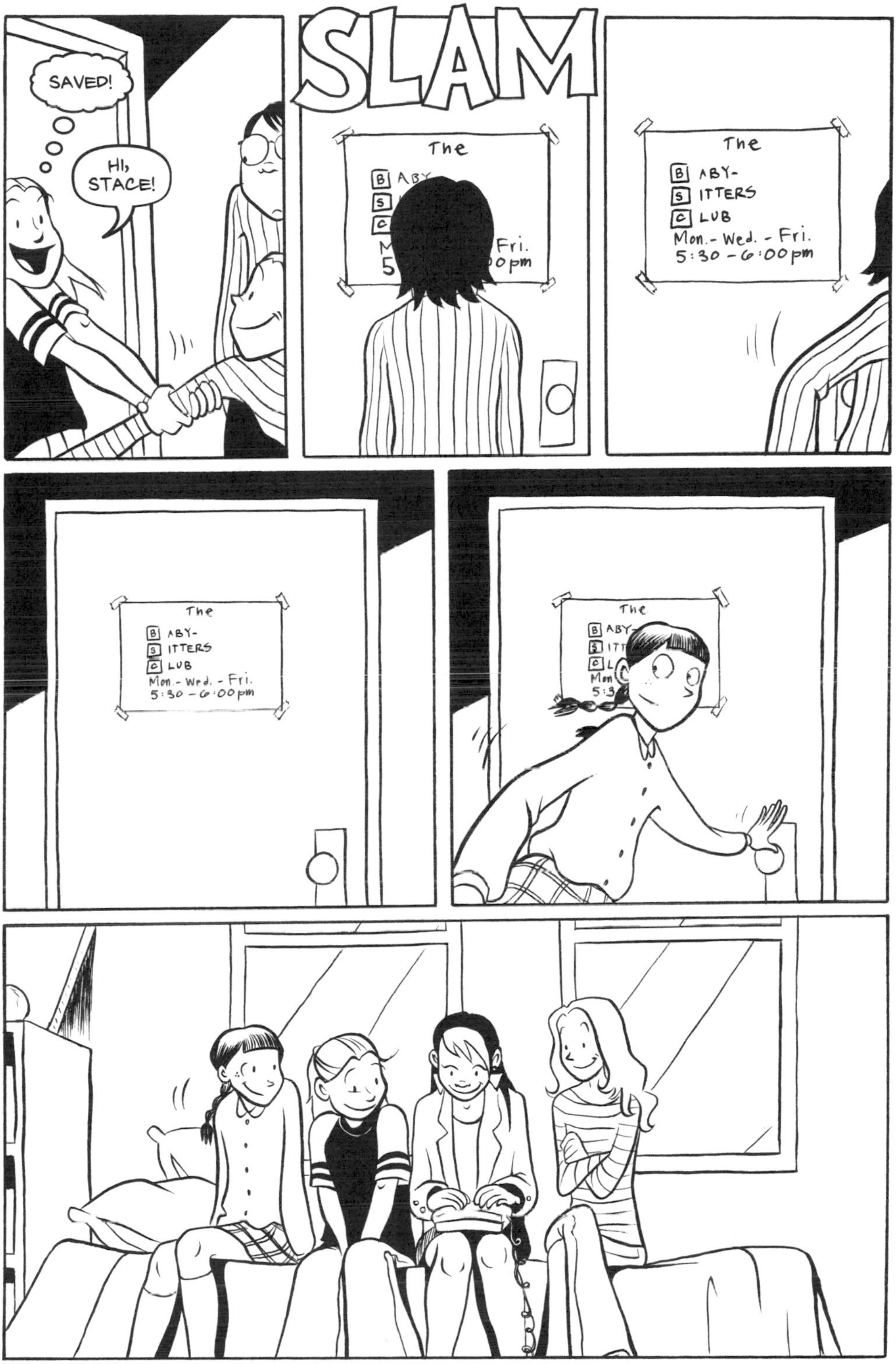
SAVED!
HI, STACE!
SLAM
The
B ABY-
S ITTERS
C LUB
Mon.-Wed.-Fri.
5:30-6:00pm

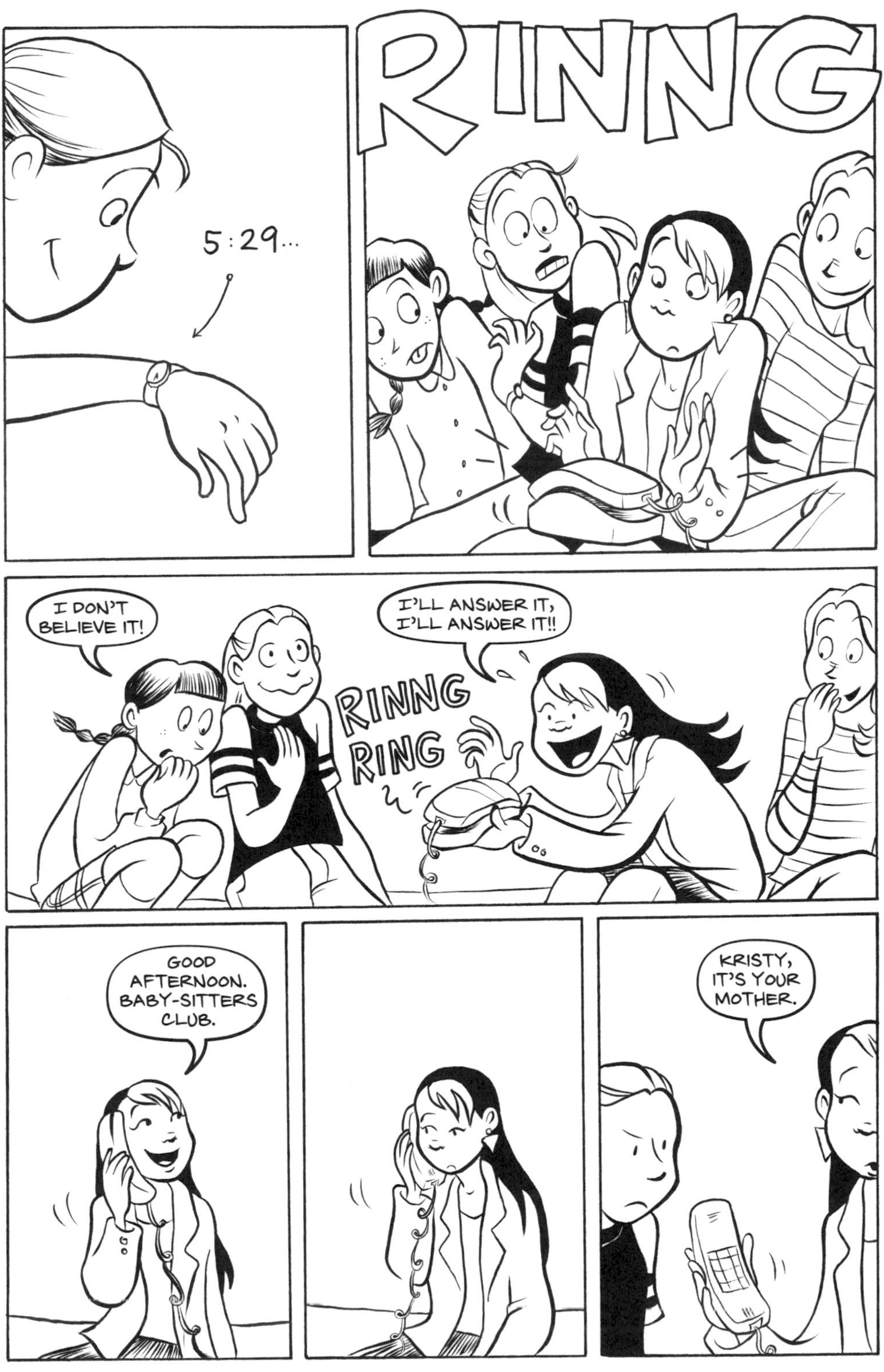
5:29...
RINNG
I DON'T BELIEVE IT!
I'LL ANSWER IT, I'LL ANSWER IT!!
RINNG RING
GOOD AFTERNOON. BABY-SITTERS CLUB.
KRISTY, IT'S YOUR MOTHER.

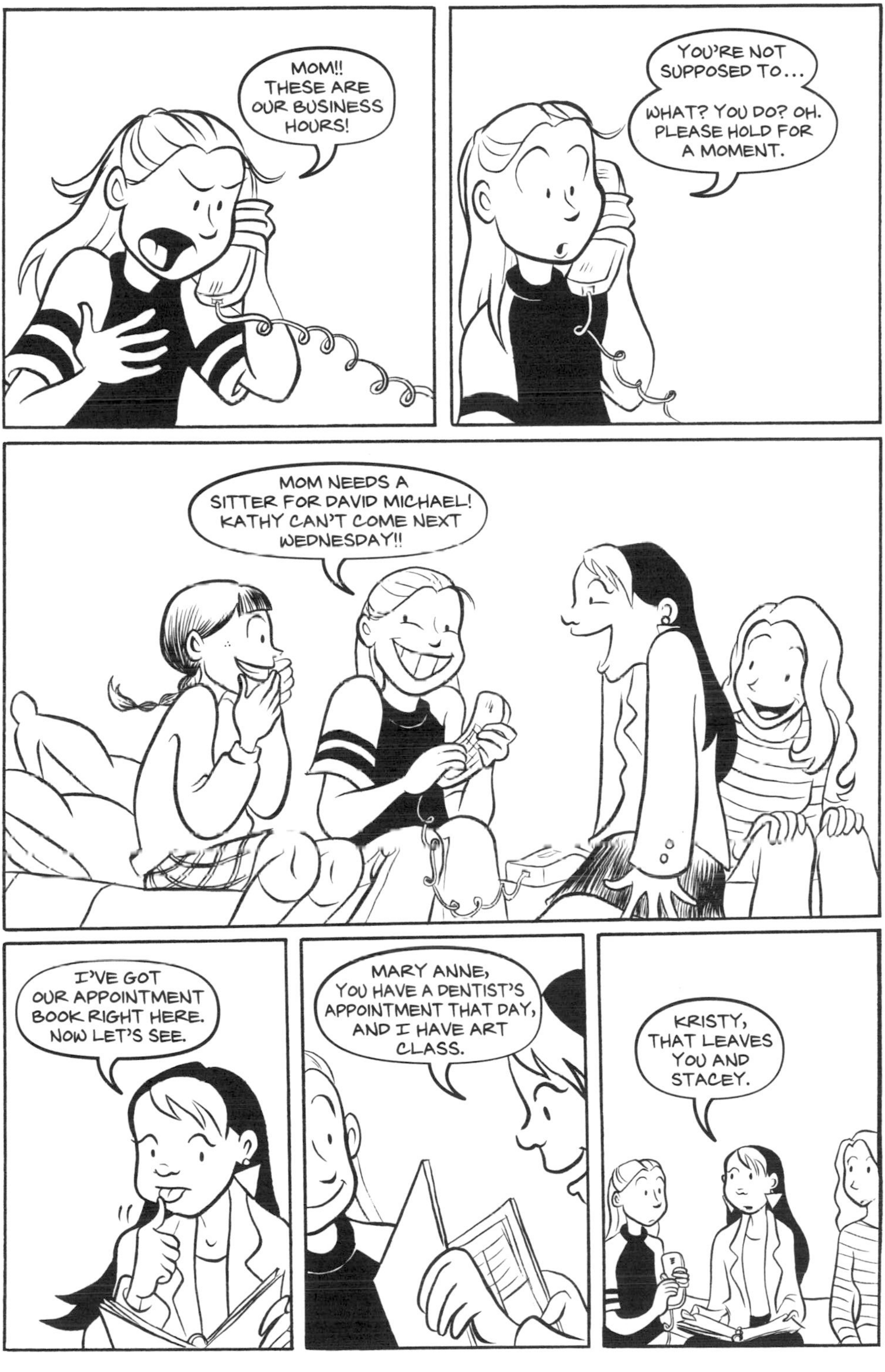
MOM!! THESE ARE OUR BUSINESS HOURS!
YOU'RE NOT SUPPOSED TO...
WHAT? YOU DO? OH. PLEASE HOLD FOR A MOMENT.
MOM NEEDS A SITTER FOR DAVID MICHAEL! KATHY CAN'T COME NEXT WEDNESDAY!!
I'VE GOT OUR APPOINTMENT BOOK RIGHT HERE. NOW LET'S SEE.
MARY ANNE, YOU HAVE A DENTIST'S APPOINTMENT THAT DAY, AND I HAVE ART CLASS.
KRISTY, THAT LEAVES YOU AND STACEY.

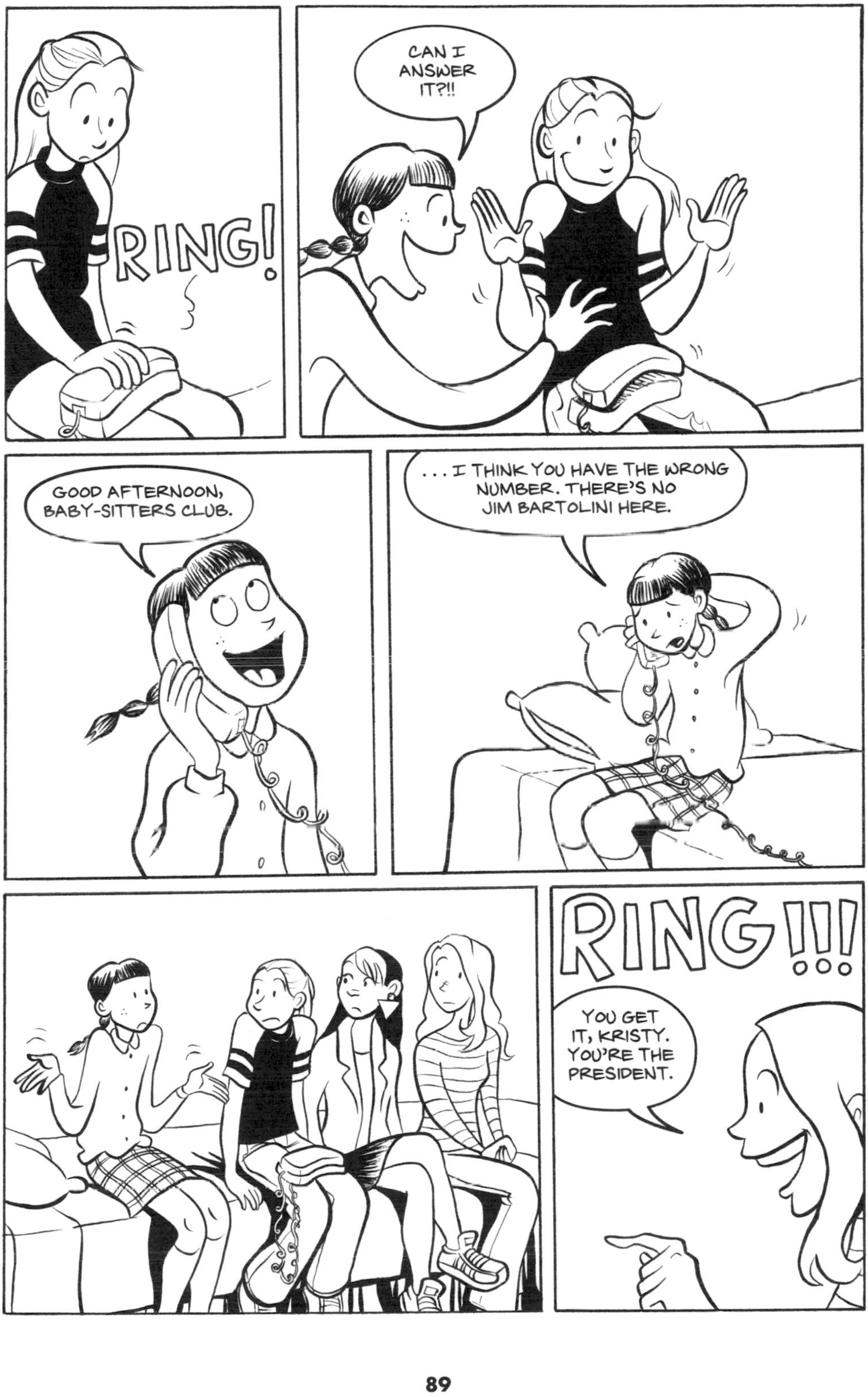
RING!
CAN I ANSWER IT?!!
GOOD AFTERNOON, BABY-SITTERS CLUB.
. . . I THINK YOU HAVE THE WRONG NUMBER. THERE'S NO JIM BARTOLINI HERE.
RING!!!
YOU GET IT, KRISTY. YOU'RE THE PRESIDENT.

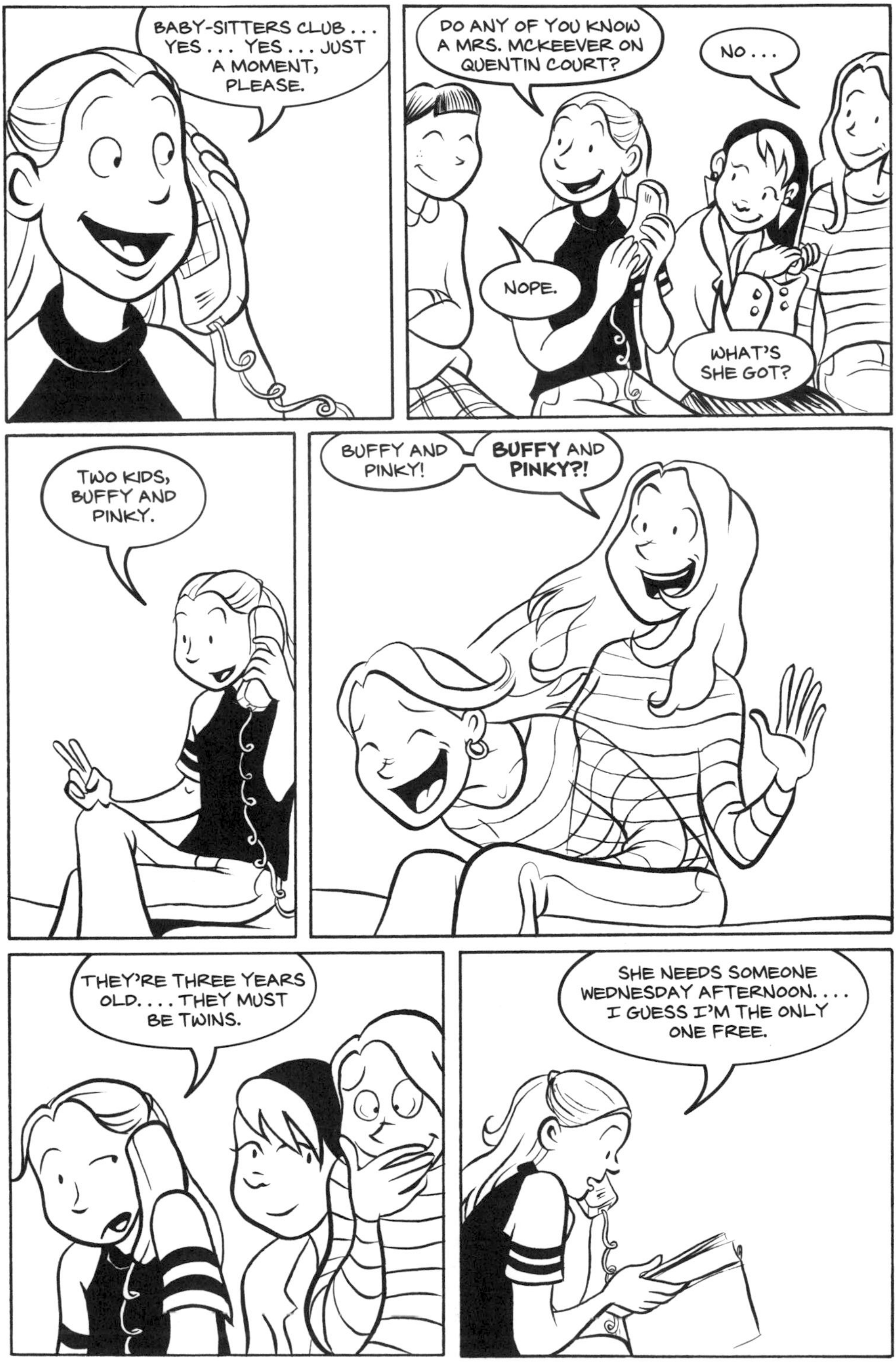
BABY-SITTERS CLUB . . . YES . . . YES . . . JUST A MOMENT, PLEASE.
DO ANY OF YOU KNOW A MRS. MCKEEVER ON QUENTIN COURT?
NO . . .
NOPE.
WHAT'S SHE GOT?
TWO KIDS, BUFFY AND PINKY.
BUFFY AND PINKY!
BUFFY AND PINKY?!
THEY'RE THREE YEARS OLD. . . . THEY MUST BE TWINS.
SHE NEEDS SOMEONE WEDNESDAY AFTERNOON. . . . I GUESS I'M THE ONLY ONE FREE.

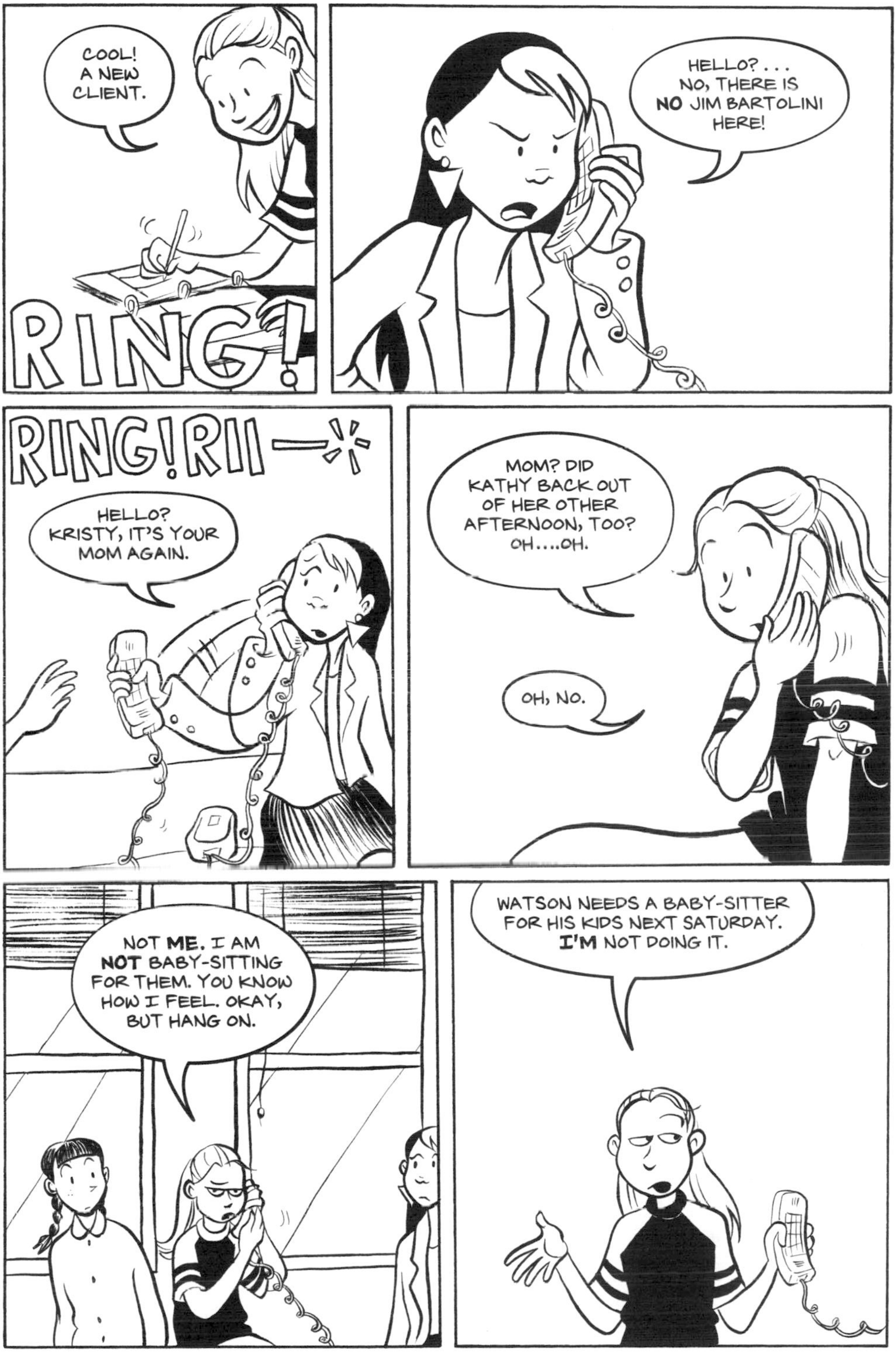

COOL! A NEW CLIENT.
RING!
HELLO? . . . NO, THERE IS NO JIM BARTOLINI HERE!
RING!RII—
HELLO? KRISTY, IT'S YOUR MOM AGAIN.
MOM? DID KATHY BACK OUT OF HER OTHER AFTERNOON, TOO? OH....OH.
OH, NO.
NOT ME. I AM NOT BABY-SITTING FOR THEM. YOU KNOW HOW I FEEL. OKAY, BUT HANG ON.
WATSON NEEDS A BABY-SITTER FOR HIS KIDS NEXT SATURDAY. I'M NOT DOING IT.

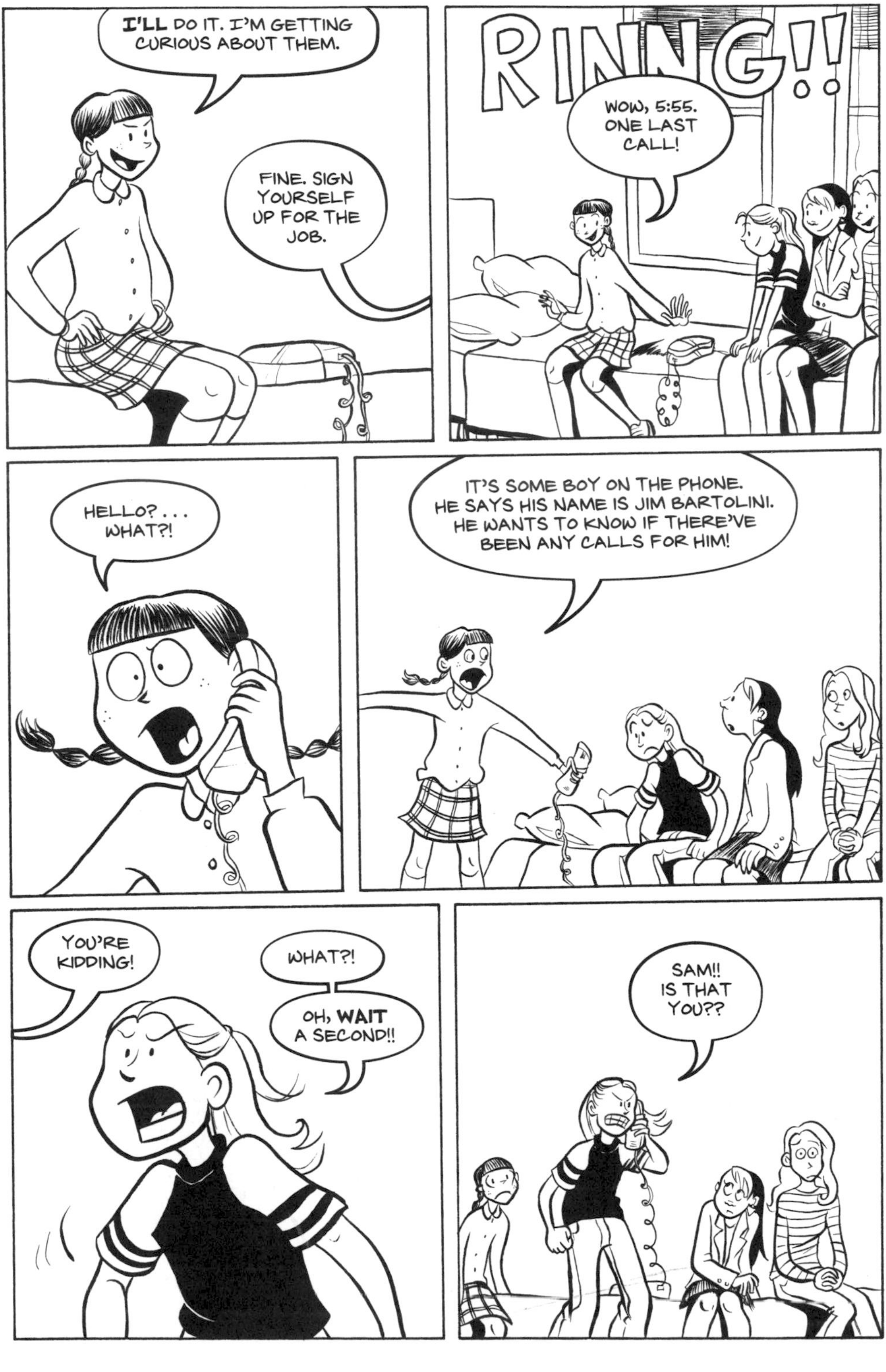
I'LL DO IT. I'M GETTING CURIOUS ABOUT THEM.
FINE. SIGN YOURSELF UP FOR THE JOB.
RINNG!!
WOW, 5:55. ONE LAST CALL!
HELLO? . . . WHAT?!
IT'S SOME BOY ON THE PHONE. HE SAYS HIS NAME IS JIM BARTOLINI. HE WANTS TO KNOW IF THERE'VE BEEN ANY CALLS FOR HIM!
YOU'RE KIDDING!
WHAT?!
OH, WAIT A SECOND!!
SAM!! IS THAT YOU??

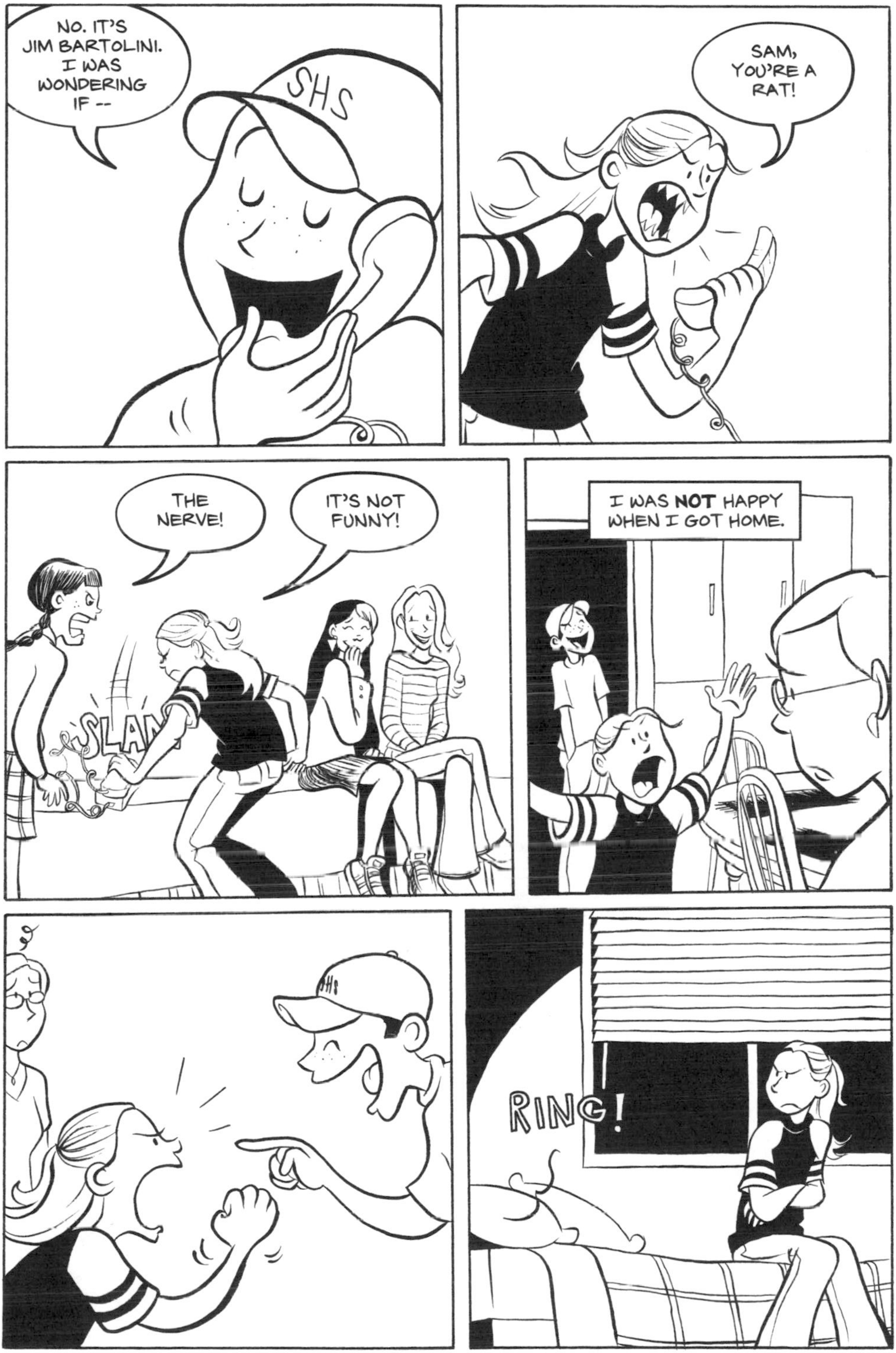
NO. IT'S JIM BARTOLINI. I WAS WONDERING IF --
SHS
SAM, YOU'RE A RAT!
THE NERVE!
IT'S NOT FUNNY!
SLAM
I WAS **NOT** HAPPY WHEN I GOT HOME.
SHS
RING!

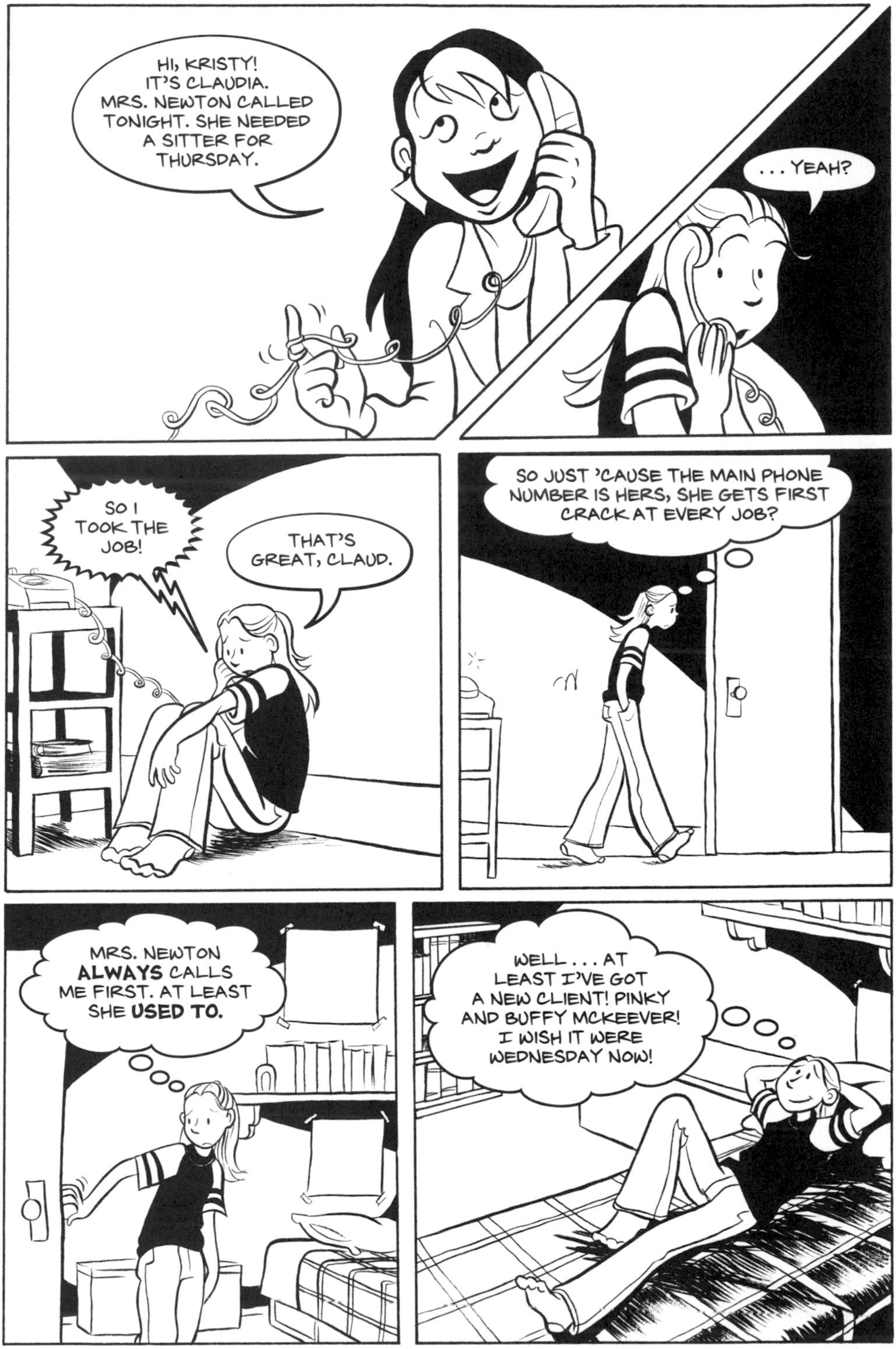
HI, KRISTY! IT'S CLAUDIA. MRS. NEWTON CALLED TONIGHT. SHE NEEDED A SITTER FOR THURSDAY.
. . . YEAH?
SO I TOOK THE JOB!
THAT'S GREAT, CLAUD.
SO JUST 'CAUSE THE MAIN PHONE NUMBER IS HERS, SHE GETS FIRST CRACK AT EVERY JOB?
MRS. NEWTON **ALWAYS** CALLS ME FIRST. AT LEAST SHE **USED TO.**
WELL . . . AT LEAST I'VE GOT A NEW CLIENT! PINKY AND BUFFY MCKEEVER! I WISH IT WERE WEDNESDAY NOW!

Chapter 7

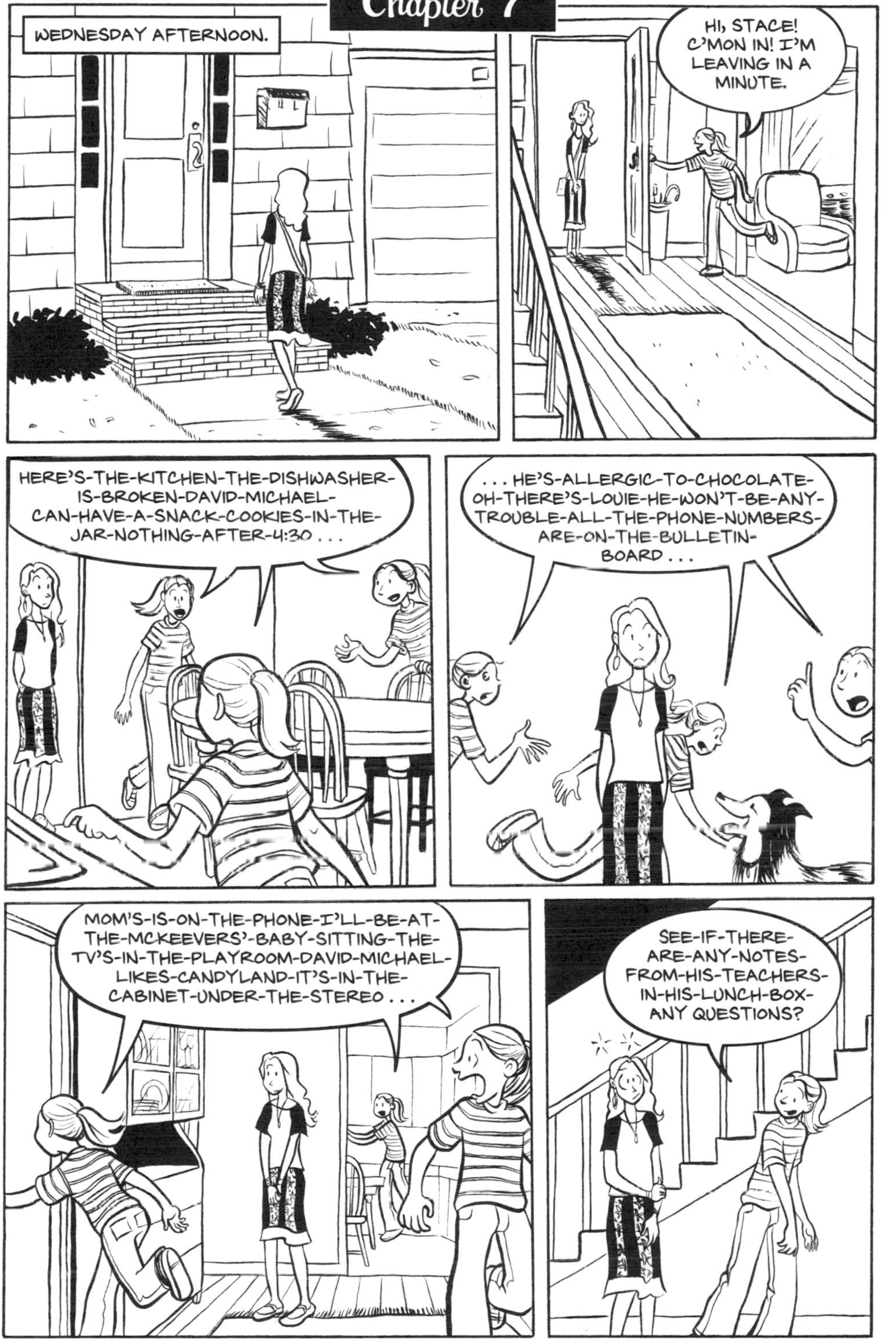
WEDNESDAY AFTERNOON.
HI, STACE! C'MON IN! I'M LEAVING IN A MINUTE.
HERE'S-THE-KITCHEN-THE-DISHWASHER-IS-BROKEN-DAVID-MICHAEL-CAN-HAVE-A-SNACK-COOKIES-IN-THE-JAR-NOTHING-AFTER-4:30 . . .
. . . HE'S-ALLERGIC-TO-CHOCOLATE-OH-THERE'S-LOUIE-HE-WON'T-BE-ANY-TROUBLE-ALL-THE-PHONE-NUMBERS-ARE-ON-THE-BULLETIN-BOARD . . .
MOM'S-IS-ON-THE-PHONE-I'LL-BE-AT-THE-MCKEEVERS'-BABY-SITTING-THE-TV'S-IN-THE-PLAYROOM-DAVID-MICHAEL-LIKES-CANDYLAND-IT'S-IN-THE-CABINET-UNDER-THE-STEREO . . .
SEE-IF-THERE-ARE-ANY-NOTES-FROM-HIS-TEACHERS-IN-HIS-LUNCH-BOX-ANY QUESTIONS?

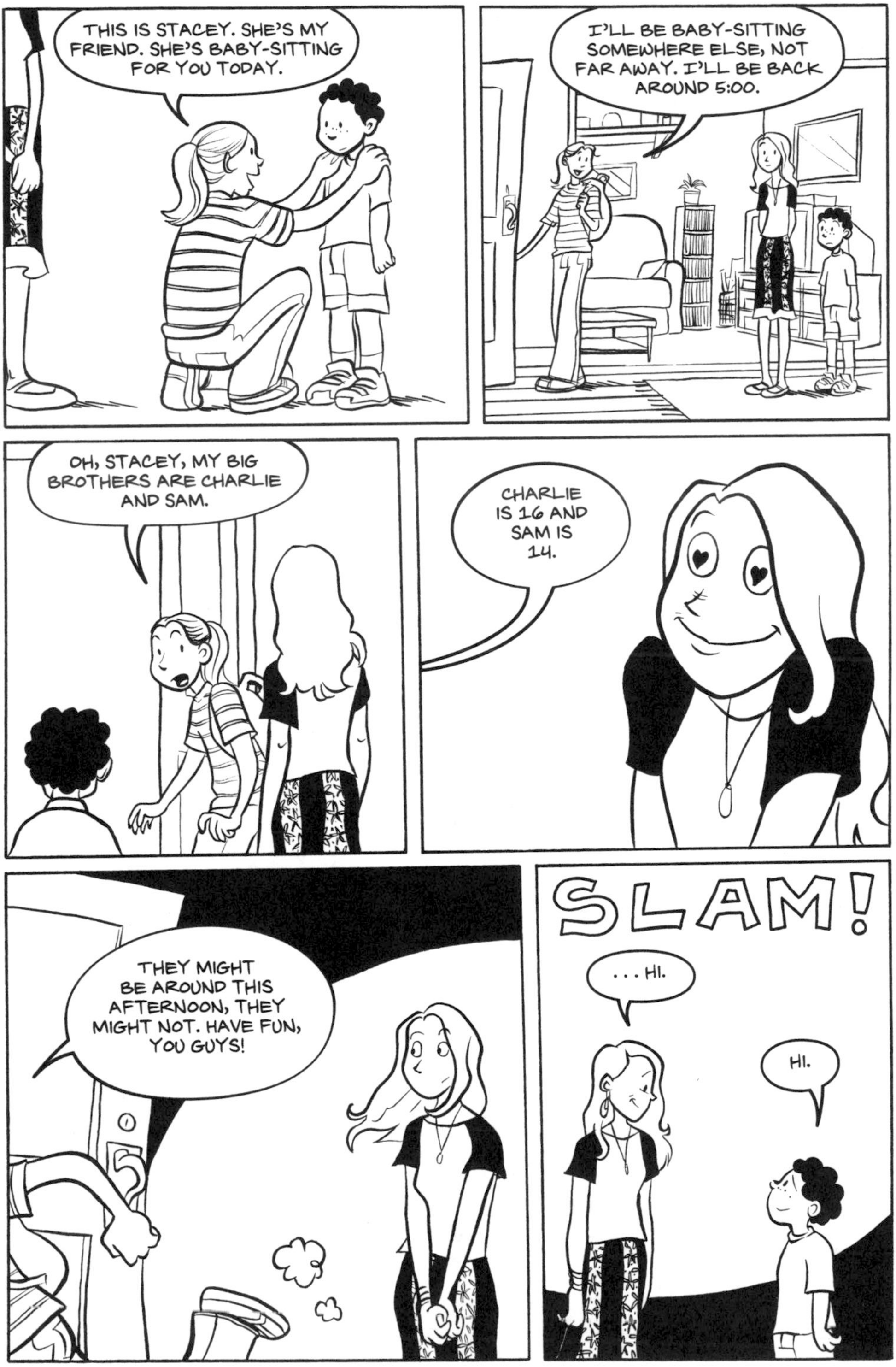
THIS IS STACEY. SHE'S MY FRIEND. SHE'S BABY-SITTING FOR YOU TODAY.
I'LL BE BABY-SITTING SOMEWHERE ELSE, NOT FAR AWAY. I'LL BE BACK AROUND 5:00.
OH, STACEY, MY BIG BROTHERS ARE CHARLIE AND SAM.
CHARLIE IS 16 AND SAM IS 14.
THEY MIGHT BE AROUND THIS AFTERNOON, THEY MIGHT NOT. HAVE FUN, YOU GUYS!
SLAM!
. . . HI.
HI.

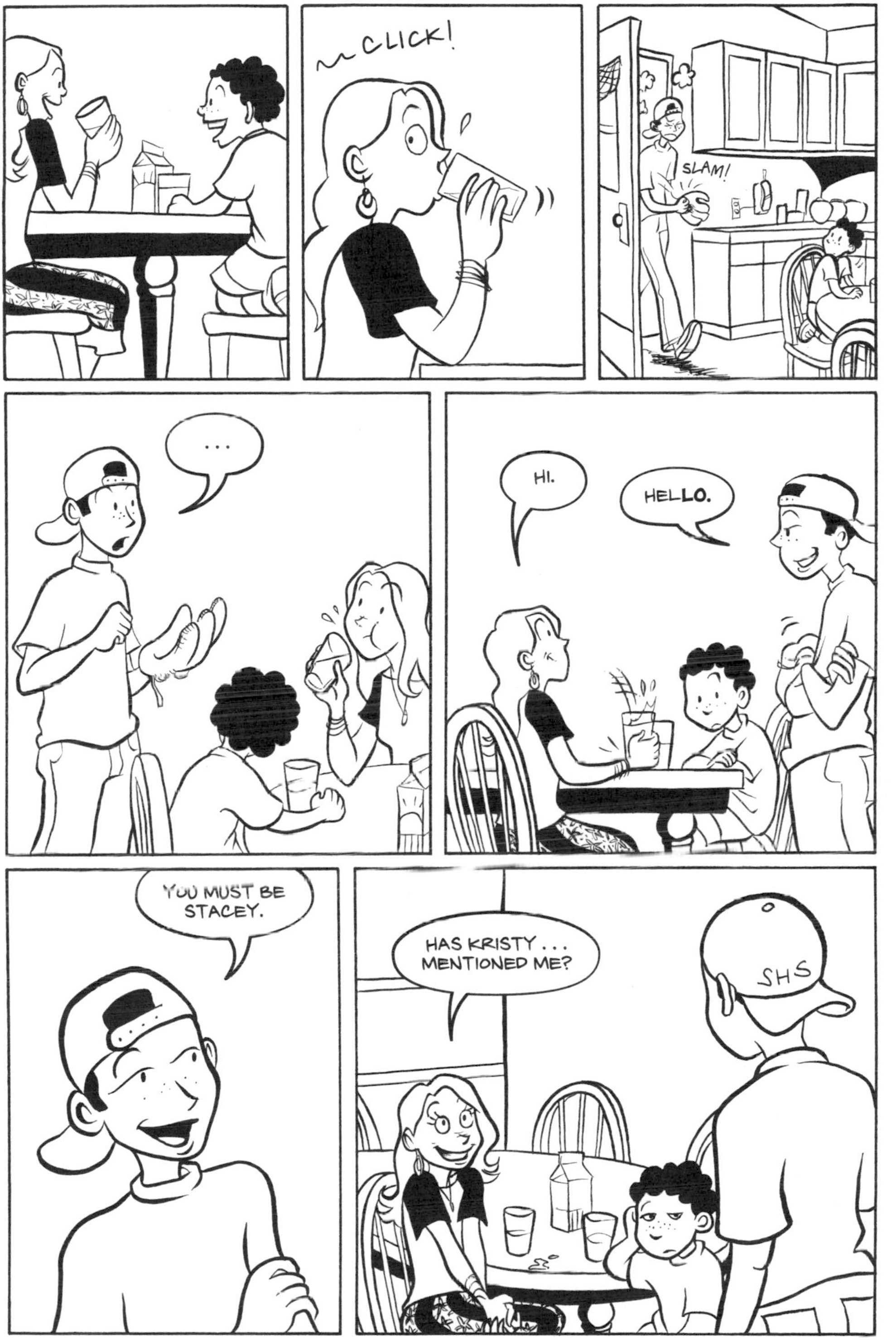
CLICK!
SLAM!
...
HI.
HELLO.
YOU MUST BE STACEY.
HAS KRISTY . . . MENTIONED ME?
SHS

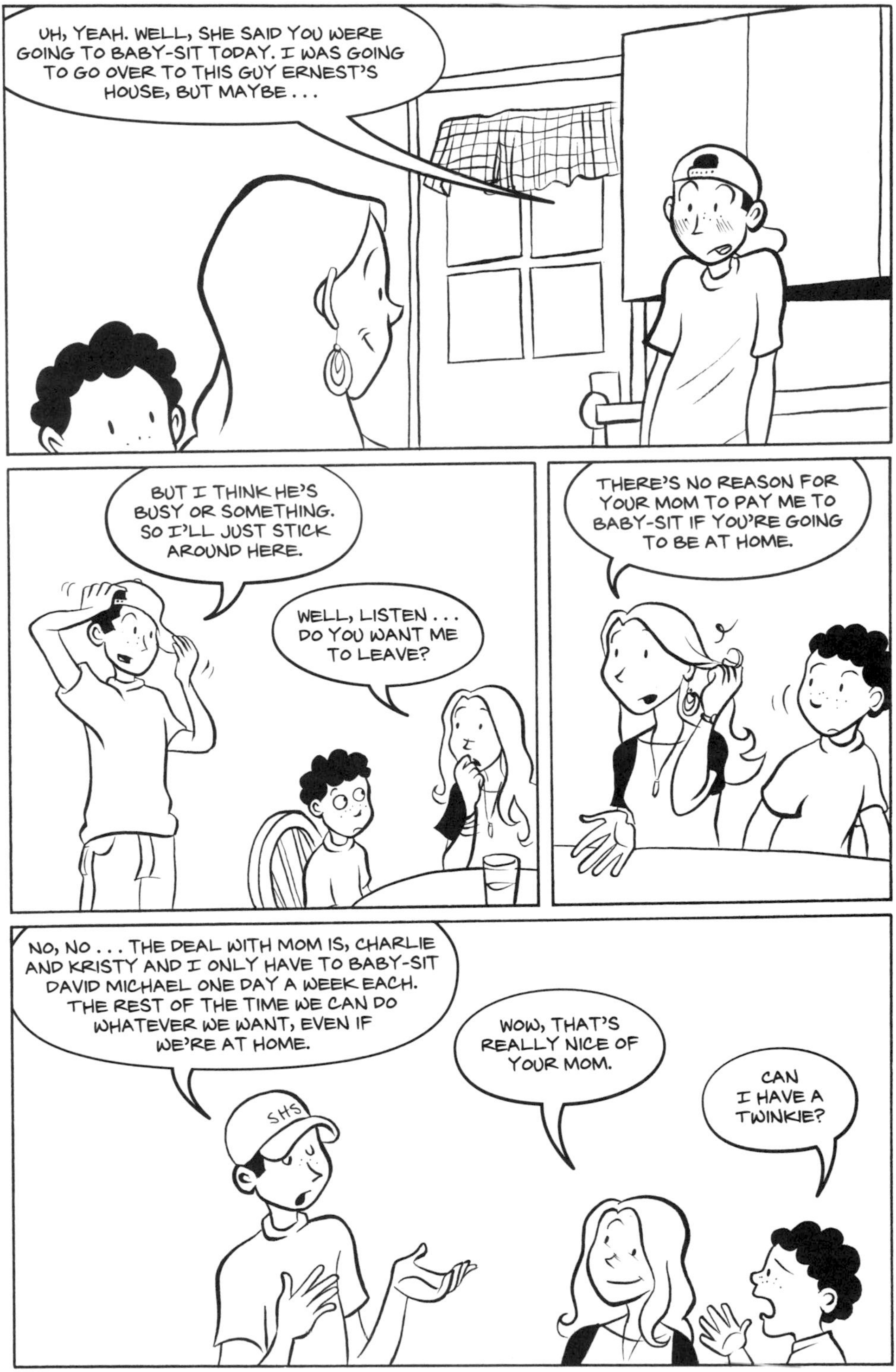
UH, YEAH. WELL, SHE SAID YOU WERE GOING TO BABY-SIT TODAY. I WAS GOING TO GO OVER TO THIS GUY ERNEST'S HOUSE, BUT MAYBE . . .
BUT I THINK HE'S BUSY OR SOMETHING. SO I'LL JUST STICK AROUND HERE.
WELL, LISTEN . . . DO YOU WANT ME TO LEAVE?
THERE'S NO REASON FOR YOUR MOM TO PAY ME TO BABY-SIT IF YOU'RE GOING TO BE AT HOME.
NO, NO . . . THE DEAL WITH MOM IS, CHARLIE AND KRISTY AND I ONLY HAVE TO BABY-SIT DAVID MICHAEL ONE DAY A WEEK EACH. THE REST OF THE TIME WE CAN DO WHATEVER WE WANT, EVEN IF WE'RE AT HOME.
SHS
WOW, THAT'S REALLY NICE OF YOUR MOM.
CAN I HAVE A TWINKIE?

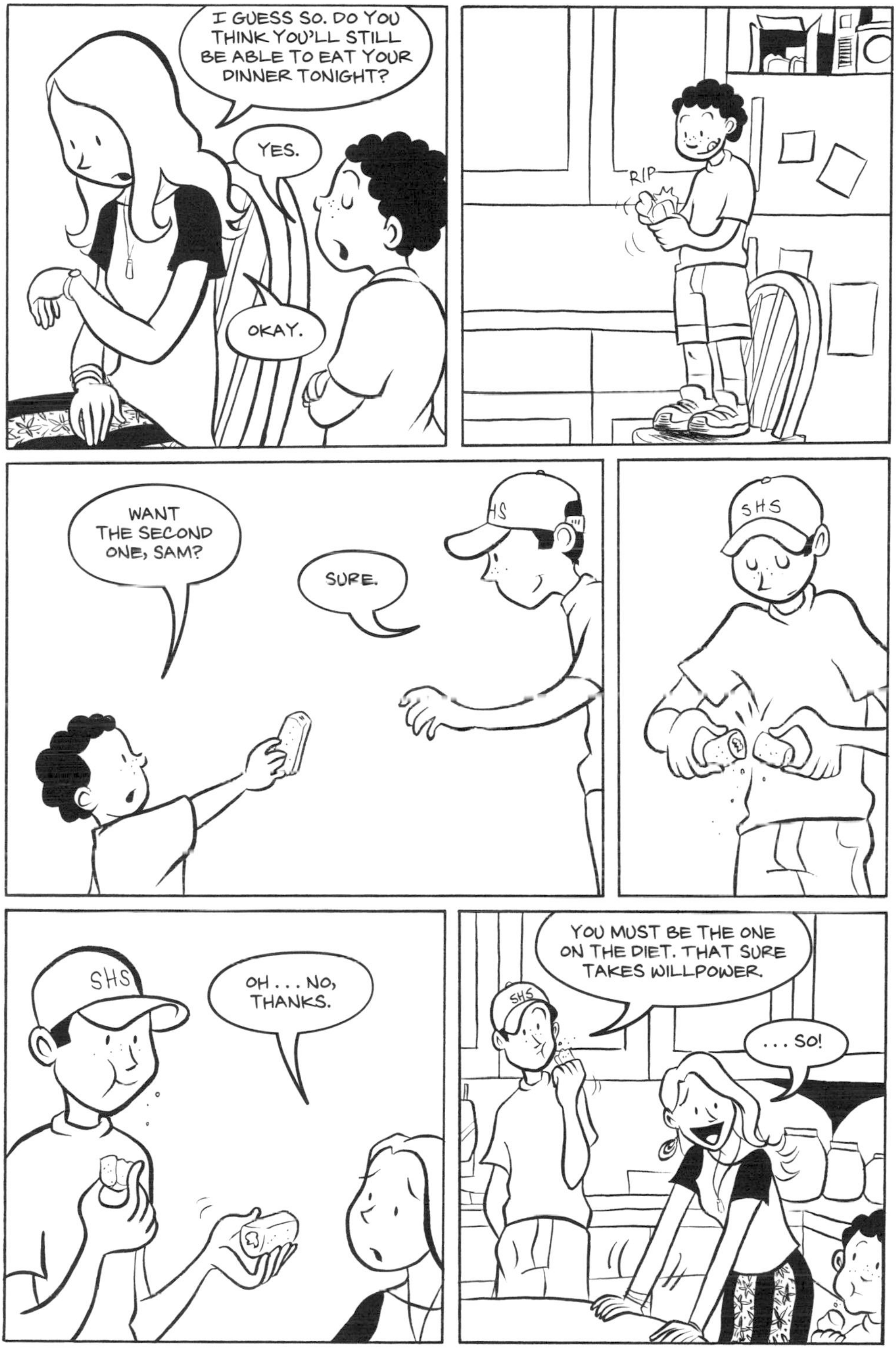
I GUESS SO. DO YOU THINK YOU'LL STILL BE ABLE TO EAT YOUR DINNER TONIGHT?
YES.
OKAY.
RIP
WANT THE SECOND ONE, SAM?
SURE.
SHS
SHS
OH . . . NO, THANKS.
YOU MUST BE THE ONE ON THE DIET. THAT SURE TAKES WILLPOWER.
SHS
. . . SO!

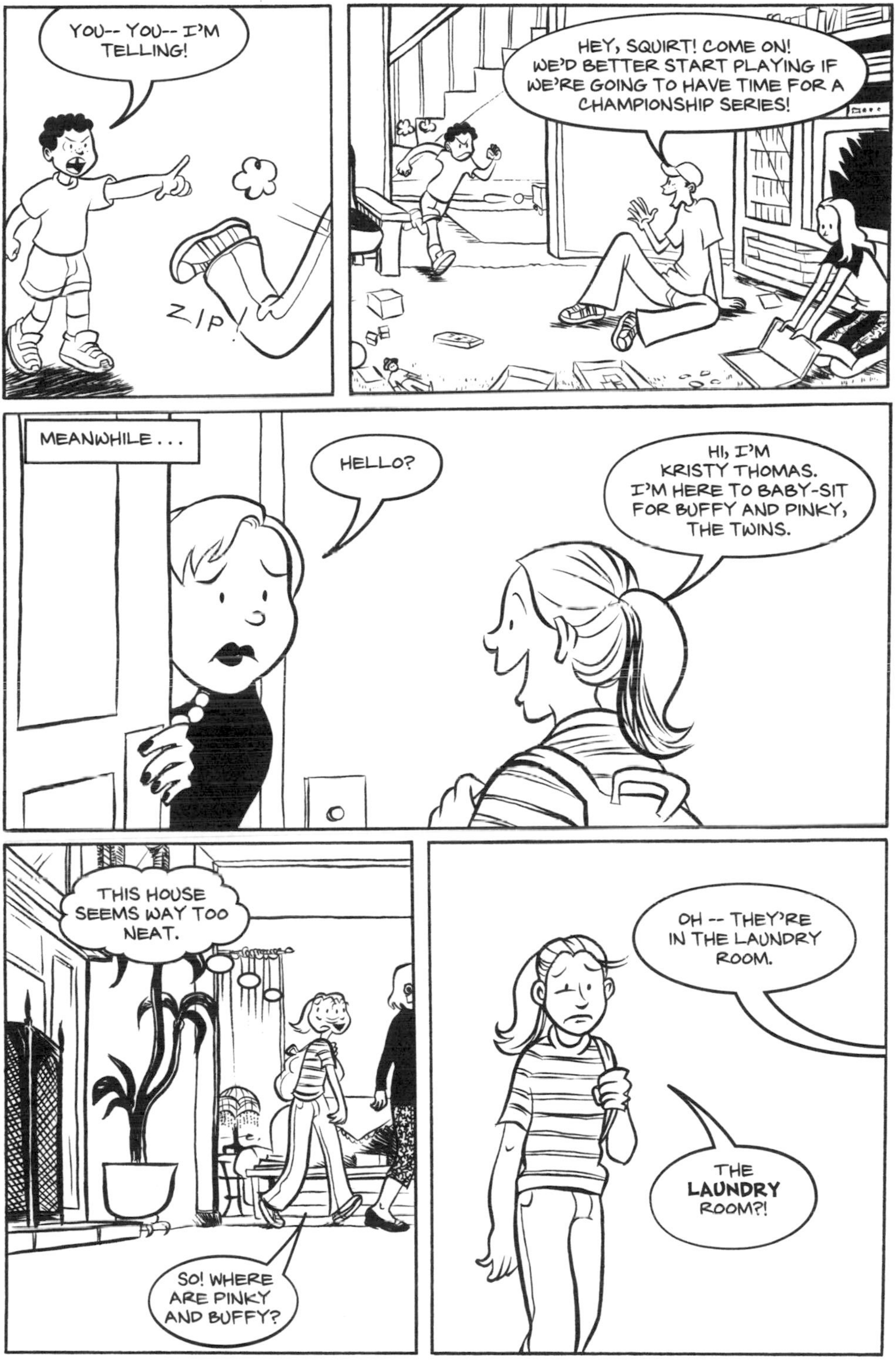
YOU-- YOU-- I'M TELLING!
ZIP!
HEY, SQUIRT! COME ON! WE'D BETTER START PLAYING IF WE'RE GOING TO HAVE TIME FOR A CHAMPIONSHIP SERIES!
MEANWHILE . . .
HELLO?
HI, I'M KRISTY THOMAS. I'M HERE TO BABY-SIT FOR BUFFY AND PINKY, THE TWINS.
THIS HOUSE SEEMS WAY TOO NEAT.
SO! WHERE ARE PINKY AND BUFFY?
OH -- THEY'RE IN THE LAUNDRY ROOM.
THE **LAUNDRY** ROOM?!

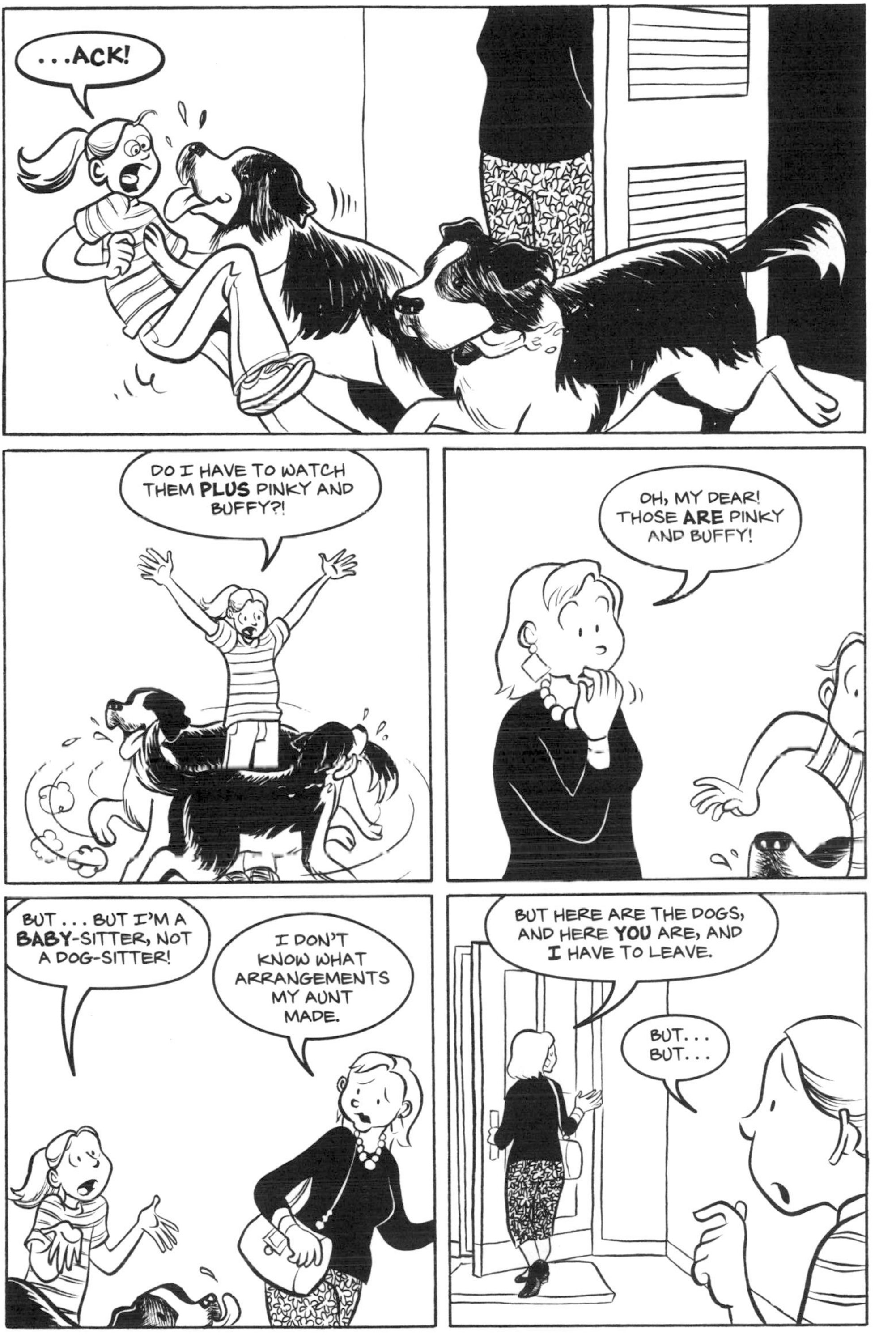

...ACK!
DO I HAVE TO WATCH THEM PLUS PINKY AND BUFFY?!
OH, MY DEAR! THOSE ARE PINKY AND BUFFY!
BUT... BUT I'M A BABY-SITTER, NOT A DOG-SITTER!
I DON'T KNOW WHAT ARRANGEMENTS MY AUNT MADE.
BUT HERE ARE THE DOGS, AND HERE YOU ARE, AND I HAVE TO LEAVE.
BUT...
BUT...

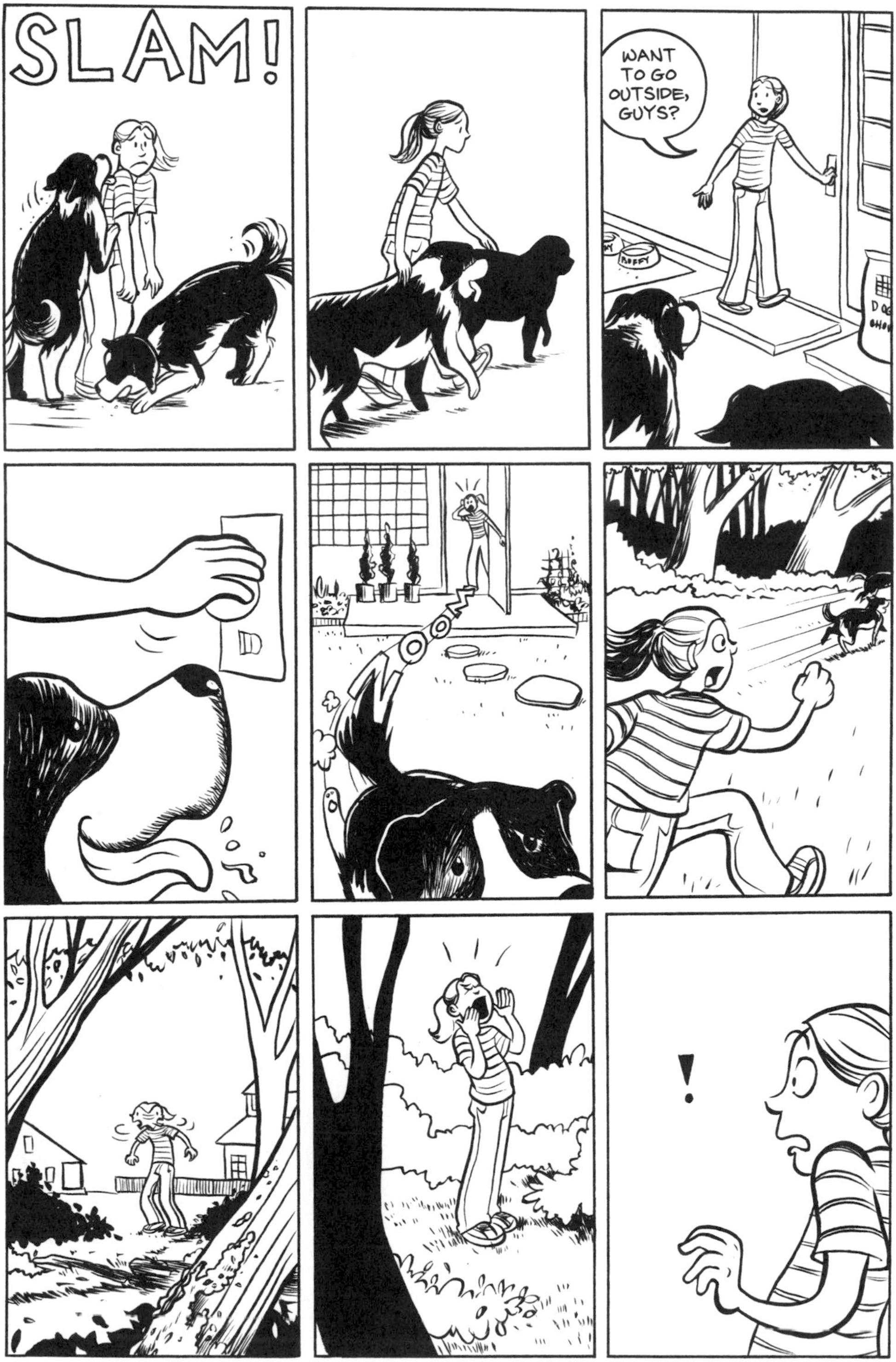
SLAM!
WANT TO GO OUTSIDE, GUYS?
BUFFY
DOG
VOOOM
!

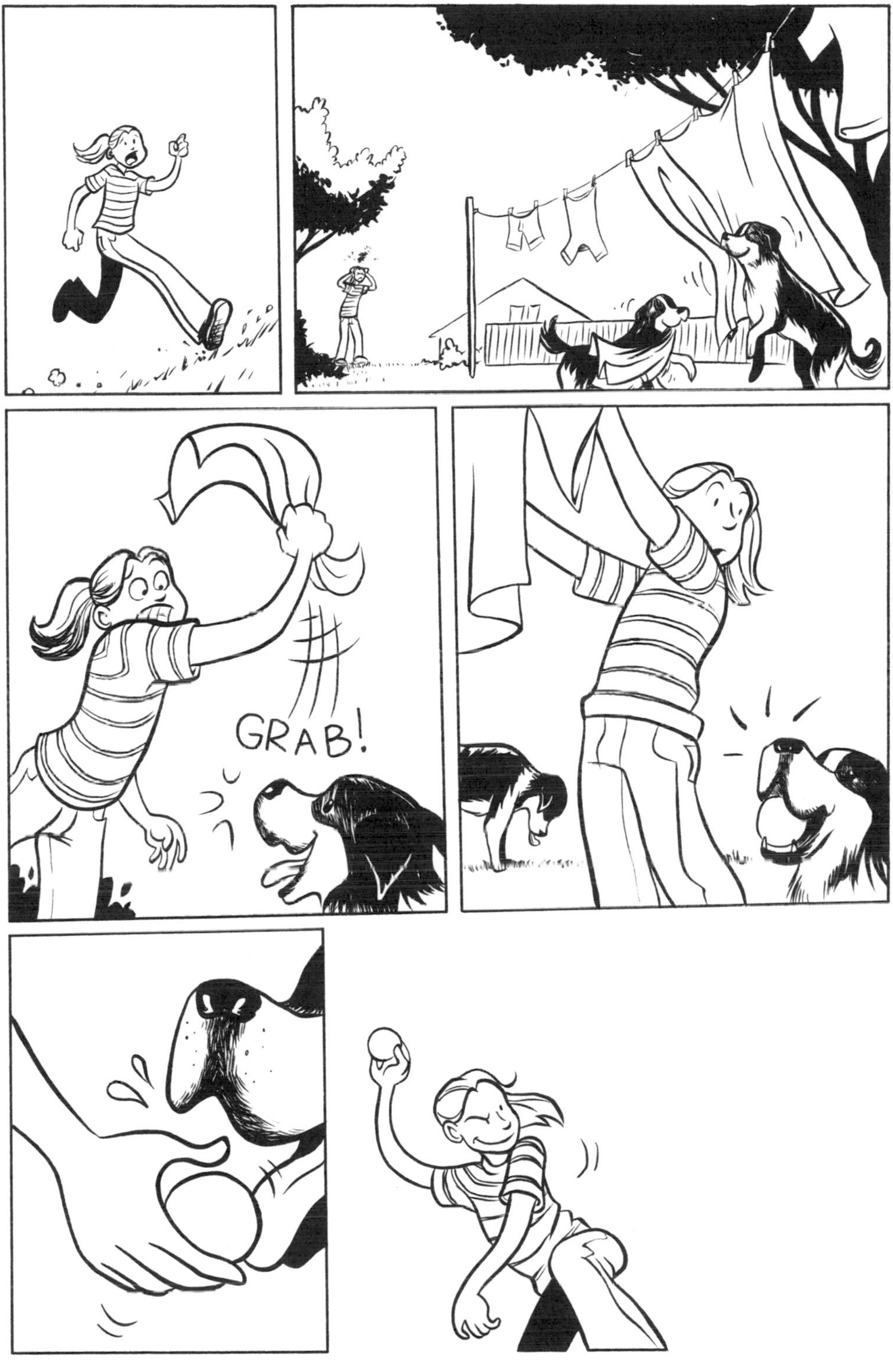
GRAB!

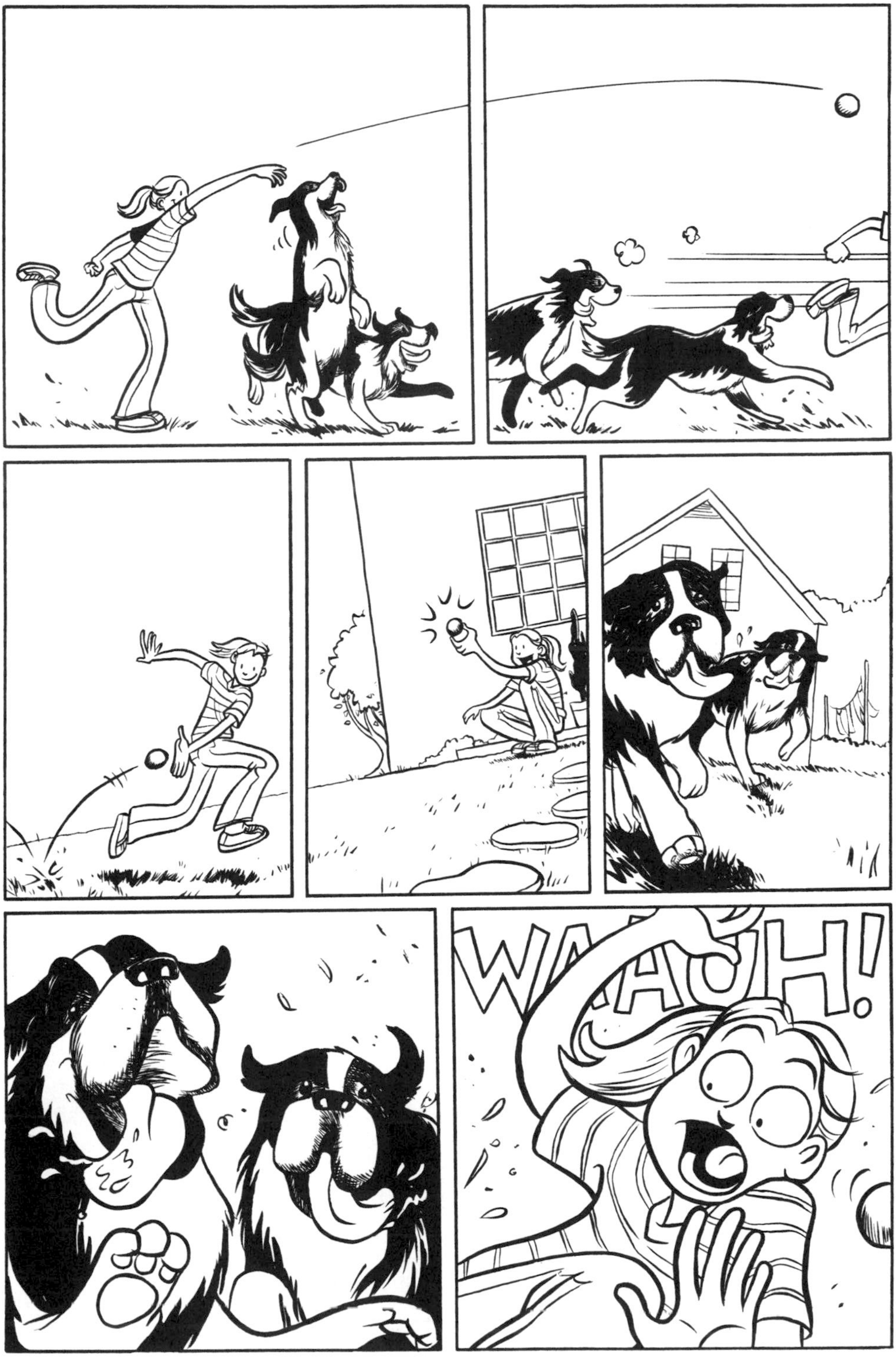
WAAUH!

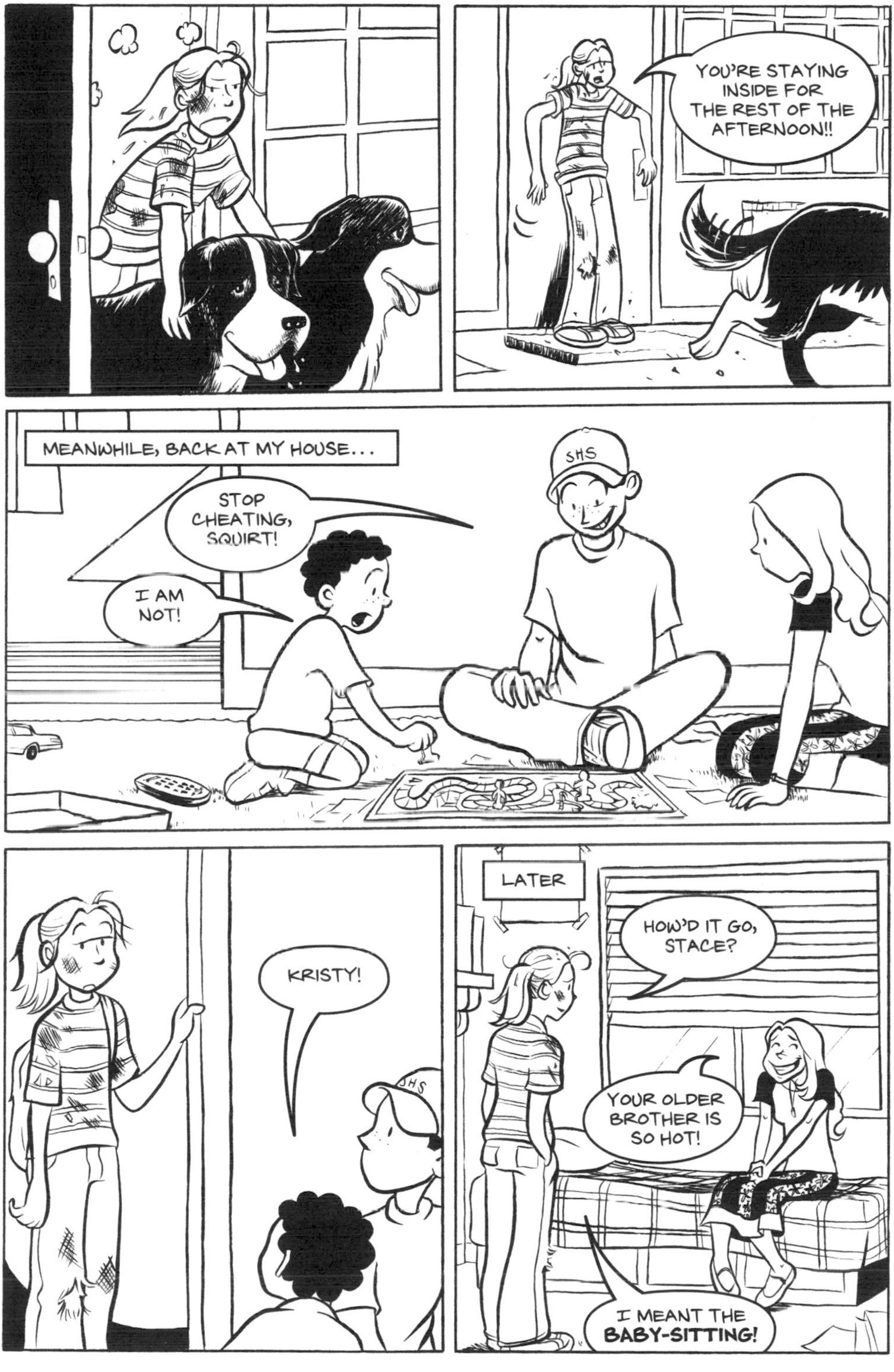
YOU'RE STAYING INSIDE FOR THE REST OF THE AFTERNOON!!
MEANWHILE, BACK AT MY HOUSE...
SHS
STOP CHEATING, SQUIRT!
I AM NOT!
KRISTY!
SHS
LATER
HOW'D IT GO, STACE?
YOUR OLDER BROTHER IS SO HOT!
I MEANT THE **BABY-SITTING!**

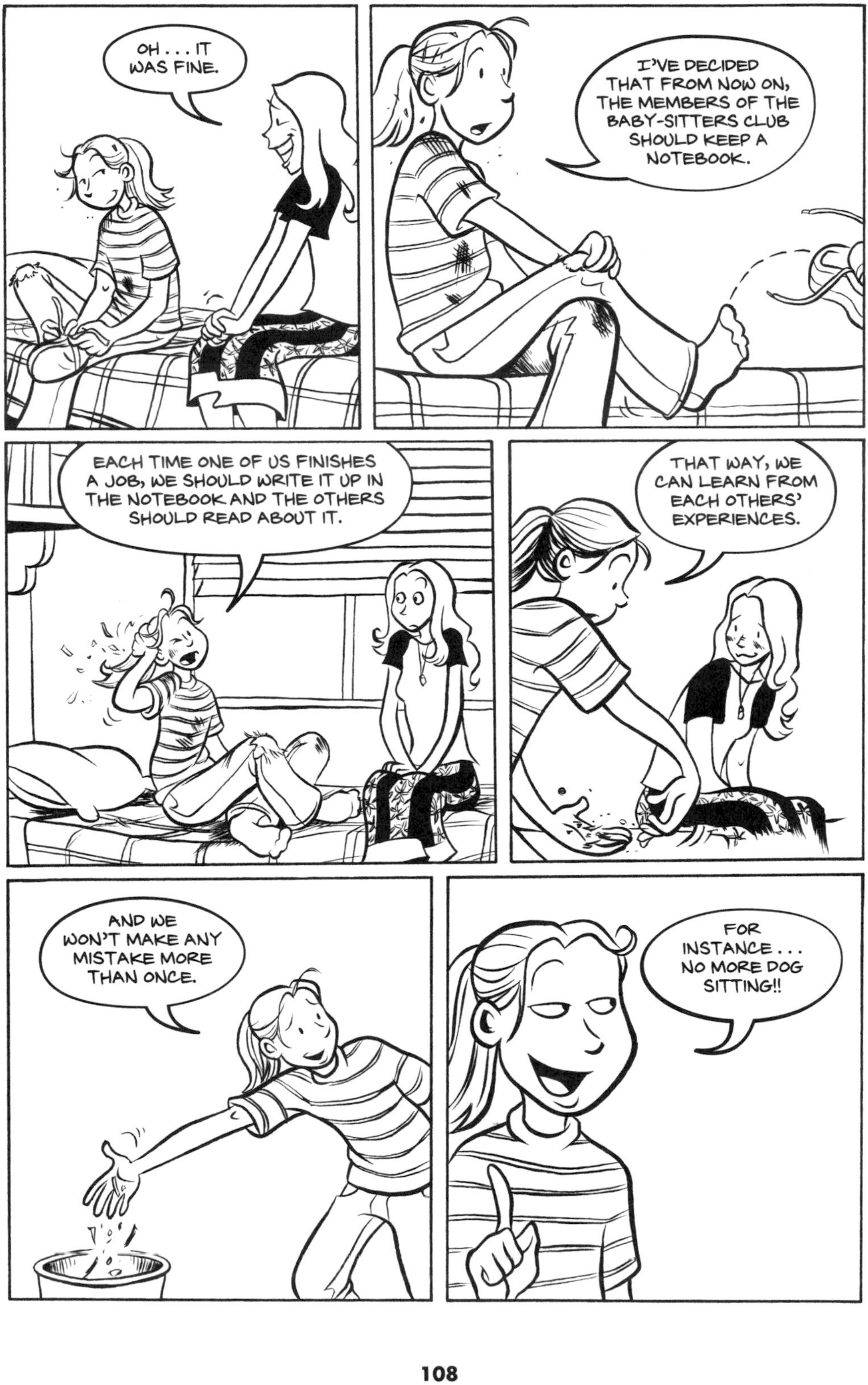
OH . . . IT WAS FINE.
I'VE DECIDED THAT FROM NOW ON, THE MEMBERS OF THE BABY-SITTERS CLUB SHOULD KEEP A NOTEBOOK.
EACH TIME ONE OF US FINISHES A JOB, WE SHOULD WRITE IT UP IN THE NOTEBOOK AND THE OTHERS SHOULD READ ABOUT IT.
THAT WAY, WE CAN LEARN FROM EACH OTHERS' EXPERIENCES.
AND WE WON'T MAKE ANY MISTAKE MORE THAN ONCE.
FOR INSTANCE . . . NO MORE DOG SITTING!!

Friday, September 26th

Kristy says we have to keep a record
of every baby-sitting job we do in this
book. My first job through the
Baby-sitters Club was yesterday. I was
sitting for Jamie Newton, only it
wasn't just for Jamie it was for
Jamie and his three cusins.
And boy were they wild!

* Claudia *

Chapter 8

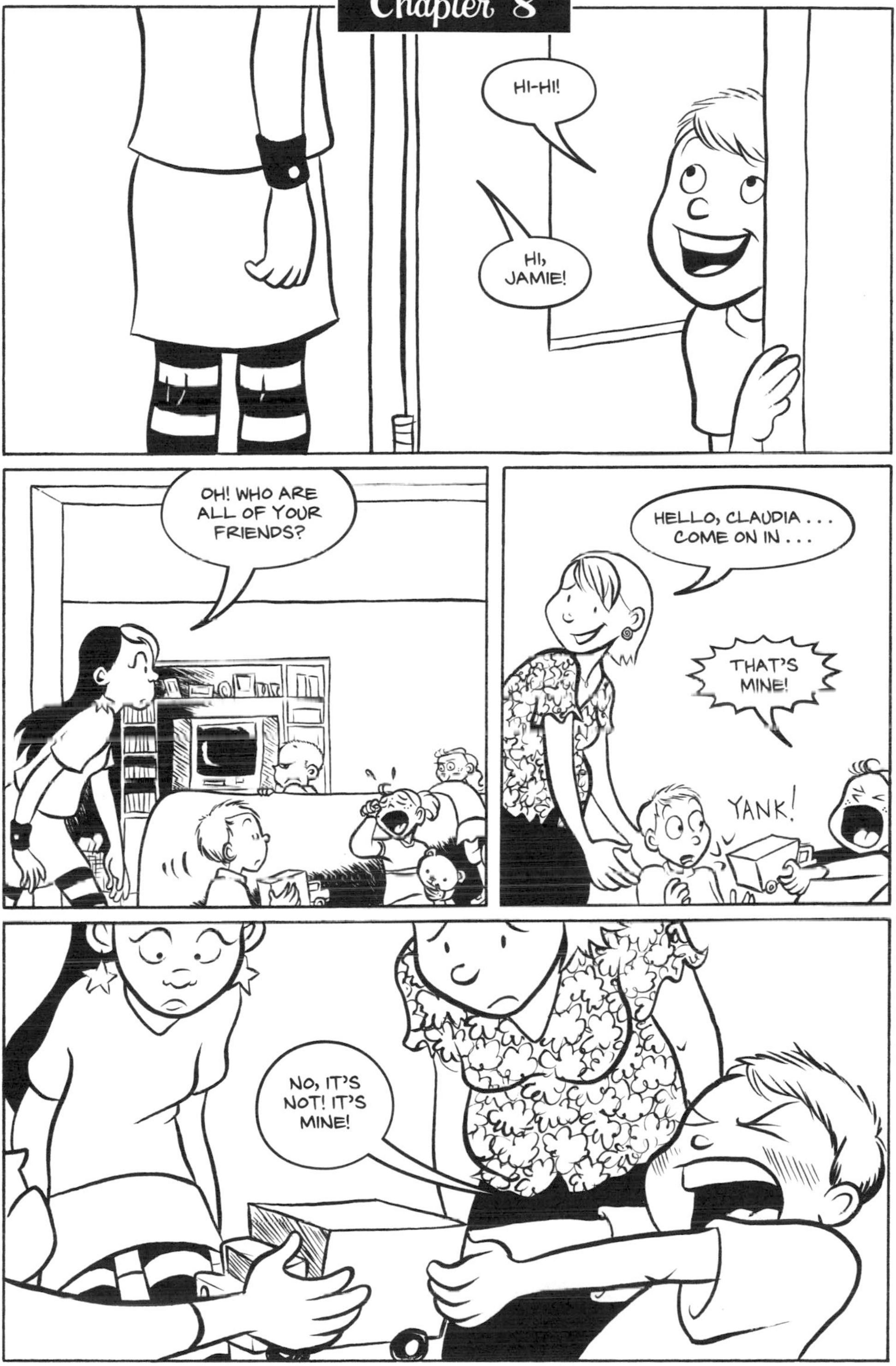
HI-HI!
HI, JAMIE!
OH! WHO ARE ALL OF YOUR FRIENDS?
HELLO, CLAUDIA . . . COME ON IN . . .
THAT'S MINE!
YANK!
NO, IT'S NOT! IT'S MINE!

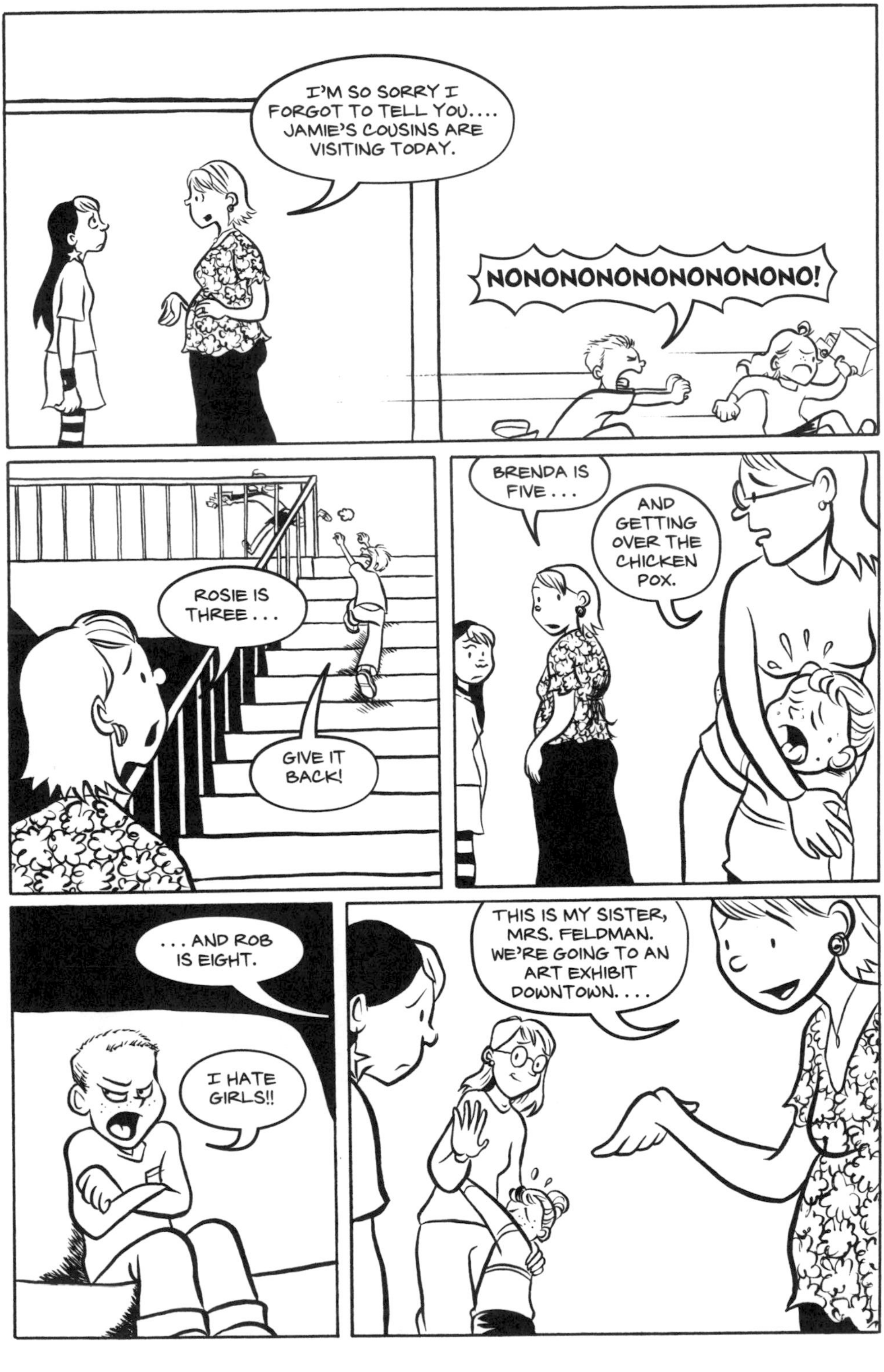
I'M SO SORRY I FORGOT TO TELL YOU.... JAMIE'S COUSINS ARE VISITING TODAY.
NONONONONONONONONO!
ROSIE IS THREE...
GIVE IT BACK!
BRENDA IS FIVE...
AND GETTING OVER THE CHICKEN POX.
...AND ROB IS EIGHT.
I HATE GIRLS!!
THIS IS MY SISTER, MRS. FELDMAN. WE'RE GOING TO AN ART EXHIBIT DOWNTOWN....

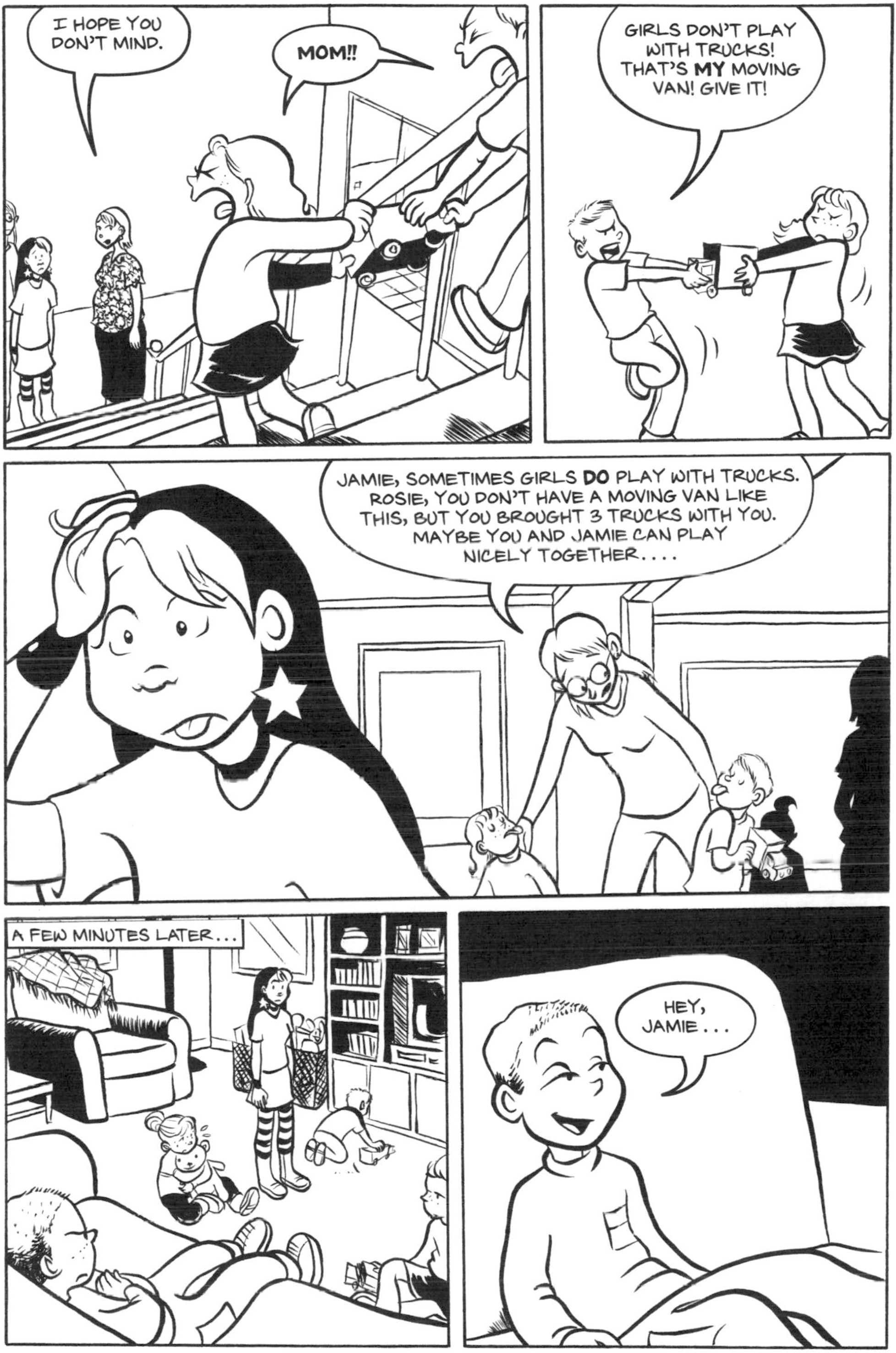
I HOPE YOU DON'T MIND.
MOM!!
GIRLS DON'T PLAY WITH TRUCKS! THAT'S **MY** MOVING VAN! GIVE IT!
JAMIE, SOMETIMES GIRLS **DO** PLAY WITH TRUCKS. ROSIE, YOU DON'T HAVE A MOVING VAN LIKE THIS, BUT YOU BROUGHT 3 TRUCKS WITH YOU. MAYBE YOU AND JAMIE CAN PLAY NICELY TOGETHER....
A FEW MINUTES LATER...
HEY, JAMIE...

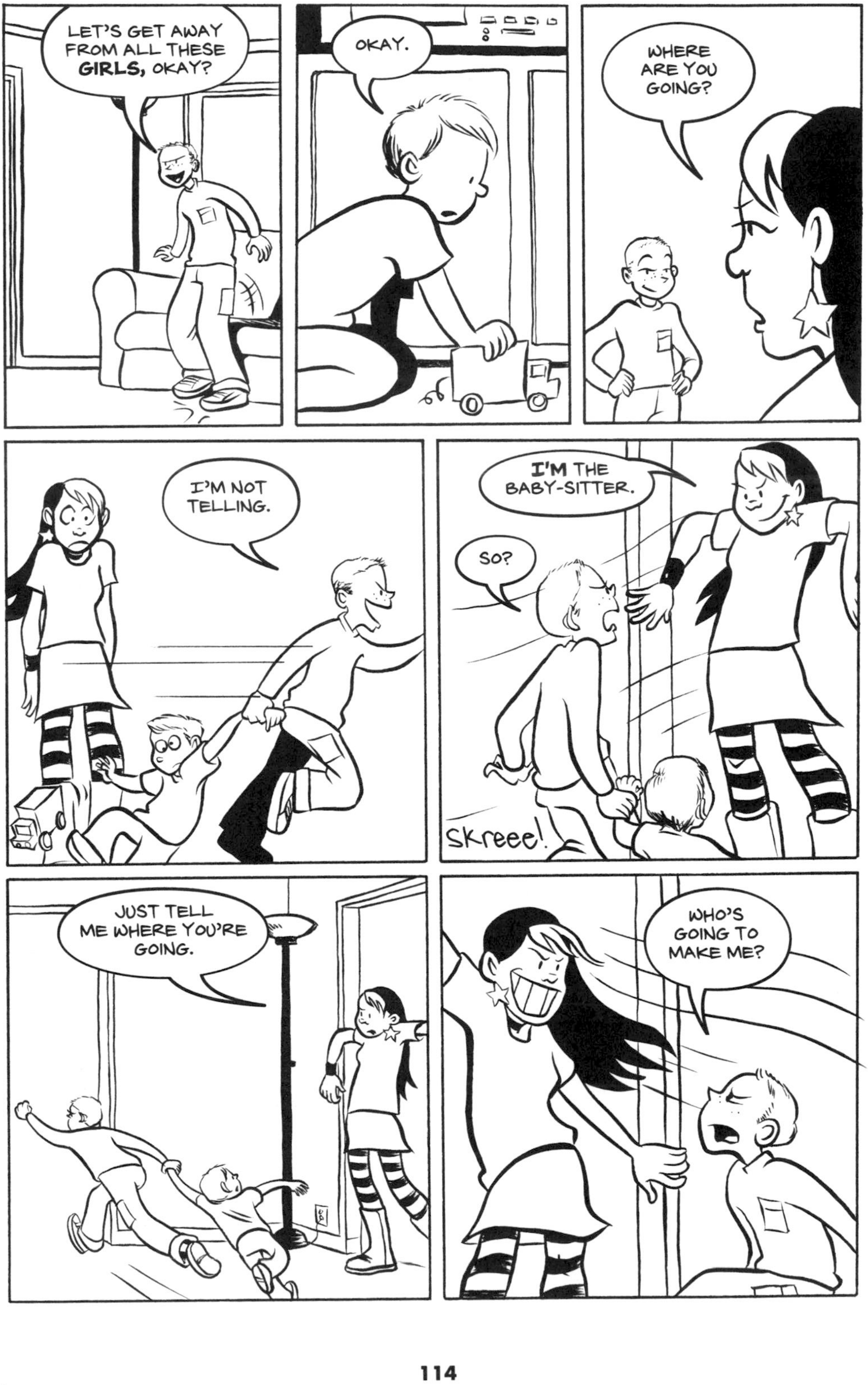
LET'S GET AWAY FROM ALL THESE **GIRLS,** OKAY?
OKAY.
WHERE ARE YOU GOING?
I'M NOT TELLING.
I'M THE BABY-SITTER.
SO?
Skreee!
JUST TELL ME WHERE YOU'RE GOING.
WHO'S GOING TO MAKE ME?

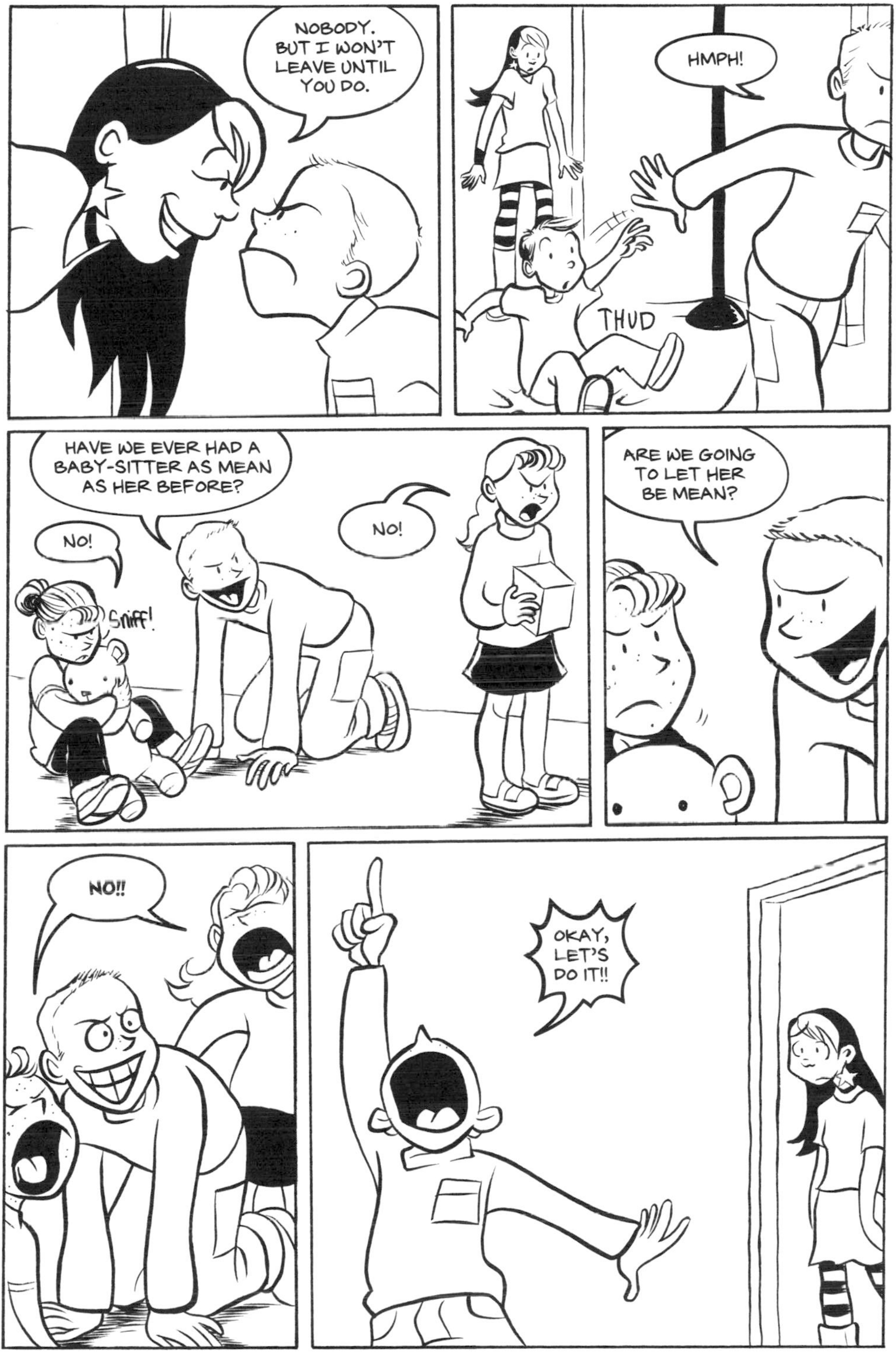
NOBODY. BUT I WON'T LEAVE UNTIL YOU DO.
HMPH!
THUD
HAVE WE EVER HAD A BABY-SITTER AS MEAN AS HER BEFORE?
NO!
NO!
Sniff!
ARE WE GOING TO LET HER BE MEAN?
NO!!
OKAY, LET'S DO IT!!

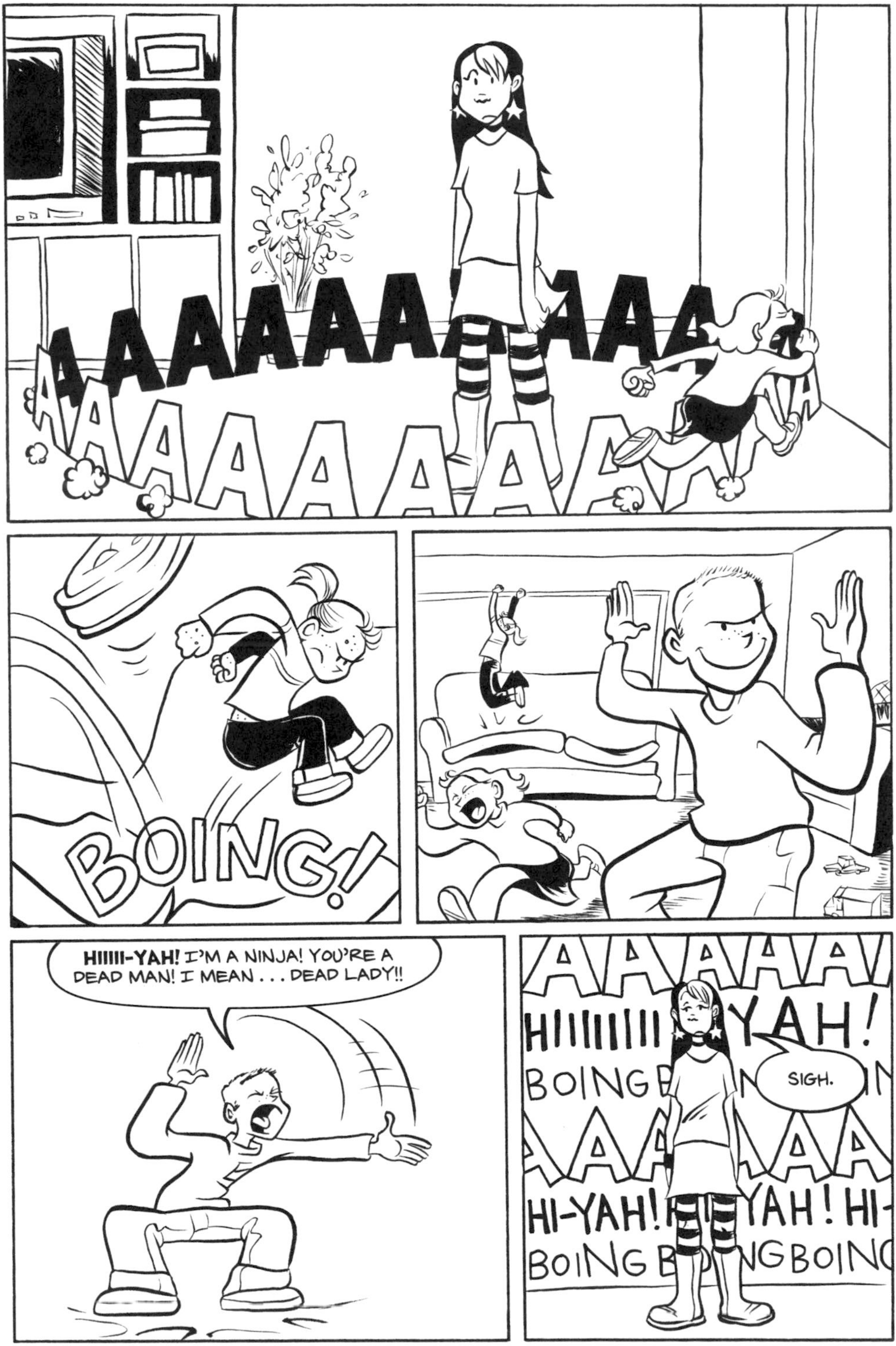
AAAAAAAAAAAAA
AAAAAAAAAAAA
BOING!
HIIIII-YAH! I'M A NINJA! YOU'RE A DEAD MAN! I MEAN . . . DEAD LADY!!
AAAAAA
HIIIIIIII YAH!
BOINGBOING
SIGH.
AAAAAA
HI-YAH! HI-YAH! HI-
BOING BOING BOING

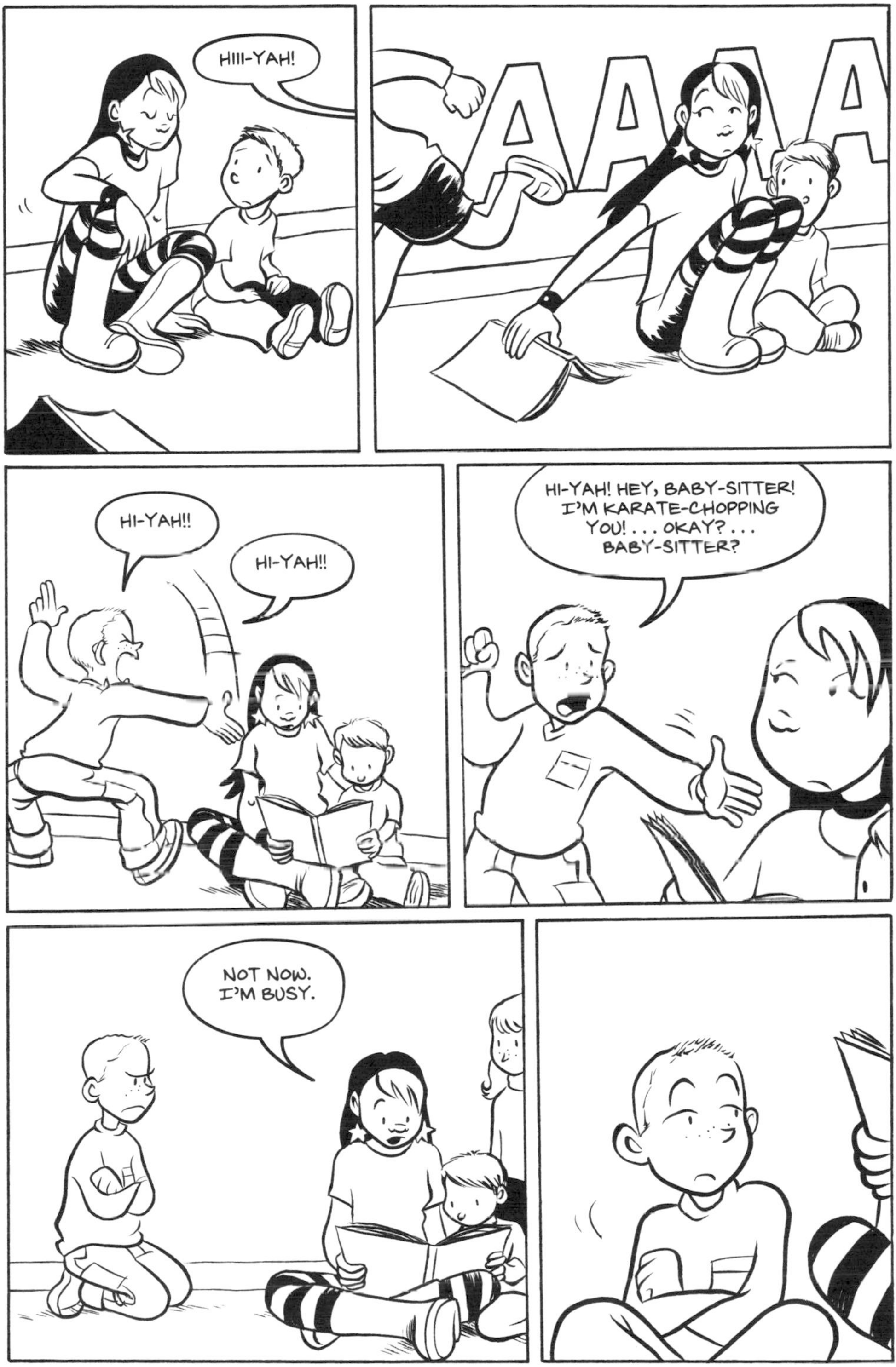
HIII-YAH!
AAAA
HI-YAH!!
HI-YAH!!
HI-YAH! HEY, BABY-SITTER! I'M KARATE-CHOPPING YOU! . . . OKAY? . . . BABY-SITTER?
NOT NOW. I'M BUSY.

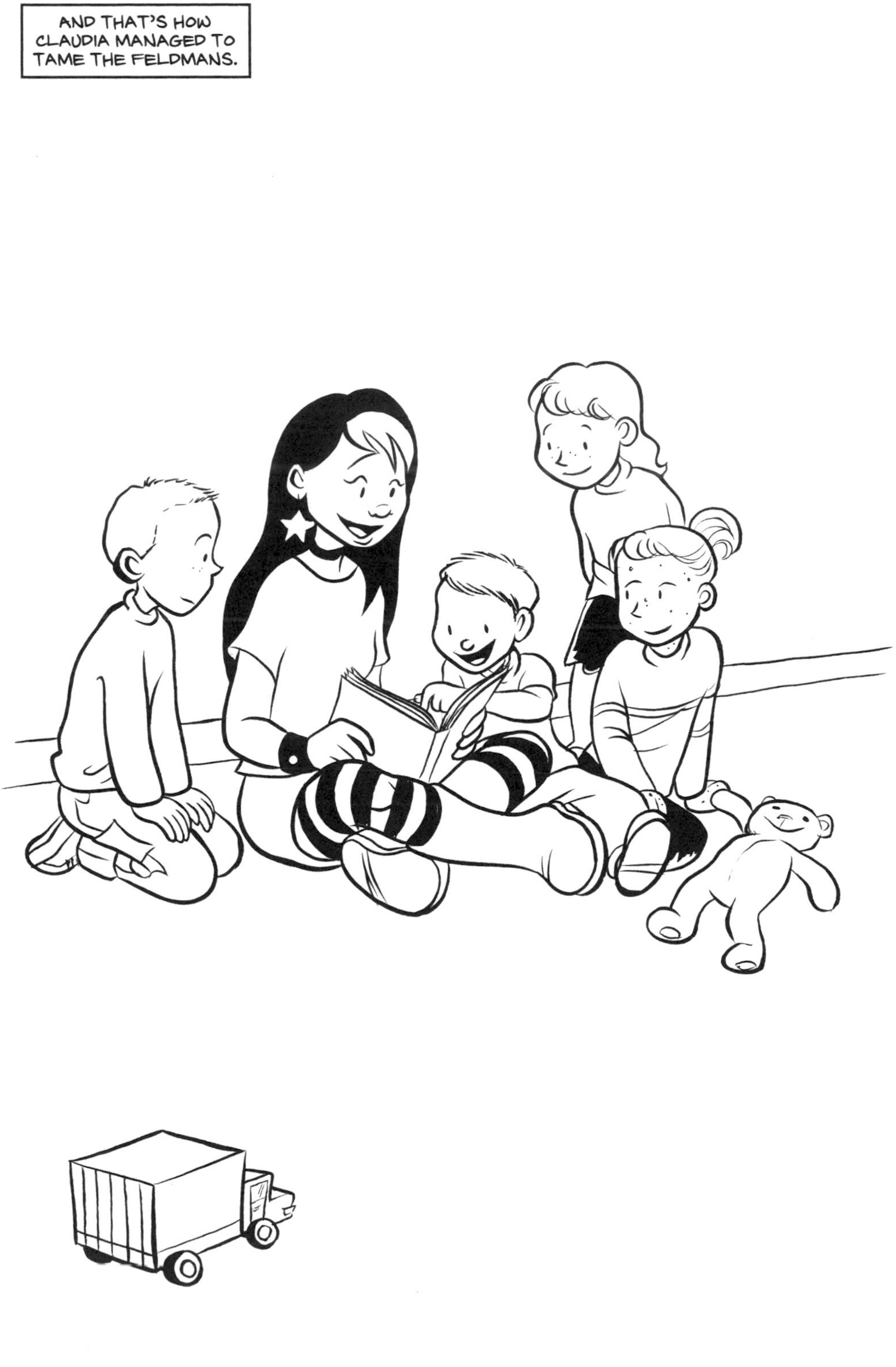
AND THAT'S HOW CLAUDIA MANAGED TO TAME THE FELDMANS.

Saturday, September 27

I don't know what Kristy always makes such a fuss about. Watson's kids are cute. I think Kristy would like them if she ever baby-sat for them. Are you reading this, Kristy? I hope so. Well, this notebook is for us to write our experiences and our problems in, especially our problems.

And there were a few problems at Watson's house...

Mary Anne

Chapter 9

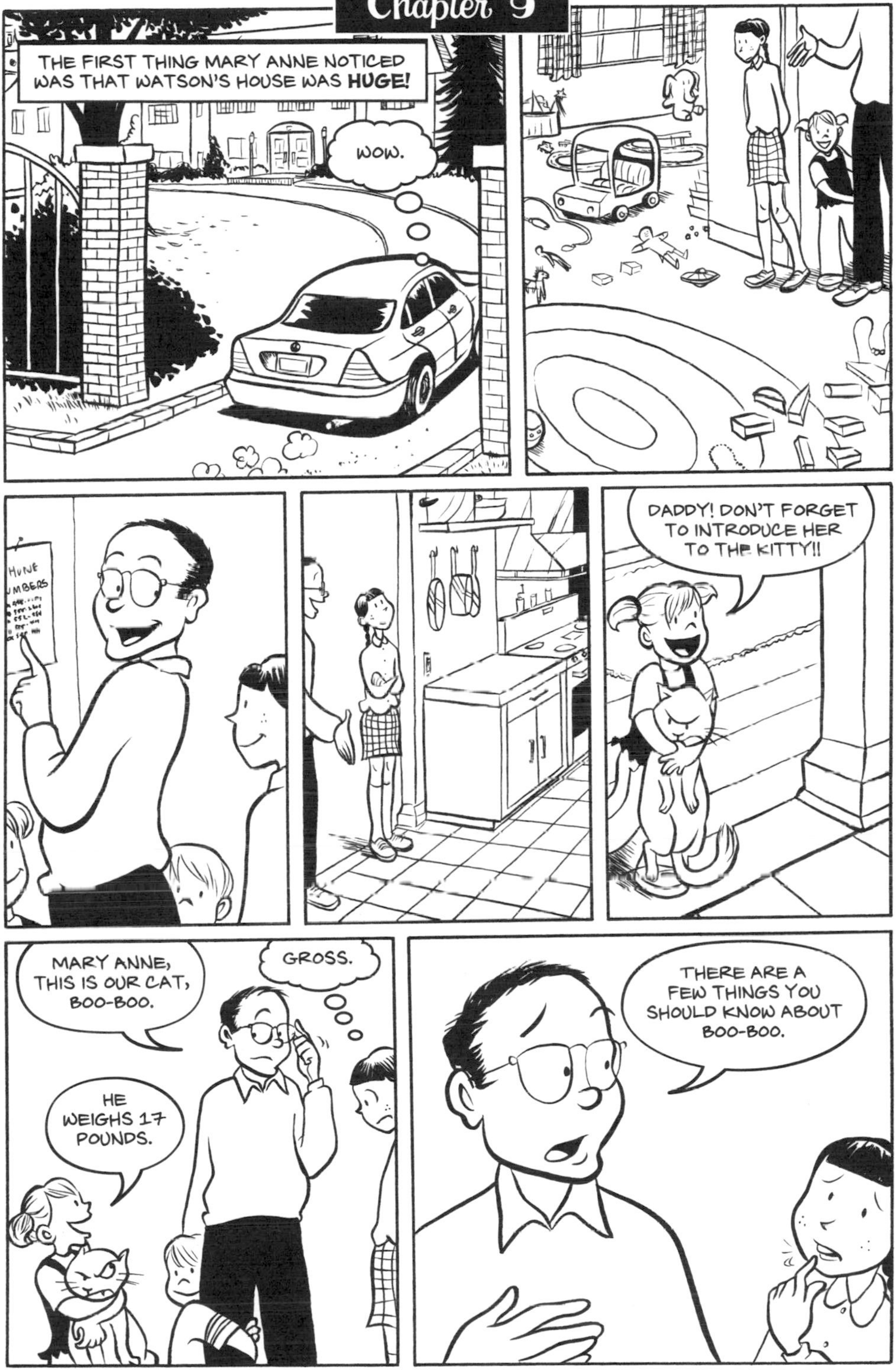
THE FIRST THING MARY ANNE NOTICED WAS THAT WATSON'S HOUSE WAS **HUGE!**
WOW.
DADDY! DON'T FORGET TO INTRODUCE HER TO THE KITTY!!
MARY ANNE, THIS IS OUR CAT, BOO-BOO.
GROSS.
HE WEIGHS 17 POUNDS.
THERE ARE A FEW THINGS YOU SHOULD KNOW ABOUT BOO-BOO.

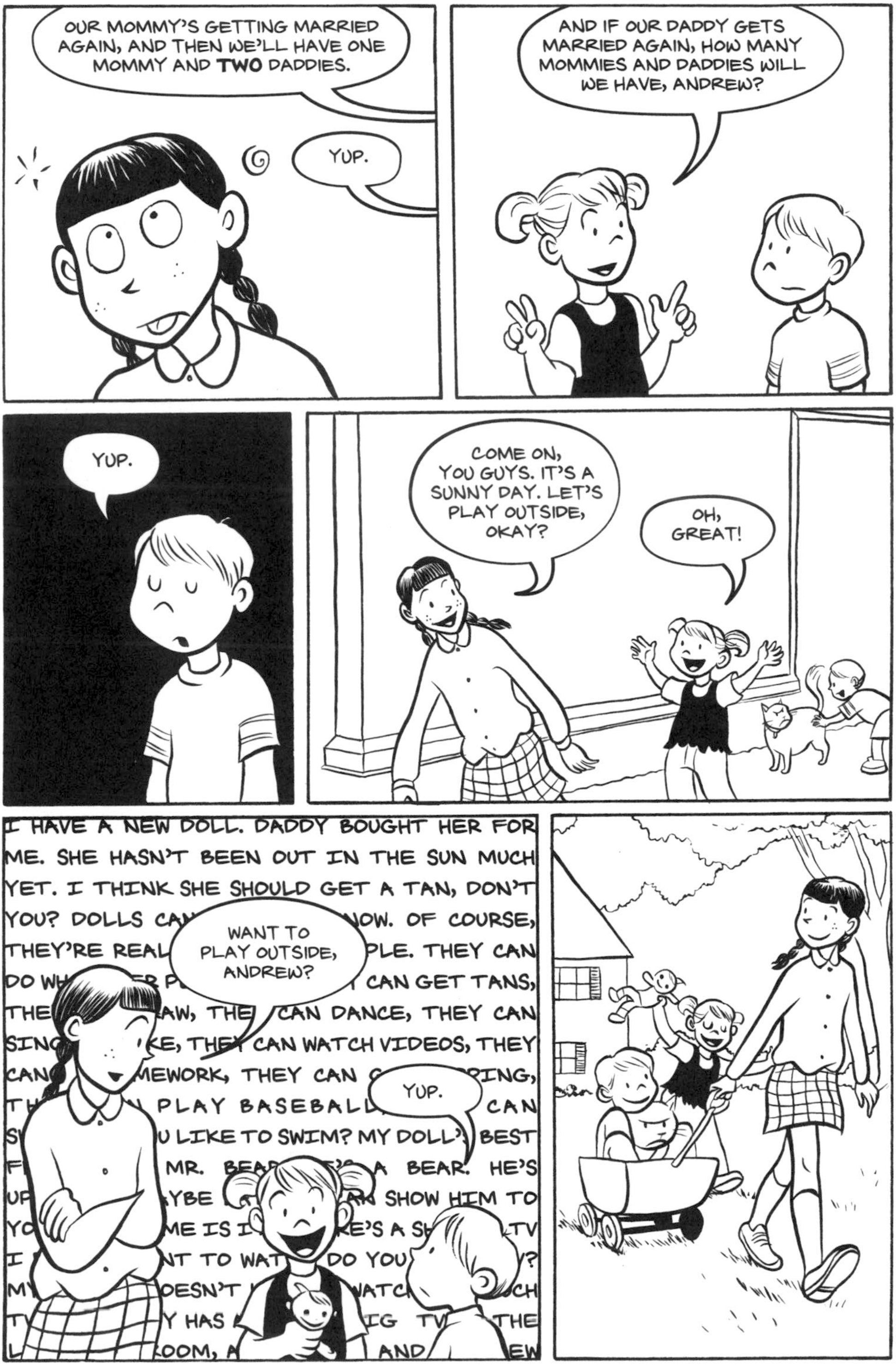
OUR MOMMY'S GETTING MARRIED AGAIN, AND THEN WE'LL HAVE ONE MOMMY AND **TWO** DADDIES.
YUP.
AND IF OUR DADDY GETS MARRIED AGAIN, HOW MANY MOMMIES AND DADDIES WILL WE HAVE, ANDREW?
YUP.
COME ON, YOU GUYS. IT'S A SUNNY DAY. LET'S PLAY OUTSIDE, OKAY?
OH, GREAT!
I HAVE A NEW DOLL. DADDY BOUGHT HER FOR
ME. SHE HASN'T BEEN OUT IN THE SUN MUCH
YET. I THINK SHE SHOULD GET A TAN, DON'T
WANT TO PLAY OUTSIDE, ANDREW?
YUP.

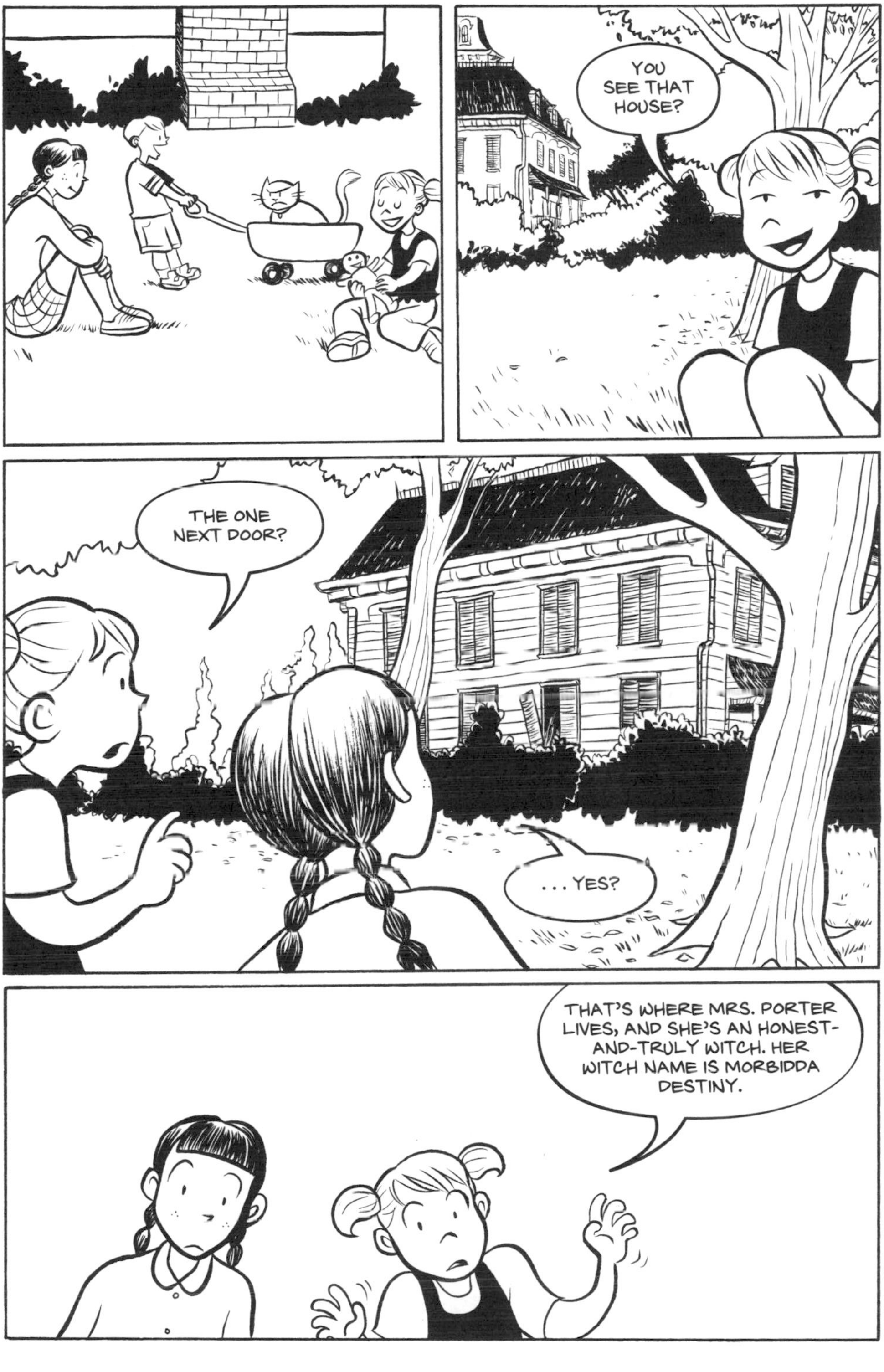
YOU SEE THAT HOUSE?
THE ONE NEXT DOOR?
. . . YES?
THAT'S WHERE MRS. PORTER LIVES, AND SHE'S AN HONEST-AND-TRULY WITCH. HER WITCH NAME IS MORBIDDA DESTINY.

126

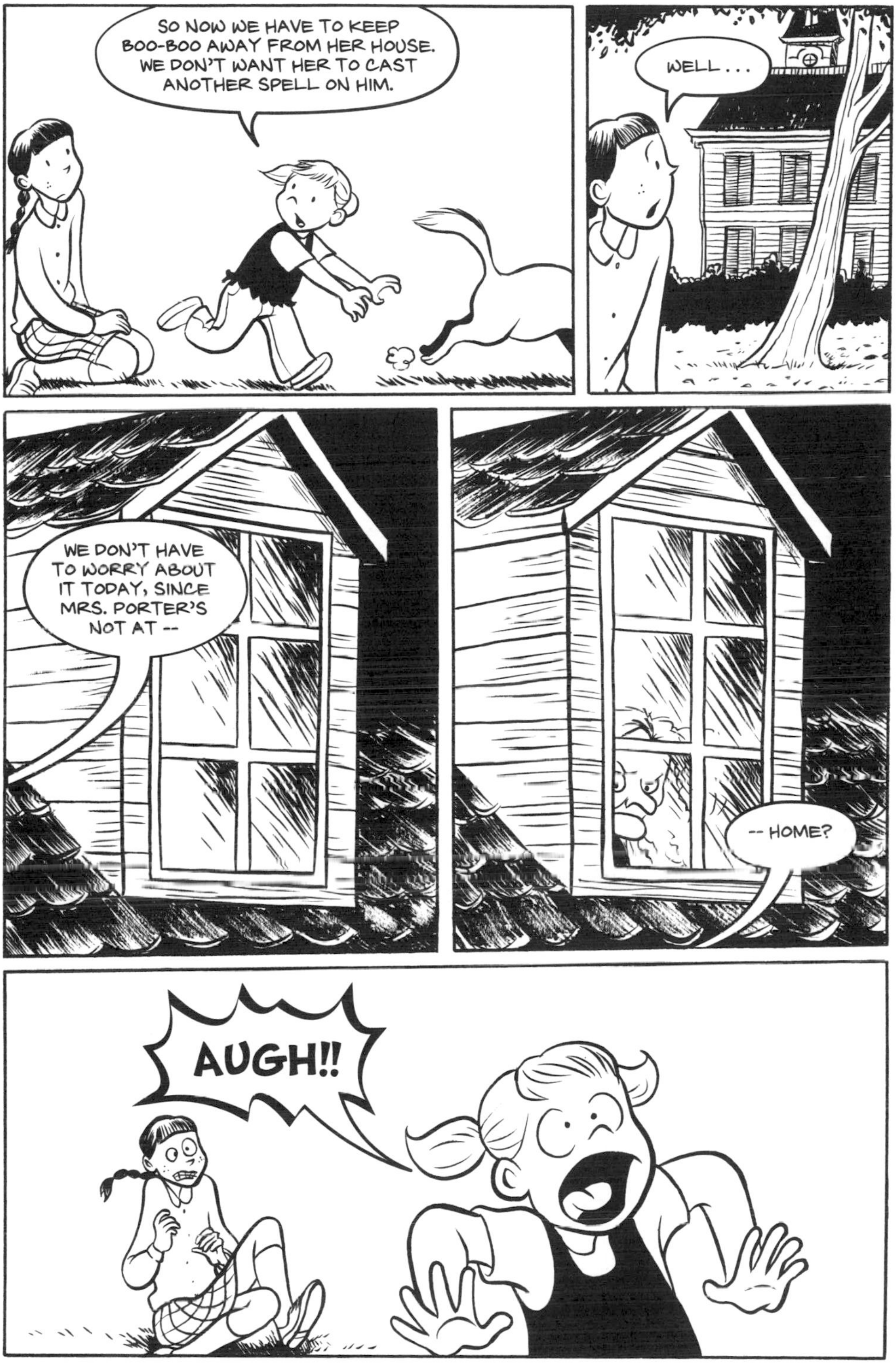
SO NOW WE HAVE TO KEEP BOO-BOO AWAY FROM HER HOUSE. WE DON'T WANT HER TO CAST ANOTHER SPELL ON HIM.
WELL . . .
WE DON'T HAVE TO WORRY ABOUT IT TODAY, SINCE MRS. PORTER'S NOT AT --
-- HOME?
AUGH!!

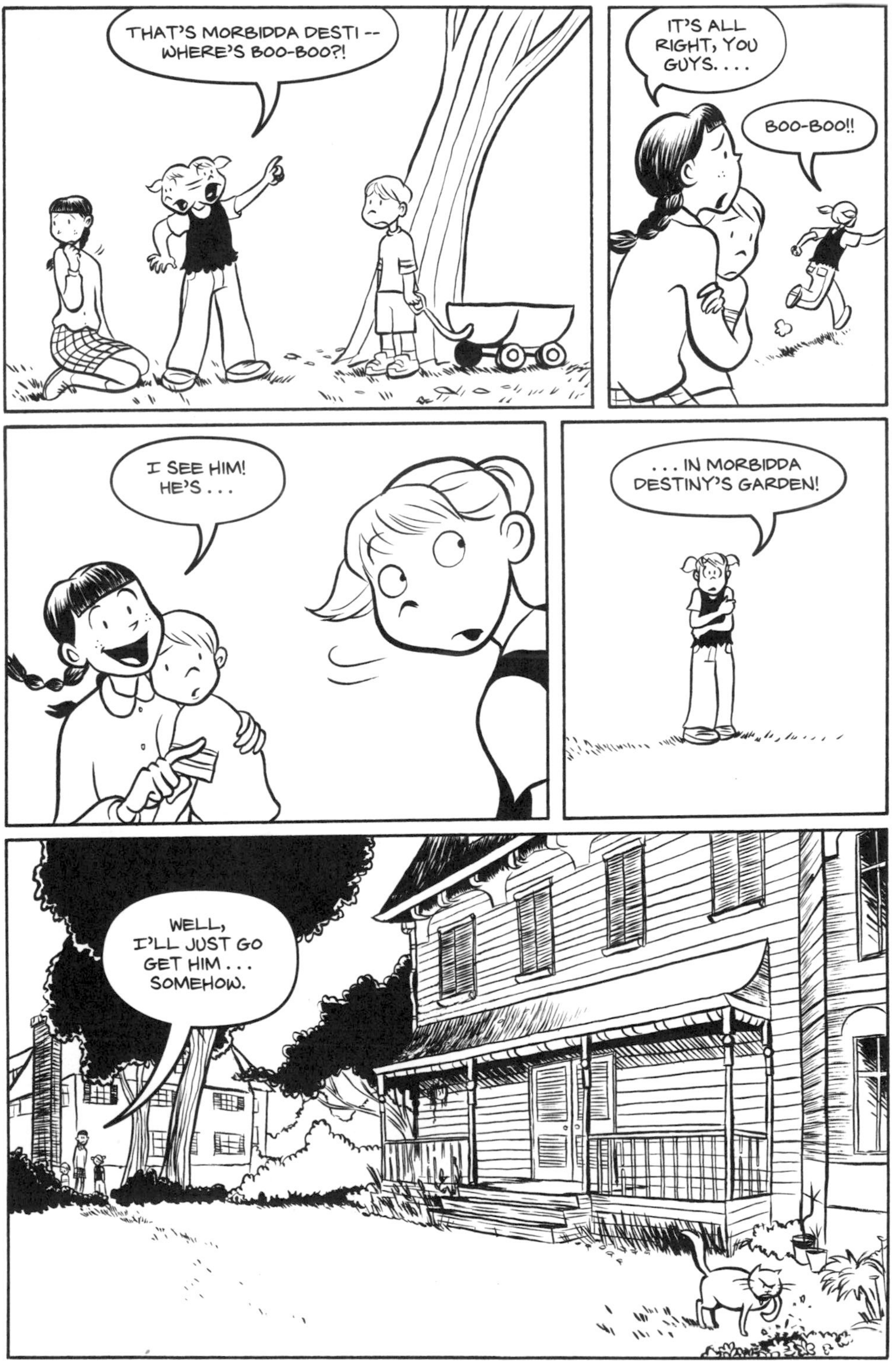
THAT'S MORBIDDA DESTI -- WHERE'S BOO-BOO?!
IT'S ALL RIGHT, YOU GUYS. . . .
BOO-BOO!!
I SEE HIM! HE'S . . .
. . . IN MORBIDDA DESTINY'S GARDEN!
WELL, I'LL JUST GO GET HIM . . . SOMEHOW.

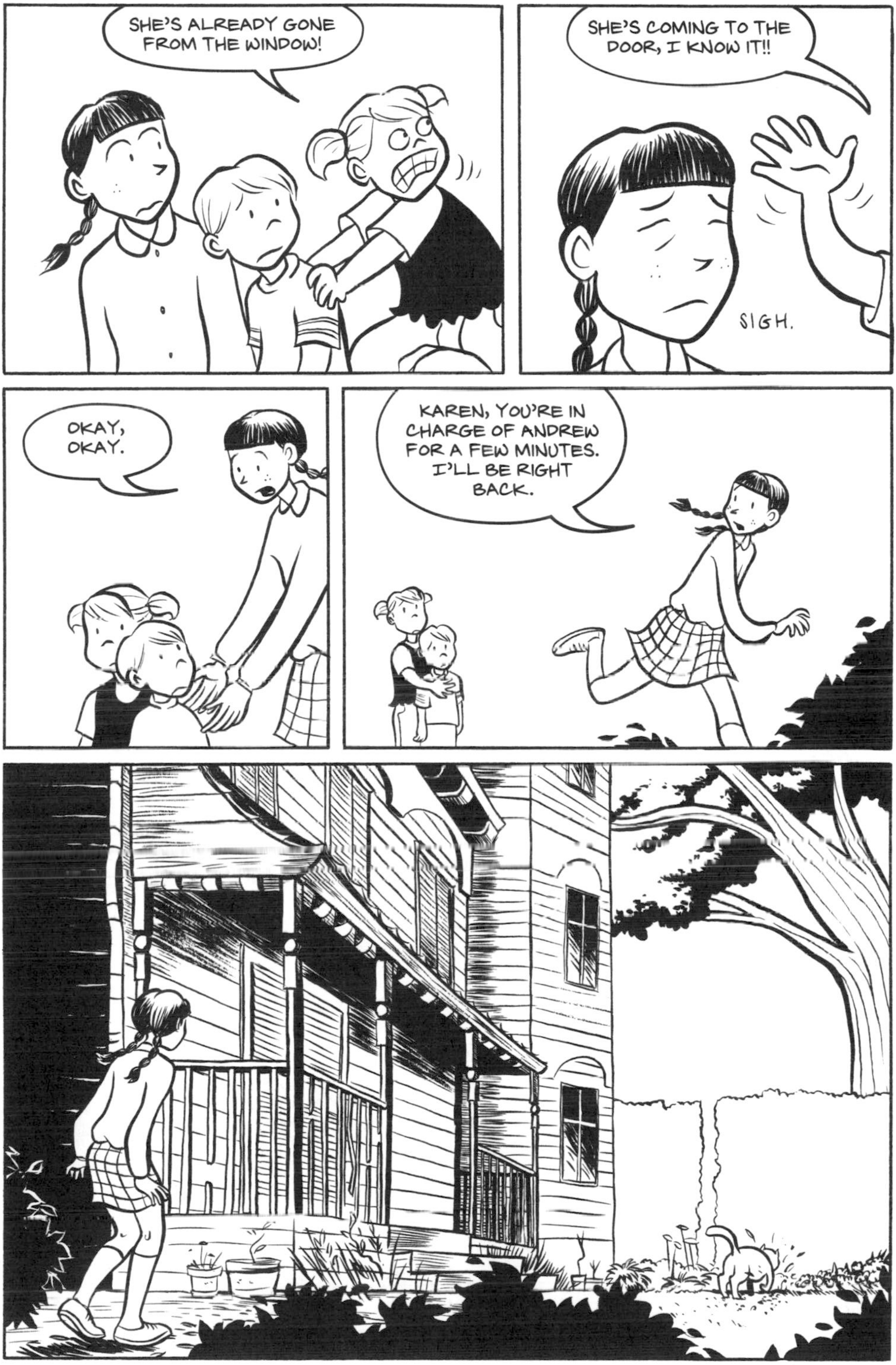
SHE'S ALREADY GONE FROM THE WINDOW!
SHE'S COMING TO THE DOOR, I KNOW IT!!
SIGH.
OKAY, OKAY.
KAREN, YOU'RE IN CHARGE OF ANDREW FOR A FEW MINUTES. I'LL BE RIGHT BACK.

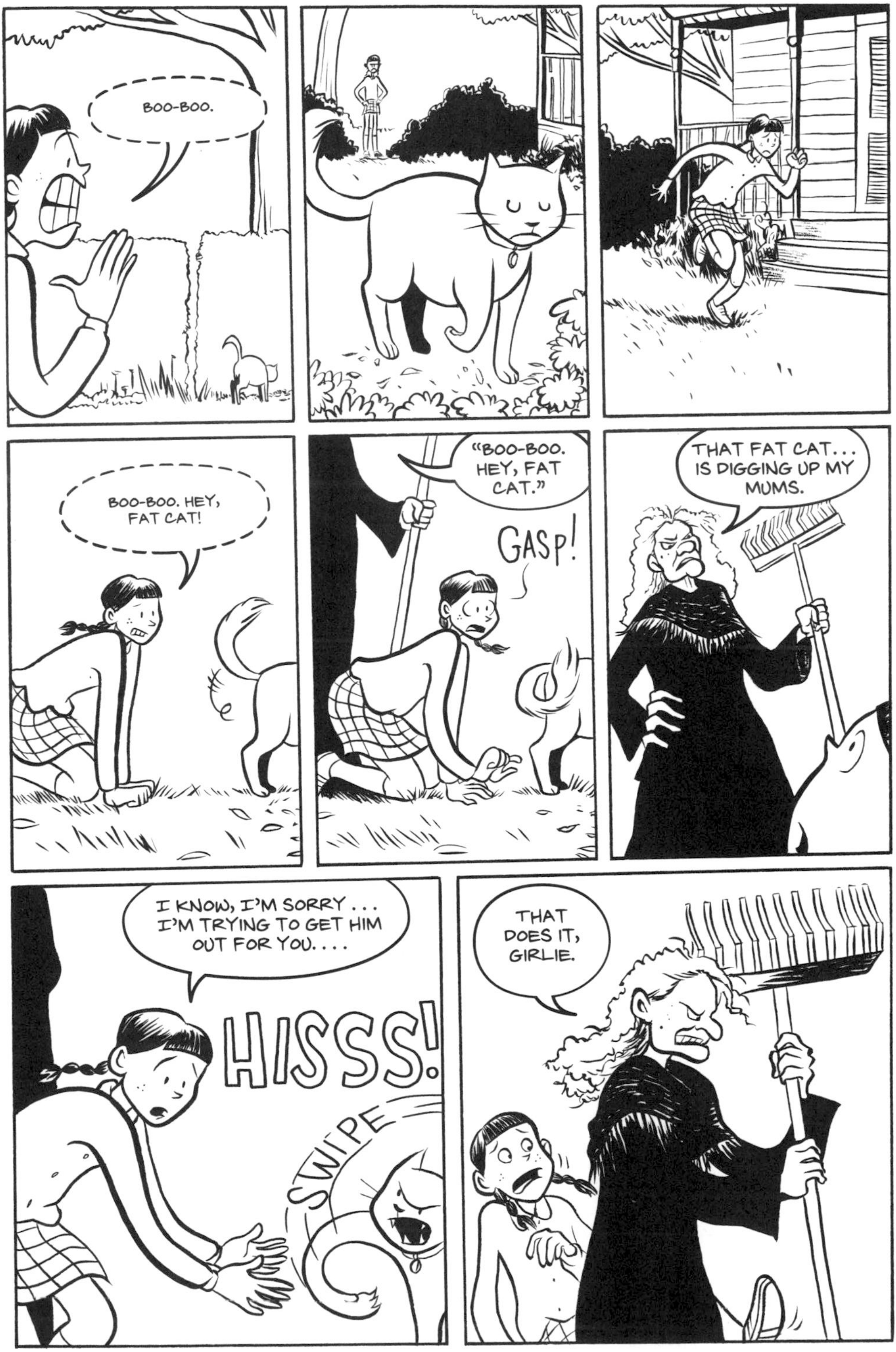
BOO-BOO.
BOO-BOO. HEY, FAT CAT!
"BOO-BOO. HEY, FAT CAT."
GASP!
THAT FAT CAT... IS DIGGING UP MY MUMS.
I KNOW, I'M SORRY... I'M TRYING TO GET HIM OUT FOR YOU....
HISSS!
SWIPE
THAT DOES IT, GIRLIE.

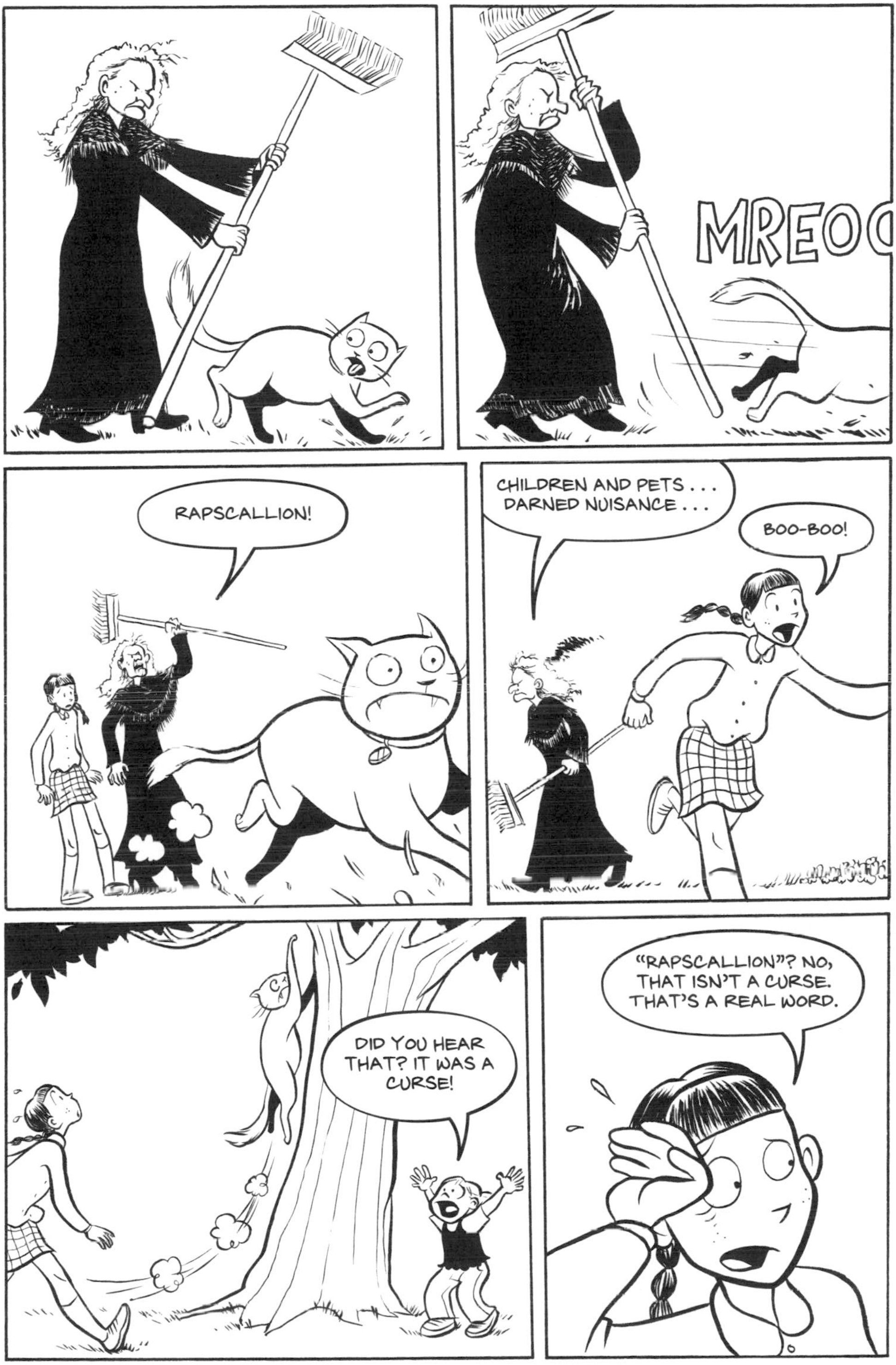
MREOO
RAPSCALLION!
CHILDREN AND PETS . . .
DARNED NUISANCE . . .
BOO-BOO!
DID YOU HEAR THAT? IT WAS A CURSE!
"RAPSCALLION"? NO, THAT ISN'T A CURSE. THAT'S A REAL WORD.

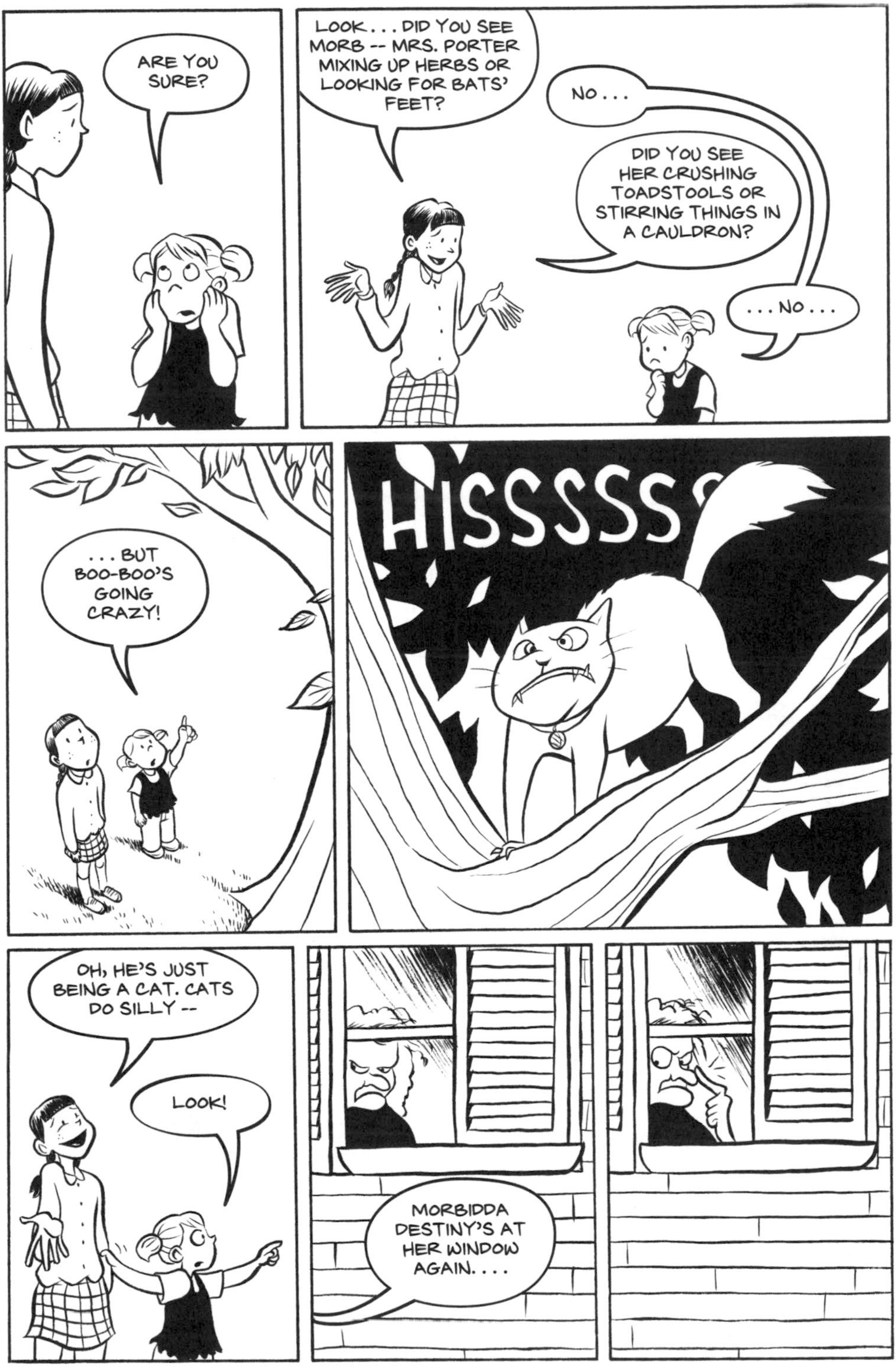
ARE YOU SURE?
LOOK . . . DID YOU SEE MORB -- MRS. PORTER MIXING UP HERBS OR LOOKING FOR BATS' FEET?
NO . . .
DID YOU SEE HER CRUSHING TOADSTOOLS OR STIRRING THINGS IN A CAULDRON?
. . . NO . . .
. . . BUT BOO-BOO'S GOING CRAZY!
HISSSSS
OH, HE'S JUST BEING A CAT. CATS DO SILLY --
LOOK!
MORBIDDA DESTINY'S AT HER WINDOW AGAIN. . . .

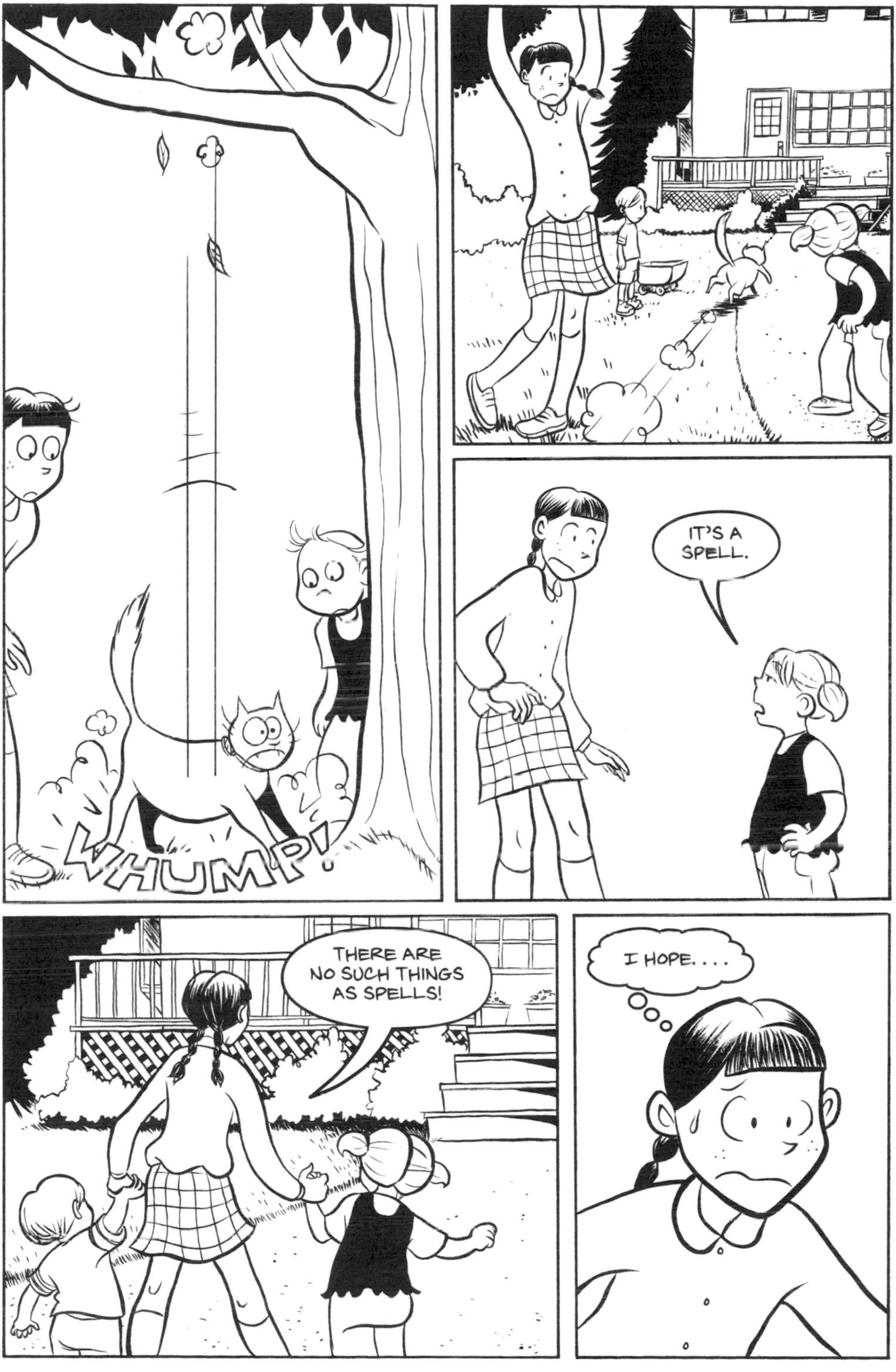
WHUMP!
IT'S A SPELL.
THERE ARE NO SUCH THINGS AS SPELLS!
I HOPE. . . .

Chapter 10

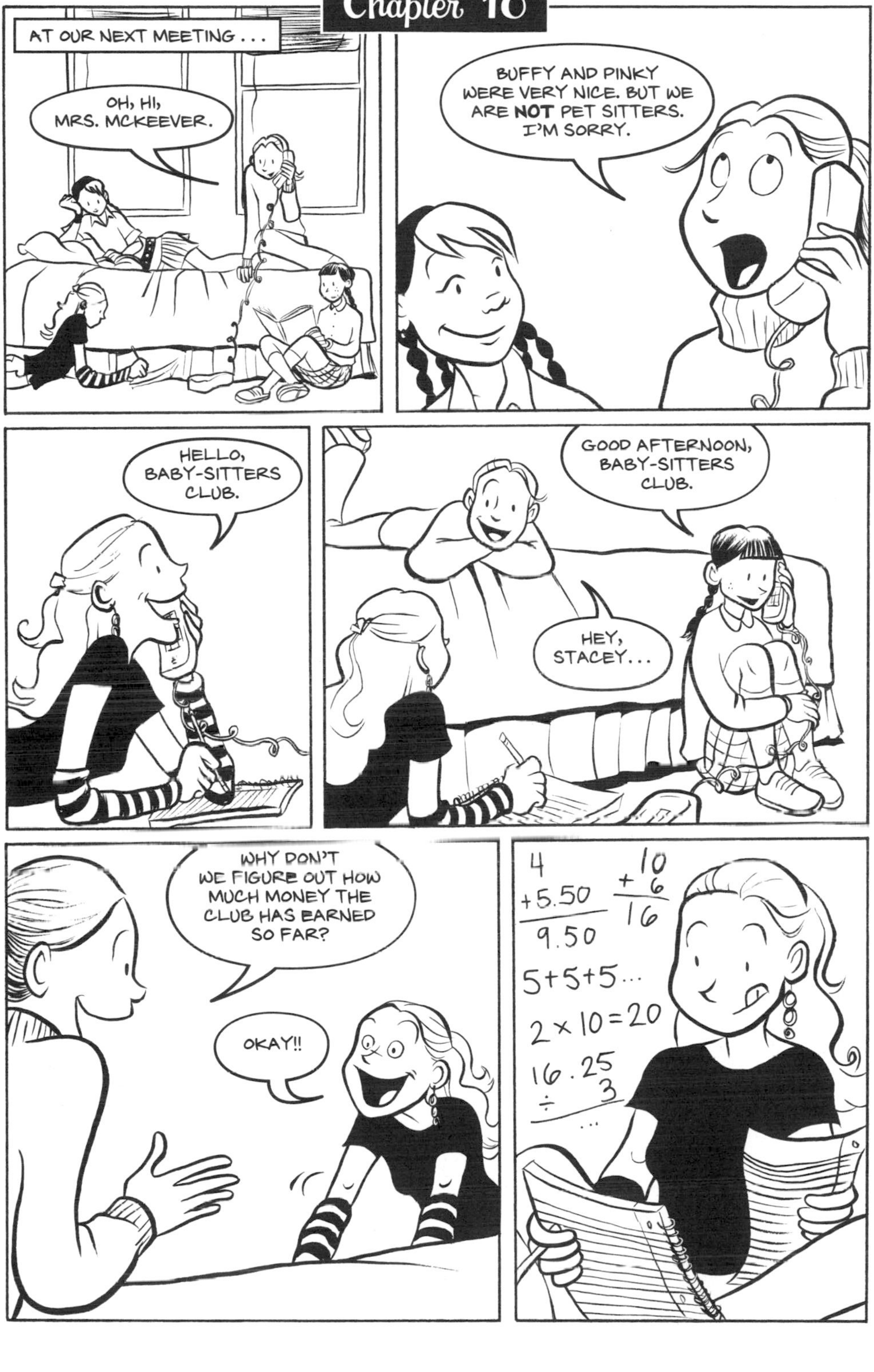

AT OUR NEXT MEETING . . .
OH, HI, MRS. MCKEEVER.
BUFFY AND PINKY WERE VERY NICE. BUT WE ARE **NOT** PET SITTERS. I'M SORRY.
HELLO, BABY-SITTERS CLUB.
GOOD AFTERNOON, BABY-SITTERS CLUB.
HEY, STACEY...
WHY DON'T WE FIGURE OUT HOW MUCH MONEY THE CLUB HAS EARNED SO FAR?
OKAY!!
4
+5.50
9.50
10
+ 6
16
5+5+5...
2 × 10=20
16.25
÷ 3
...

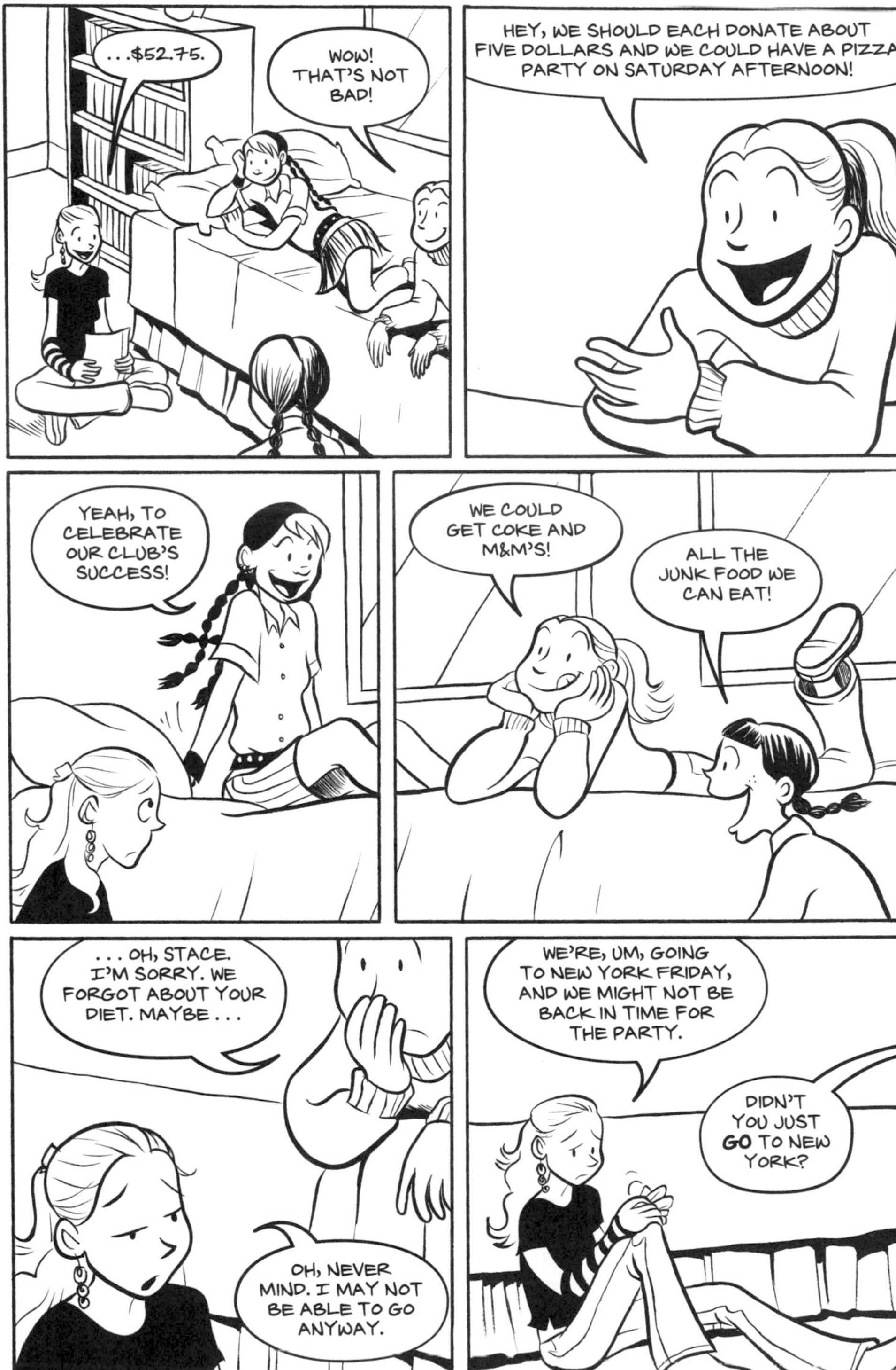
. . . $52.75.
WOW! THAT'S NOT BAD!
HEY, WE SHOULD EACH DONATE ABOUT FIVE DOLLARS AND WE COULD HAVE A PIZZA PARTY ON SATURDAY AFTERNOON!
YEAH, TO CELEBRATE OUR CLUB'S SUCCESS!
WE COULD GET COKE AND M&M'S!
ALL THE JUNK FOOD WE CAN EAT!
. . . OH, STACE. I'M SORRY. WE FORGOT ABOUT YOUR DIET. MAYBE . . .
OH, NEVER MIND. I MAY NOT BE ABLE TO GO ANYWAY.
WE'RE, UM, GOING TO NEW YORK FRIDAY, AND WE MIGHT NOT BE BACK IN TIME FOR THE PARTY.
DIDN'T YOU JUST **GO** TO NEW YORK?

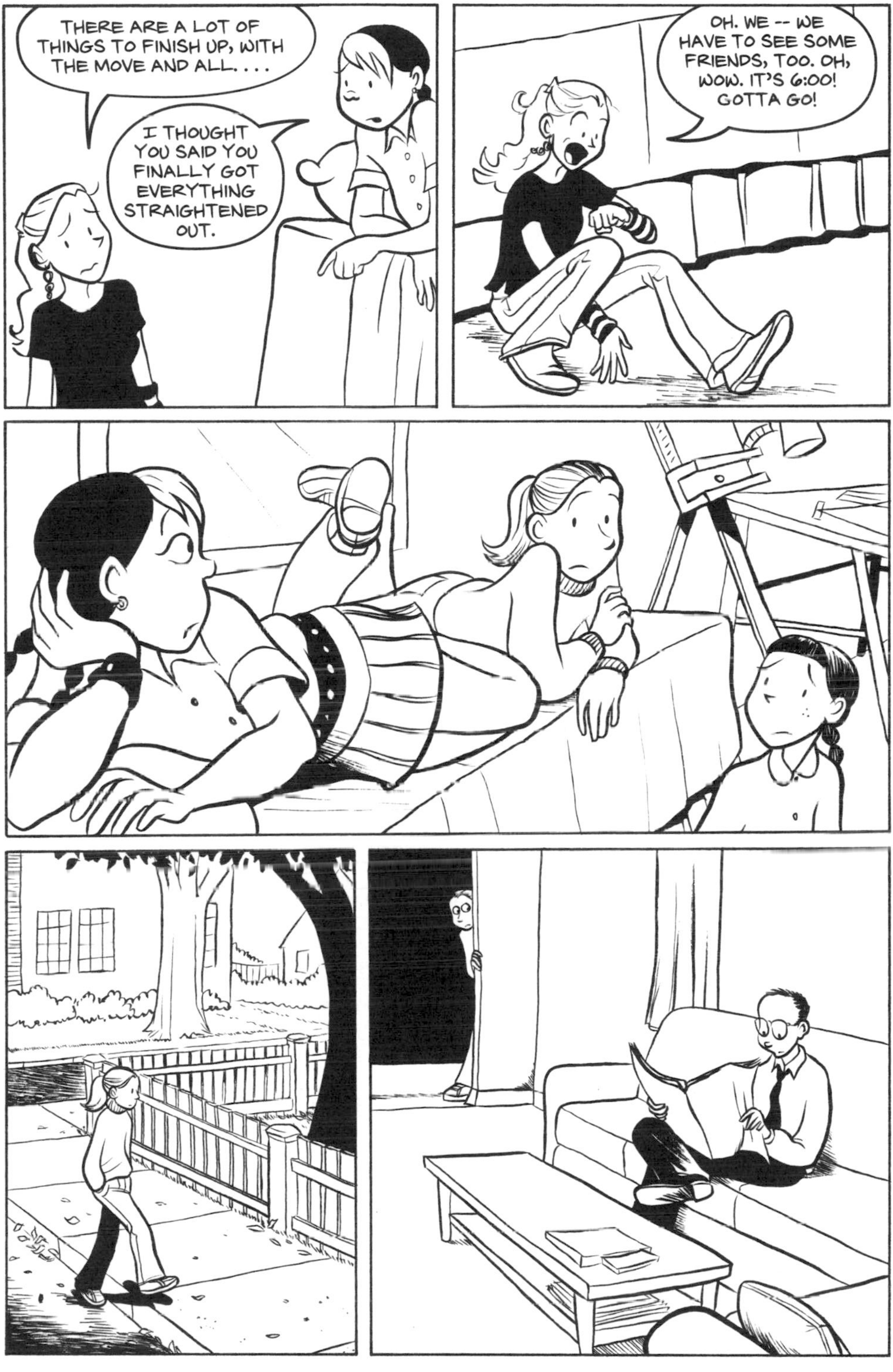
THERE ARE A LOT OF THINGS TO FINISH UP, WITH THE MOVE AND ALL. . . .
I THOUGHT YOU SAID YOU FINALLY GOT EVERYTHING STRAIGHTENED OUT.
OH. WE -- WE HAVE TO SEE SOME FRIENDS, TOO. OH, WOW. IT'S 6:00! GOTTA GO!

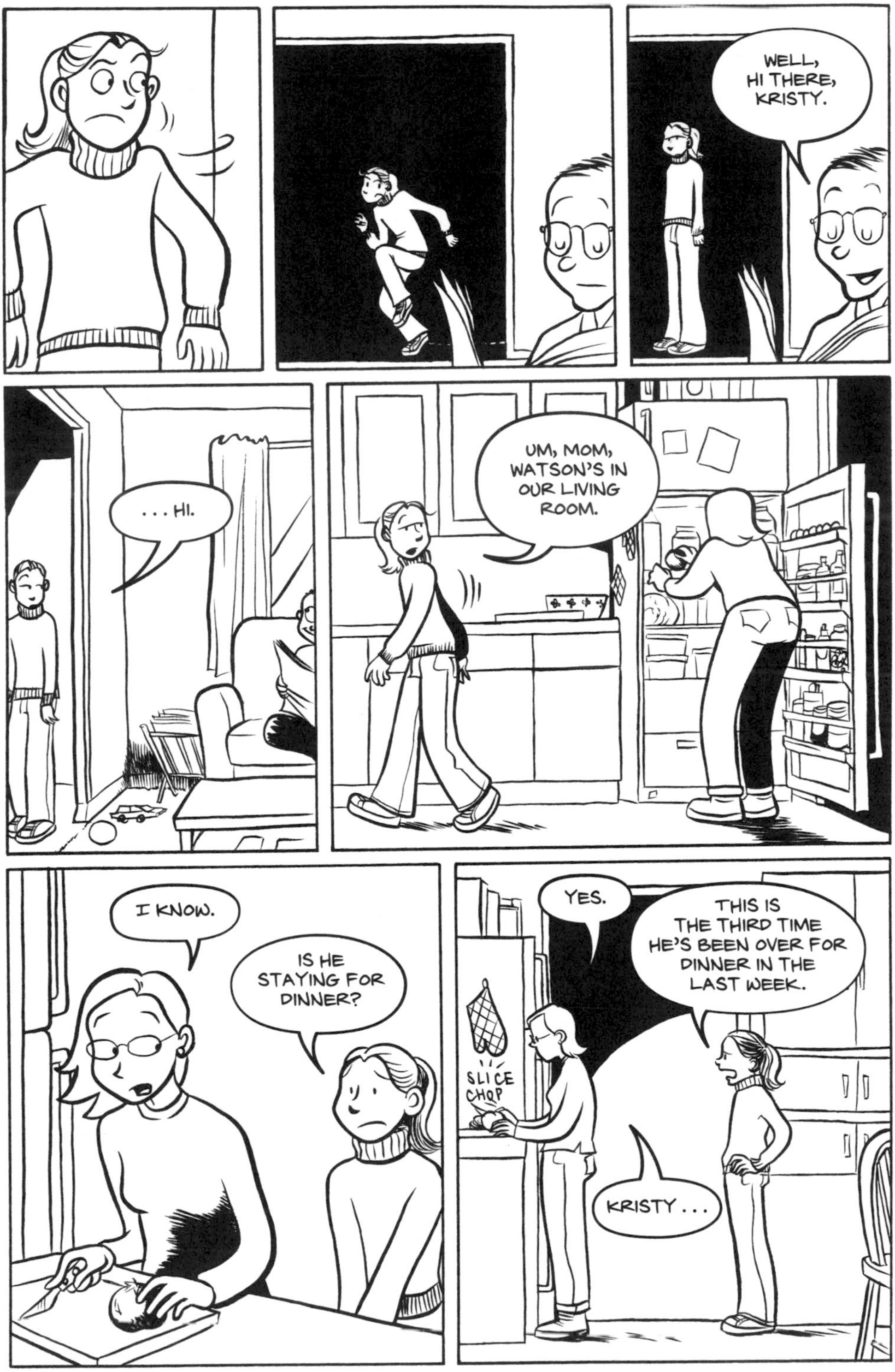
WELL, HI THERE, KRISTY.
. . . HI.
UM, MOM, WATSON'S IN OUR LIVING ROOM.
I KNOW.
IS HE STAYING FOR DINNER?
YES.
THIS IS THE THIRD TIME HE'S BEEN OVER FOR DINNER IN THE LAST WEEK.
SLICE CHOP
KRISTY . . .

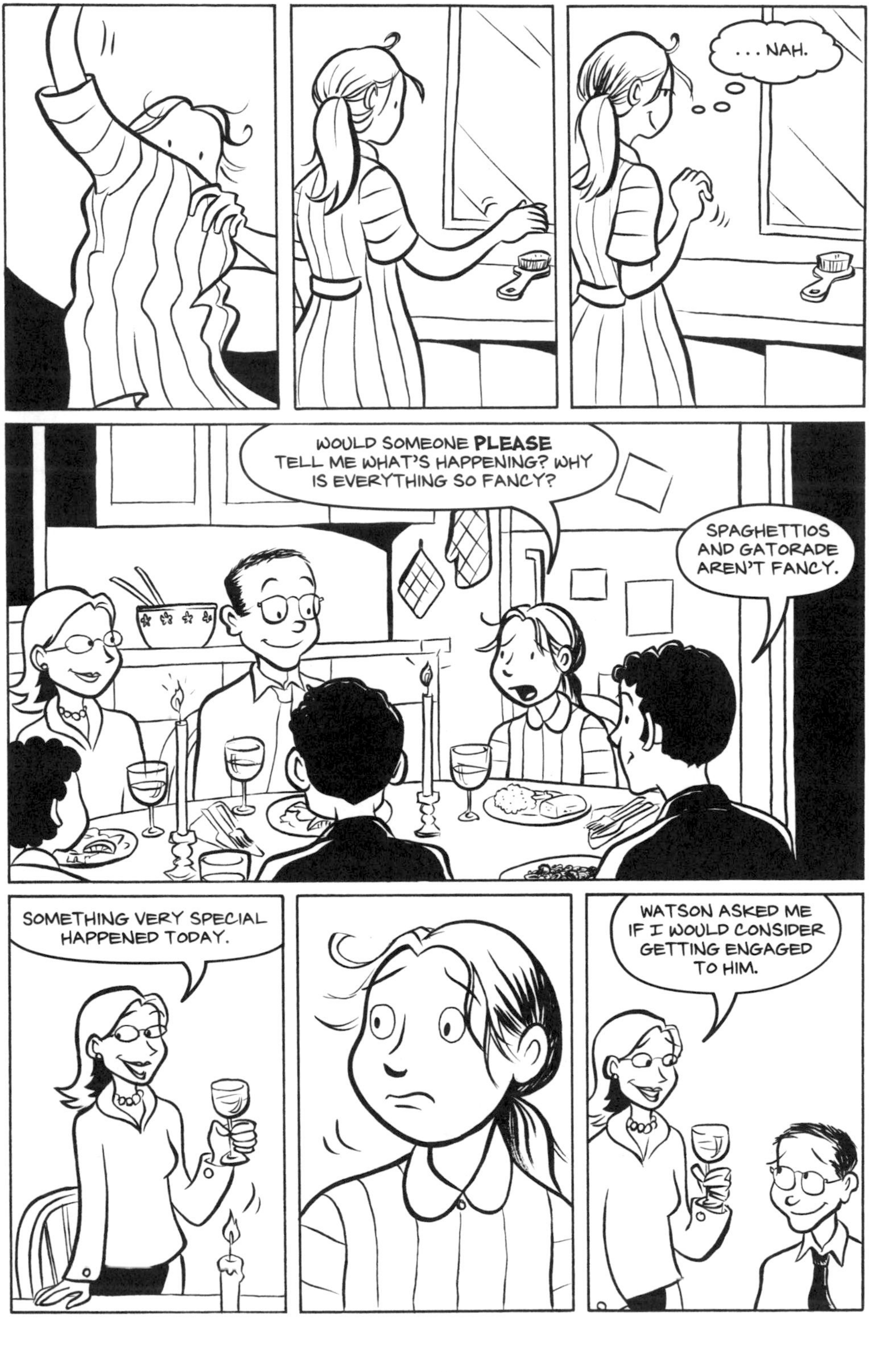
. . . NAH.
WOULD SOMEONE **PLEASE** TELL ME WHAT'S HAPPENING? WHY IS EVERYTHING SO FANCY?
SPAGHETTIOS AND GATORADE AREN'T FANCY.
SOMETHING VERY SPECIAL HAPPENED TODAY.
WATSON ASKED ME IF I WOULD CONSIDER GETTING ENGAGED TO HIM.

147

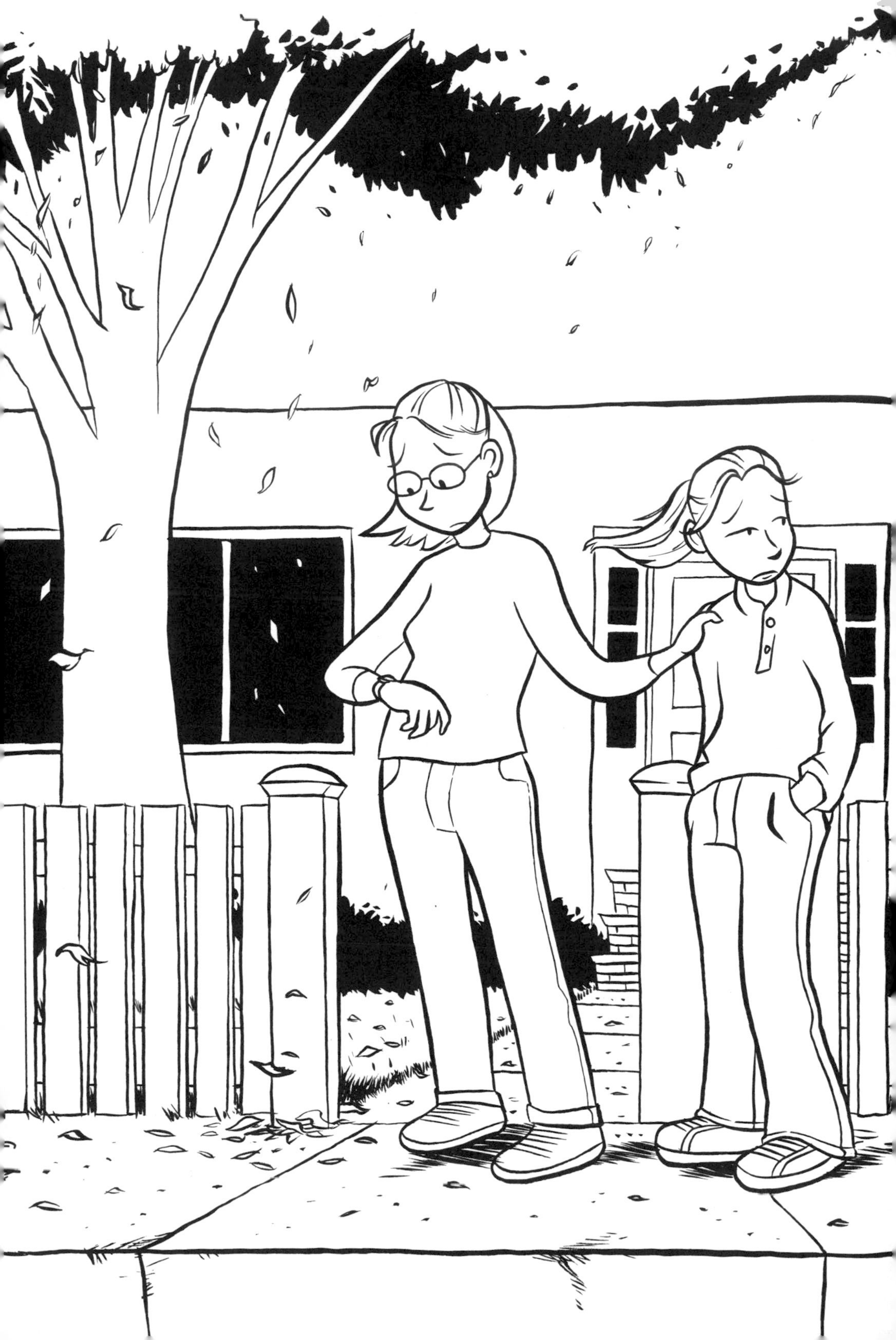

Chapter 12

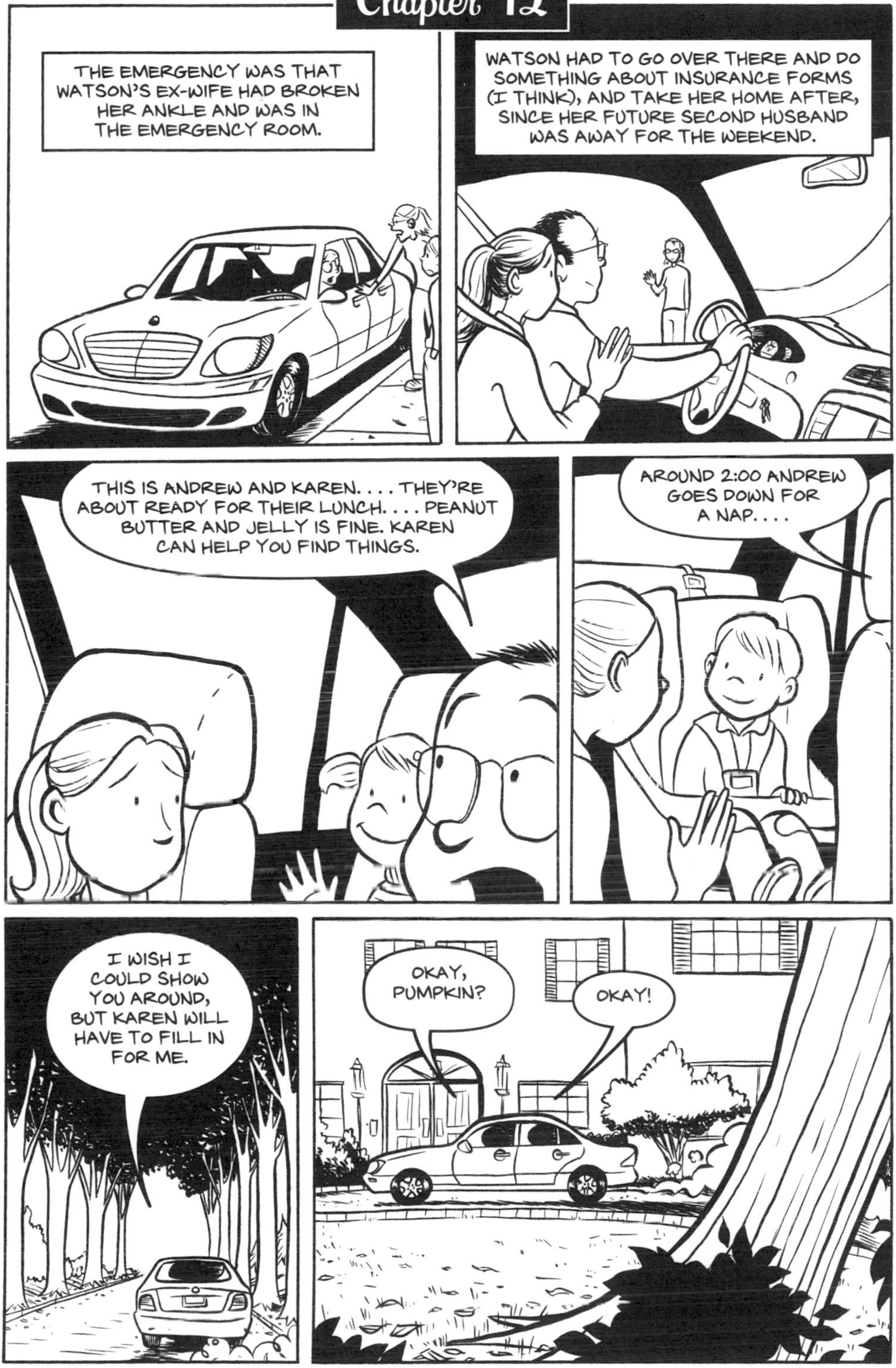

THE EMERGENCY WAS THAT WATSON'S EX-WIFE HAD BROKEN HER ANKLE AND WAS IN THE EMERGENCY ROOM.
WATSON HAD TO GO OVER THERE AND DO SOMETHING ABOUT INSURANCE FORMS (I THINK), AND TAKE HER HOME AFTER, SINCE HER FUTURE SECOND HUSBAND WAS AWAY FOR THE WEEKEND.
THIS IS ANDREW AND KAREN. . . . THEY'RE ABOUT READY FOR THEIR LUNCH. . . . PEANUT BUTTER AND JELLY IS FINE. KAREN CAN HELP YOU FIND THINGS.
AROUND 2:00 ANDREW GOES DOWN FOR A NAP. . . .
I WISH I COULD SHOW YOU AROUND, BUT KAREN WILL HAVE TO FILL IN FOR ME.
OKAY, PUMPKIN?
OKAY!

153

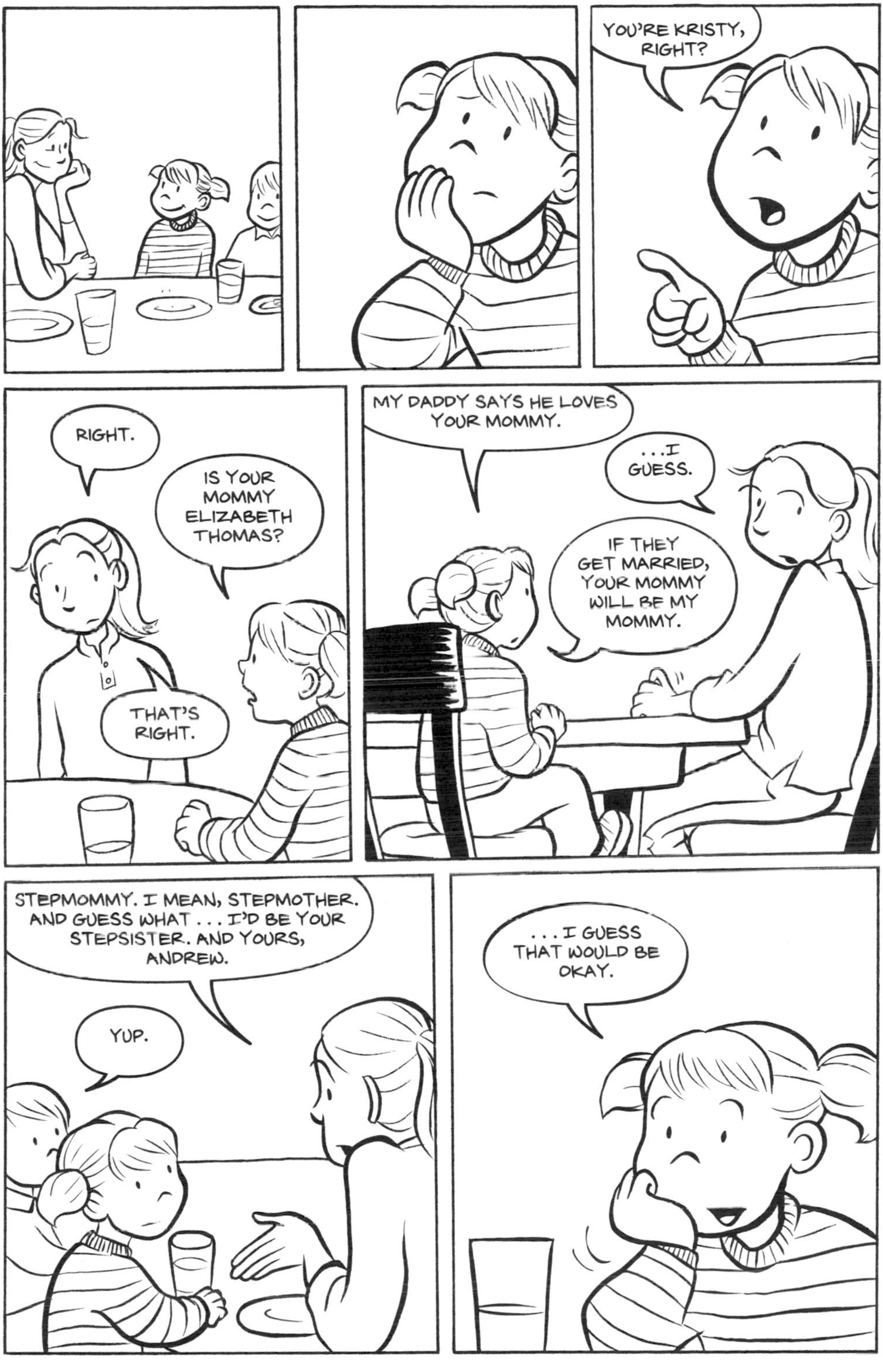
YOU'RE KRISTY, RIGHT?
RIGHT.
IS YOUR MOMMY ELIZABETH THOMAS?
THAT'S RIGHT.
MY DADDY SAYS HE LOVES YOUR MOMMY.
. . . I GUESS.
IF THEY GET MARRIED, YOUR MOMMY WILL BE MY MOMMY.
STEPMOMMY. I MEAN, STEPMOTHER. AND GUESS WHAT . . . I'D BE YOUR STEPSISTER. AND YOURS, ANDREW.
YUP.
. . . I GUESS THAT WOULD BE OKAY.

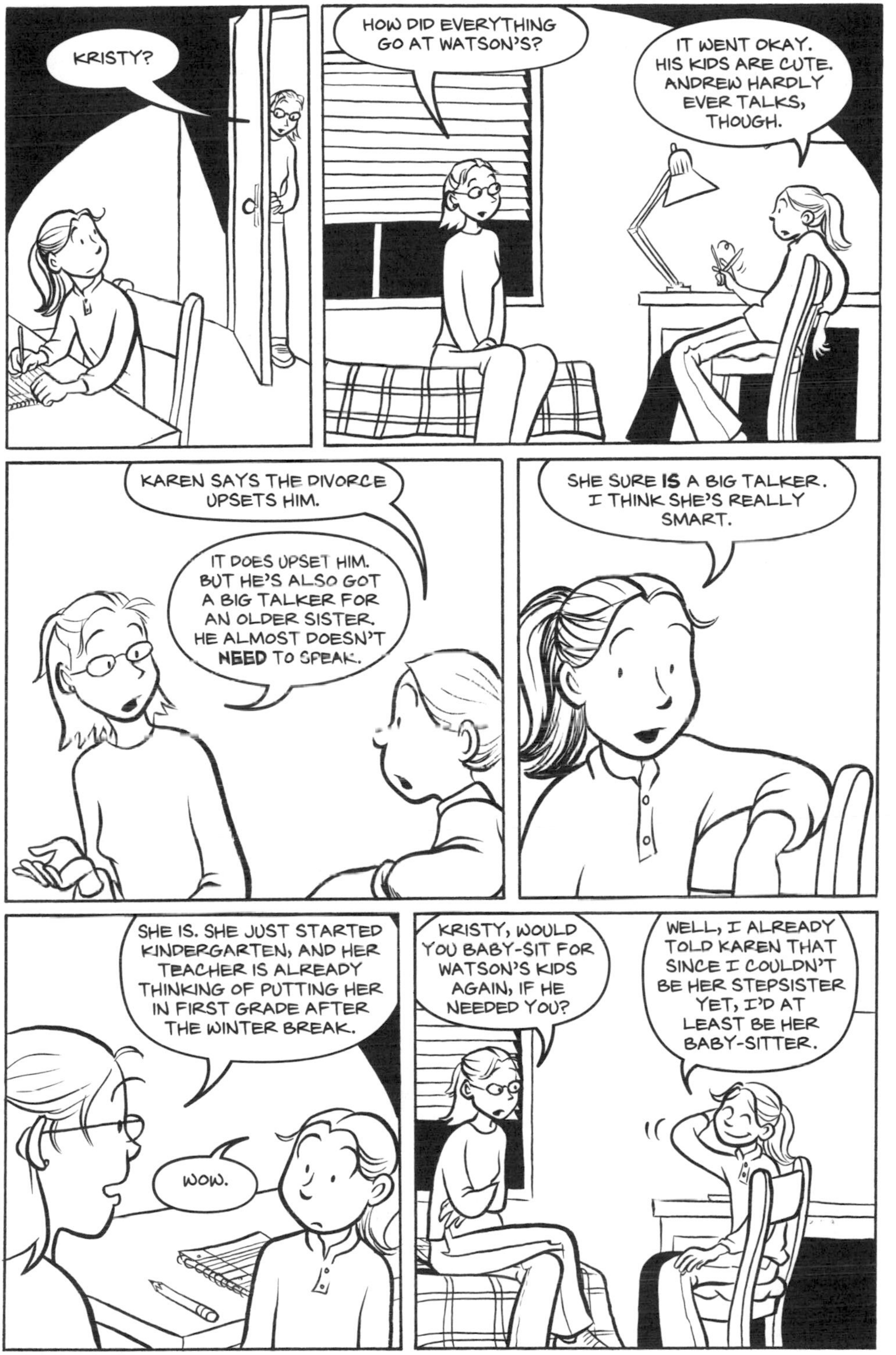
KRISTY?
HOW DID EVERYTHING GO AT WATSON'S?
IT WENT OKAY. HIS KIDS ARE CUTE. ANDREW HARDLY EVER TALKS, THOUGH.
KAREN SAYS THE DIVORCE UPSETS HIM.
IT DOES UPSET HIM. BUT HE'S ALSO GOT A BIG TALKER FOR AN OLDER SISTER. HE ALMOST DOESN'T **NEED** TO SPEAK.
SHE SURE **IS** A BIG TALKER. I THINK SHE'S REALLY SMART.
SHE IS. SHE JUST STARTED KINDERGARTEN, AND HER TEACHER IS ALREADY THINKING OF PUTTING HER IN FIRST GRADE AFTER THE WINTER BREAK.
WOW.
KRISTY, WOULD YOU BABY-SIT FOR WATSON'S KIDS AGAIN, IF HE NEEDED YOU?
WELL, I ALREADY TOLD KAREN THAT SINCE I COULDN'T BE HER STEPSISTER YET, I'D AT LEAST BE HER BABY-SITTER.

Chapter 13

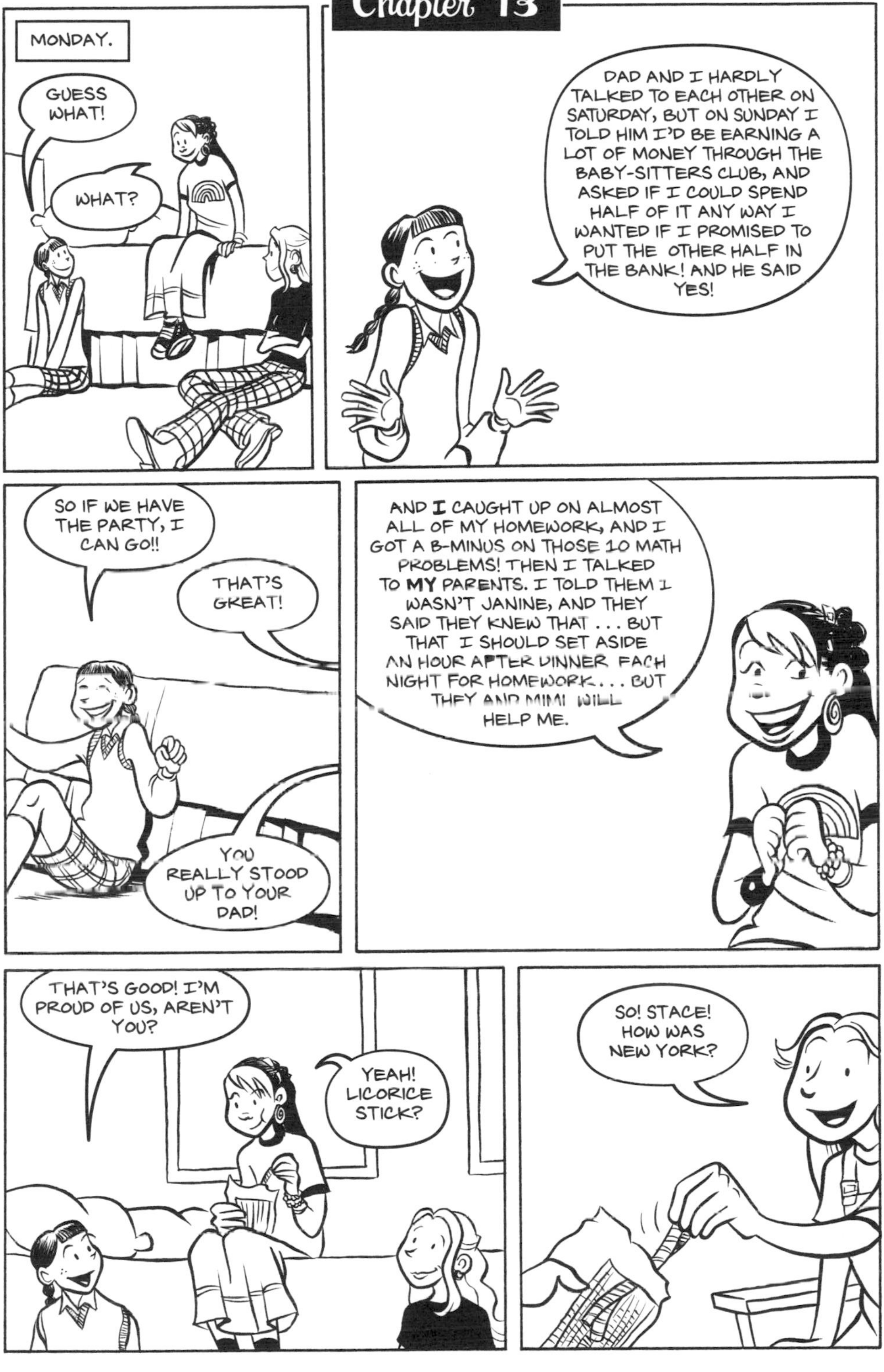
MONDAY.
GUESS WHAT!
WHAT?
DAD AND I HARDLY TALKED TO EACH OTHER ON SATURDAY, BUT ON SUNDAY I TOLD HIM I'D BE EARNING A LOT OF MONEY THROUGH THE BABY-SITTERS CLUB, AND ASKED IF I COULD SPEND HALF OF IT ANY WAY I WANTED IF I PROMISED TO PUT THE OTHER HALF IN THE BANK! AND HE SAID YES!
SO IF WE HAVE THE PARTY, I CAN GO!!
THAT'S GREAT!
YOU REALLY STOOD UP TO YOUR DAD!
AND I CAUGHT UP ON ALMOST ALL OF MY HOMEWORK, AND I GOT A B-MINUS ON THOSE 10 MATH PROBLEMS! THEN I TALKED TO MY PARENTS. I TOLD THEM I WASN'T JANINE, AND THEY SAID THEY KNEW THAT . . . BUT THAT I SHOULD SET ASIDE AN HOUR AFTER DINNER EACH NIGHT FOR HOMEWORK . . . BUT THEY AND MIMI WILL HELP ME.
THAT'S GOOD! I'M PROUD OF US, AREN'T YOU?
YEAH! LICORICE STICK?
SO! STACE! HOW WAS NEW YORK?

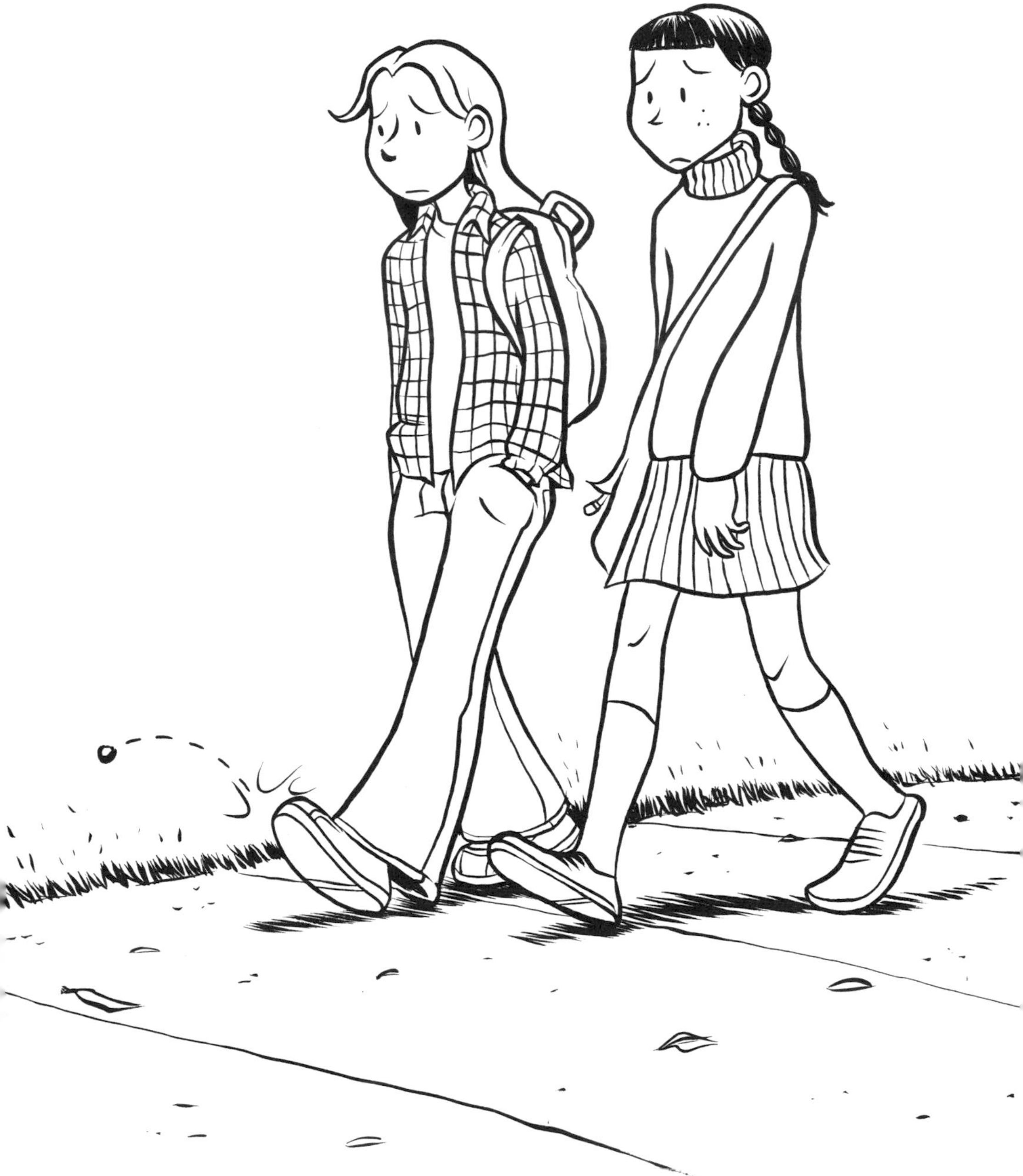

Chapter 14

STONEYBROOK MIDDLE SCHOOL

FALL FAIRE OCTOBER 3

CLAUDIA?

HMPH.

DO YOU STILL WANT TO HAVE OUR CLUB MEETING TOMORROW?

...I GUESS SO. SURE.

OKAY... WE'LL SEE YOU THEN.

'BYE.

172

174

SO I THOUGHT MAYBE I SHOULD COVER UP WHAT WAS WRONG WITH ME. MOVING HERE SEEMED LIKE A CHANCE TO START OVER.

BUT **NOT** TELLING YOU GUYS WAS WORSE THAN TELLING MY OLD FRIENDS.

WELL . . . YOU DON'T HAVE TO TELL **ALL** THE KIDS. WE KNOW, BUT WE SEE YOU MOST OFTEN.

MAYBE YOU COULD SORT OF KEEP QUIET ABOUT IT AT SCHOOL . . . BUT NOT LIE ABOUT IT.

THAT'S TRUE.

THANKS, YOU GUYS.

I THINK WE SHOULD HAVE A SLUMBER PARTY ONCE A MONTH.

183

185

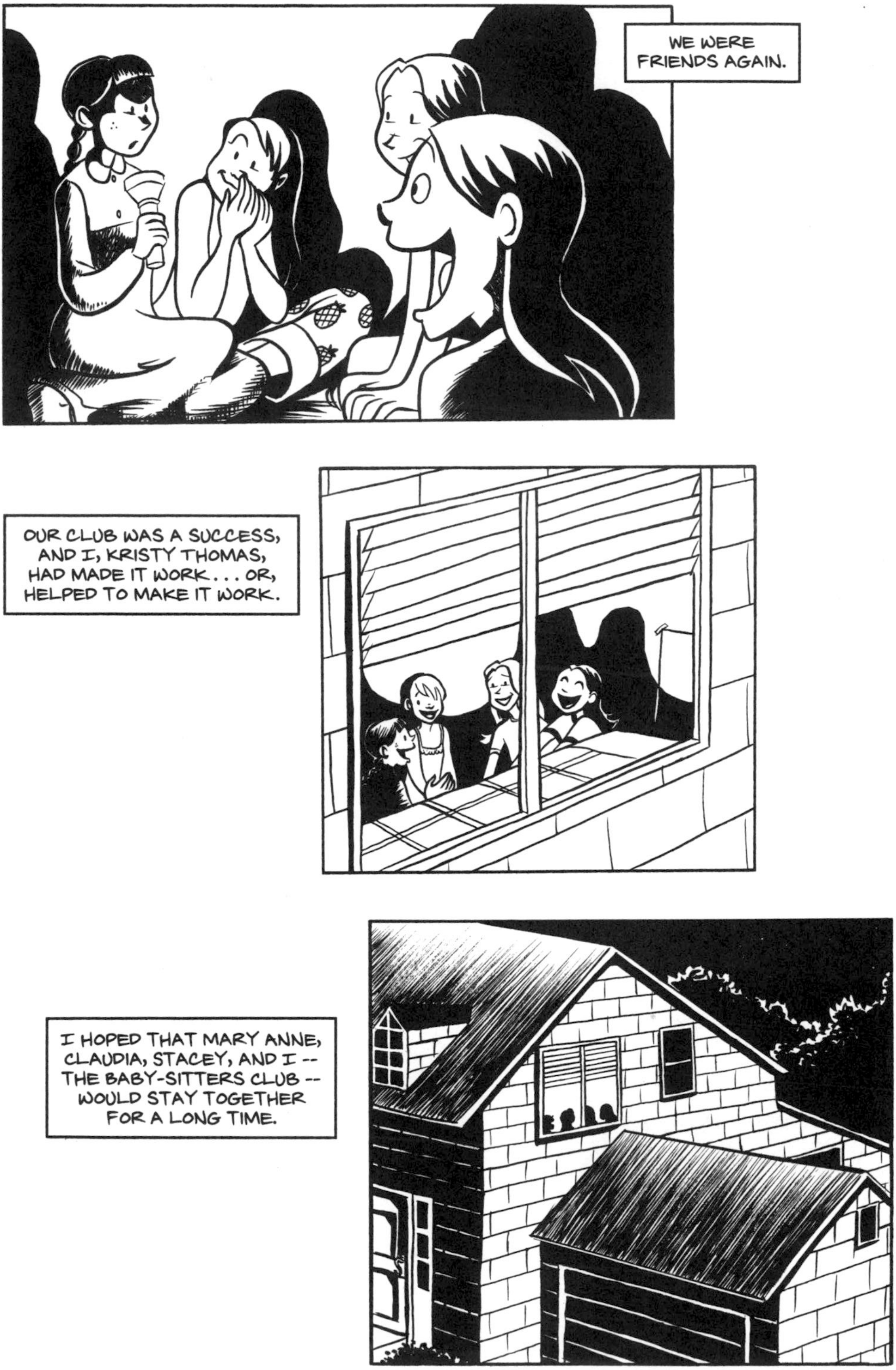
WE WERE FRIENDS AGAIN.
OUR CLUB WAS A SUCCESS, AND I, KRISTY THOMAS, HAD MADE IT WORK . . . OR, HELPED TO MAKE IT WORK.
I HOPED THAT MARY ANNE, CLAUDIA, STACEY, AND I -- THE BABY-SITTERS CLUB -- WOULD STAY TOGETHER FOR A LONG TIME.

Ann M. Martin's

The Baby-sitters Club is one of the most popular series in the history of publishing, with more than 175 million books in print. She is also the author of the acclaimed novels *Belle Teal*, *A Corner of the Universe* (a Newbery Honor Book), *Here Today*, and *A Dog's Life*. She lives in New York.

Raina Telgemeier

grew up reading comics, baby-sitting, and reading The Baby-sitters Club in San Francisco. She graduated from the School of Visual Arts in New York City. Her comics have been nominated for the Ignatz and Eisner Awards, and her illustrations have been featured in magazines, books, and newspapers. Raina currently lives in Queens, New York.

Meet Stacey

STACEY, THE NEW GIRL IN TOWN, IS FACING LIFE AND BABY-SITTING PROBLEMS LEFT AND RIGHT. LUCKILY, SHE HAS HER BABY-SITTERS CLUB FRIENDS TO HELP HER DEAL WITH WHATEVER IS THROWN HER WAY!

The BABY-SITTERS CLUB
The Truth about Stacey

BY ANN M. MARTIN
ADAPTED AND ILLUSTRATED BY RAINA TELGEMEIER

Available Fall 2006

AND LOOK FOR THESE OTHER GRAPHIX SERIES:

Queen Bee by Chynna Clugston
Bone by Jeff Smith
AND COMING SOON:
Goosebumps by R.L. Stine
Amulet by Kazu Kibuishi

graphix

an imprint of
SCHOLASTIC

www.scholastic.com/graphix

BSC2T